P9-CCV-434

Romantic Times praises Norah Hess, Winner of the Reviewer's Choice Award for Frontier Romance!

JADE

"A wonderful romance complete with surprising plot twists, plenty of action and sensuality."

BLAZE

"Norah Hess continues to give readers wonderful romances filled with three-dimensional characters. Memorable!"

LACEY

"Norah Hess has done it again! You'll savor every word, yet rush to turn the pages."

WINTER LOVE

"Powerful and historically accurate as always, Norah Hess depicts the American West with all its harsh realities, yet with compassion and sensitivity."

FANCY

"The talented Ms. Hess is sure to catch your *Fancy* with this release!"

STORM

"A charming story filled with warm, real, and likeable characters."

SAGE

"Earthy, sincere, realistic, and heartwarming...Norah Hess continues to craft wonderful stories of the frontier!"

BLAZING KISSES

"Well, how goes it, Willow?" Jules asked. "How are you holding out, bouncing around in the wagon?"

"I've got a feeling I'll be pretty sore tomorrow morning."

"I could massage you tonight, take away all your aches." Jules gave her a suggestive smile and watched Willow's face for her reaction.

"Would you be willing to do that every night?" Willow asked.

"Yes. Every night, all night."

It was like a dash of cold water in the face when Willow stood up and, dusting off her seat, said, "I'm sorry, but I only signed on as your housekeeper, not to replace your mistress." And while Jules stared at her, she started to climb into the wagon. She caught her breath when Jules sprang to his feet, grabbed her arm and jerked her off the wagon wheel. He spun her around and brought her up solidly against his chest. With an arm clamped tightly across the back of her waist, he pulled her into the vee of his spread legs. With his arousal throbbing against her femininity, he bent his head and settled his lips on hers in a searing kiss that left Willow weak.

Other *Leisure* and *Love Spell* books by Norah Hess:
MOUNTAIN ROSE
JADE
BLAZE
TENNESSEE MOON
HAWKE'S BRIDE
KENTUCKY BRIDE
LACEY
FANCY
FOREVER THE FLAME
WILDFIRE
STORM
SAGE
KENTUCKY WOMAN
DEVIL IN SPURS
WINTER LOVE

Willow

NORAH HESS

LEISURE BOOKS NEW YORK CITY

*In memory of my father, Raymond Poe,
who taught me to love the written word.*

A LEISURE BOOK®

April 1998

Published by

Dorchester Publishing Co., Inc.
276 Fifth Avenue
New York, NY 10001

ISBN 0-8439-4373-4

Printed in the United States of America.

Willow

Chapter One

The door slammed shut behind the young woman who burst through it. Her eyes wild with anger and fear, she clutched her torn bodice together.

"Willow, what's wrong?" her mother cried anxiously as she rose from her seat before the fireplace. When the only answer she received was footsteps running down the hall to the bedrooms, Ruth Ames followed them.

"Have you argued with your father again? Has he struck you?" She grabbed the arms of the slender figure and turned her around. Her gaze fastened immediately on the torn dress, the missing buttons, and then traveled up to the flushed, tear-stained face. "Please tell me that your father didn't do this."

"No, Ma, he didn't, but he knew that Buck was trying to force himself on me and he didn't say a word."

Willow pulled the ruined garment over her head and wadded it into a ball. "I don't know which one of them I hate worse," she said through gritted teeth.

"Willow!" Ruth gave a shocked exclamation when she saw the long scratches on her daughter's throat and breasts. "Did that brute do that to you?"

"Yes, Ma." Willow walked across the floor and picked up a pitcher of water from the small washstand. As she filled a matching basin with water she said bitterly, "And Pa wants me to marry him." She pulled the white camisole over her head, and after giving a short, humorless laugh, she added, "Not only wants me to, demands that I marry Buck Axel."

Willow soaped a washcloth and moved it carefully over her scratched breasts. "I can't marry him, Ma," she cried despairingly. "My life would be a hell on earth living with that monster."

The misery in her daughter's voice made Ruth's thin hands clench into fists. Her lovely Willow had fought off the attentions of their neighbor for three years. It hadn't been easy, what with her father badgering her at every turn to marry the man whose ranch abutted theirs.

Ruth knew why her husband was so insistent that his twenty-two-year-old daughter marry the forty-year-old man. Buck Axel had a creek that ran with water the year round. She had overheard him threaten Otto with the loss of water for his cattle if he didn't make his strong-willed daughter marry him.

That was all her husband needed to daily prod his daughter to marry the man who had bought the neighboring ranch three years before. A sadness came into Ruth's eyes. She knew that Willow would have left home long ago if it wasn't for her. Her only child had stayed on, taking her father's abuse to make things easier on her mother.

Otto Ames had a quick, furious temper that found its outlet in physical violence, and Ruth was the recipient most times. But usually Willow was there, jumping to her defense and often suffering blows herself in the process.

But now that Willow was being forced into a marriage that made the girl's blood run cold, Ruth would stiffen her spine and do something about it.

When Willow had changed into a nightgown, Ruth patted the space on the bed beside her. "Sit down, honey. I have something to tell you."

"What, Ma?" Willow looked anxiously at the small woman. "Nothing bad, is it?"

"I hope not. I pray that it will be all good." Ruth took a deep breath and, taking Willow's hand in hers, asked, "Do you remember my telling you once about the man I should have married instead of your father?"

"Yes, I do. His name was Bob Asher, wasn't it?"

Ruth nodded, sadness coming into her eyes. "Bob's been dead now near to ten years. He left the area and went to Texas shortly after I married Otto. Over the years I kept track of him through a friend who lived in the vicinity of the big ranch where Bob found employment. Before a year was out, he married the rancher's daughter, the man's only child. Before another year passed, his wife bore Bob a son.

"They had no other children. According to my friend, Bob's wife was on the frail side and she passed away when their boy was ten years old, just three years after her own parents died from pneumonia one winter."

"What has all this got to do with me, Ma?" Willow gave her mother a confused look.

Ruth took a deep breath and said slowly, "Two weeks ago I wrote a letter to Bob's son—his name is Jules—asking him if he would please give you a job on his ranch. I wrote that you're a fine cook and a very good housekeeper."

"Oh, Ma," Willow said, breaking in on her mother. "I wish you hadn't done that. You can't ask a stranger to take me in."

"I didn't ask him to take you in. I asked him to give you a job."

"But won't he wonder why I couldn't get a job in my own community here in New Mexico? He'll think there's something wrong with me. That I'm simple-minded or that I have a bad reputation and no one will hire me to work for them."

"He won't think that, honey. I wrote that your intended decided that he didn't want to get married and that in your embarrassment you wanted to start a new life somewhere else."

Willow shook her head. "Couldn't you have come up with something better than that?"

"I think it's a real good idea. Jules Asher is a bachelor, and if he thinks you're pining for another man, he won't bother you."

When Willow got over the shock of what her mother had done, she laughed and said, "I don't know why I'm fretting about it. He probably won't even answer your letter. When did you say you sent it?"

"Two weeks ago. I expect an answer any day."

"If it does come, aren't you afraid Pa might get it and read it?"

Ruth shook her head. "I told Jules Asher to address it to Smitty."

Smitty Black cooked for the cowhands at the ranch and was a longtime friend of the Ames women. Over the years he had kept silent his love for Ruth. There wasn't anything he wouldn't do for her, including shooting her husband if she should ask him to do it. He, like Willow, had put up with the brutal Otto because of the man's fragile wife.

"Good old Smitty," Willow said softly, remembering the times he had comforted her after her father had punished her for no apparent reason at all. As she grew older she figured out that usually he was mad at one of the ranch hands but didn't have the courage to confront the man.

Ruth stood up. "Go to bed now, dear, and tomorrow we'll ride into Bear Tooth to see if Smitty has a letter waiting for him at the general store."

When the door closed behind her mother, Willow opened her window to let the cool spring breeze flow into the room. She shivered slightly and hurried to turn down the covers and blow out the lamp. She slid beneath the blanket and stretched out on her back, staring into the darkness. Her thoughts were on the conversation she had just had with her mother. It would be wonderful if she could leave the ranch and the hard work she had been called upon to do ever since she could remember.

According to Smitty, her father had been disappointed that she wasn't the son he had wanted and had taken his anger out on the child and her mother.

All she knew for sure was that by the time she was ten years old, she was spending eight to ten hours a day out on the range, herding cattle, doing everything a cowhand had to do. All the hands pitied her but didn't dare show it. A couple of men tried to help her once, and Otto had become furious. He didn't say anything to the men, but she was made to work hours after everyone else had ridden to the cookhouse for the evening meal.

Consequently, she had grown up tough in body and hard of mind. She had tender feelings for only two people. She adored her little frail mother and was very fond of Smitty. In the winter, when there was little to do, she spent a lot of time in the cookhouse, where Smitty shared many of his recipes with her. He was a fine cook, which had a lot to do with the cowboys' staying on at the ranch. The other reason was the above-average wage Otto paid them. Ames was wise enough to know that it was the money that kept them there and not any liking the men had for him.

Willow turned onto her left side and winced. Buck's dirty fingernails had brought blood in a few places. She rolled over on her right side, and curling an arm under her head, she dared to dream of fleeing the ranch, of making a new life for herself. She would hate leaving her mother, but she knew the little woman would insist that she did.

Maybe with me gone, Willow thought, Pa won't have cause to treat Ma so harshly. Most times he gets angry because she's trying to defend me. If Ma stayed out of his way whenever she could, she would save herself a lot of abuse.

Her thoughts turned to the rancher in Texas. What kind of man was this Jules Asher? Her mother had said that she imagined he was around thirty-three or thirty-four. Why was he still single? she wondered. Most serious-minded men married in their late twenties and had started a family by thirty-three.

As her eyelids began to droop, Willow hoped that he wasn't like Buck Axel. Mean and cruel.

The next morning, early, Ruth shook Willow awake. Excitement sparkled in her eyes. "Come on, honey, get up. We want to get an early start to the village. I feel it in my bones that there will be a letter for me—for Smitty, that is."

"It might not be good news, Ma," Willow cautioned as she swung her feet to the floor and stood up. "Don't be too disappointed if your old friend's son has no place for me on his ranch."

Ruth shook her head. "I just know that he won't refuse to give you a job. If he's anything like his father, he'll find a place for you."

"That's what bothers me. I don't want him making a place for me out of pity."

"I'm sure he wouldn't do that. His ranch is huge, and he must need a lot of people to help him run it. I have no doubt that you'll earn whatever he pays you."

It was a beautiful spring day when Willow and Ruth rode out for the village of Bear Tooth. On the way, Ruth kept up a constant gay chatter. Willow wished that she wasn't so excited. The little woman could be setting herself up for a big letdown. There might not even be a letter waiting for them, and even if there was one, it might not contain the news her mother wanted to hear.

But Ruth's high spirits were still with her when they entered the general store. She kept up a running conversation with the genial shopkeeper as she made a few unnecessary purchases. When everything was totaled up and she handed the man what she owed, Ruth casually said, "I don't suppose there's any mail for the ranch?"

"As a matter of fact, there is." The man reached under the counter and brought up an envelope. "It's for Smitty." He handed Ruth the white missive with the old cook's name on it. "I wonder who that ole coot knows in Texas?"

"I believe he has a cousin living there," Ruth said in a calm voice that belied the excited tremor in her hands. "Come on, Willow," she said, gathering up her purchases, "let's get on home. There's a lot of work waiting for us to do."

I didn't know you could be so wily, Ma, Willow thought as they mounted and rode out of the village.

Ruth drew rein when they came to a stand of cottonwoods, out of sight of the village. "I can't wait to see what he's written," she said, swinging to the ground.

Willow remained mounted as her mother tore open the envelope, freed a sheet of paper from it, and began to read out loud:

"Dear Mrs. Ames,

It took me a while to figure out who you were. When my father talked about you, he always used your maiden name.

"As it happens, I can give your daughter a job. I'm in need of a housekeeper. When she reaches the small town of Coyote, anyone there can direct her to the X-Bar ranch.

Regards,
Jules Asher."

"There you are, honey." Thankful tears glimmered in Ruth's eyes. "I told you he wouldn't let us down."

"He didn't waste any words, did he?" Willow said sardonically.

"Well, what more could he write, not knowing us," Ruth said in defense of the unknown man. "The important thing is that you have a place to go, and you'll never have to worry again about having to marry that awful Buck Axel. Let's get on home and start making plans."

Chapter Two

A moth flitted around the lamp, drawn to the flame that lit the cookshack. Three people sat at the end of a long table, leaning toward each other, talking earnestly.

"It's out of the question for you to make this trip alone, Willow," Smitty said firmly. "I know the Big Bend Country. There are four or five different tribes of Indians in the area, not to mention the outlaws that hole up there. If any of them should come upon you, we'd never see Willow Ames again."

As the reality of Willow's departure sank in, Ruth had become uneasy about her daughter striking out alone. Willow knew nothing about the terrain she must travel through, the rivers she might have to cross or the people she might encounter.

But it was imperative that her daughter go. This

might be her only chance to escape Otto Ames and Buck Axel. In desperation Ruth had turned to her old friend, Smitty. She knew that in his younger years, before being gored in his right leg by a longhorn, he had worked on ranches in Texas. He could draw a map for Willow.

His arthritic finger tapping the letter Ruth had given him to read, Smitty said, "Coyote was just a dusty spot on the plains when I rode through it once several years ago. I don't expect it has changed much since then. It's not too far from El Paso, a good-sized town. That's where the cowboys go when they want to whoop it up a bit."

"How far is Coyote from here?" Willow asked.

"I'd say a couple days' ride. Plenty of time for a person to get his scalp lifted if he don't know how to move through Indian country."

Ruth choked back a lump in her throat and tried to blink away her tears. But Smitty saw the one that escaped and ran down her cheek. "Don't cry, Ruth." His gnarled hand reached out to hers. "I know it's important that Willow get away from here, and I'm gonna help her do it."

"You are, Smitty?" Ruth looked at him hopefully. "How are you going to do that?"

"I'm gonna take her to this Jules Asher's ranch." He smiled at the wide-eyed Willow.

"Bless you, Smitty Black." Ruth turned her hand over and squeezed his callused palm. "Willow and I will always be in your debt."

The aging cook's face showed how moved he was by Ruth's affectionate gesture. He would walk barefoot to Coyote for the woman he had adored for so long.

"But Smitty," Willow said anxiously, "if Pa should learn that you helped me to run away, he will fire you."

"Yes, he would. That's why we must give a lot of thought to how we're gonna pull this off."

Both women kept their eyes on Smitty's face as he thoughtfully tapped the tabletop. Finally into the tense silence he said, "I've got to leave the ranch a couple days before you do, Willow. I'll tell the old bastard that I want to go to Abilene to attend a cousin's funeral. That's in the opposite direction from the way we'll be travelin', Willow. I'll say that I'll be gone for a week so as to give us plenty of time to get to this ranch and for me to get back here.

"He won't like it, but he'll let me go. He knows that half his men only stay here because of the grub I serve them."

"Where will you stay until it's time for you and Willow to head out for Coyote?"

"There's that old run-down line shack that's never used anymore. It's just a few miles this side of the Rio Grande. The river runs past Coyote and we'll be following its course."

"Smitty, we can never repay you for this kindness." Ruth's eyes were tearing again as she brought the cook's hand up to her cheek. "You will be saving Willow from a life of pure hell."

The cook's adam's apple bobbed up and down and the hand Ruth held trembled. He couldn't believe he was touching her face.

"What should I bring?" Willow asked, breaking in on his ecstasy.

After he had swallowed a couple of times and Ruth had released his hand, Smitty cleared his throat and got out the words. "Just your clothes and a gun. I'll see to the grub and bedrolls."

"When will you leave?" Ruth asked.

"I'll tell Otto I'm leaving when he comes home from Buck Axel's place tonight. I'll take off then around midnight."

"And I'm to meet you at the line shack in a couple of days?"

"Yes. Make it at early dawn before the ranch is awake. I think you two should leave now. Otto will be comin' home any time now."

Smitty had supposed right. Ruth and Willow hadn't been in the house more than five minutes when they heard Otto riding in. They peered through the window of the dark kitchen and watched Smitty leave the cookshack and talk to him. They heaved a sigh of relief when the burly rancher continued on to the barn and Smitty, as though he knew they were watching, gave them a quick wave.

The following two days didn't lag as Willow had thought they would. Her father had ordered that she and her mother take on Smitty's duties while the cook was away. Preparing three meals a day for fifteen cowpunchers, and washing dirty dishes and pots and skillets later, sent them to bed at night completely exhausted. They wondered aloud to each other how Smitty could do it with his lame leg.

Willow was thankful she had packed her few articles of clothes in her saddlebag before Smitty left.

She doubted that she would have had the energy to do it now.

Finally, the last supper she would help her mother to make had been eaten and the cowboys left. She faced the future with mixed emotions. Tomorrow morning she would be leaving a life that hadn't been easy. But at the same time she would be leaving behind a mother whom she loved dearly. She worried also that her father would make the little woman carry on with the cooking until Smitty returned.

Willow had told Ruth to pretend that she was overwhelmed at her daughter's disappearance and to take to her bed. If that didn't make him sympathetic to her pretended grief, at least it would keep him from thinking that his wife had abetted his daughter in her flight. Ruth had said that she would try that, but Willow knew she wouldn't. Her mother was too afraid to open her mouth to her husband.

It was a sad pair who washed the dishes and pots and then swept out the cookshack floor. Willow would be leaving at dawn.

There was a nip in the air as Willow and Ruth made their tired way to the house. "Don't forget to take along a jacket in the morning," Ruth said, and then added in worried tones, "I hope Smitty will bring along enough blankets. It still gets quite cold outdoors in the middle of the night."

"I'm sure he will, Ma. Please don't worry. I'll be fine. And yes, before you can remind me for the hundredth time, I'll write to you as soon as I get settled in." Willow put her arm around Ruth's waist and kept it there until they stepped up onto the porch.

Ruth changed into her nightclothes while Willow

made a pot of coffee. They couldn't stand the strong black brew that the cowhands preferred, and each evening they looked forward to a cup made to their own liking.

As they sat before the fire sipping from heavy white mugs, neither woman had much to say to the other. If they spoke of what was on their minds, tears would start falling. Neither wanted that.

When Ruth tried to hide a yawn, Willow laughed softly and said, "Go to bed, Ma. You're half asleep."

"I think I will." Ruth heaved her tired body out of the chair. "I'll see you in the morning, dear," she said, bending and kissing Willow's cheek.

Willow wanted to grab her mother and hug her tightly. It would be a long time before she would see that sweet face again. She was saying her good-bye now and would be gone tomorrow morning when her mother came to awaken her.

When Ruth's door had closed, Willow picked up her cup and carried it to her bedroom. She sipped occasionally as she changed from her dress to a shirt and riding skirt. She would not be going to bed tonight. She would sit beside the window, staring into the darkness until the sky lightened.

Willow pulled a straight-backed chair up to the window and turned out the light. A few minutes later, as she sat in the darkness, she heard the kitchen door open, then her father's lumbering tread as he made his way to his bedroom. She heaved a sigh of relief. She had put out the light just in time. Had he seen her room lit up, he would have barged in and demanded to know why she wasn't in bed.

I'll never miss him, she thought as Otto's door

banged shut behind him. Had she or her mother made that kind of noise while he was sleeping, they would have felt the weight of his hand.

When his boots hit the floor with a thud, Willow took up her vigil.

The night wore on and Willow made two silent trips to the kitchen to refill her cup with coffee. She needn't be so quiet, she thought wryly the last time she passed by Otto's door. Most likely the men in the bunkhouse could hear his loud snoring.

At last the sky turned a dark gray and Willow left her post. She strapped on her Colt, shrugged into a lightweight jacket and dragged her packed saddlebag from under the bed. Holding her breath, she slowly opened the door, stepped out into the hall and then barely closed the door behind her. Otto wasn't snoring now, and he might have heard the click of the doorknob had she closed the door completely.

As noiseless as an Indian, Willow walked through the parlor, avoiding the boards she knew squeaked when walked on. She stepped out onto the porch and paused a moment to send a searching glance toward the stables and the area around them. When she saw that the bunkhouse was dark, she descended the two steps.

In the semi-darkness she hurriedly saddled her mare Cream Puff, and after settling the saddlebag onto the horse, she swung into the saddle. She kept Cream Puff at a walk until they were out of hearing distance of the ranch, and then headed her toward the line shack at a gallop.

Smitty was standing in the shadows, waiting for Willow when she rode up. "All set?" He smiled up at her. When she nodded, he led his little quarter horse from behind the building and swung into the saddle.

"Let's hit the trail," he said and headed the horse in the direction of the Rio Grande.

The sun was rising when when they walked their mounts across the shallow river. Smitty laughed and said that he never could figure out why it was called Grand. "Maybe because of its length," he suggested. "It is a long son of gun. It borders all of New Mexico and Texas. It never gets very deep, though, even after the spring rains."

It was a beautiful day as they followed the contours of the river. The sun was bright and the air cool. They galloped the horses in between intervals of restful walking. At noon Smitty drew rein and dismounted. "I don't know about you, but I'm hungry," he said.

"So am I. What have you got in the grub sack?"

"Nothin' fancy. Just some beans and salt pork."

"No coffee?" Willow sounded disappointed as she took up the reins of both horses to lead them to the river for a drink of water.

Smitty grinned. "Don't get into an uproar. That was the first thing I packed."

Later, as they relaxed around a fire only big enough to brew the coffee and heat the beans, Smitty asked Willow if she'd had any trouble leaving the house that morning. She said that she hadn't, and the talk turned to the area where she would be working.

"There ain't many ranches there," Smitty said. "Ain't many people either. I already told you about the Indian tribes. There are mountains, eight and nine thousand feet tall. They get snow up there in the winter. Big Bend country is my favorite part of Texas."

"Do you think I'll like it?"

"I think you will. You'll maybe get lonesome sometimes, especially in the winter when a blue norther comes in and a person don't dare stick his nose out very long at a time. But one good thing, you'll be free of your Paw and that bastard, Buck Axel."

Willow nodded. "That alone will make me like it."

"You look ready to nod off." Smitty began gathering up everything they had used for lunch. Handing the dishes to Willow, he said, "Take these to the river and wash them while I put out the fire and pack up again."

Smitty kept his horse to the same pace he had set during the morning. The sun moved steadily to the west, and when it was getting close to sinking behind the horizon, Willow called his attention to four horsemen a mile or so to their right. An oath ripped through his lips as he drew rein.

"Yaquis!" he exclaimed, looking wildly around for some cover. He saw nothing but flat land. He remembered then that half a mile back they had passed a clump of trees. It would be a perfect place to hide if they could ride back there without being seen by the Indians.

As Smitty watched the half-naked braves, he realized that the red ball of the setting sun was behind him and Willow. If the Indians should look in their direction, the bright glare would blind them to their presence.

He turned his horse around and motioned Willow to follow suit. A fast sprint soon brought them to the stand of cottonwood. After guiding their mounts in among the close-growing trunks, Smitty slid out of the saddle and peered out on the range. The figures of the Indians were growing smaller as the braves rode peacefully along, showing no evidence that they had seen the two white people.

"We'll stop here for the night," Smitty said. "It will be a dry camp, though. I don't dare make a fire to brew a pot of coffee or warm a can of beans. They would smell the wood smoke and come to investigate."

The sun had gone down by the time they had chewed some beef jerky, washed down with water from their canteens. Forgoing a cigarette for the same reason he hadn't built a fire, Smitty looked at Willow and said, "Why don't you spread out your blankets and get some sleep. I'm gonna sit up a while, keep an eye open."

Willow's exhaustion overshadowed her fear of the Indians. She had barely climbed into her bedroll before her eyes were closed.

Willow awakened to the sun on her face and the delicious aroma of brewed coffee and frying meat. She pushed aside the blanket and sat up. "I take it you feel it's safe enough to build a fire," she called laughingly to Smitty's back as he hunkered before a fire, tending to sizzling salt pork.

Smitty turned around and smiled at her. "I saw them ride out half an hour ago. They're probably huntin' for buffalo."

When Willow had visited the back of a large tree trunk, then washed her face and hands in the river, she sat down before the cookfire and accepted the filled plate Smitty handed her.

After she had finished eating, she smiled and said, "That was the best meal I ever had."

When he had taken a couple of drags on the cigarette he'd just rolled, he said, "This is the best smoke I've ever had." They both laughed, and then Smitty said, "We'd better break camp and get goin'."

Since they had eaten a late breakfast, Smitty and Willow didn't stop to make lunch. Instead they chewed strips of beef jerky as they rode along. They stopped once so that the horses could drink from the river and rest awhile.

It was near sundown when they rode into El Paso. "What should we do, Willow?" Smitty asked as they rode down the dusty main street. "If the Asher ranch is any distance from here, we'll be arriving there in the middle of the night."

"Regardless of how far it is, I'd like to have a bath and get into some clean clothes before we arrive. I've slept and sweated in this outfit for two days. I want to meet my boss looking clean and decent."

"All right then, we'll go to that hotel over there, get ourselves a couple of rooms and eat supper in their dining room. How does that sound?"

Willow looked across the rutted street to the weathered, false-front building whose sign over the double doors proclaimed, EL PASO PALACE. "Sounds good to me," she said, her mind on a tub of hot water.

They dismounted in front of the Palace, and after looping their reins around a hitching rail that ran half the length of the narrow porch, they entered the hotel, each carrying a saddlebag.

When Willow's eyes became accustomed to the semi-gloom, she saw that her surroundings had none of the grandeur the sign over the door had led her to expect. But the place was clean and the floor carpeted. She followed Smitty to the front desk. The young man standing behind it raised his head from a paper he was reading and frowned at the aging man in the dusty, sweat-stained clothing.

Smitty ignored the look that said he had wandered into the wrong part of town and announced gruffly, "Me and my niece need a couple rooms."

"I'm pretty sure we're all filled up," the clerk began, then found himself looking into the barrel of a pistol. His face grew pale and he smiled nervously as he adjusted his glasses and stuttered, "I could—er—be—be mistaken. Let me—let me take a look at the guest book."

After barely looking to see if there were vacant rooms, the clerk said, "Oh, yes, I see that I do have two rooms for rent."

"I thought you might," Smitty drawled and shoved his gun back into the holster. "Now where are they?"

"At the head of the stairs to your right."

When the keys were handed over, Smitty gave the young man a hard look and ordered, "Send up a tub and hot water to the lady's room. Pronto."

"Yes, sir. Right away, sir."

Willow smothered a giggle as she and Smitty climbed the stairs. Her old friend had scared the soup out of the arrogant, self-important clerk with his high, starched collar.

Willow's room was like the hotel lobby. Nothing fancy, but neat and clean. "I'm right next door,"

Smitty said. "While you get cleaned up, I'll take the horses to the livery, then check out the town. Maybe stop in that saloon across the street and have a drink."

On his way downstairs, Smitty passed two hotel maids coming up. One lugged a tin hip-bath; the other carried a pail of hot water in each hand. His lips curled in satisfaction. It was surprising what a pistol could do.

Willow smiled her thanks to the maids as they emptied the water into the tub. "I'll need more water than that," she said. "It will take two pails to wash the dust and grime out of my hair."

"*Sí, señorita.*" White teeth flashed in the pretty face of the youngest girl.

While Willow waited for the additional water, she walked over to the window and pushed aside the curtain so she could look down on the street below. There weren't many people about, and she thought it must be supper time. Most people had gone home to eat.

She watched two garishly dressed women with painted faces come out of the saloon and walk up and down the boardwalk. Drumming up business, she imagined.

Her attention was caught then by a beautiful black stallion walking proudly down the middle of the street. Never had she seen such an animal. Her gaze lifted to the man who rode him, a man who looked as arrogant as the stallion.

She studied his face when he drew rein alongside the women and took off his Stetson. He was as handsome as his mount, she saw, with unruly black hair and a crooked smile. But he was hard looking. There was an aloofness about him that said he lacked humility. He certainly wasn't her type of man.

Willow pulled the drapes together at a soft rapping on her door. The rest of her water had arrived. She tipped each girl a coin and locked the door when they left. Picking up the saddlebags from the floor, she laid them out flat on the bed and took from one her underthings, stockings and a pair of black slippers. From the bottom of the bag she brought out a glass bottle of rose-scented bath salts and a comb and brush.

After unstrapping the other bag, she took from it a carefully folded dress of sprigged muslin, blue in color. She gave it a couple of hard shakes to remove some of the worst wrinkles before spreading it on the bed.

At last she was ready for her bath. When she had removed her soiled clothing, she sprinkled some bath salts into the water and then stepped into the tub.

As she washed her face and throat with the washcloth provided by the hotel, her thoughts wandered to the handsome man with the hard-looking face. Had he gone with one of the women to her room? she wondered. If so, what kind of lover was he?

"Oh, for heaven's sake," Willow scolded herself impatiently, "stop thinking such things about a man you'll never see again."

She finished her bath, toweled off her body, and started on her hair. It took two latherings and rinsings before she was satisfied that it was clean. She slipped into the old worn robe she had brought along and sat in front of the open window brushing and combing the blond strands until they looked like shimmering silk lying on her shoulders. When she had put on the clean underclothing she had laid out and pulled the dress over her head, she stepped in front of the wavy mirror of the dresser and began doing up the tiny buttons of the bodice, which outlined her breasts and narrow rib cage. She frowned at the amount of breast showing above the low-cut neckline. She had worn the dress twice before, but each time she had tucked an inch-wide strip of lace around the neck to hide the cleavage it revealed.

Willow sighed. She had forgotten to add the lace to her saddlebag. There was nothing she could do but wear it as it was.

When ten minutes had passed and Smitty hadn't returned yet, she picked up her wrist purse and left the room. She would wait for him out on the porch. He should be coming any minute.

Chapter Three

Jules Asher stepped out of the mercantile just as Willow took a seat on the bench directly beneath the lantern fastened on the wall. Its light shone on her delicate face and the silky blond hair that fell around her shoulders and midway down her back.

Lord, but she's a beauty, the rancher thought. In his experience, the only unattached females who roamed El Paso at night were soiled doves, and he wondered why she chose to sell her body. Wherever she came from, there must have been any number of men who would have wanted a wife like her.

He wondered also how Big Jane, the proprietress of the only whorehouse in town, had come to recruit this gem. She hadn't had her last week when he'd visited the pleasure house. And why had the madam sent such a beauty out onto the street to hustle up business? All this one had to do was walk through the waiting room at Big Jane's place and the news would spread like wildfire that there was a new girl in town. A girl so beautiful it made a man weak just to look at her.

Jules straightened up from his leaning stance against the wall. He would be the little lady's first customer tonight. No, not her first. Her only customer for the night. A man would take a long time getting his fill of her.

His spurs clinking, he walked the short distance to the hotel and stepped up onto the porch.

"Howdy, little lady," he said in his deep, rich voice as he removed his Stetson.

Willow looked up and gave a start. The handsome cowboy she had watched from her window stood looking down at her. Up close he was almost disreputable-looking. A grub-liner, she thought disdainfully, strangely disappointed as she took in his whisker-stubbled face, the battered hat he held in his hand, his dusty clothes and scuffed boots.

She gave him a short nod and looked away.

"It's a fine evening, isn't it?" The cowboy set a foot on the edge of the bench and leaned his arm across his bent knee. When she continued to ignore him, he pressed, "Would you care to have supper with me in the hotel dining room? The food is real good."

Willow felt a surge of impatience building inside her. The man was as arrogant as he looked. She turned her head and looked into his dark, wicked eyes and said coolly, "No, I would not care to have supper with you."

"That's fine." His white teeth flashed again in a wide

smile. "We can get right down to business then. Shall we amble over to Big Jane's place and get settled in?"

"Who is Big Jane?" Willow gave him a sharp look, suspicion growing inside her.

"Come on now, honey, don't play coy with me." A coolness had come into the annoying man's voice. "You know damn well who Big Jane is. You work for her."

"At the moment I don't work for anyone." Willow jumped to her feet.

"Hey, that's better yet." The tall man stood up also, the warmth back in his voice. "I'd like to spend the entire night with you. How much would you charge me?"

Willow stared at him a moment, her mouth open. He thought she was a soiled dove! Without fully realizing what she was doing, she lifted her hand and her palm popped like a pistol shot as it smacked across his face.

Jules's hand went to his stinging cheek. "Why, you little bitch!" he grated out.

"How dare you!" Willow exclaimed. Pushing past him, she hurried back into the hotel.

Jules stood, still nursing his cheek as he watched her until she disappeared up the stairs.

So, she has set up shop here in the Palace, he thought. She thinks she's too good for a dusty, down-at-the-heels cowboy, does she? Probably she only does business with bankers and shopkeepers, men in neat suits and smelling of bay rum.

In his hurry to leave, Jules almost knocked down an elderly man coming up the steps. "Sorry, old timer," he said remorsefully when he saw that the old cowboy had a decided limp. "Are you all right?" His hand went out to steady the other man.

"I'm fine, young feller," Smitty said gruffly. "Go tend to whatever business you're in such a hellfire hurry to get to."

Jules grinned as he watched the old man stump into the hotel. The crusty old fellow probably worked there. Sweeping out the lobby and emptying out cuspidors. No wonder he was so crabby.

Jules stood on the sidewalk a minute trying to decide what to do with the evening. He was pretty well beat from helping his men brand mavericks all day and didn't look forward to the fifteen-mile ride to his ranch. Also, he didn't look forward to listening to his Aunt Jess and his housekeeper Nina trade insults with each other. The two women went at it hammer and tongs. He couldn't wait till the new housekeeper he'd hired arrived, so he could send Nina packing.

He stepped down onto the dusty street. He'd stop in at the saloon and have a few drinks, then rent one of the rooms upstairs and spend the night there.

"It's about time you got back," Willow said grumpily when she opened the door to Smitty's knock. If he hadn't been late returning, she wouldn't have had that run-in with the insulting cowboy who had taken her for a lady of the evening.

"I wasn't gone all that long," Smitty shot back. "I didn't know you was all that hungry."

"Well, I am." Willow picked up her small bag from the bed where she had angrily tossed it on her return from her upsetting conversation with the hateful cowboy. "I hope they still have some food left in the kitchen," she said, brushing past Smitty and heading down the hall toward the stairs.

"For cryin' out loud." Smitty stumped along behind her. "It's only a little past six o'clock."

The dining room had several customers when Willow and Shorty entered it, mainly men. Smitty wondered why they kept ogling Willow, and why her face looked so cross.

When they had been seated by a rosy-cheeked, teenaged country girl, they both ordered the chicken dinner, something they weren't used to having. Smitty ate with an eager appetite, but Willow just pushed the food around on her plate. Smitty knew she was out of sorts, but he never paid much attention to women's moods. They changed all the time and a man could go crazy trying to figure them out. Willow would be in a better mood tomorrow, or she wouldn't. The sun would still come up in the east and set in the west.

Before they left the dining room, Smitty asked the young lady who had served them how to get to the Asher ranch. All the time the waitress gave him instructions, her eyes were on Willow. It was obvious she was speculating as to why the striking blonde was going to Jules Asher's ranch.

The directions Smitty received were very simple. They were to head out of town and follow the dirt road that would take them straight to the ranch. It was just fifteen miles.

When Jules had stepped through the batwing doors of the saloon, he was greeted by four men from neighboring ranches who made room for him at the bar.

When Archie, the bartender, had asked him what would be his pleasure, on the spur of the moment, he'd ordered a bottle of whiskey and a glass. Now, after sharing a few drinks, he wanted some privacy. His companions didn't feel insulted when he took his bottle to a table slightly to the left of saloon's big window and sat down. They understood that once in a while a man liked to be alone when he drank. There were times when he had something on his mind that he wanted to mull over.

Without fully realizing it, Jules wanted to watch the hotel across the street. He wanted to see how many men would enter it and climb the stairs to the little cat's room.

When midnight arrived and he was the only man left in the barroom, and not a single man had visited the building he watched, Jules gave up his vigil and asked Archie for a key to one of the rooms upstairs.

The next morning, early, when Willow and Smitty met for breakfast in the dining room, he didn't think his companion looked much more pleasant than she had the night before. As they ate ham and eggs, he remarked, "I hope you're not worried about the job that's waitin' for you. You're a hard worker and you'll do just fine."

"I hope so, Smitty." Willow gave him a wan smile. "I don't know how many people are living there, how many I'll have to cook for and clean up after. What if I don't please this rancher and he turns me out later? Where would I go? I can't go home and marry Buck Axel."

"Accordin' to your Maw, Asher is a bachelor, so

there shouldn't be any younguns runnin' round."

"I wouldn't mind children. I like young ones. It's bossy adults I'm worried about."

"Well," Smitty said when he had drunk the last of his coffee, "there's no use wonderin' about it. Let's get on out there and find out."

As they loped their horses toward the dim outline of the distant mountain, they passed hundreds of longhorns along the way. "This Asher must be pretty well off," Smitty opined.

"It looks that way," Willow agreed and grew more nervous of what she would find at the man's ranch. She imagined that a man of wealth would expect high-quality work.

It was mid-morning when they reached the foothills of Davis Mountain and began to climb an area that was sparsely covered with pine and mesquite. Before long they rounded a huge rock formation, and a sprawling Spanish-style adobe house stood in front of them. A wall of the same material, some three feet tall, surrounded the building, broken by a wide arch in the center. Hanging on two short chains was a sign with the name "Asher Ranch" burned into the wooden board.

Reining in outside the wall, they tied their mounts to a heavy hitching rail. "Quite a fancy place, ain't it?" Smitty said from the side of his mouth as they stepped into a tiled courtyard and walked beneath a wide portico leading to a heavily built door of dark wood. All was quiet inside, and the only sound outside was an old hound who gave a mixed sound of greeting as he barked and wagged his tail at the same time.

"Hello, fellow." Willow held her hand down for him to sniff and the dog danced around her, begging for attention.

"Let's see if there's anyone around here," Smitty said and pulled the rope of a bell attached to the wall. He waited a minute, and when no one answered his summons he lifted his hand to tug the rope again. Just then the door opened. A cross-faced, dark-haired woman stood before them. She looked at Smitty with cool disdain.

"If you're looking for a handout, go to the cookhouse." Her gaze went over Smitty's dusty clothes, his scuffed boots.

"Now look here, you . . ." Smitty began, but Willow stepped out of the shadows.

In a voice of quiet dignity, she said, "We're not looking for something to eat. I don't know if it's any of your business, but I'm here at Mr. Asher's invitation to be his housekeeper."

At first an uncertain look came into the woman's eyes as she gave her attention to the tall, slender girl with the long blond hair. Then jealous anger blazed in her dark eyes.

"Hah!" she sneered. "Housekeeper, is it? Why don't you come right out and say that you're here to warm his bed. *I'm* his housekeeper."

"Not anymore, you ain't," an aged voice cackled behind the woman. "You'll be movin' on when Jules gets home."

"You don't know what you're talking about, you knotty old stick." Enraged, she turned on an elderly, white-haired woman who walked with the aid of a cane.

The little woman with the bright, bird-like eyes that were full of delighted laughter said, "Don't you wish I didn't know what I was talking about." She pushed past the soon-to-be ex-housekeeper and gave Willow a wide, toothless smile as she held out her hand and said, "I'm Jess Miles, Jules's aunt."

Willow shook the small, dry hand and said, "I'm happy to meet you Mrs. Miles."

"Call me Aunt Jess." She directed a sly look at the other woman who had apparently never been allowed that familiarity. "That's Nina."

Willow turned to Smitty. "Aunt Jess, meet my friend, Smitty Black. He cooks for my father's ranch hands."

The frail little woman and the old man smiled at each other, both careful not to squeeze the other one's hand too hard.

"I've forgotten my manners. Come inside." When Willow and Smitty stepped into the wide entrance hall, Jess gave her arch enemy a rap on the ankle with her cane. "Bring some coffee to the family room, Nina," she ordered. "Fresh brewed. None of that left-over stuff you usually give me."

Before she flounced off, Nina gave the aunt a malevolent look that revealed her hatred. But Jess's only rejoinder was a cackling laugh as she led Willow and Smitty into a large, tiled great room.

What a beautiful room it will be once the dirt and grime have been removed, Willow thought as Jess motioned with her cane for her and Smitty to have a seat. As Smitty laid Willow's saddlebags on the floor beside the chair he had taken, the old aunt saw the new housekeeper's glance moving over the room.

"It looks awful, don't it?" she said. "That lazy Nina hasn't lifted a hand in here for over a month. It's about time my nephew hired someone to take real charge of his home. That one in there ain't worth spit when it comes to workin'. She's only good for—" Jess stopped her tongue before finishing what she was about to say. But Smitty knew what she was thinking and gave her a knowing look that made them grin at each other and ignore the questioning look Willow gave them.

"Would you like to see the rest of the house while we're waitin' for our coffee?" Jess asked.

"I'd like that." Willow stood up, but Smitty said he'd just as soon stay where he was.

The house was large and handsome. Besides the great room there were four large bedrooms, a dining room and the kitchen, which they didn't enter. There were tiles throughout, with colorful Mexican and Indian rugs scattered about. The furniture was in the Spanish style, as was the pottery.

Dust and dirt clung to everything, including the curtains and heavy drapes. The windows were so gritty with grime that Willow couldn't clearly see through them.

The tour completed, Jess said, "I'll tell Pedro, the blacksmith's helper, to send his wife over to give you a hand scrubbing down the place. Once you get on top of the dirt, it won't be hard for you to keep the place up."

"I don't mind the scrubbing," Willow protested. "I don't need any help."

Jess shook her head. "It wouldn't be right for you to clean up after that lazy Nina."

They were walking back toward the great room when Jess asked, "Are you a good cook, Willow?"

"I think so. Smitty taught me a lot and gave me some of his secret recipes."

"Do you know how to cook spicy food?"

"I'm sorry, Jess, but I don't."

"Good girl." Jess beamed at her. "Me and you are gonna get along just fine."

When Willow and Jess walked into the family room, they heard loud voices coming from the kitchen down the hall and saw Smitty sitting on the edge of his seat, his head turned that way, listening.

"Smitty—" Willow started to tell him not to listen to a private quarrel, but Jess held a finger to her lips and whispered, "Shh, I want to hear this."

"You might as well stop yelling," a male voice said firmly. "If you have no place to go, you can move into the cabin until you find a new job."

Willow leaned forward now and listened. The man's voice was vaguely familiar.

Nina's sharp voice challenged, "I don't know why I can't stay here in the ranch house. There are four bedrooms. And another thing—why do you feel you need a different housekeeper?" Her voice softened. "Don't I keep you satisfied anymore?"

"If you want the truth, no, your work is unsatisfactory."

Nina's voice rose again. "I don't think that woman is here to keep house for you. I think you've brought her here to replace me in your bed."

A brief hush fell in the kitchen. Then the man was saying in a deadly calm voice, "It's none of your business why she's here, but these are the reasons I'm replacing you as my housekeeper. Number one, I want a woman who will keep the house clean and cook me nourishing meals. My stomach is all torn up from eating the spicy hot dishes you cook. Number two, the house looks like a pigsty, and number three, Aunt Jess doesn't like you and wants you out of her home."

A big smile spread across Jess's face when she heard that. "As for the woman visiting my bed, I've never seen her, and I have reason to believe she's as ugly as a mud fence."

"Hah! Do you think I am stupid? You know damn well you've seen her."

"Look, I've had enough of your carrying on. If you don't want to stay at the cabin, I'll take you back to El Paso, where I found you serving drinks in a casino."

"Oh, all right. I'll go to the cabin," Nina gave in sullenly.

"You know where the place is. I'm going to go meet this Ames woman while you pack your duds."

The three eavesdroppers sat back in their chairs, trying to look as though they hadn't heard a word when they heard heavy footsteps coming down the hall.

His face flushed and tight with anger, Jules strode into the great room and came to a sharp stop. The startled look that came into his eyes showed that he hadn't been aware of a listening audience to his and Nina's row. His gaze was drawn to Willow immediately, and they exclaimed in unison, "You!"

"Do you two know each other?" Jess asked, confusion on her face.

"We haven't officially met," Jules said coolly, "but our paths have crossed."

"That's right," Willow agreed in a voice equally cool. "Mr. Asher propositioned me last night."

"What do you mean, he propositioned you?" Smitty bristled, perching on the edge of his seat.

"I mean he offered me money to sleep with him."

"Jules, tell me you didn't do such a thing!" Jess was on the edge of her seat now, too.

"Hell, Aunt Jess, I didn't know who she was. She was sitting outside the hotel all dressed up. What was a fellow to think?"

"If he could think," Willow said contemptously, "he might have thought that the woman was waiting for someone, and I don't mean some stranger who would come along and offer to buy her services in his bed."

"Why didn't you tell me about this?" Smitty demanded of Willow as his eyes bored into Jules.

Willow shrugged. "It wasn't important," she said scornfully. "I thought he was a down-at-the-heel saddle tramp without a dime in his pocket. Anyway, I was starving and all I could think of was eating supper." Her eyes dared Smitty to mention her agitated state all through the meal or her lack of appetite.

Jules opened his mouth to make some kind of cutting remark, but Jess cut him off. "Well, now that's all straightened out," she said. "So, Jules, meet Smitty Black. He brought Willow here. He'll be leavin' in the mornin' to return to his job as a cook at the Ames ranch."

When the men had given a cool nod to each other, Jess looked at Willow and asked, "Do you want to see the kitchen now?"

Willow nodded and stood up. As she followed the old woman out of the room, Jules watched her through half-closed eyes. His new housekeeper had a supple grace that was delightful to watch. He squirmed as his loins tightened.

"She sure is good to look at, ain't she, Asher?" Smitty hadn't missed the way Jules's eyes had followed Willow as she left the room. When Jules made himself shrug indifferently, the old cook warned, "Only to look at, nothing else. If anybody ever hurts that girl in any way, some dark night he'll feel my knife in his back."

Jules started to laugh at the notion of this old man wielding a deadly blade, but then he saw that the warning wasn't uttered in a show of bravado. Smitty Black's expression said that he meant every word he said.

"Don't worry, old timer. I never have cared for wildcats."

"I'm glad to hear that," Smitty said, and the subject was dropped.

"While we're waiting for lunch, would you like to go down to the corral and look at my Arabian horses?" Jules asked.

As the two men left the hacienda and walked toward the stables, Willow and Jess were surveying the kitchen.

"What a mess," Jess said in disgust. "It's a wonder me and Jules didn't get food poisonin' from the food that come out of here." She sighed. "The old Mexican woman who used to keep house for Jules kept this kitchen so bright and shiny, me and Jules took all our meals in here. It was a sad day for us when she went to live with her daughter."

"It will be that way again," Willow assured Jess, "but not today," she added, looking at the large black range, which was covered with splattered, baked-on grease.

And the table looked equally bad, she thought. Dirty dishes and the remains of last evening's supper were still sitting on it. Her feet slid on a patch of grease as she walked to the sink. When she saw it stacked with pots and pans and skillets, she sighed. Where to start in this unbelievably dirty kitchen?

"I guess the first thing to do," she said, rolling up her sleeves, "is to start on these cooking utensils, then scrub down the stove and table."

"I expect so," Jess agreed. She had discarded her cane and was now bustling around with an energy she hadn't had in months. She took an apron from behind the stove and handed it to Willow. "This belonged to Maria. It's clean. That Nina never wore a cover over her dresses."

Willow lifted the lid on the water reservoir and was surprised to find it full. The water was only warm, however, and she would need it very hot to get the grease off the items stacked in the sink.

While Jess built a fire in the cookstove, Willow filled two large pots with water from the tank and set them on the stove to heat. As she waited for steam to rise from the cast-iron containers, she started scraping dried food off the plates and bowls that littered the table. Then she stacked them and set them aside to be washed later.

It took Willow and Jess close to two hours to scrub

the stove and table, then the dishes and cooking utensils.

But at last, after changing the water three times, the job was done and Willow was wondering what to serve for lunch.

"Why don't you fry some ham, scramble some eggs and make some bakin' powder biscuits," Jess suggested. "Jules hasn't had food like that for months. He'd really enjoy it."

"So would I," Willow remarked as her hungry stomach growled. "Where do you keep your supplies?"

"In the larder, through that door to your right."

Willow opened the door to a good-sized room that was dry and cool. The thick stone walls made it ideal for storing staples and perishable foods.

As Willow glanced around, she was surprised that such a well-to-do man didn't have his storeroom better stocked. Most of the many shelves were empty. She noted that there was an ample supply of bagged beans, rice, corn meal and flour. Also strings of hot peppers and cans of tomatoes.

On a bottom shelf there were a few potatoes that were sprouting eyes half an inch long, and hanging from the ceiling was a ham, which had never been cut into, and a slab of bacon in its original state.

She looked at Jess, frowning. "Who does the ordering of supplies?"

"It's always been the housekeeper's job. It's not hard to figure out who has been doin' that for a while."

"I wonder where the eggs are?" Willow searched among the bags and cans of tomatoes.

"There should be a fresh dozen around here somewhere," Jess said. "The farmer who supplies us eggs and milk and butter, and vegetables in the summer, dropped them off the day before yesterday. We had to throw away three dozen that Nina let spoil because she didn't want to cook them. Not once did she make us a decent breakfast."

"Well, you're going to have a decent lunch," Willow said with a smile, "for I have found the eggs. They were jammed behind some jars of jelly that evidently Nina didn't want to bother with either."

"If that don't put the lid on it," Jess exclaimed angrily. "She was hidin' them from Jules in case he told her to fry some for him."

By the time Jules and Smitty returned from the stables and washed up on a small porch off the kitchen, the table had a bright flowered cloth on it, and in the center was a large platter with scrambled eggs on one side and thick slices of ham on the other. Next to it was a napkin-lined basket of biscuits, flanked by a bowl of red gravy.

Willow was filling the cups with clear, dark coffee when the men entered the kitchen and sat down at the table.

"Biscuits!" Jules almost moaned his pleasure as he took two and placed them on his plate. "I'd almost forgotten what they looked like."

Willow and Jess gave him a scornful look, which he didn't miss. He knew what they were thinking: that he had given up good hearty meals in order to sleep with his housekeeper. He knew that it might look that way, but they were mistaken. He had put up with Nina because he had been too busy working the ranch to go looking for a new housekeeper. Mrs. Ames's letter had been a godsend.

Everyone was hungry and the only sound in the room was the scraping of silverware being put to use. There wasn't even a break in the eating when Nina walked into the kitchen and announced that she was riding into El Paso to begin looking for a new job. Willow and Smitty glanced up at her, but Jules and Jess kept on eating. Nina shot a glance at the table, the cloth on it and the mouth-watering food everyone was shoveling into their mouths. With a toss of her head and a curl to her lips, she flounced through the kitchen door.

Jess stopped eating long enough to mutter, "Good riddance to bad baggage."

Lunch was finished and coffee had been served when Jess said, "Nephew, tell Pedro to send his wife over to give Willow a hand getting the worst of the dirt off everything. That Nina has left the place disgustingly dirty."

Avoiding looking at Willow, Jules nodded. A short time later he nodded again when Willow, refilling the coffee cups, stopped at his chair waiting to see if he wanted more.

He watched her tilt the pot over his cup, her slender, tanned fingers curled around its handle, and the thought of them on his body made him almost jump from his chair. He hoped that Willow wouldn't glance down and see the growing bulge in his trousers.

Damn, he swore silently. *What is wrong with me?* He had known many women and none of them had ever affected him as this one did. And Willow was grieving for a man who had practically left her at the church door.

He couldn't imagine any man being fool enough to do that. Just making love to Willow every night would be enough for him. The thought of holding that tall, slender, softly naked body against his own, her breasts flattened out against his bare chest, made sweat pop out on his forehead.

By the time Jules left the table, he was wondering if he hadn't made the biggest mistake of his life by letting Willow Ames become his housekeeper.

He knew in the same breath that he wouldn't have it any other way. For he felt that in time she would forget the damn fool of a man who'd jilted her, and when she did, Jules Asher would be ready to slide in and take his place. Lord, he hoped it didn't take her too long. How long could a man go around with a perpetual arousal pressing against his fly?

Pedro's wife, Rosie, came to the hacienda just as Willow and Jess were finishing cleaning up the kitchen. She was young, pretty and a little on the plump side. She had a ready smile and was eager to please.

When Jess had introduced the two young women, she took herself off to her room for a rest and a nap. "You don't have to bother with my room," she said. "I saw to it that Nina kept it clean."

Willow and Rosie pitched in then. "We'll change the bed linens first," Willow said and directed Rosie to Nina's old room. The thought of touching that one's sheets revolted her.

When all the soiled sheets and pillowcases had been taken to the small laundry room off the kitchen,

Willow and Rosie went from room to room, taking down limp drapes and curtains, which joined the rest of the things to be washed. The windows were washed then, the tiled floors scrubbed and the heavy, dark furniture polished to a high gloss.

While Willow cleared away a winter's accumulation of ashes from the big fieldstone fireplace and scrubbed the raised hearth, Rosie gathered up all the bright Mexican scatter rugs and took them outside, where she hung them over a clothesline and beat the dust and grit out of them with a wide, long handled beater.

It was nearing four o'clock and time for Willow to be thinking about starting supper when she and Rosie looked at each other with wide, pleased smiles on their lips. They had worked like dogs, but the results of their labor were impressive.

"Now the hacienda looks like it did when old Maria took care of it," the pleasant young woman said. As she was leaving, she paused at the kitchen door and asked shyly, "Shall I come tomorrow to help you do the laundry? There is a mountain of things to be washed."

Willow saw the hope in the beautiful dark eyes and realized that more money in Rosie's household would be welcome. She didn't know how her boss would feel about paying for extra help, but if he objected, she would pay Rosie from the small amount of money she had brought with her.

"I'd be happy to have your help, Rosie." She smiled. "Shall we get an early start?"

"I'll be here bright and early, *señorita.*" The young woman's eyes shone with excitement as she took off to walk swiftly to the stables where her husband worked.

"Where do Rosie and her husband live?" Willow asked Jess a short time later when the old woman came in from a small, walled patio off the kitchen, where she had been sunning herself.

"They live with Pedro's brother and his wife and eight children in a three-room shack near the Rio Grande. I guess it's a constant struggle to feed so many mouths. Still, every spring the sister-in-law has another baby in her belly."

"Why do they keep having more when it's hard to feed the ones they have?"

Jess gave a short laugh. "Accordin' to Pedro's brother, it's because they're strict Catholics. But it's my opinion that the fool thinks it makes him a big man, being able to keep his wife expectin' all the time. He don't seem to understand that any man can do that if he wants to. There's nothin' manly about it. The manly thing to do is not to have a passel of younguns you can't take care of. His father used to brag that he sired fourteen children on his wife. He stopped boastin' the day Jules's father reminded him that half of those children had died young, and that his wife had died when she was thirty-four from so many pregnancies. That shut the braggart up, at least around my brother-in-law. A couple years later he got himself killed in some Mexican whorehouse."

Later, as Willow turned steaks in the frying pan and mashed potatoes for supper, she wondered what kind of husband Jules Asher would make. Of course, first some fool would have to marry the arrogant devil.

Chapter Four

When Jules stepped out of the bunkhouse, a full moon had risen, flooding the ranch buildings with a soft, yellow radiance. He stood in the shadow of a large cottonwood his grandmother had planted beside a two-room adobe house that was to be her home for ten years while the ranch of today was being built.

His gaze focused on the sprawling hacienda that had replaced the little adobe, which had been added onto and was now a part of the bunkhouse.

He imagined Willow asleep in the room across the hall from his, and pictured himself curled behind her, holding one of her perky little breasts, which would just fit his hand.

He dreamed on. They made long, slow love time and again, her throaty moans mingling with his harsh breathing as his hips rose and fell in the valley of her hips.

With a soft oath, Jules became aware of his breathing now and found it harsh and fast, as it had been in his imagination. Also, he had an erection so hard, it threatened to pop the buttons off his fly. He looked over his shoulder at the small cabin where Nina now resided. A light shone in the window. She was still up, no doubt waiting for him. He sighed. He knew she would welcome him in her bed, despite their harsh words earlier. But, somehow, the vision of a tall, slender woman with long blond hair made Nina's lush charms less appealing.

Willow gave a blissful sigh as she sank back in the hip-tub of scented water. It felt heavenly as the heat penetrated her tired and sore muscles. She had put in a day's work as hard as any on her father's ranch.

There was a difference, though. Today she had worked hard, but at her own pace, enjoying the task of uncovering the beauty of the fine old furniture hidden beneath dirt and grime. At home her father had made a drudge out of her, always driving her to do more, never satisfied until he had pushed her until she was ready to drop.

Everything about the Asher ranch house was different from her home in New Mexico. There the floors were wide, untreated boards with a few rag rugs scattered about, so thin and worn that one's feet were always tripping over them. The few pieces of furniture were constructed from such cheap wood that no amount of polishing brought a shine to them.

The bedrooms were sparsely furnished with a bed, dresser and washstand. There were no heavy drapes at the windows, no colorful spreads on the beds.

As Willow finished her bath and dried off with a soft, thick towel, she hoped that her work would satisfy her overbearing boss so that she could stay on in this beautiful house.

When she had slipped on a thin, worn gown, she looked at the tub of water and decided that she would drag it out onto the porch tomorrow and empty it. She wasn't quite ready for bed, though, so she walked down the hall, through the kitchen—sparkling clean now—and out onto the small patio.

In the deepening twilight, she sat down on an ornate stone bench and leaned back, unaware that a tall, lean man stood nearby, gazing at the house, having erotic thoughts of her.

How was her mother tonight? she wondered as the old hound came and by down at her feet. Ruth was probably as worn out as Willow had been before her bath. Pa would have been outraged at her disappearance and would have taken his anger out on the frail little woman. He would have ordered that, since she wouldn't tell him where his worthless daughter had gone, her mother could do her work.

Pain clouded Willow's eyes. There was no way bone-thin Ruth Ames could do half the work Willow did in a day. Tears glimmered in her eyes. If only she could free her mother from the life of misery she had lived for so long. There must be a way, and somehow she would find it.

The sound of footsteps crunching on the hard-packed soil roused Willow from her dreary thoughts.

Was the gate locked? She stood up and as quietly as possible walked to the wrought-iron gate and peered through it.

In the moonlight she saw the receding back of her boss. Where was he going at this time of evening? she wondered. She felt a jolt in her midsection when he turned onto the path leading to a small house where a light shone in the window. Nina now lived there. He was going to visit her. He might have moved the woman out of his house, but he hadn't moved her out of his life.

She was so upset that Jules was having a rendezvous with the woman, she was hardly aware of returning to the bench and sitting down. "I don't even like the man, so why should it bother me that he will make love to her tonight?" she asked herself angrily.

The more Willow thought, the more confused she became. Finally she gave up in frustration and went back into the house. In her room, she turned back the covers and crawled onto the softness of the mattress. Worn out physically and emotionally, she fell asleep almost immediately. Consequently, she missed hearing Jules walk down the hall to his room a very short time after she had seen him going to Nina's place. She would have treated him less coolly the next morning had she known that he had found himself completely unmoved by the other woman.

Willow was up early the next morning, but not before Smitty. When she walked into the kitchen, he was sitting at the table sipping a cup of coffee.

"Mornin', Willow." He smiled at her. "I brewed a pot of coffee. Sit down and have a cup with me."

"Goodness, Smitty." Willow combed her fingers through her tangled hair. "What time did you get up? It's not even daylight yet."

"I know, but I'm anxious to get goin'. Things are gonna be hellish for Ruth at the ranch, and I want to get back there and help her all I can."

Willow filled a cup with the steaming brew and carried it to the table. When she sat down, she looked at Smitty and asked bluntly, "Are you in love with my mother, Smitty?"

Smitty's weathered face reddened and he opened his mouth to deny such a foolish thought. Instead, much to his surprise, he answered quietly, "Yes, I am. I have been for years. She's the one that has kept me working for that bastard husband of hers. You don't know what hell it has been for me to stand by helpless while your pa abuses her."

"I know." Willow patted the hand that clenched the coffee cup so tightly. "I've felt that way all my life. I feel so guilty, leaving her there alone with my father. Only the threat of marriage to Buck Axel made me go away."

Smitty nodded. "You were right to leave. Eventually Otto would have had his way."

"Smitty," Willow said earnestly, "We've got to think of a way to get Ma out of there. She's worn out and won't live long if she stays."

"I know that, girl, and I'll do something, even if it means shooting Otto Ames."

"You musn't do that, Smitty." Willow looked alarmed. "You'd hang."

"It would be worth it if I could end Ruth's misery."

"That's not the answer." Willow finished her coffee

and stood up. "We must think of something else. For the time being I'm going to fry some slices of ham, and boil some eggs for you to take with you when you leave. Where are your saddlebags?"

"Over there in the corner." Smitty jerked a thumb over his shoulder. "Maybe you can fill an extra canteen with coffee. There might be an evening when I don't dare build a fire."

"That's right," Jules said from the doorway, making Willow start at his unexpected appearance. "Stay sharp when you make night camp, Smitty," he continued. "As a general rule Indians don't attack once the sun goes down. They have the notion that if a brave gets killed then, his spirit wanders forever. But a person can never be sure. A young brave not set yet in the beliefs of his people might sneak up on you in the dark."

"Yeah, I know." Smitty nodded. "I've had that happen to me." He started to speak of the experience but went no further when he saw that Jules's attention was elsewhere.

Jules, fascinated, was watching Willow slice ham. His gaze moved from her satin-smooth face to the pale blond hair that hang around her shoulders and down her back in disarray. He longed to stretch out a hand and let his fingers smooth the tangles from it.

But it was her slender, willowy shape that held his interest the longest. Her robe, worn thin from countless washings, clung to her breasts, then dipped in at her tiny waist where it was tightly belted, then followed the gentle curve of her hips. They weren't voluptuous, like Nina's, Jules thought, just wide enough to cradle his.

That's wishful thinking, he told himself. She won't even look at me, let alone welcome me between those long legs.

Willow was an unforgiving woman, but he was going to work on that. She was different from any female he had ever known, and come hell or high water, he was going to have her.

When he saw that Willow wasn't going to serve him coffee, Jules stood up and walked to the stove, seeming to accidently brush a hand against her rear as he walked past her. She gave a start and turned an angry look on him, but his features were bland and she gave him the benefit of the doubt. Maybe the touch of his hand had been unintentional.

"Should I make you some breakfast?" she asked Smitty as he finished his second cup of coffee.

"No, thank you, Willow, I ain't hungry yet. I'll eat one of them sandwiches later on in the mornin' as I ride along."

"I'm not hungry either." Jules's white teeth flashed in a wide smile as though Willow had inquired if he wanted breakfast also. "I'll eat a little later, after I've shaved."

Smitty hid a grin when Willow started packing the trail grub into his saddlebags as though Jules hadn't spoken. He wished he could stay on a little longer, just to watch the battle of wills between those two. It would be very interesting, and hard to predict which would be the winner. Both were strong-willed. It was easy to see that Asher wasn't used to being rebuffed by women, and he knew for a fact that Willow didn't have much use for men, so she wasn't going to be swayed by any sweet talk from the rancher.

When it was time for Smitty to leave, there was a wetness in Willow's eyes as she followed him outside. He already had his horse saddled and waiting.

"Give Ma my love," she said when he had mounted, "and tell her I'll be thinking about her all the time and planning the day when we will be together again."

"I'll do that, girl, and you be careful of that randy boss of yours. He's hot to get you in his bed."

"Hah!" Willow snorted. "We both know that won't happen, don't we?"

"Keep that thought, Willow," Smitty said, and lifting the reins, he rode out just as the sun touched the eastern rim of the prairie.

Willow blinked back tears and watched the last link to her mother disappear on the horizon. Would she ever see her old friend again, or her sweet little mother?

She wiped her eyes and walked back into the kitchen. To her surprise, Jules had poured himself another cup of coffee and was still sitting at the table. He wants to bait me some more, she thought grimly, and the irritation she felt sounded in her voice when she asked, "Do you want your breakfast now?"

"No, I'm still not hungry, and I haven't shaved yet. I only wanted to tell you that last night's supper was the best I've had in a long time, and that my home hasn't looked so good since I can remember. Old Maria did the best she could, but the last few years she wasn't up to all the work the place demanded to make it look its best. I wanted to have some woman come in from town and give her a hand, but she felt insulted when I mentioned it."

Willow recognized that her boss was trying a new

approach to soften her up. She gave an inward contemptuous laugh and said, "I can understand that an elderly woman's pride and lack of strength would keep her from giving the place the attention it deserves, but what excuse do you have for Nina not keeping your home clean? She's young, and looks very strong to me."

A mixture of embarrassment and anger stained Jules's face. Willow was right, but it wasn't up to her to chastize him. In his outrage, he spoke words that he immediately wished he could call back.

"Nina wasn't here to do housework."

Willow gave him a look that shriveled him to his toes. "I see," she said with a curl of her lips. "You hired her for the express purpose of heckling and tormenting your aged aunt. I can't see how she could possibly be of any interest to you otherwise."

Jules blundered on in his rage, "That's because you're not a man."

"Hah!" Willow shot back at him. "If I were a man, I wouldn't want anything to do with the likes of that one. There's nothing special about her. In fact, she's very common. In all ways, I expect."

Jules knew he was losing the battle and was thankful when Aunt Jess tapped her way into the kitchen. "Drat it!" she exclaimed. "I wanted to see Smitty off."

"You just missed him, Aunt Jess." Willow pulled a chair away from the table. "Sit down and I'll pour you a cup of coffee."

"How are you this mornin'?" Jess looked at her nephew, who still showed traces of anger in his eyes.

"I'm fine, Aunt Jess. How are you feeling?"

"I'm feelin' fine as a fiddle. Had my best night's

sleep since I stopped eatin' Nina's food. I bet you slept better after that fine supper Willow served us."

Jules ignored the last part of Jess's remark. He hadn't slept well at all despite the fact that his stomach felt fine. The thought of the beauty sleeping across the hall from him had kept him awake for most of the night.

Jess transferred her attention to Willow when a cup of coffee was set before her. "Honey, did you ask Rosie to come help you with the wash today?"

Willow darted a look at Jules's tight face before answering, "Yes, I did, if that's all right."

"Of course it is. There's a pile of dirty clothes in the washroom that almost touches the ceiling. That Nina only washed clothes twice all the time she was here." She looked at her nephew. "I never could figure out why you kept her on."

"Maybe you never thought about it too hard, Aunt Jess," Willow said sardonically. "Maybe Nina has hidden assets."

Jess would have jumped up and down in her glee had she been able to. She had gotten the results she had aimed for. Willow wasn't afraid to stand up to her nephew, to let him know what she was thinking. Jules had finally met his match.

When Jules only glared at her, his face growing darker, Jess said, "We're real short on rations. I think Willow should ride into Coyote and lay in some supplies."

Jules pushed away from the table, his chair scraping on the tiles. "Put everything on my tab at the store," he answered as he stomped out of the room.

Willow and Jess looked at each other and fought

back the laughter that rose in their throats. "I don't think that rooster is too happy with us, Willow," the old woman whispered, her little black eyes glittering with mischief.

"I know. Isn't it a shame." Willow's pretended dismay sent them both into loud laughter.

Jules slammed his bedroom door against their merry mirth.

"I think we've pulled enough feathers out of his tail, don't you?" Jess wiped the tears from her eyes. "He looked ready to strangle us both."

"I guess we have for the time being." Willow wiped her own eyes. "There's always tomorrow."

Jess agreed, then added, "I shouldn't rag him like that, but he's so dratted arrogant. I can't help bringin' him down a peg or two ever once in a while. Show him he's not as special as he thinks he is sometimes."

She tamped tobacco into her pipe then and struck a match to it. When she had drawn on the long stem a couple of times, sending smoke curling around her face and white hair, she said, "In all honesty, though, I reckon Jules has a right to feel a cut above the average man. Since he was old enough and strong enough to round up cattle, he has worked like a slave, building this ranch into the biggest and the best in the territory."

Willow was saved from having to make an agreeable response to Jess's observation by the arrival of Rosie. She was thankful. She didn't think she could have uttered the words Jess might have expected her to say. In her opinion, just because Jules Asher had worked had to have the finest ranch around didn't justify his stepping on people's feelings, saying to them whatever entered his mind.

"I am ready to start, *señorita*." Rosie smiled at Willow. "Do you have a big pot to heat water in?"

"I expect so." Willow looked questioningly at Jess.

"There's a big iron kettle right outside the washhouse, and a fire pit to build a fire under it," Jess said, "and there's tubs and washboards waiting beside the dirty clothes. If I was you, girls, I'd do the washing outside. It can get mighty hot in there, what with the hot water and the exertion of scrubbing out the dirt."

An hour later the clothes had been carried outside and sorted, and hot water was steaming in the washtubs. Both women were bent over washboards, and bed linens and towels hung from two clotheslines stretched between trees.

Willow had just hung up a shirt when Jess called from the kitchen patio that it was time for a coffee break.

"Aunt Jess, you shouldn't have done this," Willow scolded when she and Rosie sat down at the table and found ham and scrambled eggs waiting with the coffee. "You're going to start your hip to aching if you move around too much."

"It didn't take much walkin' to fry some meat and scramble some eggs," Jess scoffed as she poured coffee for the three of them. "Actually, three years ago when I broke my hip, the sawbones in El Paso told me not to sit around after the bone mended. He said that I should exercise it. At the time I didn't think he knew what he was talkin' about, but I'm beginnin' to change my mind. It seems the more I move about, the less I hurt."

"If you're feeling that good, Miss Jess, maybe you can give us a hand with the wash," Rosie teased.

Jess grinned and gave the girl a rap on the knuckles with her spoon. "And maybe you would like to muck out the stables when you've finished the wash."

"Oh, no!" Rosie pretended dismay. "I couldn't do that. I'm too delicate."

The women's laughter rang out, and Jules, working at breaking a two-year-old mare, stopped and listened. He hadn't heard his aunt laugh like that in a long time. And Willow's throaty laughter started a stirring in his loins.

"You know, Willow," Jess said when the last of the late breakfast had been eaten and they were drinking their coffee, "I think you should get freshened up and ride into Coyote and pick up the supplies. I'll give Rosie a hand with the rest of the wash."

"I don't think you should do that, Aunt Jess."

"That's right, Miss Jess," Rosie said. "There's not that much to do. I can have it finished in less than an hour."

"Well, if you're sure, Rosie." Willow stood up, "I'll wash my face and change my clothes."

"You do know how to handle a team and drive a buckboard, don't you, Willow?" Jess asked.

Willow gave a short laugh as she remembered that she had been barely nine years old when her father ordered her onto a wagon seat, handed her the reins and ordered her to drive into town to pick up some blocks of salt. She had felt as if her thin arms were being pulled out of their sockets as she strained to control the big, strong work horses.

"Yes, Aunt Jess, I'm an expert at handling a team."

"I had a feelin' you would be." Jess nodded admiringly as she filled her pipe and lit it. When she had it going to her satisfaction, she said, "I wrote out a partial list of the things we need. Before you leave, check it and add whatever I've forgotten. It's been a long time since I've gone marketing."

Fifteen minutes later, her face washed and her hair brushed, Willow scanned Jess's supply list, added a few more things, and then left the house.

Jules saw her coming toward the barn and stopped what he was doing. He leaned against the snubbing post and watched her long legs stride along in a knee-length, split riding skirt.

He noticed after a while that the stable hands were ogling Willow in the same way he was, and it angered him. He pushed away from the post and strode up to the men.

"Don't you have something better to do than standing around?" His words were like pistol shots and the ranch hands jumped to attention and hurried away to their designated jobs.

When Willow came up to him, Jules smiled and remarked, "You have a nice day to ride into town."

"Yes, I do," she answered, thinking to herself that it was the first time he had ever spoken to her in a genial voice with no mockery or innuendo in his tone.

Jules looked at her delicate, tanned arms and asked, "Are you sure you can handle a team?"

"Oh, yes." Willow forgot that she didn't like the man and smiled at him. "I've done it hundreds of times."

"You don't look old enough to have done that," Jules teased lightly. "How old are you?"

"Why, Mr. Asher, you should never ask a woman her age." Willow's amber-colored eyes sparkled at him.

"I thought a man was supposed to stop doing that when the woman was over forty." Jules's eyes smiled back at her.

"Well, in that case, I'm twenty-two."

"And still single." Jules shook his head. "Now that's a surprise. Were all the men blind in your area?"

This was the first time Willow had ever flirted with a man, and she liked it. Her father had never allowed any young men to come courting her. Her mother had claimed bitterly that he was afraid of losing a ranch hand he didn't have to pay. That had all changed, though, when Buck Axel bought the ranch next to theirs.

Jules heard the bitterness in her voice when she answered, "Something like that, I guess." For the first time in his life Jules felt the sting of jealously. She was thinking about the man who had jilted her. If only she would let him, he could make her forget that man ever existed.

He had learned one thing in the last few minutes. If he wanted to make any headway with the beauty, he must stop heckling her and start showing her some respect.

"I've been thinking," he began and then swore under his breath. Nina had come up beside him and possessively linked her arm in his. Before he could pull away from her, Willow was walking off, her chin in the air and her back held ramrod straight.

"What do you want?" Jules asked abruptly, untangling his arm from Nina's.

"I only wanted to say good morning to you," she said, looking woefully at the irritated rancher. "I didn't know that I wasn't allowed to speak to you."

"You can stop that poor-me act right now, Nina. If you ever pull a trick like that again, I'll give you ten minutes to pack your duds, whether you have another place to go or not."

Nina stared after Jules as he strode away, going toward the barn. "You're hot for the long-legged blonde right now," she muttered, "but you'll come back to me when you discover that proud beauty won't take care of your needs the way I can." She returned to the small cabin when she saw Jules disappear into the barn.

Jules stepped inside the big building and saw two of his men hitching up the wagon for Willow. In their excitement at being so close to her, they were bumping into each other, laughing as they tripped over each other's feet.

He cleared his throat and the men froze. "I'll take care of that for Miss Ames," he said, his voice gruff.

The men dropped the trace chains and faded into the dark recess of the barn. Willow climbed up on the tall wagon seat and sat there in cool dignity, ignoring Jules as he finished the hitching of the horses.

"All set." He smiled up at her a minute later.

"Thank you." Willow's tone was as cool as her attitude. She unwound the long reins from the woodstock and slapped them on the horses' wide rumps. As they moved out, Jules stood watching the buckboard bounce and rattle over the rutted dirt road as Willow skillfully handled the team. In his mind he cursed the day he'd ever laid eyes on Nina. She had purposely interrupted when she saw that he and Willow were on friendly terms.

The prairie stretched before Willow, flat and treeless, extending out of sight. She let the team choose their own pace as she held the reins loosely in her hands.

The air was warm and brisk, and her tired body welcomed the gentle motion of the well-sprung wagon seat. Several times she heard the lowing of cattle but never came in sight of them.

The drawn-out bawling of the longhorns triggered thoughts of her father's ranch, and of her mother. Smitty would be almost home by now and soon he would assure the little woman that her daughter was settled in at the Asher ranch.

That would please Ma, she thought, but what price had her mother paid for her release? Had her husband struck her when he learned that their only child had left home? He would have been angry enough to have done that. It wouldn't be the first time he'd lifted a hand against her.

And what about Buck Axel? Now that she was out of the man's reach, what would his attitude be toward her father? She doubted that they would even be friendly anymore. She felt that neither man really liked the other. Each wanted something the other one had. Buck wanted her, and Pa wanted the assurance that he could always water his cattle in the river that ran through the Axel ranch.

The single-street town of Coyote appeared in the distance, and Willow broke off her unpleasant thoughts. As she drew nearer and the buildings stood out, she counted seven sleeping under the warm sun.

Riding down the street in ankle-deep dust, she learned which building held what.

On one side was a saloon, one horse tied up in front of it. Next to it was a barber shop with a sign on its side that read, "Doctor's Office Upstairs." At the end of the street was a stable.

Across the street from those places of business was a cafe, the general store which had brought her here, then an empty lot and a small schoolhouse. Next to it was a church.

All the buildings were weatherbeaten, and Willow imagined that none of them had ever known paint.

As she pulled the team in alongside the porch of the mercantile and set the brakes, she glanced at another wagon hitched to the side of the store. When she climbed to the ground, she glanced inside the vehicle. It held bushel baskets of farm produce. The sight of big red tomatoes made her mouth water.

Willow stepped up on the board sidewalk and started to walk inside the store. She was nearly knocked down by a man who came hurrying out onto the porch. If he had not shot out his hands and grabbed her, she would have gone over backward into the street.

Steadied by strong, yet gentle hands, Willow gazed up at a very handsome male who looked a few years older than she. His hair was black, in need of a trim, and he had the bluest eyes she'd ever seen. He was of medium height and muscular build.

"Are you all right, miss?" she was asked anxiously. "I'm afraid I wasn't watching where I was going."

"I'm fine," Willow assured him with a smile. "I'm afraid I wasn't paying much attention to where I was going either. I had my eyes on those big red tomatoes in that wagon."

"Those are mine," the young man said. "I supply the grocer with vegetables, milk, butter and eggs; then in the fall I bring him apples, pears, squash and pumpkins. Also I bring beef and pork when he needs them."

Willow had a sudden thought. "Do you sell to the Asher ranch?"

"I sure do. You're not the new housekeeper there, are you?"

"Yes, I am. I took over my duties yesterday."

"If you don't mind my saying so, you don't look like a housekeeper."

"Well, I am," Willow said coolly, her chin coming up in the air. Was he assuming that she was more than a housekeeper? Did he think she would play a role like the one Nina had played in the rancher's life? Probably was *still* playing, according to what she had seen last night.

"I only meant that you're too young and pretty to be doing a menial job," the farmer hurried to explain.

"This menial job, as you call it, is honest work and I don't feel ashamed doing it. Would you think better of me if I was serving drinks to a bunch of drunks in a saloon?"

"Heavens no! I wouldn't want to see you doing that. I wish you'd forget everything I said. It came out all wrong."

He looked so repentant that Willow relented. "They're forgotten." She smiled at him. "We'll start all over. When will you be coming to the ranch?"

"Tomorrow morning," he answered eagerly. "And I

hope you buy more produce from me than the other . . . housekeeper did," he laughingly joked. "About all she bought was tomatoes and hot peppers."

"I'll be taking some of everything you grow. Fresh vegetables are very important in a person's diet."

Willow offered her hand to the young man. "My name is Willow Ames."

"I'm Thad Wilson." When he released her hand, he tacked on with a smile, "Bachelor."

A fleeting dimple flashed in Willow's cheek as she said, "Maiden."

"Well," Thad said reluctantly, "I guess I'd better get this stuff inside."

"I guess you'd better. There's a man in there giving you impatient looks." Willow grinned at him, and then walked into the store.

"Mornin', Miss," a balding, middle-aged man said with a genial smile. "I saw you ride in and recognized the team. Come from the Asher ranch, did you?"

"Yes, I did." Willow returned the friendly smile. "I'm the new housekeeper there, and"—she paused to take the grocery list from her vest pocket—"and I need to make quite a few purchases from you."

"Fine, fine. Jules ain't been doin' much business with me lately. Mostly beans and rice."

"I'm going to need more than that, Mr.—" Willow hesitated as she handed over the long list of provisions she needed.

"The name is Herbie Jackson," the pleasant, middle-aged grocer said.

Willow gave him her name; then, as the storekeeper began gathering and piling the items she needed on the counter, she wandered around the store, noticing that Herbie carried most things a rancher or his wife might want. She and Thad passed each other several times as he went back and forth to his wagon, carrying in bushels of produce. Each time they smiled at each other.

When Thad had brought in the last of his vegetables, Herbie paused in filling Willow's order to pay the young farmer for the half-dozen baskets of vegetables lined up to the right of the counter.

"You can go now," he said brusquely after handing over some bills. "I'll carry Miss Ames's groceries out to her wagon."

That he didn't like being dismissed so summarily showed in the darkening of Thad's brow. He had no excuse now to hang around the long-legged beauty.

"I'll see you tomorrow then, Miss Ames," he said, and left the store without a word to Herbie.

Were there bad feelings between the two men? Willow wondered. She tested the grocer by saying, "Mr. Wilson seems like a nice young man."

"Yes, he's very polite," Herbie said. Then he asked, "Do you want any of these vegetables for your supper?"

Willow knew he wasn't going to say any more about the young farmer, so she nodded that she did.

"I'd like some of those string beans, and some potatoes and half a dozen ears of sweet corn. Just enough for tonight's supper."

When Herbie had totaled up what she owed, Willow told him to put it on the Asher tab. When that had been done, she helped him carry everything out to the wagon.

As the team backed the wagon out and Willow

headed them out of town, she called back, "I'll probably see you next week, Mr. Jackson."

"Call me Herbie," he called after her, and then watched the wagon until it rolled out of sight.

"She's gonna stir up a bunch of trouble," he said with a grin. "Jules ain't gonna like it at all when men come courtin'. I wonder if he's still got that Nina out there at the ranch to soothe him ever once in a while. I'd bet my store the new housekeeper ain't gonna take care of his personal needs.

"Yep," he said as he walked back into the store, "things are gonna be real interestin' round here."

Chapter Five

As the buckboard bounced along, Willow found herself comparing Thad Wilson and Jules Asher.

The young farmer was open-faced, with no subterfuge in his clear blue eyes. There was nothing ruthless about him, unlike Jules. Yet the rancher's dangerous aura only added to his attractiveness.

Willow became aware that the team and wagon were beginning to cast long shadows, and she glanced up at the sun. It had traveled some distance westward and she cracked the whip over the backs of the horses. She had been gone from the ranch for almost three hours.

When the buckboard rattled into the barnyard, Jules came striding from the stables, his face dark with anger. "Do you realize you've been gone for over three hours?" he demanded before she pulled the team to a halt. "I was just getting ready to go look for you. What kept you so long?"

As Jules railed at her, his voice harsh, Willow thought of Thad and his slow, soft speech. She jumped to the ground and gave Jules a look that silenced him. Ignoring his anger and his question, she said coolly, "Have one of your men bring the supplies to the house, will you?"

Silenced, Jules watched her walk away, her boot heels kicking up little puffs of dust. No matter how good his intentions, he always ended up making her angry with him.

He hurried after her, catching up to her a short distance from the hacienda. "Look, Willow," he said, walking alongside her, "I know I spoke harshly to you back there, but I've been worried that something might have happened to you. I was afraid you ran into some renegade Indians, or even rustlers. We haven't had any trouble with either for over a year, but nevertheless, I should have had someone accompany you."

They had reached the portico by the time Jules finished explaining himself. Willow paused at the covered archway. Looking up at him, she saw concern for her in his eyes. Surprisingly, he had been worried about her.

"I admit that I could have been home sooner," she said. "I spent too much time in the store talking to Herbie, and I dawdled on my return."

She had spoken in softer tones and Jules heaved a silent breath of relief. Maybe he hadn't lost too much ground after all. "I daydream once in a while too," he said. The laughter lines around his eyes deepened.

That was highly unlikely, Willow thought, but all she said was, "I'll take someone with me the next time I go to town." She slapped the pocket of her riding skirt. "I do carry a gun, you know."

Amusement glittered in Jules's eyes. "Do you know how to use it?"

"I certainly do," Willow answered, remembering the secret hours Smitty had spent teaching her and her mother how to draw and shoot straight. They had never perfected the fast draw, but if their target was close enough, they would hit it every time. Smitty had declared that if ever they had to defend themselves against animal or man, they could hit the heart dead center.

"I bet you do," Jules said with a grin. Then he added jokingly, "I'd better watch my step around you."

"That's right," Willow answered, but she didn't smile as she walked into the portico, leaving Jules with a puzzled look on his face.

Had she just given him a warning? he wondered with a frown.

"Jules was gettin' quite concerned about you, Willow," Jess said when Willow walked into the kitchen. "I never saw him so worked up before."

"I know. I saw him when I came in. I'm not to go to Coyote alone anymore."

"That's not a bad idea. Did you buy everything you wanted?"

"Yes." Willow's teeth flashed in a pleased smile. "For supper tonight we're going to have fried chicken, mashed potatoes and gravy, corn on the cob and string beans. For dessert we'll have apple pie. How's that sound?"

"It sounds so good that the way my mouth is waterin', my teeth are gonna wash out onto the table. All eight of them."

After they had laughed at Jess's sally, the old lady became sober-faced and asked, "You didn't forget my pipe tobacco, did you?"

"Nope, I didn't. It was the first thing I bought."

"You're a good girl, Willow Ames," Jess said softly. "Unlike Nina, who always called my pipe a smelly old thing and said she was going to throw it into the fireplace the first time she could get her hands on it. You ain't said a word against it."

"I kinda like the smell of it. Smitty smokes a pipe."

"I know. Smitty is a fine man."

Willow hid her look of amusement from the old lady. Clearly, if a man smoked a pipe, he was all right in Jess's opinion. "I'm going to change clothes now, then come back and start on the pies," she said before Jess could continue talking about Smitty. "Someone will be bringing in the supplies pretty soon. Will you show him where to put everything?"

When Willow returned to the kitchen after having changed into a blue gingham dress, cut low across her breasts and showing just a hint of cleavage, she found that it was Jules who had driven the team up to the house and was in the process of unloading the wagon. Jess sat puffing on her pipe as she watched him put the things away.

As Willow tied an apron around her narrow waist, Jules looked up from storing some staples in a bottom cupboard and asked, "What are we having for supper?"

With a straight face, Willow answered, "I'm making hot tamales and burritos."

When Jules didn't say anything, only groaned, Jess said with a wink at Willow, "I hope you don't use as much hot pepper as Nina does."

"You'll like them fine, Aunt Jess. An old Mexican woman taught me how to make them."

Jules seesawed back and forth, wanting to tell Willow to please make something else, but he was afraid of riling her.

Willow could have sworn that his shoulders sagged a little when he left the kitchen to drive the wagon back to the barn. Her laughter pealed out, and Jess's high cackle joined it.

The spicy aroma of flaky-crusted pies filled the kitchen an hour later as Willow lifted them from the oven and placed them on the window ledge to cool. She turned her hand then to cutting up the dressed chicken she had bought from Herbie. When she had dredged the pieces with flour she dropped them into a waiting skillet of hot grease to brown on all sides before placing a lid on them.

Jess was peeling the potatoes, so she began shucking the cobs of tender corn. As she carefully picked the corn silk from between the rows of kernels, she wondered what her mother was making for supper. There was the possibility that she wouldn't be cooking tonight. If Smitty was back, he would bring her a plate of what he had prepared for the cowhands. Pa seldom ate at home.

An hour later the table in the kitchen was set with china and flatware. When Willow heard the tinkling sound of Jules's spurs on the tiles of the kitchen patio, she began dishing up the hot food.

When Jules had washed up outside and stepped into the kitchen, the expression that came over his face made both women laugh. "So," he said, laughing with them, "you played a little trick on me, I see."

"I just couldn't resist," Willow said. "Aunt Jess had mentioned that both of you were tired of spicy food, so . . ."

The way Jules ate his supper, asking for seconds, pleased Willow more than she wanted it to. She asked herself why she should care one way or the other whether he liked what she put on the table. And she was annoyed with herself for blushing when he complimented her on supper, saying that her fried chicken was the best he'd ever eaten.

When Jules had walked through the kitchen door and out onto the small patio, Willow darted a look at Jess. Had the sharp-eyed old woman seen her heightened color? It appeared that she hadn't, since she was busy tamping tobacco into her pipe. Aunt Jess was very much against her nephew's involvement with Nina, and Willow didn't want her thinking that the new housekeeper had her eyes on her nephew. She felt that Jess liked her, and she wanted to keep it that way. She liked this job and didn't want to lose it. She needed it if her plan to bring her mother to Texas was to be successful.

The next morning when Willow, Jess and Jules were finishing a breakfast of ham and eggs and hot biscuits, Jules looked out the window at the sound of wagon wheels. "It's the sodbuster," he said. "Isn't he a little early, Aunt Jess?"

"Yes, he is, by a couple hours." She looked at Willow. "Do you know what you want from him?"

"Pretty much." Willow stood up, ready to go outside and look over what Thad had brought.

"You don't have to go." Jules stood up also. "Tell me what you want and I'll get it."

"Don't be ridiculous." Willow laughed. "You'd probably pick up the first thing you saw."

"Well, what would you do?"

"First I'd test everything for freshness, color and tenderness," Willow answered as she went through the door, Jules at her heels.

"Good morning, Thad," she said, smiling at the young farmer as he jumped from the wagon to the ground. "I hope you have brought some of that delicious corn that I bought from Herbie yesterday."

Thad nodded a good morning to Jules, and when the rancher ignored him, he turned back to Willow. "I sure did, and other things too." He jumped up on the wagon bed and held his hand down to help Willow up beside him. "Look things over." He gestured to the different bushels of tomatoes, corn, string beans, green onions and an assortment of greens. To one side, in a small basket, were eggs and a crock that held butter.

"My mom churned it fresh this morning," Thad explained to Willow. "And the milk is fresh also." He gestured to a canvas-covered gallon jar.

Jules, his face growing darker by the minute, leaned against one side of the patio arch watching Willow and the handsome farmer as they talked and laughed while Willow examined and chose the items she wanted.

Jess, looking out the kitchen window, was afraid of what her nephew might do when Willow and Thad continued to talk in low tones even after she'd made her purchases. Jess couldn't understand what they were saying to each other, and the way Jules had cocked his head to listen, she didn't think he could either, which was probably making him all the more angry.

When his eyes narrowed to slits, she thought to herself, "It looks like my nephew has finally met a woman who will take away his bachelor days. But my, how he will fight it. He'll be worse than a yearling bein' dragged to a branding fire."

Finally Jules could take no more. He strode over to the wagon, and as he hefted a basket of vegetables, he growled to Willow, "Are you going to lollygag all day? I'm sure you have work to do in the house." When she shot him an angry look, he knew too late that he had said the wrong thing to her. Would he never learn to curb his tongue where she was concerned?

And though he knew he had stepped out of line with Willow, he continued with his reckless words when she followed him into the kitchen. "You had an awful lot to say to the sodbuster. Don't let his good looks make a fool out of you."

"The way you did just now?" Willow snapped.

"I don't see it that way, and I want you to get one thing straight. I'm not going to have a bunch of men hanging around the house, chasing after you."

Hot, angry tears smarted Willow's eyes. How she

hated this arrogant, low-minded man. If only she felt free to slap his hateful face, to scratch the sneer off his lips. But she must take his insults if she was to help her mother.

She wheeled and stamped out of the kitchen.

When her bedroom door slammed shut, Jess looked at Jules, shaking her head. "What's gotten into you, nephew? You can't treat Willow like she's a bonded slave. She's a grown woman who can talk with young men if she likes. If you keep it up you're gonna lose the best cook and housekeeper you can ever expect to find. If she leaves because of your insults, and you bring Nina back as our housekeeper, I'll leave with the girl."

She gave Jules a thoughtful look and then asked sharply, "Is that what you have in mind, Jules? Do you want that whore back in the house?"

"That's a ridiculous question and you know it." Jules raked his fingers through his hair. "I don't know why I railed at Willow. Maybe it's because I don't trust that romeo farmer. I'd hate to see her taken in by his handsome looks, his soft words and ready smile."

"Willow has been fooled by a man once. She'll know if Thad Wilson is not to be trusted." After a short pause Jess said, "I think what's bothering you is that you're jealous. Deep down you want Willow for yourself, and you're fightin' against it."

"Hah!" Jules snorted a laugh. "You mean marry her, tie myself to one woman? That will never happen. My freedom is too important to me."

Jess drew impatiently on her pipe. "Your freedom is gonna be poor company when you're an old man with no wife and no children or grandchildren to lighten your days. You remember me saying this when you're old and sittin' alone in front of your fire."

The old lady stood up and left Jules sitting at the table. He jumped slightly when the second door slammed shut. *I've got both women angry with me now,* he thought grimly, and took off for the stables. There he would find release for the emotions roiling inside him by working at breaking in a big bay stallion he had captured the week before.

Capturing and breaking bangtails to the saddle had started out as a kind of hobby for Jules. It had an excitement that cattle didn't bring to a man. Then word came that Montana and Wyoming were in need of the hardy and durable mustangs that made ideal mounts for cowboys. Properly trained, they made perfect cutting horses.

Also, droves of burros were being exported to the mines in Colorado. He hadn't tried his hand at rounding them up though. "Let the teenagers have fun doing that," he had remarked.

When he entered the corral, lasso in hand, Jules stood a moment, waiting for the right time, and then, swinging the rope gracefully over his head, he dropped the noose around the neck of the handsome bay.

The instant the stallion felt its touch, he lowered his head, trying to shake it off, but Jules had anticipated the movement and gently tightened the rope. With a snort of defiance, the animal settled back on his haunches, pitting his strength against his captor's. With patience and comparative ease, Jules got the horse over to the corral gate, opened it, and then vaulted lightly upon the bay's back.

The moment he felt Jules's weight the stallion uttered a scream of rage, and raised himself upright on his hind legs, trying to shake the weight off his back. He stood still for a moment, then dashed furiously out over the plains. Jules didn't try to hold him back, but let him run until he finally stopped, his head hanging low. An hour later he trotted back to the stables quietly, as though he had been used to having a rider on his back all his life.

"You've got yourself a fine horse there, Jules," said his cook, Amos, who had watched the mad ride over the plains. "You ought to put him to that fancy mare you bought last spring. I bet you would get a real nice foal from her."

"I've been thinking the same thing," Jules agreed. "The bay has good blood lines."

As the two men walked toward the cookhouse, Amos asked, "Will you be starting the cattle drive as you planned next week?"

"Yes. Have you laid in the supplies you'll need?"

"Yeah, I'm all set. The chuck wagon is packed, all ready to go," Amos said.

Jules always started his drive in the spring, so that the cattle could graze fresh grass as they moved slowly north. Spring was also a good time to avoid flash floods.

One thing Jules never did was to take cows or calves on a drive. The steers were easier to drive and could maintain a rate of fifteen miles a day. He liked his cattle to be strung out in a long line so they could be drifted instead of driven.

He calculated he would be moving a herd of three thousand and would need to take along a dozen drovers, one of these a trail boss, an experienced professional who had made several such drives. His trail boss was Rooster Garr, a strong, quiet man who stayed mainly to himself. He was nearing fifty and had never been married.

Each hand would have a string of eight to ten horses, and that meant the need of a wrangler. He was usually a young hand, who was expected to know every horse in his band and to which hand it belonged.

As Jules walked toward the house after leaving Amos at the cookshack, he was in a deep study. On the one hand, he looked forward to the cattle drive. He enjoyed eating his meals around a roaring campfire, listening to and watching the cowboys horse around, telling tall tales. Also, he found it restful to sleep under the stars for a while.

On the other hand, he was reluctant to be away from the ranch for so long. He had seen the gleam in the farmer's eyes as he talked to Willow, and he knew what such a look meant. Thad Wilson was hot to have the beauty. In his own absence the man would come courting her, and by the time he returned to the ranch, she could be gone, a sodbuster's wife.

He wished he could remain at the ranch and sweet-talk her himself. But even as the thought entered his mind, Jules knew he had to go on the drive. He had built the ranch up with hard work, and one of the reasons for its success was his personal involvement in every aspect of the business. He couldn't change that now.

Chapter Six

The five days Willow had been at the Asher ranch had passed swiftly for her. She was still in the process of cleaning out corners, getting rid of the accumulation of dirt and grime. She had washed windows, polished furniture and hung clean drapes and curtains. But the hacienda was beginning to regain the splendor it had once had in the days of Jules's mother.

A fact he often mentioned.

Things were much better between her and her boss lately. He was quite pleasant to her these days, and sometimes she forgot how unpleasant he could be if he wanted to.

Thad had come calling one evening, and though Jules hadn't liked it, he hadn't said anything when she and Thad went for a walk in the moonlit evening. He had, however, followed them out onto the patio and she had felt his eyes boring into her back as they walked away.

When she and Thad walked homeward an hour or so later, she saw the glowing tip of a cigarette under the portico, then saw it arch into the air as it was flipped away.

But when they arrived at the vine-covered archway, it was empty. She'd had a feeling, though, that Jules was standing at a window, watching them. She had been tempted to lift her face to Thad, inviting a good-night kiss, but she hadn't. It wouldn't have been fair to the young man. She had sensed that he had been working up the nerve to do just that, and she suspected that, given any encouragement, he would be all over her. And she wasn't ready for that. He was the first man she had walked out with, and she needed time to learn this courting business.

Willow left off her recollections as she finished ironing the last piece of clothing in the laundry basket. It was one of several shirts she had pressed for Jules.

As she folded it and laid it on top of the others, Jess walked into the kitchen. "You've been at this all mornin'," she scolded. "It's time you stopped and had a bite of lunch. Sit down here at the table and I'll make you a sandwich."

"I can do it, Aunt Jess," Willow protested as she pushed the flatirons to the back of the stove to cool before putting them away.

"No, I'll do it," Jess insisted. "Now do as I say."

Willow didn't argue further. She had learned that once the old lady decided something, there was no changing her mind. Anyhow, she was ready for a rest.

The amount of shirts and trousers she had ironed for Jules gave testimony that Nina hadn't washed clothes for weeks.

"There, put that under your belt," Jess said a short time later as she placed a thick beef sandwich before Willow. "Do you want coffee or milk to wash it down?"

"I'll have coffee if there's any left in the pot."

There was, and after Jess set her own sandwich on the table, she filled two cups.

"You've certainly brought this place up to snuff, Willow," the old lady said after a few bites of her sandwich. "It does my heart good to see my sister's home looking like it should. She was always so proud of it."

"Have you always lived here, Aunt Jess?"

Jess shook her head. "I didn't come here until after my sister passed away. Before that I lived on a small ranch my father left to me years ago."

Willow looked at her, surprised. "Do you still own it?"

"Oh, yes. I like to know that it is there in case I ever need it."

"Where is it, and who runs it for you?"

"It's about twenty miles north of here. There ain't much to runnin' it. I have a few hands to tend my three hundred head of cattle, and as for the ranch house, I have a Mexican couple livin' there. They take care of the milch cow and some chickens. They raise a garden for their own use."

Envy flashed through Willow's mind for an instant. Jess spoke so casually about her holdings, whereas she felt it would be a bit of heaven to own such a place, a place where she could bring her mother to live in peace after so many years of hell.

While Willow was pondering why some had so much, while others had neither wealth nor peace of mind, Jess spoke on another subject.

"I guess Jules and his men will start the cattle drive to Kansas in a few days. He told me last night that they had all the calves and cows separated from the steers, and that tomorrow they would start hair-branding the unmarked yearlings."

"I don't think I'm acquainted with the term 'hair-branding.'" Willow wrinkled her brow. "How is that done?"

"The animals are branded with a light slash of the branding iron that only touches the hair. It's to be on the left side behind the shoulder. It takes extra time, but an honest rancher will do it, branding only his own cattle, leaving his neighbor's longhorns alone."

That would not be my father's way, Willow thought contemptuously. He would not waste the time hair-branding, but would claim every steer, cow and calf he saw.

Buck Axel was the same way. That was one of the reasons her father got along so well with the man she feared and despised. She still couldn't shake off the dread that somehow Buck would find her and drag her back to her father's home. By now he and Pa would have come to the realization that all they had to do to make her come around was to threaten her mother with bodily harm. A shiver feathered down Willow's spine at that thought. It was unbearable to imagine her frail little mother being beaten. But it was equally impossible to consider being married to the cruel Buck Axel.

Smitty had told her some awful things about the rancher—how he treated the poor Indian woman whom he kept in virtual bondage by setting a man to watch the house while he was away so that she couldn't escape. It was rumored by some of his men, who had peeked through a window, that he made her go around without her clothes when he came home from work, and that they often heard her screaming in pain.

And Pa had to know this because he spent many evenings at Buck's place. Maybe he even abused the woman himself. Willow stared down into her coffee. How could a man want his daughter to marry such a monster?

"That's a strange name your mama gave you, Willow," Jess said suddenly. "How did she come up with it?"

Willow chuckled. "It's short for Wilhamina, my grandmother's name. I've never been called that, though."

"Willow suits you. You're tall and slender and move so gracefully, just like the willows that hang over the river."

"Thank you, Aunt Jess." Willow laughed. "I've never been compared to a tree before, but willows are nice trees."

Jess grinned. "I've heard one man refer to you as a long-legged witch, and once in a while as a damned beauty."

"I don't suppose I have to guess who said that," Willow replied.

"I guess not." Jess's eyes twinkled as she filled her pipe and put a match to it. "There's one thing about my nephew," Jess started to add, and then stopped short when shouts and yowls of pain came from outside.

"What in the world!" Willow exclaimed. She jumped from her chair and rushed outside, with Jess following her as fast as she could.

They found the cook on the ground, cradling his right foot in his hands, a grimace of pain on his pale face. Two stable hands and the young wrangler knelt around him.

"What's wrong, Amos? What has happened to you?" Jess panted anxiously.

"He must have sprained an ankle stepping in that hole over there," the wrangler answered for the cook.

"Sprained, hell," Amos shouted. "The damn thing is broke."

"Let me look at it." Willow knelt and, taking the injured foot in her hand, said, "One of you men help me get his boot off."

"No! I couldn't bear havin' you pull it off," Amos objected loudly.

Willow looked at the men ready to help her. "One of you fellows will have to cut it off."

"Oh lord, I just bought them two weeks ago," Amos complained as a sharp blade sliced through his boot from top to bottom.

"Don't carry on so," Jess scolded as Willow carefully removed the boot. "We'll buy you a new pair."

One look at the rapidly swelling ankle told Willow that Amos was right. The ankle was broken. She looked up at the wrangler. "Ride to town and bring back the doctor. Tell him to bring splints for a broken ankle."

"Pick him up and carry him inside the cookhouse," Jess ordered. "Give him a glass of whiskey and make him as comfortable as possible until the Doc gets here."

The two stable men had taken hold of Amos when Jules rode up. "What's wrong?" He climbed from the saddle and hurried over to the huddled group.

"Amos stepped in a hole and broke his ankle," Jess answered. "Sammy just left to fetch the doctor. The men were getting ready to carry him inside."

"I'll do it," Jules said brusquely, and bending down, he gathered the slight body up in his arms and strode into the cookhouse, where Amos's quarters were located in the back of the building. Jess followed him, but Willow stayed outside. She wasn't needed, and besides she hadn't been asked to go along.

When she returned to the house, she put away the garments she had ironed, then got out the ingredients to make pie dough. There was a can of peaches in the larder room. She would make a cobbler for their supper tonight.

Half an hour later, when the dessert was ready to go into the oven, Willow glanced through the window and saw the doctor drive up in his buggy, the wrangler riding alongside him. Pulling the horse in, the middle-aged doctor climbed from the buggy and hurried inside the cookhouse, carrying a small black bag and a bundle of short splints. She was peeling potatoes when Jess returned to the house.

"Broke his ankle in two places." Jess plopped down in a chair and pulled her pipe from her dress pocket.

"He was cussin' a blue streak when I left. He's mad at himself for breakin' his ankle and leavin' Jules without a cook for the cattle drive."

"I expect Jules is doing a little swearing too," Willow remarked.

"Surprisingly, he's not. But you can see that he's worried about where to find a cook on such short notice."

"I'm sure he'll think of something," Willow said as she began to shuck the husks off six ears of corn.

"I can't imagine what. There's not a hand on the ranch capable of doin' much more than brewin' a pot of coffee and heatin' a can of beans."

"What about Nina? She could cook for them."

"Didn't you know? Jules sent her packin' a couple days ago. It cost him a little money. Jules said she raised quite a ruckus when he told her to go."

"Serves him right," Willow said sharply. "Maybe he'll think twice before he moves another woman into his home."

"I'm sure he will," Jess said, thinking to herself that if Jules had his way, his long-legged witch would be the last woman to move into his home. Of course, right now he was fighting the idea.

Willow was telling her stupid heart to slow down, that it didn't make any difference to her that Nina was gone. She glanced out the window and saw Jules and the doctor leaving the cookhouse. The two men stood a moment on the narrow porch, talking. Then the doctor climbed into his buggy and Jules walked toward the house.

"Here comes your nephew now," she said to Jess.

Jules looked tired and discouraged when he walked

into the kitchen. "Would you pour me a cup of coffee, Willow?" he asked as he pulled a chair away from the table and sat down.

"How long will Amos be laid up?" Jess asked.

"He has to stay off his foot for two weeks. Then he can start walking around a bit with the aid of crutches."

"Well, he sure can't go on the cattle drive," Jess said, a worried frown on her wrinkled face. "What are you gonna do for a cook?"

"I don't know." Jules sighed heavily.

Willow was as surprised as Jess and Jules when she said, "I can be the camp cook."

"You cook for seventeen men?" Jules laughed.

Willow was tempted to pour the coffee over his head at the sarcasm in his voice. He was so arrogant, he naturally thought a man was superior to a woman in all ways.

She checked her rising temper and said calmly, "I've done it for my father many times."

"How many men did you cook for?" Jules asked disbelievingly, "a half dozen?"

"No, Mr. Know-it-all," Willow retorted. "I've made meals for twice that many men."

"Well, nephew, it looks like your problem has been solved." Jess's eyes twinkled. "I can't think of any reason that Willow can't fill Amos's shoes. Maybe even do his job a little better. And I can cook for Amos and the few men left behind to keep an eye on the place."

"Are you sure you're up to doing that, Aunt Jess?" Jules looked doubtful.

"I'm sure. I've been feelin' quite spry lately . . . since Willow moved in with us."

"All right then, I guess it's settled. Willow will go with us on the cattle drive. I'll pay you extra, of course," Jules said. "Since you've done this before, I guess I don't have to give you any instructions."

"No, you don't, but I'd like to check out the wagon, see that it will be carrying everything I might need."

"I'm sure it is well equipped." Jules gave Willow a frowning look. "Amos has been preparing the chuck wagon for years."

"What about the hoodlum wagon? Who takes care of that?"

"Brian Winterspoon, the driver. He's been doing that for years also. Do you want to inspect his wagon too?" Jules's voice was sharp. He was still smarting from the new title Willow had given him.

"No, Mr. . . . Asher, I don't. As long as he's got enough wood in it for me to cook with."

Jules gave her a narrow-eyed look. She had almost called him a know-it-all again. But as she gazed back at him, her eyes were innocent, so he didn't call her on it.

He looked at Jess and said, "We've spent half the day hunting for calves that are too young to keep up with the herd. We're driving them in close to the ranch where they can be fed. Will you see to it that the stable hands take care of them while I'm gone?"

"I will. If they lose one head, I'll take a whip to them."

Jules gave an amused twist of his lips and stood up. "I believe you would," he said and left the kitchen.

That evening Willow sat on the kitchen patio, the old hound, as usual, lying at her feet. A tiny frown was etched in her forehead as she gazed at the moths fluttering around the wall lamp. She was having second thoughts about her rash offer to cook on the cattle drive.

What had made her do it? It was hard work, bouncing along in the chuck wagon, keeping ahead of the herd, choosing the right spot to build a fire and make the meals. And about those meals. A cook had to prepare hot meals no matter what, even after hail storms and stampedes, not to mention the big suppers after day-long drives. She would be beat when she rolled up in her blankets at night.

When she asked herself again why had she volunteered to cook for a bunch of cowhands, she wondered if it had anything to do with a desire to be near her brooding, handsome boss.

Agitated at such a notion, she jumped to her feet. *I'd be loco to want that,* she told herself.

Nevertheless, a tall, dark man hovered in the background of her dreams that night.

The next morning when Willow made breakfast for Jules, only a few words passed between them. She had learned that he, like herself, only grunted answers to any question put to him until he had had a second cup of coffee.

When he finished eating his bacon and eggs and hot biscuits and was having that second cup of coffee, Jules cleared his voice and said, a little nervously, "I hate to ask this of you, but would you cook for the hands until we leave on the drive?"

"I had planned on doing that," Willow answered, rising and gathering up Jules's plate and cup. "I guess I'd better get over to the cookhouse and fire up the stove." She glanced out the window and saw that the sky was turning pink. "The men will be expecting breakfast before long."

"Jimmy, Amos's helper, will show you where everything is and give you a hand when you need him. He cleans up the kitchen after all the meals."

Willow nodded, and after hesitating a moment, Jules grunted, "I'll see you later then," and walked outside.

When Willow opened the door to the cookhouse a short time later, she found a tall, gangly teenager waiting for her. He had built a fire in the big black range and had a gallon-sized pot of coffee brewing.

"You're Jimmy, aren't you?" She smiled at him.

"Yes, miss." Jimmy shyly ducked his head.

"I'm Willow. I guess we'd better get started cooking up something for that bunch still asleep in the bunkhouse."

For the next hour Willow didn't move from the stove as she fried pounds of bacon and dozens of eggs. In between she stirred up a batch of biscuit dough and slid a tray into the oven. When the sun was peeping over the horizon, and Jimmy heard the men washing up outside, he set the table and then helped Willow dish up the hot food. To say that the cowboys were surprised to see the beautiful housekeeper at the stove would be an understatement. They could be more aptly described as stunned. They'd had distant glimpses of the new housekeeper, but for most, this was their first up-close view of her, and the blond beauty silenced their tongues and gave them two left feet as they knocked into each other, fumbling for their chairs.

Unaware of their shy glances, Willow began frying

stacks of flapjacks while Jimmy poured coffee around. When the only sound heard was the scraping of knives and forks, Amos called from his quarters, "Jimmy, ain't the men come in for breakfast yet?"

Jimmy grinned, and picking up a cup of coffee, went through the door and into the room where the cook lay on his narrow cot. He was back in time to place two platters of flapjacks on the table and replenish the coffee cups.

When everyone's hunger had been sated at last, a few braver cowhands mumbled, "Thank you, miss," as they left the kitchen.

When Jimmy started clearing the long table, he said, "Amos would like to speak to you before you leave."

Willow smiled wryly as she took off the big apron she'd found hanging on a peg beside the stove, and then rolled down her sleeves. She had a pretty good idea what the cook wanted to speak to her about. His chuck wagon. A good cook was always loath to have another poke around his domain.

"Good morning, Amos," Willow said when she poked her head around the door. "May I come in?"

"Come on in, miss." Amos scooted up in bed until he leaned against the wall. When she stepped into the room, he gave her an appraising look and then motioned her to sit down in the chair pulled up to his narrow bed. "Jules tells me that you're gonna take over my job while I'm laid up. But if you don't mind my sayin' so, you don't look strong enough to do it."

"I'm stronger than I look, and Jimmy will be helping me."

"The men are a rowdy bunch and you'll hear a lot of cussin' goin' on."

"Yes, I expect so," Willow answered, but didn't add that she hadn't heard any swearing from the men this morning.

"Now, about my chuck wagon. I have a special spot for everythin' and I don't want you changin' it. When I get back on my feet, I'll expect everything to be the same as I left it. Do you savvy what I'm sayin'?"

"I understand." Willow nodded. "I'll be very careful not to change anything."

The cook's tone softened when he realized that Willow wasn't going to give him any trouble. "Most of the men are hogs when it comes to food. You'll have to lock up your supplies between meals. And don't leave anything out that they can get their hands on."

"I'll remember that. Thank you for the warning."

"I guess that's about it then. Have a good trip." When he scooted back down in the cot, silently dismissing Willow, she grinned crookedly. Leaving the room, she closed the door quietly behind her.

"He wanted to warn you not to mess up the chuck wagon, didn't he?" Jimmy asked, in soap suds up to his elbows as he washed dishes, pots and pans.

Willow gave a small laugh and said, "I think I'll go inspect it now."

She climbed into the covered wagon that had been parked behind the cookhouse. As she walked down the center aisle between supplies packed on either side, she found that Amos hadn't forgotten the essentials to make good, hearty meals. He had an ample supply of everything, which should last until they arrived at their destination, where the wagon could be outfitted again. Of course, there was always the danger of the wagon rolling over and supplies being dumped on the ground, or of its being swamped with water in a river crossing.

But there were a few things of her own she wanted to add. Things she had brought with her from home. There were special herbs for stews and roasts and maple syrup to add to the tomatoes that would go into her special baked beans. And her own cast-iron bean pot in which the beans would simmer slowly all day.

And one other thing. The cowboys back home had loved the cookies she always brought along. Big cloth bags filled with oatmeal raisin treats.

She hopped down from the wagon and strode to the house. She would start baking as soon as she straightened up the house.

"My, somethin' sure smells good in here." Jess sniffed the air as she came into the kitchen. "What are you bakin', Willow?"

"Cookies. I'm going to take them with me on the cattle drive. Taste one." Willow motioned to the rows of cookies lined up on the table, cooling.

"Land's sake, how many are you gonna bake? You've baked near to a hundred already."

"Before I'm finished I'll have triple that amount. I'll give them to the men when I can't bake them a dessert for some reason. The cowboys back home loved them."

"I can see how they would," Jess said after dipping one of the sweets in her coffee to soften it up. Her eight teeth didn't allow too much chewing on anything so crisp.

As she watched Willow dropping spoonsful of cookie dough onto a flat pan, she remarked, "You're a hard worker, Willow. I don't understand why some man hasn't snapped you up before now. Ain't there any single men where you come from?"

"Oh, there's plenty of them. The thing is, my father never allowed any of them to come around. I think he was afraid of losing his workhorse. Anyway, that's what Ma always said."

"From your tone, I'd say you ain't overly fond of your paw."

"That's putting it mildly." Willow slammed the oven door on the pan of cookies she had just shoved inside it. "He's a cruel, unfeeling man. He has always hated the fact that I was born a girl instead of the boy he wanted. He has the nerve to blame my poor mother and has made her life a living hell."

It was quiet in the kitchen for a while as Willow prepared another pan of dough and Jess studied her angry, flushed face. Finally the old lady spoke.

"Is that why you came here, Willow . . . to get away from your father?"

"Yes." Tears suddenly gathered in Willow's eyes, and as they ran down her cheeks, she sobbed, "I feel so guilty, leaving Ma alone with him. He browbeats her so. She's so frail and helpless."

"Don't blame yourself for that, honey," Jess implored her. "Your mother is the one who wrote Jules, asking him if he could find a job for you here on the ranch."

Before Jess finished speaking, Willow realized that she had just contradicted what her mother had written in her letter. She was supposed to be heartbroken because the man she had expected to marry had changed his mind. Should she try to explain everything to the old lady who had treated her so kindly, or keep silent, hoping that she hadn't noticed the difference between the letter and what she had just heard?

"Nevertheless"—Willow swiped a hand across her wet eyes—"it is my dream to bring my mother out of New Mexico."

"I'm sure you'll work something out. We'll talk about it when you get back from the cattle drive. In the meantime, try to concentrate on the hard work that lies ahead of you."

Jess was right, of course, Willow thought later as she pulled the last batch of cookies from the oven. She was in no position to help her mother now. She would be better off financially when the drive was over. A good trail cook was paid more than a top cowhand. Her shoulders sagged. She still wouldn't have nearly enough money to provide a home for her mother.

Chapter Seven

"Don't forget to take along a jacket, Willow," Jess said as she shuffled into the kitchen wearing her ratty old robe and a pair of heavy socks on her feet. "It's right cool on the plains in the early morning hours."

"I remembered." Willow jerked her thumb over her shoulder in the direction of the door. "It's over there hanging on the peg."

Jess poured herself a cup of coffee and sat down at the table. After appraising Willow by the lamplight, she nodded and said, "I see you know how to dress for the trail. Where did you get them britches?"

"Jimmy loaned them to me."

"I must say you look better in them than he does. He ain't got no butt to fill them out the way you do."

"They are snug against my rear, but it was either

Jimmy's or borrow a pair of Jules's. You can imagine how they would fit me."

Jess grinned as she filled her pipe. "The way the men are gonna ogle you, my nephew will probably wish that you were wearing a pair of his pants."

"If that does happen, I doubt that he will even notice."

Jess gave Willow a look that said she was simple, but let the subject drop. Instead, she said, "Whenever you come near some town, drop me a line, will you? I'd like to know how you're gettin' along."

"I will, Aunt Jess. If I'm not too tired, I'll try to write something every night—a kind of journal to send to you."

"Oh, you're gonna be tired, honey. You're gonna be draggin' at the end of the day."

"I know I'll be beat the first few days, but I'll toughen up."

Both women looked at the door when they heard the jingle of spurs on the tiled patio floor.

"Are you ready to go, Willow?" Jules walked into the kitchen, then stopped to stare at her hip-hugging trousers. Where dresses and riding skirts had only hinted at the gentle curves of her hips and long legs, the tight male attire left nothing to the imagination. His men would fight over her all the way to Kansas.

He was about to order her to get back into a dress, but two pairs of female eyes dared him to say it. In the end he walked around the table and, dropping a kiss on his relative's wrinkled cheek, said softly, "You take care of yourself, Aunt Jess, and don't try to do too much while I'm gone. In case you need me, send a letter to one of the small towns I've written down here." He fished a piece of paper out of his vest pocket. "I'll check in each one to see if there's a letter waiting for me."

"You take care, too, Jules, and make sure you look after Willow. We don't want to lose the best cook and housekeeper in all of Texas."

Jules didn't say that he would or that he wouldn't as he left the kitchen and stepped out into the early dawn.

"I don't think he likes your outfit, Willow." Jess cackled her glee. "He's gonna be worse than a mother hen with one chick, keepin' an eye on you around his men."

"You're wrong, Aunt Jess," Willow scolded. "The men aren't going to approach me—and if they did, Jules wouldn't notice it."

Before Jess could respond to Willow's remark, Willow bent over and she, too, kissed her wrinkled cheek. "Be careful not to do too much, and take your nap every afternoon."

Taking her jacket off the wall peg, Willow stepped outside into pandemonium. Horses were neighing and Sammy, the wrangler, was yelling and swearing. At least a dozen horses had gotten away from him and were running through the yard, trampling flower beds and knocking over pots of bright red geraniums. When the horses headed for the barnyard, Jules, swearing as loudly as Sammy, sprang into the saddle and raced away to head the animals off.

From the high seat of the chuck wagon, Jimmy grinned down at Willow. "Ole Sammy is gonna get his butt chewed out. The boss don't let a feller make too many mistakes, and a wrangler ain't allowed to make but one. The remuda is too important on a cattle drive. Our cowpokes change their mounts six or seven times a day."

"I'm glad it's not us at the receiving end of his anger," Willow said, climbing up onto the wagon and taking the reins from Jimmy when she sat down.

"Yeah, he can be pretty mean when he gets riled up." Jimmy grinned and sat back as Willow snapped the long reins over the horses's backs. They had started to move out when Willow heard her name shouted. She yelled, "Whoa," when she saw Thad Wilson racing his horse toward the wagon.

"I was afraid I'd miss you," Thad said, a little out of breath as he pulled up alongside the wagon and smiled at her. "I wanted to say good-bye and to give you this." He took a bag from the saddle horn and handed it to her. "It's apples from last fall. I thought you might enjoy eating them as you ride along."

"I will, Thad. Thank you very much." She laid the bag down at her feet.

"I'm going to miss you." Thad gave her a woeful look.

"I'll be back before you know it."

"I'd like to come calling on you then . . . maybe on a regular basis?"

Before Willow could answer him, Jules raced his horse up to the wagon, his face as dark as a thundercloud. "Why are you still here, Willow?" he shouted, ignoring the farmer. "You're holding us up. If you know so much about cattle drives, you should know that the cook always leads off."

Willow did know this, and she was embarrassed and angry at herself. And put out at Thad too. He had caused her delay. She said a short good-bye to him and whipped up the horses.

As the wagon bounced and rattled across the plain, Jimmy said with a laugh, "You just got a rear-chewin' too."

"It probably won't be the last one either," Willow muttered, snapping the reins and calling on the team to move faster.

After about fifteen minutes of driving the team as fast as she thought was safe, Willow looked back and saw that the long line of cattle was about a quarter of a mile behind her. She pulled the team in to a brisk walk.

Jimmy, who had braced his feet on the floorboard and was clinging desperately to his seat, let out a whoosh of relief. "Boy, Willow, there was a couple times when I thought I was going to be bounced to the ground."

Willow's lips twisted wryly. "There were a few times when I thought I might too."

The sun was fully risen now, and Jimmy said, "It looks like we're gonna have a nice day."

"It would seem so. Is the hoodlum wagon behind us?"

Jimmy craned his neck to look behind them, and said, "Yeah, about a hundred yards behind us."

A pair of strong mules pulled the hoodlum wagon, which was filled to capacity with wood for the many campfires that would be made. There would be no fuel to be found on the plains, except for cow chips. If she could help it, Willow wouldn't cook a meal on dried cow dung.

"Who is driving the wagon?" she asked Jimmy.

"My pard, Brian Winterspoon. We've been workin' on the Asher ranch since we was fourteen."

"Don't you fellows have any family?"

"I don't. Not that I know of. My folks died from influenza one winter when I was thirteen and I was sent to live in an orphanage. Me and Brian got tired of bein' hungry and cold all the time, so one night we lit out, headin' west. Brian has an older sister somewhere in Texas. He thinks she's workin' in some saloon. His ma and pa are dead too."

Willow's heart went out to the two boys, who were on the edge of manhood. Nothing but hard work lay ahead of them. They would eventually become cowhands and punch cattle the rest of their lives.

But she knew better than to express any sympathy to Jimmy. He would resent it, she knew. So she only said, "I guess the two of you are kind of like family then."

"Yeah." Jimmy grinned. "I guess we are. Kinda like brothers."

When the talkative teenager had not spoken for several minutes, Willow glanced at him and she smiled slightly. His head lolled to one side; he was sound asleep. She imagined that being excited about the cattle drive, he had probably slept little last night.

Feeling a hunger pain, Willow dug into the cloth sack at her feet and pulled out an apple. When she bit into it, she found it crunchy and juicy. What was she going to do about the young man who had given her the fruit? she wondered. He had more or less come right out and said that he wanted to court her.

Was she ready for that? She chewed thoughtfully. She didn't think so. Although he was handsome and thoughtful and very sweet, she didn't really know him.

But he had a house and a farm. A place to take her mother. It was something to think about.

Willow glanced up at the sky and saw by the sun that it was nearing eleven o'clock. When on a long cattle drive, the cowhands had their first meal of the day around that time. They would start getting hungry now, since the only thing that had hit their stomachs that morning was coffee on arising.

She started looking for a likely place to make camp and before long spotted an ideal site.

A quarter mile or so away there was a line of willows. Where willows grew there was water. She turned the horse's head in that direction, at the same time telling Jimmy to wake up.

Pulling the team up beside the hanging foliage of the trees, close to a shallow, swiftly running stream, Willow began taking from the wagon the items she needed to prepare the late morning meal.

Then, as she cut up a whole slab of salt pork and opened several cans of beans, dumping them into a large pot, Jimmy went about building a fire.

He began by digging a wide hole in the gravelly soil at the river's edge and lining it with rocks. In the center of it he then laid two large, flat rocks to support a pot, skillet and coffee pot. Brian arrived with the hoodlum wagon just as he finished and together they built a fire in the cooking pit.

Willow smiled a greeting at Jimmy's friend, and then took over the cookfire. Half an hour later, when the cowboys came straggling in, she had crisp salt pork and a pot of beans sitting on the tailgate of the wagon. Along with the steaming food were two loaves of sliced sourdough bread and a stack of tin plates and cups. Flatware stuck out from the top of a tall jar. The large pot of coffee was warming on some hot ashes.

For the next several minutes Willow filled plates and handed them to the men, while Jimmy poured coffee.

The men were shy and polite, as they had been the morning before. Each one mumbled a "Thank you, miss," when she handed him a heaping plate of meat and beans.

Willow shook her head. These men were rough souls, unafraid of anything, yet a decent woman could freeze their tongues and turn them into awkward boys.

When the cowhands' hunger was sated and they had gone back to the grazing herd, Willow wondered why Jules hadn't come in to eat. Was he still put out at her for holding up the start of the drive?

She shrugged her shoulders indifferently. If he got hungry enough, he'd come in. When Sammy the wrangler came in to eat, she called to Jimmy and Brian, "Come on, fellows, and fill your plates. I don't know about you, but I'm starving."

The four of them were sitting in a group, talking and laughing as they wolfed down the food on their plates, when Jules arrived, coming through the willows. When Willow stood up to fix him a plate, he motioned her to stay put and busied himself filling a plate from the tailgate. He joined Willow and the teenagers then and dug into the food the same way they had.

Jules's stomach had been making empty rumbling noises all the while he stood back among the trees watching Willow move about the cookfire. He had groaned inwardly every time she bent over the pot or skillet, her shapely rear clearly defined in the tight borrowed trousers. He clenched his fists when she stretched up to the wagon for something and her breasts strained against the material of her shirt. He had grown so hard with wanting her that he'd stayed hidden until his men left and he had gained control of himself.

By the time all five were having a second cup of coffee Jules had relaxed, and the young men saw their boss in a light they had never seen him in before. Jules laughed and joked with them and gently teased Willow, saying that the meal he had just eaten wasn't as good as she usually provided. She had come back at him with a twinkle in her eyes, demanding what he expected from beans and salt pork.

It came time for Sammy to get back to the remuda, and Jimmy gathered up the dirty dishes, pot and skillet and took them to the stream to scrub them with sand. He talked Brian into helping him and while they horsed around, sloshing water on each other as they took care of scouring everything, Willow and Jules were left sitting alone.

Willow leaned lazily against a wagon wheel, and Jules remained sitting cross-legged on the ground. "Well, how goes it, Willow?" He smiled as he asked. "How is your butt holding out, bouncing around in the wagon?"

"I've got a feeling it will be pretty sore tomorrow morning."

"I could massage it for you tonight, take away all its aches." Jules gave her a suggestive smile and watched Willow's face for her reaction.

Hope leaped inside him when it looked as though she was considering his offer. A stirring started in his loins at the thought that he might be able to slide his hands over her smooth flesh.

"Would you be willing to do that every night?" Willow asked.

"Yes. Every night, all night."

It was like a dash of cold water in the face when Willow stood up and, dusting off her seat, said, "I'm sorry, but I only signed on as your housekeeper, not to replace Nina." And while Jules stared at her, she started to climb into the wagon. She caught her breath when Jules sprang to his feet, grabbed her arm and jerked her off the wagon wheel. He spun her around and brought her up solidly against his chest. With an arm clamped tightly across the back of her waist, he pulled her into the vee of his spread legs. With his arousal throbbing against her femininity, he bent his head and settled his lips on hers in a searing kiss that left Willow weak.

Releasing her and pushing her away, he ground out, "You're nothing but a tease, Willow Ames. If you're not interested, just say so without the games."

He stamped off, disappearing into the trees, leaving Willow staring after him, her fingers on her burning lips. Flustered by the sensations coursing through her, she hurried the teenagers along, and in less than twenty minutes they were pulling out.

Jimmy tried to engage Willow in conversation, but when she only answered him in monosyllables, or not at all, he gave up and, leaning back in the seat, nodded off.

Her feet propped on the splash board, her elbows on her knees and the reins held loosely in her hands, Willow continued to go over in her mind the way Jules had kissed her.

She had never been kissed by a man before, not even a peck on the cheek from her father, and she didn't know what to make of Jules's demanding lips. The kiss had to have been motivated by pure lust, she told herself. He didn't know her well enough to have any tender feelings for her. Thank God she hadn't had time for any response to his embrace. Otherwise she hated to think what she might have done.

Like kiss him back or press herself against that hot, throbbing part of him.

She was thinking how thankful she was that she hadn't had time to make a fool of herself, when up ahead she spotted a deer browsing on grass. She pulled the team in and nudged Jimmy awake as she drew the rifle from its sling behind her.

"Take the reins," she said, "and hold the team still. I'm going to take a shot at that deer."

Excitement glittering in his eyes, Jimmy gripped the reins firmly as he whispered, "Do you think you can hit him, Willow? He's pretty far away."

"I don't know," Willow answered as she rested the rifle on her shoulder and pressed her cheek against the stock, the muzzle trained on the unsuspecting animal.

Jimmy held his breath, watching Willow's fingers tighten on the trigger, then squeeze it.

The deer dropped in its tracks and Jimmy let out a

whoop that startled the team into motion. "Boy, that was some shot, Willow, especially for a girl. Who taught you how to shoot like that?"

"Our cook back home. He was a hired gun as a young man."

"I'd like to meet him some day, have him show me how to bring an animal down at such a distance."

"I wish you could meet him, too, Jimmy," Willow said, a touch of sadness in her voice. She wished both Smitty and her mother were safe in Texas with her.

When they arrived where the deer had fallen, Brian pulled the hoodlum wagon in behind them. "Get your skinnin' knife out, pard," Jimmy called, "we're gonna have venison steak for supper tonight."

Willow smiled and shook her head as Jimmy sang her praises while the two boys skinned and gutted the deer. "She put the bullet right behind his ear, killin' him instantly," the teenager bragged.

When the carcass was loaded into the hoodlum wagon, a fast glance behind her showed Willow that the distance between the chuck wagon and the herd had shortened considerably. She whipped up the team and was soon out of sight of the cattle.

It was a couple of hours to sunset when Willow made camp, further up the same stream where she had made lunch. The first thing on the agenda was to have Jimmy and Brian carry the slain deer to the tail-gate of the wagon. She took her own special butcher knife from a box and sliced nineteen steaks off one of the haunches. When those had been set aside, she set Jimmy to making a cookfire. While she waited for that to be done, she cut some meat into cubes for tomorrow night's supper. And if the meat didn't spoil, she would serve the men a venison roast the third night.

When the herd came in sight and was allowed to stop and graze, Willow had the tender steaks waiting, and she was pulling nineteen potatoes from the fire's hot ashes. The vegetables the men would be offered were steamed squash and sliced tomatoes. For dessert she would pass out cookies with their coffee.

When the men began to come in, their faces wet from a visit to the stream, Jimmy couldn't wait to tell them about Willow's long shot. "She just put the rifle to her shoulder and squeezed the trigger and that buck dropped in his tracks."

The cowboys looked at her shyly, respect for her marksmanship in their eyes. A few got up the nerve to compliment her as she filled their plates. Each time she answered, "It was just a lucky shot. I probably couldn't do it again in a hundred years."

"Don't believe that," Jimmy declared. "A gunman taught her how to shoot."

Jules walked into camp in time to hear Jimmy's last remark and to see the alarmed look that came into Willow's eyes. Did the boy know what he was talking about, and why was Willow suddenly looking nervous?

How would Willow know a gunman? he asked himself. As for that, how well did *he* know Willow Ames? Her mother's letter had only said that her daughter was leaving home because of a broken engagement. Could this gunman be that man?

He was still smarting from the way Willow had led him on and then rejected him. No other woman had ever done that to him.

When Jimmy came up to him and started to tell him about Willow's great shot, he cut him off. "I heard you telling the men. Fill me a plate and bring it to me, will you?" he added, sitting down several paces behind his men, who were eating their supper close to the campfire. And though he mentally called them fools as they stole looks at the beautiful cook, all the time he ate he also watched her out of half-closed eyes.

Chapter Eight

A couple of weeks had passed since the cattle drive pulled out from the ranch. Everything had been going smoothly. Most of the men had lost their shyness around Willow, and some even talked and joked with her. Willow liked them all with the exception of one man—Joe Becker, a cowboy who never changed his clothes and seldom shaved. She was very nervous around him and tried to avoid him.

He had looked vaguely familiar until the evening when Jimmy was singing her praises about her shooting and that a gunman had taught her how to shoot. She had happened to look at Joe Becker while Jimmy was going on about the deer and caught the alert look that came into the man's eyes. She could almost see the wheels turning in his head as he tried to place her. At the same time she remembered why he looked familiar. She had seen him once at her father's ranch.

He was a cousin to Buck Axel. If he made the connection between her and Buck, he would give away her whereabouts to his relative. She had asked herself repeatedly what she should do. Run again? But run where?

Every night those questions ran through her mind as she suffered nightmares in which Buck and her father chased her, demanding that she marry the man she so despised.

On the fourteenth evening of the cattle drive, as the men were topping off their meal with a cup of coffee and a smoke, one of the men asked, "Shouldn't we be comin' to a town pretty soon, boss?"

"There's a small cow town a couple days' ride from here," Jules answered.

"That's good. I'm ready to cut the dust in my throat with a belt of whiskey," another man said.

"You men know the rule about drinking on a cattle drive. You can have one drink apiece, then back to the herd."

Willow remembered her promise to send Jess a letter the first chance she got. She would write it tonight and put it in the envelope that held the brief happenings of the day which she had jotted down each evening.

"Have you fellers noticed them dark clouds gatherin' in the north?" a tall, skinny cowboy asked. "I bet we get rain tonight or tomorrow."

"I hope so." Jules flipped his cigarette butt into the fire. "If it doesn't rain soon, the grass is going to dry up like dust balls. I sure as hell don't want to drive a herd of skin and bones to the holding pens."

A short time later, Willow left the men and went to the chuck wagon. She struck a match to the lantern hanging from a peg and dug a notepad and a pencil from a box under the tall seat. After a thoughtful minute, she wrote:

Dear Jess,

Everything has gone well. I do miss my soft bed, however, and my talks with you. Believe it or not, a woman with nineteen men around her can get very lonesome. Some of them would like to be friendly, to talk to me, but of course Jules doesn't allow that to happen. So I make do with the company of Jimmy, Sammy and Brian. You can imagine how entertaining that is. But it appears they have adopted me, and I guess that's better than having them play tricks on me.

I hope that all is well with you and that you're not working too hard. I look forward to being with you again.

Love,
Willow

Willow had just turned down the lantern wick and stretched out in her bedroll when she heard Jules tell his men good night, then heard his footsteps go past the wagon. She knew that, as usual, he would spread his blankets close to the wagon. She was especially glad of his nearness tonight, for Joe Becker seldom took his leering eyes off her. If Jules wasn't nearby, her sleep wouldn't be too sound. Her last thought before nodding off was of her mother and her longing to see the gentle little woman.

Whoever had said it might rain was right. It was around two o'clock in the morning when Willow awakened to a cold, wet wind on her face. She leaned up on her elbows and peered outside.

There had been no thunder or lightning to warn of its approach, but the rain had arrived. It was blowing sideways in stinging wet sheets. She felt sorry for the men, who had no protection against the deluge. They would be soaked to the skin.

She was about to close the canvas flap when she saw Jimmy and Brian loping toward the wagon. She barely had time to roll out of the way as the pair stormed inside.

"We thought you might let us wait out the rain with you, Willow," Jimmy said, his teeth chattering.

"Well, yes, I guess so." Willow didn't have the heart to order them back outside. "But let me get farther back in the wagon. You're dripping water all over me."

She had barely pulled her bedroll to the very back of the wagon when it gave a bounce and Sammy arrived. With a sigh, she sat up, and said, "Jimmy, light the lantern."

In its dim light she thought to herself that she had never seen a sorrier-looking sight in her life. Three gangly, drenched teenagers gazed at her through the water dripping off their heads.

"Jimmy, you know where we keep the towels and blankets," Willow said, concern in her voice. "You fellows have to get out of those wet clothes before you catch pneumonia. When you've got them off, towel yourselves dry and then roll up in a blanket." She lay back down and turned on her stomach to give them some privacy.

The wagon shook as the three awkward teenagers bumped into each other as they disrobed, dried off, and then wrapped the warmth of dry blankets around their shivering bodies.

Willow gave a sigh of relief when the lantern was put out and it grew quiet in the wagon. "Just call me Mother Goose," she muttered before falling back to sleep.

The rain on his face had awakened Jules. With a curse he sat up, wondering where to go. There was nowhere to go. Only prairie surrounded them. Maybe Willow would give him shelter in the wagon, he was thinking, when he saw Jimmy and Brian bolting for the wagon. Before he could yell, "Stop right there!" they were inside. A minute or two later he saw Sammy running in the same direction. When lantern light flared inside the shelter, he heard Willow saying something and decided to leave it up to her whether the boys stayed or left. A few minutes later, the light went out and it grew quiet.

Jules pulled the tarp from beneath his bedroll and sprinted to the chuck wagon and crawled underneath it. Damn, he thought when he found that his trail boss and another cowhand were already there.

When Willow awakened at her usual time, it was quiet outside. As she stepped over and around her three sleeping guests she realized the rain had stopped.

She shook Jimmy's shoulder. "Come on, Jimmy, get a fire going so we can make breakfast."

Jimmy sat up and looked at her out of sleep-filled

eyes. "I'll be right there," he muttered, then shook awake his companions.

Everywhere Willow stepped was a quagmire of mud. But Jimmy managed to get a fire going in the pit that supper had been cooked in the night before.

While the coffee brewed, Willow fried extra bacon and flapjacks. The men lined up in front of the hoodlum wagon to wait their turn to get dry clothes. They had a hard day's work ahead of them.

None of the men took the time to shave, only bolted down their breakfast and hurried off to see how the cattle had fared.

Jules had checked on them as soon as he crawled out from under the wagon. He found the herd wet, but peacefully grazing. His spirits were high when he walked into camp. For the first time in days, he smiled at Willow and spoke.

"That was quite a gully-washer we had, wasn't it?" he said as she filled a plate for him.

"It sure was. I can't remember ever seeing it rain so hard."

"You had company, I noticed."

"Yes." Willow smiled. "They were half-drowned." After a while she added on a sad note, "They're not as tough as they pretend. Last night they were three young boys, bewildered and looking for someone to care for them."

"I know," Jules agreed. "They haven't had anyone to look after them for a long time. It looks like you've become their adopted mother."

"I hope not," Willow laughed. "I can't take care of myself half the time."

Jules gave her a smoldering, rakish look. "I know

someone who would love to take care of you."

"You do, do you?" Willow said coolly, then added, "I'm not interested."

"Not even a little bit?"

"Not in the least."

"How long are you going to pine for that man?" Jules demanded.

"What ma—" Willow began, but she caught herself and corrected, "I'm not pining for a man." She looked anxiously around, wishing Jimmy would put in an appearance.

"Like hell you're not. You won't let another man get near you."

"You mean I won't let Jules Asher get near me."

"All right, let's say you won't let me get near you. Why not if you don't have another man on your mind?"

"Maybe it's because I can see you for what you are."

"And what am I?" Jules's voice was losing its bantering tone.

"You're a womanizer," Willow said bluntly. "When you meet an attractive woman, all you think about is getting her in your bed. You aren't the least bit interested in what she's like, what goes on in her mind, whether she's happy or sad, what her dreams and fears are. And the sad thing is, you don't even care."

When Willow had finished her assessment of his faults, her voice had risen and her face was flushed. Jules was equally riled up and he glared at her, angry sparks glittering in his eyes.

"At least something stirs my blood." His voice was dangerously low. "I don't have ice water in my veins like you do. You're the coldest woman I ever came across. No wonder the man you wanted to get your hooks into dropped you. Lucky for him he found out in time that beneath that beautiful shell there wasn't much substance, that you wouldn't be bringing too much warmth to the marriage bed."

They stood glaring at each other. Jules saw from the rage shooting out of Willow's eyes that she was about to spring at him.

"Don't do it," he warned. "You won't like the consequences."

"Consequences be dammed," Willow ground out and stiffened her muscles to throw herself at him.

The appearance of Jimmy and the startled look on his face made Willow pause long enough to get control of her outrage. Her arms dropped to her sides and her fingers uncurled.

"Let's get packed up, Jimmy, and get rolling," she said as calmly as she was able.

Jules stood a moment, then turned around and stamped away, his back stiff and his stride long.

Jimmy looked at Willow and knew from her stormy face not to ask any questions.

As the days passed a cold aloofness existed between Willow and Jules, which the cowhands didn't miss. They laughed among themselves that the boss had probably made a move on their cook and she must have rebuffed him in no uncertain terms. Why else would he go around snapping and snarling at everyone? After all, Jules Asher could have any woman he wanted—until now.

As for Willow, their respect for her grew. She was smart. She knew he was after only one thing and she wasn't going to have any part of it.

Willow was her usual warm self, laughing and joking with the men as she served them their meals. In the evenings before retiring, she sat with "her boys," singing with them, accompanied by a battered guitar that Brian strummed. Sometimes some of the other men would wander over and join in. Her presence in camp made many a man turn back to memories of his youth, a loving family, perhaps a girl he had left behind to become a cowboy.

When Willow saw sadness creep over some of the faces, she would suggest they sing some rollicking song that would bring smiles all around. She didn't like the sad songs either. They made her think of her mother.

And always, Jules sat off by himself, a dark scowl on his face.

Three days after Willow and Jules had had their flare-up, they came to the outskirts of Ely. A sleepy cow town in the heart of cattle country, it had profited from trade with drovers and cowboys.

There was a saloon, a bath and barber shop and a mercantile that sold everything from menswear to trinkets a cowboy might want to buy for some girl he had his eye on. Also in the store, walled off by itself, was a post office.

The cattle had been driven into a loose milling pattern and left to graze while half the men rode into town to have that single drink before returning and relieving the ones that had been left behind.

When Willow made it known that she was going to ride into town, Jimmy gave her an argument. "I don't think you should go, Willow," he said, his brown eyes serious. "There's another herd of cattle up ahead, and we don't know anything about the men who are driving them. They might not be very nice."

"I can take care of myself," Willow said confidently. "I have a letter I want to send to Aunt Jess."

"Jimmy can mail it for you," Jules said behind her.

"I know that." Willow turned around, ready to do battle. "I want to look around in the store, pick up something for Aunt Jess."

"She doesn't need anything, and I don't want you starting trouble that can only be settled with guns."

"But I—"

"But nothing. You're not going. And if you don't give me your word that you will stay with the wagon, I'll tie you to one of the wheels."

Willow knew by the cold threat in his eyes that he would do it. "Oh, all right," she gave in ungraciously. "I give you my word."

"It's for the best, Willow," Jimmy said, trying to console Willow before he set off to overtake Jules and his two friends.

The camp was strangely quiet without Jimmy following her around, always talking. Finding nothing to occupy herself with, she walked toward the wagon, thinking that she might as well take a short nap.

She had lifted one foot to the step-up board when she heard the sharp crack of a brittle twig being stepped upon. She looked over her shoulder and saw Joe Becker standing a few feet away, his loose, fat lips spread in a leering smile over his tobacco-stained teeth.

"What do you want?" she asked, frowning at him.

"I brung you a purty." He dangled a string of gaudy beads on his finger as he walked closer to her.

Willow managed to keep the uneasiness out of her voice as she said, "Thank you, but I don't accept presents from men."

"I bet if Asher brung you something, you would take it."

"Then you'd lose your bet."

"What about my cousin Buck? You're promised to him."

"You're mistaken again. I have no intention of marrying him."

"You will. Buck always gets what he wants. And he wants you in the worst way."

"If you believe that, why are you buying me gifts?"

"Because I'm gonna have a taste of you before he makes you his bride."

Willow's irritation turned to panic when suddenly she was shoved from behind and boosted over the wagon seat so that she landed on her back on the floor. The breath was knocked out of her, and before she could cry out, Becker's big body was on top of her, pinning her down, his fingers clawing at the neck of her shirt.

She was helpless from the waist down, his weight making it impossible to move. But her hands were free, and she raked her nails across his face. Becker let out a yell of pain and slapped her hard across the face, then captured her wrists and held them in one hand. And though she twisted and turned, trying to shake him loose, she was helpless to stop him from ripping open her shirt and clawing her breasts from her camisole.

"My, ain't they purty," he said, licking his lips. "I'm sure gonna have a fine time suckin' on them." He leered down at her as he pinched one of her nipples.

"You're hurting me," Willow cried out.

"That ain't nothin' to the way my cousin is gonna hurt you when you're married to him. He's gonna keep you naked and tied to the bed. So you just be good to ole Joe, cause he ain't that mean if he don't have to be."

Willow hadn't called out yet; she had saved her energy to fight Becker off, but when he snaked down his hand and ripped open the fly of his trousers, she screamed, and in desperation managed to free her hands. Again and again her hard little fists hit him in the face, but all the while his hands were busy, trying to strip her trousers off.

Finally, sheer will could no longer support Willow's failing muscles. She was exhausted and breathing fast. With her last strength, she opened her mouth and screamed as loudly as she could.

Becker swore an ugly oath. Doubling up his fist, he clipped her hard on the chin. With a sigh, she wilted into unconsciousness.

Jules hadn't been able to banish the image of Willow's disappointed face when he told her that she couldn't go into town. He knew it wasn't fair that she had to stay behind. She had worked hard, preparing good, nourishing meals. And it wasn't easy handling a big strong team and bouncing along in a wagon all day.

But had he allowed her to go to town, there would have been trouble. Some men always made fools of themselves over a beautiful woman. If any male accosted Willow on the street and one of his men saw it happen, there would be gunfire and one or two men could end up lying dead in the street.

But what's to keep me from bringing Willow into town and staying with her while she looks around? he thought. *I'll do it,* he decided, turning his horse around. *I'll go get her right now.*

Jules was nearing the camp when he heard Willow scream. The hair rose on the back of his neck. Had a bull wandered away from the herd and walked into camp? The older longhorns could be meaner than hell if they found a person on foot. Or maybe she had been bitten by a rattlesnake.

When his horse thundered into camp, he recognized Becker's horse cropping grass nearby. "The rotten bastard," he ground out, his eyes glinting with cold rage. He almost ripped the wagon seat off to get to the man.

Startled, Becker looked up when Jules's feet landed beside him. His face went dead white, and his eyes fixed on Jules in dread fascination. "She lured me on," he whined, putting up his hands to ward off what he knew was coming. "I didn't want to get in the wagon with her, but she insisted. She—"

The fat man didn't get to finish his sentence. Jules's rock-hard fist smashed into his mouth and nose, sending blood and teeth flying. Becker was grabbed by the arms then and lifted off Willow. With one heave Jules sent him flying over the wagon seat, landing hard on his rump. Jules followed him, and for several minutes his punishing blows landed on Becker's face.

With a promise of more violence in his eyes, Jules panted, "Get on your horse and ride the hell out of here. If we ever run into each other again, pull your gun, for I will draw mine."

When Becker had pulled himself into the saddle and ridden away, Jules climbed back into the wagon.

He knelt beside Willow and his heart thudded. She was so pale, her long lashes were a startling black on her cheeks. Had the bastard killed her? When his trembling fingers picked up her wrist to feel for a pulse, he saw the angry looking scratches on her breasts. He wished with all his heart that he had shot Joe Becker. If he ever saw him again, he would.

When he felt a steady beat in the slender wrist, he drew a breath of relief. She was alive. He looked more closely at her limp body. Her shirt was ripped and all the buttons gone, but the trousers were intact. Becker hadn't had time to tear them off her. For the first time, he was thankful for their snug fit.

He drew the shirt together, and then began to gently pat her cheeks, urging softly, "Wake up, Willow. He's gone. It's me, Jules. Open your eyes and look at me."

Willow's lids fluttered, and then her amber-colored eyes stared up at Jules. She gave a glad little cry and reached her arms to him.

Jules leaned down and gathered her trembling body into his arms, holding her tightly against his chest. And while she clung to him, he stroked her hair, her cheeks, murmuring the kinds of words one spoke to a frightened child.

Finally the tremors that had shaken her body eased somewhat, and when Willow lifted her head to gaze up at Jules, she found her lips mere inches from his. He caught a sharp breath, and cupping a hand to the back of her head, he brought his lips down and settled them over hers.

It began as a gentle, soothing kiss, but soon deepened into urgent pressure that demanded a like response. A sensation she had never known before surged through Willow. On their own, her arms lifted to clasp Jules's shoulders as her lips stirred with the same urgency as his. With his lips still fastened on hers, Jules eased her back down and stretched out beside her.

The hungry pressure of the kiss continued as they strained against each other. Finally, out of breath, Jules broke the sensuous contact. Willow held her breath as his head lowered and his lips parted against her throat. They lingered there a moment and then slid slowly to her breasts, where he planted gentle kisses on the scratches Becker had put on the white flesh. His tongue then caressed her sensitive, swollen nipples as his hands slid restlessly over her ribcage. Willow made a low, throaty sound when his hot mouth settled over one breast. She tightened her arms around his shoulders when he drew the hardened nipple between his lips and began to suckle it like a man dying of thirst. When the hardened nub became swollen, he switched to its twin. While he was giving it the same attention, Willow was moaning and thrashing her head. She wanted more, but was not quite sure what it was her body was demanding.

Then Jules was lifting his head and rising to his knees. He removed her boots, then gently eased her trousers down over her hips, pausing to kiss her smooth, flat stomach before stripping them down her legs. Her torn shirt and camisole came next, then her underwear.

As he drew off his boots, then shucked off his clothes, he didn't take his eyes off her slender, lovely body. Willow had leaned up on her elbows to watch him disrobe, and she stared in fascination at his long, hard arousal, which throbbed and jerked in anticipation of burying itself inside her warmth. She knew now what it was her body wanted. It wanted to be filled with every inch of Jules.

Still in a storm of passion, Willow reached eager arms to him when he inserted a knee between her legs, parting them for his entrance inside her. A moment later all her desire died when he entered her with a hard thrust of his hips. She gave a pained cry and tried to push him off her.

"I'm sorry, Willow." Jules's body grew still. "I had no idea you were still a virgin." He gently stroked her hair off her forehead. "It will stop hurting in a minute," he said. "I promise."

He didn't know if it would or not. He had never had a virgin before. A good feeling rose inside him. No other man had ever been there before him.

Jules bent his head to lick his tongue over a nipple, then drew it into his mouth. He had roused her to a fever pitch this way before; maybe it would work again.

It took but moments before he was proven right. Willow was making little moaning noises in her throat and was caressing his shoulders and back. He slid his hands under her hips and began to move slowly inside her. When she made no outcry and lifted her long legs to wrap them around his waist, he increased his pace, his thrusts long and rhythmic.

Willow responded by eagerly lifting her hips to receive fully each long drive of his hips. Jules felt as if he would climax immediately. But he gritted his teeth and continued to drive inside her. He wanted it to be good for her, too.

When he felt the walls of her femininity tightening around him, he increased the bucking of his hips and rode a crest that left him weak and drained. Never had he experienced a release so all-consuming.

Tremors were still shaking Willow's body. He drew her close in his arms and stroked her back until she lay quietly, her breathing even again.

Chapter Nine

Five weeks passed before the Asher herd had been driven across Oklahoma and on into Kansas. Another few days and they would reach their destination in Wichita.

Willow mopped at her sweating face with a clean dish towel as the chuck wagon rattled along. It was summer now, and the sun's rays beat down unmercifully on man and beast. She mentally promised herself that this was the last cattle drive she would ever make.

A little smile twitched the corners of her lips. She was safe in thinking that. Mrs. Jules Asher wouldn't be expected to drive a chuck wagon, or cook for a bunch of hungry cowhands. She would stay home, keep the house spotless and cook her husband good, nourishing meals.

And best of all, her little mother would be a part of her life again. Jules and Aunt Jess would like her gentle mother. Everybody who knew her liked Ruth Ames.

Except for Ruth's husband, that was. Sometimes it seemed that he hated his wife. Certainly he didn't respect her. If a man didn't respect his wife, he couldn't really love her.

And that was the mistake Mama had made in her marriage. She had never stood up to her bully of a husband. Otto was the sort of man who took advantage of the weak and the helpless, riding roughshod over them.

But time was growing short for Otto Ames to mistreat his wife. As soon as they returned to the ranch and she and Jules were married, they would ride to her father's ranch and take Mama away. Her father would never stand up to Jules.

Jules. Willow's eyes grew soft. The nights spent with him had made the hot days bearable. Their passion for each other had only grown with time. It seemed the long hours of making love were never enough. She thought with a smile that it was a good thing that Jules had to leave the wagon at a decent hour to keep from being caught there by Jimmy or one of the other teenagers. They would wear each other out otherwise.

"I don't want to leave you," Jules would complain as he drew his trousers on. "I'm never going to leave you once I get you home. If I live to be a hundred, I'll still want to make love to you."

"And I'll be ready for you," she always answered.

And I will be, Willow thought. It took but a touch

of Jules's hand, a smoldering look from across the evening campfire, and a raging desire to be in his arms rose inside her.

He had taught her many things about lovemaking during those hot, steamy nights. Things she had never dreamed happened between a man and a woman. At first she had been timid and bashful, but now everything they did to each other seemed natural and right to her. She was as eager as Jules to explore the pleasures they could bring each other, kissing and getting to know every inch of each other's bodies.

Willow made herself stop thinking of Jules. Desire for him was building inside her, and it was several hours before darkness when the camp would sleep.

Willow let her mind wander to other things, once stopping to wonder if Joe Becker had showed up at her father's ranch yet. She wouldn't be surprised to find her father and Buck Axel waiting for her when she returned from the cattle drive. But having her father find her didn't frighten her anymore. Jules would soon send them packing.

"That's what I said, Buck. Your intended is drivin' a chuck wagon and cookin' for a bunch of cowhands on a cattle drive to Wichita," Joe Becker told his cousin.

"Who owns the outfit?" Otto Ames demanded.

"An arrogant bastard from Texas. He owns a big spread near El Paso."

"How in the hell did Willow get there and hire on to cook for a bunch of men?" Buck paced angrily back and forth. "It don't make sense."

"She was this Jules Asher's housekeeper first. Then

the day before they were supposed to go on the trail, the cook there broke his ankle. Miss Ames offered to replace him. Said she had done for you a couple times, Otto."

"His housekeeper, huh?" Buck said suspiciously. "I wonder if she's his bed warmer too."

"I wouldn't be surprised. He's a right good looker. These bruises you see on my face and my two missing teeth are his work. He went crazy mad because he thought I was lookin' at Willow. After he beat me up, he fired me. Said if he ever seen me again he'd shoot me."

"When are we gonna go after her, Otto?" Buck asked.

"We can't go now, Buck. We're gonna start our own drive day after tomorrow. Anyhow, there's no hurry. We know where to find her when we're ready. As soon as we get back, we'll go get her."

"And then what?" Buck growled, giving Otto a hard look.

"Then we'll have a wedding." Otto's eyes narrowed in determination.

"You've been sayin' that for months and nothin' has happened yet. I'm gettin' damned tired of waitin'."

"There won't be no waitin' this time. I've learned that all I have to do is slap her mother around a few times. The girl will do whatever I want her to do as long as I leave my sickly wife alone.

"But I sure would like to know who helped Willow run away. There had to have been some thought to it, some plannin'." A hard glint came into Otto's eyes. "And I've got a pretty good notion that sweet Ruth and that damn Smitty are at the bottom of it."

Otto climbed onto his mount's back. "I'll come over to your place later, Buck." His lips curled in a leer before adding, "Make sure you've got that squaw all nicely tied up. Right now I'm gonna go home and start doin' some questioning."

The cousins watched him ride away, Buck practically rubbing his hands together at the prospect of finally making Willow his wife. And if he didn't find her still virgin, she would pay dearly for sleeping with another man.

Joe Becker cleared his voice and asked, "You still got the same woman at your place, Buck?"

"Naw. I wore that one out. Besides, I put a baby in her belly. I sent her back to her people. I've got a new one now. Had her for a couple weeks."

"Do you mind if I take a crack at her? I ain't had a woman in months."

"Go ahead. But don't wear her out. You heard Otto. He'll want to use her when he gets here."

It was nearing sundown and Ruth was sitting on the porch, hoping to catch a cool breeze as she rested her tired body. She had been working since sunup, mucking out stables and spreading fresh hay on the floors. That was just one of the many jobs she had to do these days. Everything that her daughter had done once, her husband demanded that she do now.

Ruth rested her head on the chair back with a tired sigh. She couldn't have done a third of the work without the help of Smitty and the stable hands. As soon as Otto rode away in the mornings, they made her sit down while they did what was necessary.

A spasm of pain flickered across Ruth's face when

she began to cough. It was summer, but the cold she had caught last spring lingered. Her health was failing rapidly, she knew, and she longed to see her daughter once more. But that was out of the question. Willow was safe from her father and Buck Axel, and in order for her to see her again, her lovely girl would have to come home. And that must never happen.

Ruth's body stiffened when she saw her husband striding toward the house, his face dark with anger. She gripped her hands tightly together. She saw the threat in Otto's tightly coiled body.

She let out a yelp of pain when he jumped up on the porch, grabbed her by a thin arm, and jerked her out of the chair.

"What's wrong, Otto?" she begged as he dragged her, stumbling, down the porch steps. "Where are you taking me?"

"I'm takin' you to the cookhouse. Me and you and that sneakin' cook are gonna have a little talk."

"What in the hell is goin' on?" Smitty burst through the cookhouse door when Otto gave Ruth a jerk that brought her to her knees.

"I'll tell you what's goin' on." Otto shoved Smitty away when he would have helped Ruth to her feet. "I've just learned where that selfish daughter of mine is, and I'm damn well gonna find out who helped her run away. The sooner the two of you admit to helping her, the less you'll feel of my fists."

Still on her knees, Ruth began to whimper her fear and distress.

Smitty looked down at the pale face of the woman he had silently loved for so long. Throwing back his shoulders and looking into the eyes of the man he hated, he said, "I helped the girl. Ruth had nothing to do with it."

"I doubt that." Otto drew back a foot to kick his wife. "It was all her idea."

"Damn you!" Smitty's voice rose. "You kick her and I'll blow your brains out!"

"Oh, you will, will you, you old stove-up bag of bones," Otto yelled, his hand hovering over the pistol at his side. He gave Ruth a sharp kick in the side.

Ruth tried to hold back a cry of pain, but it escaped her, and at the sound of the muffled utterance Smitty pulled a gun from his apron pocket and thumbed back the hammer. At the same time Otto snatched his pistol free and two shots rang out almost simultaneously.

Smitty's shot kicked up dirt at his boss's feet, while the rancher's bullet hit the elderly man in the chest. He stood an instant; then his head sagged forward and he crumpled down into the dust. His body twitched once, and then grew still.

"Smitty!" Ruth screamed and struggled to her feet. But when she would have gone to her old friend, Otto grabbed her arm and held her back.

"Get your butt back to the house," he growled. "I'll tend to you later."

Her fist in her mouth to hold back her sobs, Ruth stumbled into the house and on into her bedroom. Throwing herself onto the bed, she let the tears flow, weeping for the man who had tried to defend her, and for the beloved daughter who would be dragged back into a life of misery.

Outside, Otto pinned his men with a threatening glower as he said, "All right, you stable hands, you saw what happened. You saw Smitty draw first. I had to shoot him in self-defense."

The men nodded reluctantly. The old fellow had drawn first, but Otto had deviled him into doing it by kicking Miss Ruth. The boss had known that Smitty's arthritic fingers would slow him down.

"One of you men ride to town and bring back the sheriff," Otto ordered; then he stomped off to the barn.

An hour later Ruth stood at her bedroom window watching the sheriff ride away with Smitty's limp body strapped across his horse. "Good-bye, old friend," she whispered and collapsed onto her bed.

When it was nearing supper time, Otto knew better than to force Ruth to cook for the hands. The men were already sullen-faced about Smitty's death, and just one wrong step from him might make them all ride away. He thought for a minute, then ordered one of his beeves slaughtered. He spent the next hour frying steaks for the men.

Otto sat off by himself as he ate his meat, not once thinking to bring his wife anything. Later, when he saddled his horse and rode away, the men spoke of this.

"One of us must bring Miss Ruth something to eat," one of them said.

"I'll make her something," said a dark and brooding man, dressed entirely in buckskins.

No one knew the half-breed's full name. He had given only the name Logan when he was hired to break horses. Otto bragged that he had the best tamer of horses in all of Texas.

Logan didn't pack a gun, but wore a wicked-looking knife at his waist. He had an unerring aim, making the men fear and respect him. But he held himself aloof from them, so none called him friend.

Logan entered the house, and in the semi-darkness felt his way to the table. Striking a match on his thumbnail, he lit the lamp sitting there. He laid a leather pouch and a piece of beef wrapped up in a neckerchief on the table and then lit a fire in the range. After placing a kettle of water to heat, he washed the piece of meat and set it aside on a plate.

When steam escaped from the cast-iron pot he took a mug from a cupboard and opened up the pouch. It contained *atole*, a mixture of wheat and brown sugar ground together. A small quantity mixed with hot water made a pleasant and nutritious drink. It would feel good in Ruth's stomach until he could make her a proper meal.

With the mug in hand, Logan opened doors until he found Ruth's bedroom. She lay on the bed in a stupor, limp and motionless. "Miss Ruth, are you all right?" He laid a hand on her shoulder, genuine concern in his voice.

Ruth stirred and turned over on her back. "It's you, Logan." She smiled in relief. "I was afraid it might be Otto."

"He's gone. Probably won't be back tonight."

"But sooner or later he'll return." Ruth shivered.

"He won't lay a hand on you when he does."

"Oh, Logan, what's to keep him from it?" Ruth said, her voice breaking.

"The bar I intend to put on your door. All you have to do is stay in here until he leaves on the cattle drive."

"But that's only delaying things for a while. He'll be back later."

"But you won't be here when he returns."

Ruth flashed him a confused look. "Where will I be, if not here?"

"You'll be in Texas with your daughter."

"You know where Willow is?" Ruth sat up.

"Yes, Smitty told me. He wanted me to know in case something happened to him. Now, I want you to sip this while I tell you about my plans to get you out of here."

Ruth sipped the *atole* and listened eagerly to Logan.

"When Otto heads out on the drive, we'll wait an hour or so before taking off ourselves in a wagon. I'll make you a pallet out of hay and place it in the wagon bed for you to rest and sleep on. You'll do just fine."

"Oh, Logan, you're making me feel fine already. I was so low in spirits, I wanted to die."

"I'm only too happy to do something for you, Miss Ruth, to return some of the kindness you have shown me. While you finish your drink, I'm going to fry you a steak and make some beef broth that will put strength back in you. We've got a day and a half to get you feeling better before we start out."

"Logan, would you please put the bar on my door first?"

Logan looked down at her, his eyes surprisingly soft in a face so harsh and unyielding. "I'll get to it right now."

Ruth had finished her drink and sat waiting anxiously for Logan to return. She couldn't rest easy until the bar was up. Otto could return any minute. She gave a startled jerk and held her breath when she heard the kitchen door open and then close.

But it was no heavy thumping of boots that came toward her door, only the soft whisper of moccasins.

Logan entered the room, carrying in his arms a long, two-inch-thick bar of wood and two heavy iron braces to hold it. "My"—Ruth smiled her relief—"you made that fast."

"I didn't have to make it." Logan's eyes had a devilish twinkle. "I took it off the barn door. I told myself that you were more important than a bunch of horses."

"I'm sure Otto would disagree with you," Ruth said, sadness in her voice.

"Otto Ames is an idiot," Logan said as he took nails and hammer to the wood that would keep Ruth safe from all intruders.

That night, after a meal of tender steak, stewed squash and sliced tomatoes, washed down with long sips of beef broth, Ruth Ames had the best sleep she'd had in a long time behind her barred door.

Twice, late in the night, Otto banged on the door, demanding that Ruth let him in. Each time, with an indifferent twitch of her shoulder, she turned over and went back to sleep. She was safe. Logan had even nailed the window shut and closed the shutters.

Chapter Ten

The morning the cattle drive began, Logan stood in the open barn door watching the last of the herd disappear over the range. When he saw the rolling dust disappear, he climbed into the wagon and drove the team up to the house, his stallion tied to the tailgate.

Ruth waited for him on the porch, a carpet bag lying at her feet. She wore a dress of blue sprigged calico, with a slatted bonnet on her head. A mixture of apprehension and excitement looked out of her brown eyes. She couldn't wait to see her daughter, but would Jules Asher frown at her arrival? Maybe he would think she was being forward, arriving without an invitation. The last thing she wanted to do was jeopardize Willow's housekeeping job. She knew that if the rancher refused to let her stay in his home, Willow would leave with her. And if that happened, how would they make a living?

When Logan came to help her into the wagon, she looked at him with anxious eyes. "Are you sure I'm doing the right thing, going to Willow? What if I cause her to lose her job?"

"Asher is not going to fire her, Miss Ruth."

"But look at me, frail and ailing, no good to anyone."

"Come on, let me help you into the wagon. You're not going to be ailing the rest of your life. By the time we reach his ranch, you'll have roses in your cheeks and be as spry as a young colt."

"Oh, Logan, I do hope you're right." Ruth sighed as the broad-shouldered man lifted her up and set her on the wagon seat.

"You're going to be all right," he said, climbing up beside Ruth and picking up the reins. "You're not to worry about anything." He looked down at her after the team pulled out and said with twinkling dark eyes, "If worse comes to worst, you've always got me to look after you."

"I couldn't ask for anything better than that." Ruth smiled up at Logan.

Ruth did improve some as the wagon rolled toward El Paso. But she still fatigued easily and spent most of the time resting on her pallet. But each night Logan prepared her a supper of wild game he shot as they rolled along, and she grew a little stronger each day. She slept well on her comfortable pallet, with Logan asleep on his bedroll under the wagon.

The morning of the day they were to arrive at the Asher ranch, it began to rain, a slow, soaking drizzle.

Logan unfolded the tarp he had brought along and made a tent-like structure to keep the rain off Ruth.

Nevertheless the rain seeped into the hay mattress and dampened the sheet and blanket that Ruth lay on. By the time they reached El Paso and inquired the way to the Asher ranch, Ruth was coughing and running a fever.

Finally, the trail-weary cowboys had herded the longhorns into the holding pens a few miles outside of Wichita. A wide smile on his face, Jules swung Willow off the wagon seat. "Have Sammy saddle you a horse so that you can ride on into town and get us a room at the Gold Crown Hotel. I'll be a while meeting with cattle buyers and haggling price."

"What about the chuck wagon? Will it be all right?"

"Don't worry about it. It will be Jimmy's concern from now on. He'll be driving it home." He ran a finger down her throat and into her cleavage. "You and I will be going home by horseback. We'll have all the privacy we want."

"And don't forget tonight in our hotel room," Willow reminded him with a look that caused a tightening in his loins.

Willow entered the lobby of the Gold Crown Hotel and felt out of place as she walked across the thick carpet to the desk directly across from the big double doors. A young man sat there, balding and bespectacled, reading a newspaper. She was conscious of how she must look, her shirt and trousers trail worn, her hat and boots gray with dust. And her face must look a fright. She'd had no way of washing it before leaving camp. The water barrel had been empty, as well as her canteen.

After one glance at her, the man in the high-collared, starched white shirt and string tie went back to reading his newspaper, completely ignoring her. Willow let a full minute go by, anger growing inside her, then she slapped her hand down on the shiny dark wood.

The clerk jumped at the sharp sound, and giving her a contemptuous look, said loftily, "We have no vacancies. Maybe you can find a room at the other end of town. You'd be more comfortable there with your own kind."

Remembering Smitty's response to similar treatment, Willow pulled her pistol from her waistband and laid it on the desk. "Look, you poor excuse for a man, I'll give you five minutes to find me a room."

She didn't think it was possible that the young man's face could become whiter, but it now looked the color of death as he turned the ledger toward her for her to sign. She thought a minute, and then with a flourish, penned Jules's name.

It was her turn to give a curl of her lips when the clerk recognized the name of the biggest rancher in Texas. "I'll give you the room Mr. Asher always uses when he's in town." He fumbled a key off a board behind him. He snapped his fingers at a pimply-faced youth, ordering, "Escort the lady to room fifteen."

"And send up some hot water for a bath," Willow called back as she climbed the stairs to the second floor. When the door was opened for her and her battered saddlebags were placed on the floor, Willow smiled and said, "Mr. Asher will take care of you later."

While she waited for the water to arrive, Willow inspected the lush, well-appointed room. How different it was from the Palace in El Paso. She paid close attention to the big bed, where she and Jules would make love tonight. A warmth spread through her body just thinking about it. When she opened up a tall wardrobe, she stared at the sheer robes and gowns hanging there. Jealousy gripped her chest. How many women had entertained Jules in this room? she asked herself, sitting down on the edge of the bed.

She suspected that there had been many women in Jules's life besides Nina. Would he tire of her after a while, and go back to looking at other women with lust in his eyes?

She told herself not to think about it, that things would be different with her. They would be married and Willow Asher would keep her husband so well loved, he'd never think of another woman.

In a short time the young man who had shown her to the room returned, carrying a pail of steaming water in each hand. When he left, closing the door quietly behind him, Willow examined several bottles of bath salts and bars of scented soap on a shelf above a stack of soft towels and washcloths. Choosing one of each, she sprinkled the salts in the water. As a floral aroma filled the room, she got out of her dusty, sweat-stained clothes and stepped into the tub.

She attacked her hair first, lathering and rinsing it twice before wrapping a towel around the wet tresses. She then began a slow, lazy soaping of her body.

When the water began to cool, she stepped out onto the floor and briskly dried herself with a towel, then wrapped another one around her body. Utterly relaxed now from the long soaking in the tub, she yawned widely. The big bed looked very inviting. She stretched out on the soft mattress and in seconds she was sound asleep.

An early darkness had descended because of the rain, and Jess lit a couple of lamps in the family room. She sat down in her favorite rocker and was about to strike a match to her pipe when she heard a thud on the kitchen door. It sounded like someone had kicked it.

She rose, took the pipe from her mouth and reached down the rifle that hung over the mantel. She walked through the kitchen, pulled aside the curtain and peered outside. She made out the shadowy figure of a man with a woman in his arms. Jess saw no threat in them and lifted the bar on the door.

When she opened the door partly, the handsome breed standing there asked, "Ma'am, does Miss Willow Ames work here?"

"Yes, she does. But she's not here right now. What do you want with Willow?"

"This lady is her mother and she's in a bad way. I'm afraid she has pneumonia."

"Oh, my goodness, bring her in." Jess opened the door wide and moved back out of the way. When Logan stepped inside, trailing water, Jess ignored the puddles he was making and said, "Follow me. We'll put her in Willow's bed."

When Logan laid the slight figure down, Jess began

issuing orders. "While I get her out of these wet clothes and into some dry ones, you go down to the bunkhouse and tell Rooster Garr that I want to see him right away."

When Logan hesitated a second, she added, "He's the oldest man there. Gray hair and mustache."

Jess had barely stripped off Ruth's damp clothes and dressed her in one of her nightgowns when Logan returned with a stockily built man in his mid-fifties following behind him. Iron-gray hair curled loosely on his head.

Rooster Garr nodded to Jess, and then he looked down at Ruth. His gaze moved slowly over her small face, its delicate bone structure and pale lips. "Poor little bird," he said softly as his big hand stroked the top of her thick brown hair. He looked up at Jess. "She needs a doctor, and fast. I'll ride into town and bring back Dr. Ordin."

Jess nodded and then said, "Wait a minute while I write a message for Willow."

Not more than a minute later, Jess returned from the kitchen and handed Rooster an envelope. "Give it to Martinez and tell him to ride to the telegraph office in El Paso. They can send the message to Wichita. Jules always stays at the Gold Crown Hotel when he finishes a drive. The telegram will be delivered to him there."

When Rooster had gone, Jess looked at Logan and asked, "Why is another woman fleeing that ranch in New Mexico?"

"They are running from its owner; Otto Ames, Willow's father and Ruth's husband. Don't ask why. It would take all night to give you the many reasons they had."

"I expect Mrs. Ames realizes what a good friend she has in you."

"I hope she does. There's nothing in this world I wouldn't do for her. I've been seriously thinking about riding back to New Mexico and putting a bullet between her husband's eyes." Turning toward the door then, Logan said, "I'm going to put the team away and get into some dry clothes. I'll be right back."

"Stop in the cookhouse first and tell our cook, Amos, to give you a plate of the stew I made for the men's supper. That is, if the hogs left any."

Logan returned to the house shortly after the doctor and Rooster arrived. The two men and Jess watched anxiously as Doctor Ordin felt Ruth's pulse, took her temperature and then listened to her chest.

When he raised his head he said, "She has double pneumonia. It appears that she's been in ill health for some time and doesn't have enough strength to fight off the sickness that has taken hold of her. She will need round-the-clock care. Every three hours she's to have a spoonful of this medicine." He held up a flat bottle of clear liquid for everyone to see. "This is to break up the congestion in her lungs. And this one"—he held up a small bottle containing amber liquid—"is for her fever. Give it to her every two hours."

Doctor Ordin closed the black bag he had carried into the house and stood up. "I'll stop by in the morning to see how she fared during the night."

When he had gone, Logan said, "I'll take the first shift."

"No." Rooster shook his head. "I'll take it while you

get some sleep. You can relieve me at midnight and sit with her until morning. And you, Miss Jess, can look after her in the daytime." He gave the old lady a keen look. "That is, if you think you're up to it."

"Of course I am, you knucklehead. Haven't I been cooking for you ever since Willow went on the drive?"

"Sorry, Miss Jess. I spoke without thinking. Now off to bed with you." Rooster was left alone then with their unexpected guest—one who was very ill. He pulled up a chair beside the bed and, sitting down, gazed at the delicate face of the woman whose breathing barely lifted the sheet that covered her. From the first, he had been drawn to this fragile woman as he had never been to one much younger. Even as ill as she was, there was a beauty and dignity in her fine features.

"Poor little bird," he whispered, "some bastard has treated you badly."

Chapter Eleven

Willow stirred and smiled in her sleep. Soft lips were dropping hot kisses on her stomach. When they moved down to one inner thigh, she held her breath expectantly. She released it with a soft sigh and whispered Jules's name when she felt teeth nibbling at the little nub of her femininity. Passion flooded through her and she came awake. She murmured Jules's name and he came to her, silent and bare of clothing. Still not speaking, he parted her thighs and crawled between them. When she lifted her legs to wrap them around his waist, he began to thrust inside her slowly. In lazy somnolence they rose and fell against each other. There was no need to hurry. No one was going to come upon them. A whole night of uninterrupted lovemaking lay ahead of them.

Much later, as Jules sat on the edge of the bed with

Willow stroking his back as he rolled a cigarette, he remembered the letter he had been handed when he signed in at the hotel. "There's a telegram for you from Aunt Jess on the table," he said.

"How nice," Willow exclaimed, sitting up and reaching for the envelope, which was somewhat smudged with fingerprints. "I wonder what she has to say."

She extracted the sheet of paper and read,

> Willow, come home as quickly as you can. Stop. Your mother is here and I'm afraid that she has pneumonia. Stop. Love Aunt Jess.

"Oh, no!" Willow cried, her face drained of color.

"What is it?" Jules took the telegram from her nerveless fingers and read it. "Ah, honey, I'm sorry," he said, putting his arms around her.

"Something awful must have happened to make her come looking for me." Willow leaned into the strength of Jules's arms.

Jules held her away, saying, "Let's get dressed and start home. You get our clothes together while I go get our mounts."

It took Willow less than five minutes to dress and get their clothes together. She hurried downstairs and out the door, there to pace back and forth, waiting for Jules to return.

Jules had already purchased their trail supplies, but he took time to fill their canteens. Altogether, in twenty minutes they were riding out of Wichita under a full moon.

"We'll ride a few hours, then stop and get some

sleep," Jules said as they reached the end of town and prodded the horses into an easy gallop.

"Must we, Jules? We can cover a lot of ground if we ride all night."

"Honey, I know you're distraught, but if nothing else, the horses have to get some rest every twenty miles or so; otherwise we'll run them into the ground before we reach the ranch."

Willow knew he was right, so she said no more. With the night wind blowing against her face, she silently prayed to God to help her get to her mother as soon as possible.

It was well past midnight when they came to a lone cottonwood standing starkly on the prairie. Jules helped Willow to dismount, then spread their blankets beneath the tree and staked out the horses nearby.

When they stretched out on the bedroll they lay spoon fashion. Willow's head rested on Jules's shoulder and his arm lay across her waist. Jules smiled wryly. This was the first time in his life he had ever held a woman in his arms with no thought of making love to her. All he wanted to do was be a comfort to Willow.

And so it went as they drew closer to El Paso and the Asher ranch. Each day they rode until it got dark, then stopped wherever they might be. Jules made supper from game he had shot as they rode along; then they would get a few hours' sleep before continuing.

A week later they spotted the Asher ranch in the distance. Willow gave a cry that was a mixture of excitement and dread as she kicked her mount into a hard gallop.

"You have the most beautiful hair I've ever seen on a woman, Ruth," Rooster said as he drew a brush through her rich brown tresses.

"Thank you, Rooster." Ruth's cheeks pinkened at the compliment. She couldn't remember the last time a man had praised anything about her. Probably when Otto was courting her, trying to impress her with empty words. She had learned soon after marrying him that he had none of the finer feelings. He could pretend when he wanted something, but once he obtained what it was he'd gone after, his true character was soon apparant.

But Rooster Garr wasn't like that. The big, burly man had tended to her with the gentleness of a caring mother. It was he who had mostly sat with her through the nights when her fever was high and fits of coughing racked her body. It was his strong arms that had held her, stroked her head, whispered encouraging words to her. It was he who daily made her some kind of broth to strengthen her.

And all those things had worked. Her fever broke and her lungs cleared, and daily she grew stronger. This morning Jess had helped her into one of her faded dresses, for Rooster had promised that today she could go out onto the veranda and sit in the sun for a short time.

She waited impatiently now for him to finish dressing her hair.

"There," the big man said, finally laying the brush aside. "You're ready for your big adventure." As Ruth laughed at his remark, she was swooped up into Rooster's arms. "You don't weigh nothing," he complained as he carried her out onto the veranda and settled her in a chair he had padded with a bright Mexican blanket. "I've got to put some meat on them little bones."

A flush stole over Ruth's face again. What did Rooster mean when he said that he had to put some meat on her bones? It sounded as though he was making himself responsible for her.

The thought excited her even as she knew it could never happen. She was a married woman, and Otto would sooner or later show up to drag her and Willow back to New Mexico.

But, oh, how she would love to have this big man take care of her. With him she could voice an opinion without fear of being struck for it.

Rooster had just came out on the veranda carrying a tray with a mug of broth on it when he and Ruth saw two horses galloping toward them.

"I think that's Jules and your daughter," Rooster said, placing the tray on a table beside Ruth. "I recognize his stallion."

Willow was off her horse before it came to a complete stop and was running to her mother's outstretched arms. Happy tears washed down their cheeks as they clasped each other.

Willow finally pulled away and gazed into Ruth's eyes. "How are you feeling, Ma? You are so thin."

"I was quite ill for a while," Ruth said as they held each other's hands. "But I had wonderful people taking care of me. Especially this fellow." She smiled up at the big man looking down at them. "He made me drink gallons of meat broth."

"Hello, Rooster." Willow smiled at the cowhand. "I can't thank you enough for taking such good care of my mother."

"No thanks needed, Willow. I enjoyed every minute of it." Rooster dropped a hand on Ruth's shoulder. "But don't forget Logan, who brought her here, and Miss Jess, who also took care of Ruth's personal needs and entertained her with stories of her youth." He grinned. "Blood-curdling tales they were, too, of Indian raids, outlaws and rattlesnakes."

While everyone was laughing, Jess came out onto the veranda with Logan behind her. "It's about time you two got home," she pretended to complain.

With a wide smile, Jules grasped his aunt's waist and spun her around until she began to beat him on the chest with her knobby fists. "Put me down, you big buffalo, before you break my ribs," she ordered, "and meet Logan."

After the two tall men shook hands, Jules turned expectantly to Ruth.

"Jules," Willow said, drawing him down beside her, "I want you to meet my mother, Ruth Ames."

Jules took the thin hand offered him. "I'm real happy to meet you, ma'am, and to see that you are recovering. Your daughter can now relax and stop worrying about you. I was afraid she was going to get sick, too, before I could get her home."

Ruth reached for Willow's hand. "Poor Willow has worried about me since she was a little girl." She looked at Willow with a sad smile. "I'm afraid we'll have to go on worrying about each other. Your father knows where you're living, and when he returns from the cattle drive and finds me gone also, he'll be in a rage when he comes looking for us."

"You don't have to go back with him," Jules said. "There're three strong men here who can see to that."

"I don't want to bring you into our troubles. Otto is a mean, vengeful man. He'll go to any extreme to get his way."

"Don't worry about that. He won't be browbeating defenseless women when he gets here. He'll be hooking horns with three determined men. He'll back off, I promise you."

"I hope you're right, but he'll be bringing his friend Buck Axel with him. That one is meaner than my husband."

"Who is this Buck Axel? One of your cowhands?"

"No. He owns a ranch next to ours. He wants to marry Willow."

Jules looked at Willow. "Is he the one you were engaged to?"

"Heavens no! He's old and fat and meaner than a rattlesnake."

"Jules"—Ruth looked shamefaced—"I lied to you in my letter. Willow wasn't engaged to marry anyone. No one jilted her. I just thought that would be a good excuse for her wanting to get away."

"Well, that clears up a lot of things." Jules smiled at Willow. "I've been trying to figure out what man in his right man would run from you."

Rooster looked down at Ruth's flushed face and said firmly, "Miss Ruth, you're beginning to tire. It's time you were getting back to bed."

"Oh, but . . ." Ruth reached for Willow's hand again.

"She can go with you. The two of you can chat to your heart's content while you're resting."

Willow and Jules looked perplexed as they moved back out of the way while Rooster gathered Ruth up in his arms. Jess and Logan paid no attention to the big man carrying Ruth away. They were used to the attention he gave the little woman.

When Willow had followed Rooster and her mother into the house, Jules looked at Logan and said, "Come with me and take a look at the wild horses I've caught."

On the way to the corral, Amos stepped through the cookhouse door. "How's the ankle?" Jules asked the cook.

"I've been hobblin' round on it. Doc says that I can start cookin' next week."

"I'm glad to hear that. The men will be coming home in a few days."

"Everything go all right on the trail?"

"Everything went along fine. Lost six head at a river crossing."

"I expect the girl had a rough time of it, handlin' the team, cookin' on an open fire. The men probably went around hungry half the time."

Jules looked down at the ground to hide his amusement. There was a hopeful note in the cook's voice that betrayed his wish that Willow had failed as a trail cook.

He crushed Amos's hopes by saying, "She did just fine. Every night she had a hot, hearty meal waiting for the men when they came in."

Amos was silent for a moment; then he grunted, "That's good," and turning around, limped back into his domain.

"I think he's afraid Willow will take his job from him," Jules chuckled as he and Logan walked on in the direction of the penned mustangs.

"You've got a fine bunch there," Logan said, leaning on the top rail of the corral. "What are you going to do with them?"

"I'll break them to the saddle, then drive them into Wyoming to sell them to ranchers."

"I've heard that they are in need of mounts there."

"Do you know anything about breaking the wild ones?"

Logan's lips twisted in a wry grin. "That's all I've done since I was twelve years old."

"The hell you say. How would you like to help me with these?"

"I might as well. I sure can't go back to the Ames ranch."

"What happened there that made you bring Ruth here?"

"Ames flew into a rage when he learned that Smitty, their cook, had helped Willow to run away. Otto taunted the old man to draw on him, and Smitty, too proud to back down, drew his gun. Of course he was slow, as Ames knew he would be. The bastard shot the old fellow through the heart.

"Although the cowhands hate Ames, they had to admit to the sheriff that Smitty drew first."

Logan paused, looking out over the range, a glitter in his dark eyes. "When the bastard knocked Ruth down and threatened that he would take care of her when he returned from the cattle drive, I decided to bring her here to be with her daughter." He looked at Jules. "He and that Buck Axel will come looking for them."

"And I'll be ready for the polecats."

In the early evening when the lamps were lit and everyone sat at the supper table, Jules looked across at Willow and saw that she had been crying. He felt that he knew why. Ruth had told her about Smitty, her old friend. He would console her about it later. When they were in bed together.

"Are you sure you'll be comfortable on that?" Ruth asked as she watched Willow make up a narrow cot with bed linens.

"I'll be just fine, Ma. Remember, I've been sleeping on the ground for weeks. This will feel like a cloud to me." Willow smiled at her mother, who had yawned several times. "You go to sleep now, and I'll see you in the morning."

Willow waited until Ruth was in a deep sleep, then quietly let herself out of the room and slipped next door to Jules.

He was waiting for her, without any clothing, his arms folded behind his head. "I thought you would never get here," he half complained, rolling over onto his side and propping his jaw on his hand.

"I came as soon as Ma fell asleep." Willow stepped out of her last garment.

Jules's eyes kindled as he gazed at the loveliness of the woman standing before him. How good her nakedness was going to feel against his.

When Willow blew out the lamp and lay down beside him, Jules said as he gathered her in his arms, "I don't like the idea of you having to sneak into my room. I want you sleeping beside me all night."

"I know," Willow said softly, "but Ma is straight-laced. She'd object to my sleeping with you. We'll just have to be content with stolen hours for the time being," she added as she put her arms around Jules's shoulders and pressed her body against his.

In the ensuing hours they made up for the nights when Jules had only held Willow in his arms. It was nearing dawn before they were exhausted and sated with each other. Each had love bites where they had explored the other's body. When Willow leaned over to kiss Jules good night before going to her cot, he was sound asleep.

"We'll be married soon," she whispered, "then I won't have to leave you like this."

Chapter Twelve

It was deep twilight when Willow stepped out onto the veranda. She sat down in the deep shadow of a bougainvillea that spilled over the roof.

She wanted to be alone, to think. If Jimmy and Sammy and Brian saw her sitting there, they would hurry over to join her. Most times she welcomed their company, their bantering and their horseplay.

But tonight she meant to do some deep thinking. She needed to consider things she couldn't give her complete thoughts to during the day because there were so many interruptions. The day after her arrival back at the ranch she had resumed her housekeeping duties. It had taken two full days to put the large house back in order, doing the things that Jess was unable to do in her absence.

Then there was the tending of her mother who,

thank God, was recovering rapidly. And there were meals to be prepared, bread to be baked. Clothes to be washed and ironed.

But she was strong and healthy and could have handled her workload easily. It was the worrying about her father and Buck Axel that was wearing her down. They were on her mind all the time, making her more jumpy and nervous as each day passed and the time for their appearance at the ranch grew nearer and nearer. She figured she had another two weeks of freedom.

A soft sigh escaped Willow. When was Jules going to set the date of their wedding?

Every night after they finished making love she waited in vain for him to speak of marriage. She had thought about bringing up the subject herself, but pride wouldn't let her. After all, the man did the proposing.

But didn't Jules realize that if she were a married woman her father would have no other recourse but to ride away and leave her and Ma alone? What was he waiting for? she asked herself. He loved her. Each night in his arms proved to her that he did.

Willow left off her worrying when she heard her mother calling her name. With a sigh, she stood up. She still hadn't done any clear thinking. Her thoughts were as muddled as ever.

Three weeks later, the moment that Willow had dreaded was upon her. It was mid-morning; she had just finished hanging up a basket of wash and was returning to the laundry room when a horse galloped up, almost knocking her down. Startled, she looked into her father's sneering face. Behind him, Buck Axel was pulling his horse to a snorting stop.

"Well, daughter," Otto grated out, "at last I've run you and that milksop mother of yours down. I'll give you ten minutes to get your duds together and get your butt on a horse. That goes for puny Ruth too."

"We're not going anywhere with you, and you can't make us."

"Can't I, though." Evil looked out of Otto Ames's eyes. "It will be the easiest thing in the world to do. By the time I knock my wife around a little, you'll be beggin' me to take you home."

"You wouldn't dare lay a hand on either of us."

"Why not? There's only an old woman in the house. Me and Buck have been watchin' the place for two days. We know that every morning Asher and that half-breed ride off together, then the cowhands leave the ranch. That leaves only the cook and a couple of stable hands near the ranch house. Now get goin'."

"Ma!" Willow suddenly screamed, "lock your door!" As she backed away, she looked around wildly for a club or anything else to use to protect herself.

"Grab her, Buck!" Otto yelled. "I'll go get her maw."

Buck was on to Willow in an instant, his arms locked around her waist, pinning her arms to her sides. But she could kick, and her sharp boot heels brought angry yelps from the fat man. From the corner of her eyes, she saw her father about to enter the kitchen patio, and she screamed again, "Ma! Lock your bedroom door!"

Willow's warning to Ruth had barely died away when there came the driving thud of hoofbeats.

* * *

Jules and Logan had been riding about an hour, looking for a wild stallion and his harem. They had about decided that they wouldn't have any luck today, that it was too hot for the wild ones to move about. They were probably holed up somewhere waiting for the cool of the evening before venturing out to graze.

Jules was about to untie the ranch horse he'd been leading, when he heard the sound of drumming hoofs. He turned around and saw a dust cloud in the distance. A wild herd was coming over the plains toward them, their heads high, their necks proudly arched, their long manes and tails gracefully flowing in the wind created by their racing hoofs. He freed the horse trotting beside him, and with a slap of his hat on its rump, the horse took off, heading for the ranch. A small pine tree attached to a rope around his neck, dragged behind him, stirring up a cloud of dust.

This was a trick an old Indian had showed Jules a long time ago. The mustangs would see the rolling dust and instinctively follow it, often right into a corral. But it worked only with small herds.

It worked today. When Jules and Logan closed the gate on the corral there were one stallion and six mares joining the twenty head already there.

"Breaking that bunch should keep us busy for a while." Jules grinned at Logan. "Let's go home for a cup of coffee before we start on them."

They had almost reached the house when Willow's terrified scream rang out. Both men sprinted to the house, separating at the veranda. Jules entered the kitchen patio and Logan slipped along the outside wall. As Jules moved quietly to the arch leading outside, he saw Ruth's frightened face at the kitchen window. He motioned her to stay where she was, then sprang through the opening.

A wild fury shook him when he saw Willow in the grip of a man who he knew instantly was Buck Axel. From his side view he saw Logan holding at bay an older man who must be Willow's father.

He shot a fast glance at Willow. She was breathing fast, obviously panic-stricken. He swore under his breath that she should be so afraid.

Jules swept his gaze to the man who held her and saw that he had a pistol in his free hand. As he stood taking the measure of a man who would pit his strength against that of a woman, Buck spoke.

"Stand back, or I'll put a bullet through your heart."

Jules's answer to the threat was a grim sneer of contempt. He looked at Willow and asked softly, "Do you hear me, honey? Can you think straight?"

"Yes." Her answer was firm.

"All right then, bend forward. Now!"

Willow reacted immediately, folding at the waist, leaving Buck's chest vulnerable to attack. Swearing at his failure to jerk Willow back in place, the enraged man raised his gun and squeezed the trigger. The bullet plowed up dirt at Jules's feet.

Swift as the blink of an eye, Jules had drawn his Colt, shooting Buck in the shoulder a split second before the man got his own shot off. He watched the man stagger back, clutching his shoulder. Then, his eyes glittering like ice, he ordered, "Lay your gun on the ground and kick it toward me."

With a sullen look on his face, Buck did as he was ordered. Jules bent and picked up the pistol and then looked at Willow. "Are you all right?" he asked. When she answered that she was, he said, "Go in the house. I'm sure your mother and Aunt Jess are anxious about the gunfire. I'll be in before long."

Jules brought his attention back to Buck. "Get on your horse," he ordered.

"What about the bullet you put in my shoulder?" Buck whined. "I'm gonna bleed to death if I don't see a doctor."

"You're not going to bleed to death. It's only a flesh wound," Jules said contemptously before saying to Logan, "Keep an eye on him while I have a few words with his companion."

Otto stood waiting, his fingers twitching from the paralysis of fear that had seized him when Jules and Logan appeared. His voice cold, Jules said, "Ames, I'm letting you go this time. But if you ever come around here again, terrifying Willow and Ruth, I'll shoot you down the same as I would a mad dog. Is that clear?"

Otto was incapable of speaking. He could only nod and hurry to scramble onto his horse. But once he was a safe distance away, he became braver and called to Jules, "I'll be back. Them are my womenfolk and I intend to get them back."

Jules drew his Colt and, smiling contemptously, shot at the horse's back hooves.

The startled animal lunged away, almost unseating Otto.

Laughing together, he and Logan entered the kitchen. Jules no sooner stepped through the door then Willow threw herself into his arms, at last letting her pent-up tears of fright flow.

"Don't cry, honey." Jules stroked her hair. "You and your Ma won't be bothered by either one of them again."

"You don't know them, Jules. They are evil men and determined to get their own way. They'll sneak in here again and shoot you in the back."

"They won't. The shot I put in Axel's shoulder has ruined his gun arm, and your father is too much of a coward to face me alone." Jules held Willow away from him. "Is Ruth all right?"

"Yes, she is. She's resting right now. So is Aunt Jess."

"You go lie down for a while, too. You've just had a bad shock. You're as pale as your white apron. Logan and I are going to have a cup of coffee and then start taming the mustangs we just brought in."

Willow lay on her narrow cot, listening to her mother's even breathing. She wished that she could nap, too, to relax her nerves, which were still raw. Those few minutes before Jules had appeared, looking like a wild man, she had thought that she and her mother were going to be dragged back to their old miserable existence, that she would be forced to marry Buck Axel.

How good and safe she had felt when suddenly Jules was there to protect her. No one had ever before intervened in Otto Ames's treatment of his womenfolk. Except poor Smitty, she amended. The poor old fellow had died because he'd tried to help Ruth. And Logan—she musn't forget him. He had been brave enough to bring Ma to her.

But Pa and Buck would be back. She knew that as

well as she knew the sun would rise in the east. Her only hope was that by that time she would be married. If she was the wife of Jules Asher, Pa wouldn't dare drag her away. But there would be nothing to keep him from forcing Ma to go with him. Not that he loved his wife; he would do it only out of pure meanness.

Willow finally gave up the hope of sleeping. She would do better to keep herself busy with something. She remembered that she hadn't finished the wash yet.

Still, as she scrubbed and rinsed and hung out everything to dry, it was all done automatically, and worrisome thoughts continued to run through her mind. How long would it be before her father returned? When was Jules going to set their wedding date? Surely after today he would realize that they should marry soon for her protection.

Willow had just finished hanging up the last basket of wet clothes when she heard the crunch of footsteps behind her. She jerked her head around and then relaxed. Thad Wilson stood smiling at her.

"I just learned that you had returned from the cattle drive," he said. "I'm happy to see you back."

"Thank you, Thad." Willow returned the handsome young man's smile. "I'm happy to be back. What have you brought me today?" she asked, leading the way past the kitchen patio to where the young farmer had parked his wagon.

"The usual vegetables, milk and eggs. I brought along a couple young fryers in case you're hungry for some friend chicken for supper."

"That sounds good, Thad, but I'm just too tired to pluck chickens."

"You wouldn't have to. I took the chance that you might want them, so I did all the messy work. They're ready to be cut up and put in the frying pan."

"In that case, I'll take them." Willow grinned at him. "Maybe the next time you come, you can bring me a stewing hen. I'm hungry for some chicken and dumplings."

Thad said that he could do that and Willow began choosing what vegetables she wanted. When everything had been put into a basket, Thad picked it up.

But before he carried the reed container into the kitchen for her, he asked with a shy smile, "Can I come over tonight and sit with you for a while? You can tell me all about the cattle drive."

Willow was ready to say that she didn't think it was a good idea, that she would be marrying Jules soon, when Jules himself came striding up from the barn.

"Hello, Wilson," he said, frowning. "Still peddling your vegetables, I see."

An angry flush spread over Thad's face at the hint of contempt in Jules's voice. He answered politely, though. "Yes, like you, I'm still working at earning a living."

It angered Willow also that Jules had spoken demeaningly to Thad. It was uncalled for. Was he by any chance jealous of the handsome younger man? she wondered. Maybe she should let Thad call on her. Maybe seeing another man interested in her would spur Jules to set their wedding date.

When Jules had disappeared into the kitchen, Willow took the basket from Thad and, smiling up at him, said, "I'll look for you around seven o'clock."

The wide grin that curved the young man's lips made Willow feel guilty about stringing him along. He was a nice person and didn't deserve to be treated so shabbily.

The three men—Jules, Logan and Rooster—did most of the talking at the supper table. When Willow had been complimented on the crispy fried chicken, the men turned to the subject of wild horses. They talked of how many of the wild ones Jules and Logan had tamed that day and how many they expected to break tomorrow.

Willow and Ruth had little to say. They were still unsettled by the scare they had experienced that morning. Ruth jumped at the slightest unexpected sound, and Willow kept replaying in her mind the terrifying minutes when Buck Axel had held her prisoner against his fat belly.

When Willow heard the clock strike six in the great room, she hurried to slice the apple pie and pour coffee. Thad would be there in another hour and she wanted the men out of the house. She was having second thoughts about having told Thad that he could return at seven o'clock. Jules might not get jealous at all. He was pretty arrogant in his knowledge of how she felt about him. He could very well just become angry and order the smitten farmer off the premises.

Willow began to wonder if Jules suspected that Thad was going to come calling tonight. He had just asked for a second serving of pie and to have his coffee cup refilled as he and Logan continued to talk horses. Jess had left the table half an hour before, and Ruth had excused herself and said good night shortly after. Rooster had left then too.

Hoping to hurry the men along, she began clearing the table. The men apparently took the hint and rose and walked outside. She breathed a sigh of relief when she heard their voices fading away on the evening air. They were going to the stables.

She flew around the kitchen, washing the dishes and putting them in the rack to dry. A quick swipe at the table and stove and she was hurrying to her room. Thad would arrive any minute and she wanted to at least comb her hair before he did.

The clock was striking seven when Willow stepped out onto the veranda and took a seat in the shadow of the hanging vines. When Thad showed up, she intended to explain to him that she was in love with Jules. That should be sufficient to make him forget about courting her.

The old hound sat at Willow's feet, sniffing at the evening breeze as the minutes ticked by. Willow heard the clock inside strike the half hour, and she wondered why Thad was late arriving. Fifteen minutes later, she decided that he wasn't coming. She was relieved. She wouldn't have the embarrassment of telling him that he would be wasting his time calling on her.

She was about to rise and go into the house when she heard Jules saying good night to Logan down at the stables. She sat quietly and he walked past the veranda without a glance in her direction. She saw him step into the small patio and disappear into the kitchen. Then she heard him speak to Jess in the family room.

"Where's Willow?" he asked.

"I guess she's gone to bed. Today was very upsetting to her." Jess knocked out her pipe and then said, "You're late coming in. What kept you? The wild ones?"

"Some of the time. The rest of the time I was setting that sodbuster straight about Willow. Can you imagine he had the nerve to get all spruced up and ride over here to court Willow?"

"Yes, I can imagine that. Willow is very beautiful, and how is anyone to know that you're interested in her? What exactly did you tell him?"

"I told him that Willow was my woman and that I'd kick his sorry ass if he ever came around here again other than to do business."

There was a short silence before Jess asked, "What are your real feelings about Willow?"

"Willow is the kind of woman I've looked for all my life. She's the sort a man would never tire of."

"I'm happy to hear that. Willow is a fine young woman. You couldn't pick a better wife."

"Wife?"

Willow heard the surprise in Jules's voice, and her heart felt as if it had dropped to her feet. She held her breath to hear what he might add to that single word.

"Aunt Jess, you know how I've always felt about marriage. It changes a man, ties him down, makes him old before his time. I haven't changed my mind about that."

"But you just said—"

"I said that I want Willow to be with me the rest of my life."

"You hair-brain, she is not the type of woman who would be satisfied with that kind of life. She will want marriage so that she can have children. She's too proud to be another Nina."

"Don't compare her to that one. Willow knows I don't think of her that way."

"How would she know that? Have you told her? After all, she cleans for you, cooks your meals and shares your bed for a few hours every night. In what way is she any different from Nina? Is it because she cooks better, keeps your house cleaner?"

"Of course not." There was a thread of anger in Jules's voice. "Nina was nothing to me. I care deeply for Willow."

"But not enough to give her your name?"

"I'll give her everything a wife could expect from a husband, but I will not give her my name."

"You're a damn fool, Jules Asher!" There was anger in Jess's voice. "I hope you lose her, and regret it the rest of your life."

Willow vaguely heard the tapping of Jess's cane on the tile floor as the old lady left the room. She had just received the worst shock of her life.

She sat on, her hands clenched in her lap, her eyes dark with the pain that gripped her like a vise. How could she not have realized, or at least suspected, that Jules had no intention of marrying her? She felt like a complete fool.

Had Nina felt that way when she was told to move on, that she was no longer wanted? And would that happen to her someday?

It would not, Willow determined. She wasn't going to wait around for it to happen. She would leave his house before he told her to.

But where would she go? Although she had saved all her wages, she hadn't been working long enough to set aside all that much.

When she heard Jules's bedroom door close, she stood up and slipped quietly into the house and on into the room she shared with her mother. When she closed the door, she drew the bolt that locked it. When she didn't join Jules, he might come looking for her, and she couldn't bear making love with him, knowing now that he didn't have any intention of ever marrying her. As it was, she felt cheap, and if she continued to share his bed, she would feel like a paid whore.

Mentally fatigued and exhausted in spirit, Willow couldn't relax in her narrow bed. Her mind kept pondering one question—where to go, where to go?

She discarded several ideas before deciding that she and her mother should go to El Paso. She would have a better chance of earning a living in a town than she would looking for employment at some ranch as a housekeeper. Most ranchers had wives to care for their homes.

That decision made, Willow finally began to relax and was about to fall asleep when she heard the door knob rattle. She became instantly alert. Would Jules leave when he found the door closed against him?

Her question was answered when she heard him ask softly, "Are you asleep, Willow?"

Willow lay quietly, barely breathing, afraid he would waken her mother. But Ruth had awakened and Willow held her breath when she heard Ruth get out of bed and walk to the door.

"She's asleep, Jules. Can I do anything for you?"

There was silence on the other side of the door for a moment, and then Jules answered, "It's not that important, Ruth. I just wanted to tell her that Logan and I are riding out in the morning to hunt mustangs up in the high country and that we may be gone for a couple days."

"I'll tell her, Jules. You be careful chasing those wild ones."

When Willow heard Jules's door close, tears slipped down her cheeks. A chapter in her life was closed.

Chapter Thirteen

The next morning at the first gray light of dawn, Willow awakened to the click of Jules closing his bedroom door. She tensed when she heard him stop at her door. Was he going to knock? She couldn't pretend to be sleeping again. He would know better.

She relaxed when he walked on down the hall, his footsteps fading as he entered the kitchen, then closed that door behind him. She rose and parted the drapes a crack so that she could see him walk past her window. It would be the last time she would ever see him.

Before he walked out of sight, Jules paused and looked back at the house. When he moved on after a moment, Willow crawled back into bed, her throat aching from the tears lodged there. She mustn't cry and wake her mother. Ruth would insist on knowing the cause of her tears, and Willow was too ashamed to tell her that the faith she had put in Jules had turned to bitter disillusionment.

As Willow lay staring at the ceiling, she heard the tapping of Jess's cane as she walked to the kitchen. Shortly after that, she heard Jules and Logan ride out. She rose, quietly got dressed and let herself out of the room, leaving Ruth to sleep on.

Jess had just finished building a fire in the range and was filling the coffee pot with water when Willow entered the kitchen. The old woman looked up. Seeing the desolation in the younger woman's eyes, she said, "Sit down, Willow. I think we need to talk."

"About what, Aunt Jess?" Willow tried to speak calmly as she sat down at the table.

"About whatever it is that is bothering you."

"What makes you think something is bothering me?"

"A couple of things," Jess answered as she spooned coffee into the pot. "There's the strained look on your face, and the fact that you didn't get up to see Jules off."

Willow made no answer as she avoided the old lady's eyes.

Jess waited a few moments and then asked bluntly, "You overheard me and Jules talking last night, didn't you?"

A sigh feathering through her lips, Willow looked at Jess and nodded.

"I'm sorry, girl. I'm ashamed of my nephew, and also surprised at his refusing to marry you. He cares deeply for you. Where he gets his crazy ideas about marriage, I have no idea. His mother and father had a good, loving relationship, as did his grandparents. It must come from that rowdy bunch he hangs around with in town. They'll never settle down either."

After a few minutes had passed, Willow said, "I'm going to have to leave here. You know that, Aunt Jess."

"I know, but where will you go? You can't go back to your father's ranch."

"No. That would be the last place I would go to. I thought maybe El Paso. I should be able to find some kind of work there."

"I don't know about that. According to what I've heard, it's a pretty rough place for a single woman to find work. Probably the only employment you could find would be serving drinks to drunks in some saloon."

"I was thinking of housekeeping work."

"I don't know about that either. Any husband who could afford that luxury for his wife would hire a young Mexican girl. They work dirt-cheap. Sometimes for only room and board. You've got to make enough to provide a home for your mother also."

Willow dropped her head in her hands and whispered despairingly, "I don't know what to do. I can't go home and I can't stay here."

The aroma of brewed coffee filled the room and Jess stood up and brought the pot to the table. As she filled the two cups sitting there, she said, "I have an idea that will be perfect for you and Ruth."

"You do?" Willow reached for the small pitcher of milk.

Jess returned the pot to the stove and sat back

down. "Remember me telling you about my small ranch?" Willow nodded. "Well, it's the perfect place for you and Ruth to live."

"But Aunt Jess, I couldn't afford to pay you rent. Besides, Jules would soon find out where I'd gone. I don't want him to know where I am. I'm afraid I'd let him talk me into returning home with him. I'd hate myself then."

"There's two ways of looking at it, Willow. First off, my place is ten miles on the other side of town and it would never enter his mind that you would be there. Second, his pride will be crushed when he learns you've left him. He may become angry and not care where you are."

"That last is what I hope happens. But, Aunt Jess, I can't sponge off you like that."

"You wouldn't be doing that. A few weeks back I received a letter from the Mexican couple who have been caring for the ranch the past ten years or so. They are getting up in years now and want to retire and return to Mexico. I've been racking my brain, trying to think who could replace them. You are the perfect one to do that. Ruth is daily becoming stronger and will be able to take care of the house and do the cooking, freeing you to run the ranch, which won't be difficult to do. I only run about three hundred head. A couple men have been tending to them, but I don't think they've been doing a good job of it lately. I lost twenty-five longhorns last winter. That wouldn't have happened if the men had got off their lazy rumps and driven the cattle in close to the ranch so that they could have been fed some hay. I'm thinkin' that they don't pay any attention to old José anymore.

"If you take me up on my offer and drive the herd to market this fall, I'll split the profit with you. How does that sound?"

"It sounds like I must be dreaming," Willow exclaimed, relief in her voice. "One thing I'm really versed in is running a ranch. I don't mean to brag, but I think I know every aspect of the business. My father had me running cattle when I was no more than ten years old."

"All right, that's settled then. I think you should start getting ready right now and leave within the hour. I'll have Rooster hitch up the wagon for Ruth to travel in. She's not quite strong enough yet to make the trip on horseback. Go wake her up and tell her whatever you want to about why you're moving. While you do that, I'll start breakfast," Jess said. Then she went outside and gave a shrill whistle. When Rooster came to the bunkhouse door, she motioned him to come to the house.

"Is something wrong with Ruth?" Rooster asked when he came hurrying into the kitchen.

"No, nothing is wrong with Ruth," Jess said impatiently. "She and Willow are moving."

"Moving?" Rooster asked, confusion on his face. "Moving where, and why?"

"Willow doesn't want this to get out, so keep your lip buttoned. They're going to my ranch. Willow is going to run it for me."

"But who's gonna look after Ruth while Willow is out chasin' cattle? In fact, who is gonna look after both of them? What if a bunch of outlaws come out of the badlands and catch them alone? They'd be helpless."

"Are you finished?" Jess threw down the knife she had been using to slice bacon. "I agree, you've given me some good arguments. I guess there's only one thing to do. You'll have to go with them."

The agitation on Rooster's face changed swiftly. His brow smoothed out and his lips spread in a wide, pleased smile. "I think that's a real good decision you've just made, Miss Jess."

"Hah!" Jess snorted. "As if you didn't have that in mind all along."

"No, I didn't. It was just—"

"Oh, shut your mouth and go hitch up the wagon. Come back to the house then and eat breakfast. Willow wants to get going right away."

Rooster had no sooner left than Willow came into the kitchen, ushering a bewildered Ruth in front of her. "Jess," Ruth said as she sat down at the table, "I don't understand why Willow wants to up and leave this lovely house—leave the good friends we've made here."

"Ma, I've explained to you why. We'll have our own home to live in, and I'll be making higher wages."

"But we'll be alone. Who is going to take care of us? What if Otto finds us?"

Jess slid Ruth a sly look. "Rooster will be with you. He'll take real good care of you and Willow."

When Ruth's face lit up and she exclaimed, "That's nice," Jess winked at Willow. Both were aware of the bond that was developing between the dainty little woman and the rough cowhand. Neither had any doubt that if necessary, Rooster would fight to the death, protecting Ruth.

Everything moved swiftly then. Willow packed her

and Ruth's belongings while Jess finished making breakfast. Rooster pulled up in the wagon when she was putting it on the table.

The early morning meal was eaten in short order with little being said by anyone. Each one was thinking of what lay ahead. It was plain to see by the soft looks exchanged between Ruth and Rooster that they were looking forward to the time they could spend together on the trail.

Jess's face was sad as she thought how she was going to miss this young woman, whom she would love to have as a daughter.

A mixture of thoughts was running through Willow's mind. There was excitement at the idea of running a ranch all on her own, making decisions, telling the men what to do. But there was also despair at leaving behind the man to whom she had given her whole being, the man who had only given her a fraction of himself. She couldn't believe that she had been such a fool. She had chosen to ignore the fact that Jules had never spoken of love although he had said many times that he would never tire of making love to her. And why hadn't she noticed that he never spoke of the children he hoped they would have?

Willow became aware that Rooster had scraped his chair away from the table and was helping Ruth to her feet. It was time to go. Time to start the journey to a new life.

Jess followed them outside, and after Ruth thanked her for her kindness, for helping to nurse her back to health, Rooster took her by the waist and lifted her onto the wagon seat.

It was time for Jess and Willow to say good-bye.

Words weren't necessary between the two women who had grown so close. Everything was said in eyes that glimmered with unshed tears.

"I'll send Logan to the ranch once a month to see how everything is going along for you," Jess said softly. "If you should need help of any kind, there's always a Mexican lad hanging around the stables. He can bring me a letter."

They gripped hands a moment, and then Rooster boosted Willow onto the wagon seat, next to her mother. He climbed up on the other side of Ruth, picked up the reins and released the brake. The horses moved out and Jess watched the wagon until it disappeared over the top of a knoll.

Willow dabbed at her wet eyes and straightened her back as she vowed never to look back again. Only heartache lay there, and she could never have a new beginning with that yoke on her shoulders.

When Ruth took her hand, squeezing it as she exclaimed softly, "Isn't it a glorious morning, Willow?" she agreed that it was and, relaxing her body, she sat back and looked over the prairie through her mother's eyes.

The sun was higher now and was beginning to burn off the mists that hovered in low spots between the knolls stretching ahead of them. The grass was green and shiny from being bathed in dew all night. Sparsely scattered across the range were clumps of ground cherry, the yellow bell-shaped flowers glistening under the early-morning sun.

Three hours later, as they skirted a small cow town that had no name, the whole land shimmered with heat as the wagon bounced along. Around noon

Rooster spotted a line of birch in the distance, and he turned the team in that direction. Before long, he had located a wide, shallow stream moving slowly over gravel and smooth stone. Jumping from the wagon, he lifted Ruth to the ground and led her to a smooth rock of chair height. "Sit here in the shade and cool off," he said, smiling down at her. "I'm gonna unhitch the horses now and let them have a drink of water."

While Rooster tended to the team, Willow spread a blanket on the ground a few feet from where Ruth perched on the rock. "Are you hungry, Ma?" she asked as she took from the wagon the basket Jess had put their lunch in.

"Yes, I am. It must be the fresh air that has whetted my appetite."

By the time Rooster led the horses back from the stream, Willow had laid out on the blanket four beef sandwiches and some apples.

With much talk and laughter the meal was eaten, and then Willow and Ruth excused themselves to walk farther into the birches. When they returned they found that Rooster had rehitched the team and was ready to head out again.

They had traveled another two or three miles when they began seeing groups of cattle grazing in the lush grass. "I wonder if they belong to Miss Jess," Rooster said. "I can't read the brand from here."

"I can't either," Willow said. Then a few minutes later, Willow said, pointing, "I think I see a bunch of buildings up past the foothills south of us. What do you think?"

Rooster squinted his eyes in the direction Willow

had indicated. "By golly, I think you're right," he exclaimed. "I can make out what looks like a barn." Turning the team's heads and slapping the reins on their rumps, he said, "Let's go take a look."

When the horses entered the shady foothills and began to climb, the air became blessedly cooler. "I pray this is Miss Jess's place," Ruth said, untying her bonnet strings and taking it off her head. "Don't the pines smell good, Willow?"

"They do indeed, Ma," Willow agreed, drawing long breaths of pine-laden air into her lungs. "I've got my fingers crossed that this will be our new home."

"We'll soon find out," Rooster said when the narrow road took them around a bend and several buildings lay before them.

A sturdy, rambling adobe house stood in the forefront of the outbuildings that stood higher up the mountain. The house was surrounded on three sides by pines that would cut off the cold wind in the winter. It was smaller than the Asher home, but was built in much the same manner, with a long veranda and a small patio to one side. Willow imagined that it led off the kitchen.

Bright flowers grew in profusion in the yard and in wooden boxes on the veranda, competing with hanging pots of vines and cascading petunias. A red flowering bougainvillea, with a trunk the size of a two-year-old sapling, had grown up the chimney at the side of the house and spread its color across the veranda roof, then spilled down the other side.

"Isn't it delightful?" Ruth clasped her hands in the folds of her dress. "I would be happy to live here the rest of my life."

"Let's find out first if this is Aunt Jess's place," Willow cautioned, as she climbed over the wagon wheel to the ground. She started walking along a gravel path and paused when the veranda door opened and an elderly Mexican woman stepped outside.

"Can I help you, *señorita*?" she asked with a smile.

"I hope so," Willow said, smiling back. "My companions and I are wondering if this place belongs to Miss Jess Miles."

"*Sí.*" The woman nodded, still smiling. "Are you friends of Miss Jess?"

"Yes, we are. She has sent you a letter." Willow took a folded piece of paper from her shirt pocket. "Can you read English?"

"A little, but not very fast." The woman took the letter from Willow.

Willow watched her slowly read the words on the paper. When she suddenly smiled, Willow suspected that she had come to the part that said Willow would be taking over the running of the ranch.

"This is good." Willow received another wide smile when the woman lifted her eyes from the letter. "I am Sofia Salazar. My husband and I are anxious to return to Mexico to live out our old age." She motioned to Ruth and Rooster. "All of you come inside and have a glass of cold buttermilk while I set out something for you to eat. You must be very tired and hungry, having traveled so far."

Sofia led them through the patio and into the kitchen Willow had suspected was there. The table, chairs and cupboards in the room were old, but still sturdy and kept in perfect condition. A bright red cloth covered the table, and a potted plant of small yellow peppers had been placed in its center.

There were pots of red geraniums on the wide window sill, which faced out onto the patio. The pots and pans hanging on the wall beside a black range were bright from being scoured after each use.

"I hope I can keep it looking like this," Ruth whispered when Sofia opened a narrow door to their left and stepped through it.

"You'll do just fine," Rooster was saying when the Mexican housekeeper returned, carrying an earthern pitcher.

"I keep all foods that spoil quickly in the larder. There is a small creek that runs through it all the year. It is always very cool in there. My vegetables stay nice and fresh in there for several days," she explained, putting the pitcher on the table, and then reaching down three glasses from one of the cupboards.

"Now"—Sofia smiled when she had poured the milk—"I will make you sandwiches."

"Don't go to that trouble, Sofia," Willow said, anxious to do a little exploring of the ranch, to meet the men who worked there. "It will be supper time soon." She glanced at Ruth, who looked a little drained. "I think Ma should lie down and take a nap while Rooster and I take a look around."

"I am a little tired," Ruth admitted as she sipped her milk.

"You can choose which bedroom you want," Sofia said, and then added, "There are three. When you are ready, I will show them to you."

Willow and Rooster finished their refreshment and left Ruth in Sofia's capable hands.

"The buildings are all in good shape, but everything

looks a little neglected," Rooster said when they had given the barn and other buildings a cursory look. "Some doors need to be tightened and a few tiles ought to be replaced on the roofs. I noticed there are some poles missing on the corral. Things that can easily be taken care of. I think it's a case of nobody caring. I'll get it fixed up in no time."

"Does that mean you are going to stay on with me and Ma?" Willow looked at the big man, hope in her eyes.

"Yes, I'd like to if it's all right with you. I don't like to think of you two women living here practically alone. And Ruth bein' fragile and all."

Willow knew that it was her mother and not herself that made Rooster want to remain at the ranch. She felt sorry for the big, gentle man, yearning for a woman he could never have. Even though her father didn't love his wife, he would never let her divorce him.

"You care for my mother, don't you, Rooster?" she asked softly. "More than just as a friend?"

Rooster's face reddened and he ducked his head. "I expect I do," he said in a low voice.

"You understand that she's still a married woman?" Willow asked gently.

"Oh, yes," Rooster said earnestly, bringing his gaze back to her. "I just want to look after her, no more. Even if she was a single woman, she wouldn't look on a rough character like me as a suitor."

Willow was about to say, "Don't be too sure of that," but she thought better of it. Why give this fine man false hope?

No more was said about Ruth when two men

stepped out of the bunkhouse and looked at them curiously. One was a tall, rangy fellow who seemed to be in his mid-thirties. The other one was older, pushing forty, also tall and lean.

"Can we help you folks?" the younger one asked as the pair walked toward them.

"I'm Willow Ames, and my friend here is Rooster Garr." Willow held out her hand to the man who had spoken.

"My handle is Denny Prater, and my pard is Hoot. Hoot Welby."

When everyone had shaken hands, Willow said, "I don't know how you men feel about taking orders from a woman, but if you stay on, that is what you will be doing. As of now, I'm taking over the running of Jess Miles's ranch. If that doesn't set well with you men, I suggest you gather up your gear and head on out tomorrow morning."

When both men had gotten over their shock, Denny Prater said with a pleased smile, "I don't see any problem with that. What about you, Hoot?"

With a wide smile on his thin face, Hoot declared, "I always wondered what it would be like, takin' orders from a pretty woman."

"You may not like it." Willow spoke coolly. "I'll expect more work out of you than you've been doing lately."

"I don't know what you mean, Miss Ames," Denny said, looking uncomfortable.

"When was the last time you checked the cattle?" Willow pinned him with stern eyes. "And speaking of them, how come you lost so many head this past winter?"

"It was a real cold winter," Hoot muttered.

"No worse than usual," Willow said firmly. "You could have driven them into the foothills and scattered hay for them."

Neither man made any more excuses and Willow asked, "Where can I find *Señor* Salazar?"

Denny nodded toward the barn. "He's probably still taking his *siesta* on a pile of hay. He'll get up when it's supper time."

That remark told Willow why everything had a run-down appearance. The old man had lost interest in the ranch, and consequently, the help did pretty much as they pleased. Which was only natural, with no one to tell them what to do.

"It's near that time now." Willow glanced up at the sky. "I'll wait until then to meet *Señor* Salazar."

Chapter Fourteen

Jules and Logan lounged around their campfire, the restlessness of stamping hooves the only sound in the darkness as they sipped strong coffee. Each man stared into the flames, thinking his own thoughts.

Jules was thinking of Willow, wondering why he hadn't been able to see her before he left the ranch three days before. Why hadn't she come to his room the night before he left? Ruth had whispered that she was asleep when he knocked on the door. There hadn't been much he could do about that. Her mother would have thought it strange if he had entered the room and shaken her daughter awake.

But why hadn't she met him for breakfast the next morning? Had she still been sleeping?

One thing he did know. He missed her. Missed her

company, missed the long hours of holding her in his arms, making love with her.

He thought of the conversation he'd had with his aunt the night before he went on the wild horse hunt. Had she been right, claiming that Willow expected marriage from him?

He shook his head. Willow was no more interested in marriage than he was. What she had seen of marriage hadn't been good, and she would be affected by that.

Besides, she was the type of woman who wasn't afraid to ask for what she wanted. If she wanted marriage, she would have said so a long time ago.

Would marriage to Willow be all that bad? Jules asked himself. His desire for other women had died after the first time he made love to her. One thing he knew for sure, he would never tire of her. Not only was she beautiful and desirable, he could talk to her as he had never been able to talk to another human being.

He glanced across the fire at his companion, who sat cross-legged, staring into the flames. "Logan," he asked, "have you ever been married?"

Logan looked up, blinked his eyes in surprise a couple of times, then after a rueful laugh asked, "Now what decent woman would marry a half-breed?"

"I think any number of women would jump at the chance to marry you."

"You're wrong, friend. Because of my mixed blood, no white father or Indian father would allow his daughter to marry me."

"If I had a daughter, I'd let her marry you."

"But you don't have a daughter." Logan reached

forward and stirred the fire. "You're not likely to have one, either, if you don't intend to get married."

"I guess not," Jules agreed and spoke no more on the subject.

But their conversation lingered with Jules. He found that it bothered him that he would never have a daughter or a son. A son who would carry on with the ranch when he was too old to do so. He wondered if Willow ever thought of that. Did she ever ask herself if she would miss having grandchildren around when she grew old? He thought of his Aunt Jess, a bitter, sharp-tongued woman with no husband or children, only a wild nephew to take care of her. Did she ever regret not marrying, having children?

His head began to ache. He had never before given serious thought to anything other than his cattle and the wild horses he chased.

"I'm going to turn in," he said, standing up and brushing off the seat of his trousers. "I'd like to get started by daylight."

Logan nodded and continued to gaze into the fire.

Jules held the lead rope that was tied to the tame horse dragging a thorny mesquite bush behind him. As the shrub bounced along, it kicked up high, rolling dust that the wild ones followed. To them, the dust was their leader and they would follow it wherever it led.

In this case, to the Asher ranch where a specially built corral awaited them.

Jules lifted the corner of the bandana tied loosely around his throat and wiped at his whisker-stubbled, sweating face. Another ten miles and they would be home. He glanced back at Logan, who was bringing up the rear of the herd. The heat never seemed to bother him. As for that, nothing ever seemed to bother the tall, stoic man. Jules often wondered what went on behind the dark eyes that gave nothing away.

He knew there was much bitterness in his new acquaintance, and he could understand that. Shunned by both races, not welcomed by either one, his life must be hard to bear. No wonder he was so good with horses. Those beautiful animals didn't care a whit about his blood lines. They only knew that he had a gentle touch and an understanding of their wild spirit.

Jules left off thinking about Logan and turned his thoughts to Willow. In another hour or so he would see her. He would grab her in his arms and hug her until she squealed for mercy. Then later, in the soft night, he would breathe and drink in the very essence of her. The night wouldn't be long enough to sate his desire for her.

A few hours of daylight were left when they topped a butte and looked down on the ranch buildings. Jules's keen eyes went to the high corral that was only used for the mustangs he captured. As he had directed before he left three days ago, the wide, sturdy gate stood open, waiting for the mustangs to be driven through it.

As the wild ones thundered toward it, no one came running to greet them. Every man on the ranch knew that to do that could frighten the horses, scatter them in all directions. Three days of hard work would have to be done all over again. And to catch them a second time would be hard, if not impossible. The lead stallion would be wiser, his trust of men gone.

When the last horse had gone through the gate and was milling around with the others, looking for an opening to escape through, Jules and Logan ran to drag the heavy gate closed.

Only then did several men come hurrying up. "Hey, boss," one man exclaimed, staring through the bars, "you sure have caught a bunch of beauties. You and Logan are gonna have your hands full, breakin' them. They act real spirited."

Jules kept looking past the cowboy, hoping to see Willow come running from the house to greet him. Hadn't she seen him ride up? he asked himself when no graceful feminine figure appeared.

She had to have heard their arrival, he thought, frowning. The hard pounding of fifteen horses' hooves could be heard a mile away. He was disappointed that Willow didn't seem as eager to see him as he was to see her.

"Fill the water trough and pitch the mustangs some hay," Jules ordered no one in particular, then strode off to the house.

Stepping into the kitchen, he called out, "Willow, Aunt Jess, I'm home." He waited for the sound of Willow's hurrying feet, but heard only the tapping of Jess's cane coming down the hall.

"Hello, nephew," Jess said as she made her slow way into the kitchen. "Did you have a successful hunt?"

"Yes, I did. Where's Willow?" he asked impatiently.

"Sit down, Jules, and I'll get you a glass of whiskey to cut the dust in your throat."

"What's going on, Aunt Jess?" Jules looked anxiously at his relative. "Did that father of hers show up again and force her to leave with him?"

When Jules didn't sit down, Jess did. She looked up at his suddenly strained face and said, "Her father hasn't been around, but Willow and her mother are gone."

"Gone? Gone where?" Jules sat down now. His aunt's words had weakened him so he was afraid his legs would buckle and he would fall to the floor.

Jess shrugged her narrow shoulders and carefully couched her answer. "I guess if she wanted you to know, she would have left us a note. I understand that she and Ruth took off shortly after you did . . . Rooster went with them."

"But you must have an idea why she went away. Did she seem upset or angry before I left?"

"Yes, to both your questions."

"Why should she feel that way?"

"She overheard our conversation about marriage the night before. I guess you were mistaken that she didn't expect marriage from you."

When Jules only stared at Jess, the old lady pointed out, "I told you that she did, but you were so sure you knew what you were talking about that I decided to let you find out the hard way that Willow was no Nina."

"She never said anything to me about marriage!" Anger began to grow inside Jules. Anger directed more at himself than at Willow. For the first time in his life, he had misjudged a woman.

He jerked to his feet and stamped out of the kitchen.

When he arrived at the corral, his face was as dark

as the clouds building in the west. "What's tied your tail in a knot?" Logan asked, grinning at him.

"Willow." Jules snapped the name. "Would you believe that she snuck away as soon as my back was turned? And that's not all—Rooster went with her and her mother. A man who has worked for me for over fifteen years."

"Rooster is pretty soft on Miss Ruth. He'd want to look after her." Logan studied Jules's tight face a moment and then asked, "Did she leave you a note, saying why she left, where she was going?"

Jules shook his head. "No note, no nothing. She just up and left."

"There's got to be some reason she'd leave without saying why. You haven't been beating her, have you?" Logan joked.

"I'd like to beat her now." Jules looked unseeing at the horses, which were slowly settling down. "According to Aunt Jess, Willow overheard her asking me if Willow and I were getting married. I said that I had no intention of ever getting married. I guess Willow had different ideas."

"You know, Jules, you're a real smart fellow when it comes to cattle and horses, but you don't know diddly about how a woman thinks. A decent one, that is. Any man with a speck of brains would know that Willow Ames is the type of woman men marry. No man should treat her like a whore."

"Hey, hold on there," Jules said, bristling. "I wouldn't treat Willow with anything but respect. I have the highest regard for her. It was my intention that she be here with me the rest of my life."

"I can't believe you are fool enough to think that

Willow would be satisfied with such an arrangement."

"That's the only kind she's ever going to get from me," Jules growled.

"It's just as well that she left then. It won't take her long to find another man who will jump at the chance to marry her."

A picture of the handsome young farmer swam before Jules. That one would marry her in the wink of an eye. A sudden thought narrowed his eyes. Had Willow gone to Thad Wilson?

"I don't give a damn where she went," he muttered to himself. Turning his back to the corral, he said with forced lightness, "I guess I'd better wash up and ride into town to find a new housekeeper."

Logan shook his head as he watched Jules walk away. "You poor devil," he said, "why don't you admit you're torn up inside?"

The sound of pounding hooves and creaking wagon wheels turned Logan's attention from Jules. He grinned when he saw two riders racing a chuck wagon. When the three pulled rein in front of him, his grin widened. All three riders were between boyhood and manhood, at the moment leaning more toward boyhood as they argued good-naturedly over who had won the race.

"You saw us, mister," a gangly blond said. "Who do you think got here first?"

"I'd say it was a dead tie," Logan answered, not about to get in the middle of a teenage squabble. "All three of you were doing some fine riding."

Logan had chosen his words wisely. The young men nodded, pleased with his decision.

The blond one spoke again as he climbed off the wagon. "We heard that Willow's mother was here and that she didn't feel very good. Do you know how she is now? Willow was awfully worried about her."

"She's coming along pretty good. I take it you fellows are just getting in from the cattle drive."

"Yeah," the blond answered; then he introduced himself and his friends. "I'm Jimmy, and that long drink of water is Sammy, and that ugly one is Brian."

When handshakes had been exchanged, Jimmy, the spokesman for the trio, said, "Let's go say hello to Willow first, and then we can take care of the horses."

"She's not there, fellows," Logan said.

"Where is she? Has she gone to town?"

"No, she hasn't gone to town. Nobody knows where she's gone. She just up and left three days ago. She and her Ma and Rooster." He wondered why the three looked so crestfallen at his news.

Jimmy stared down at the ground, a thoughtful look on his face. The other two waited for him to say something. Finally, he raised his head, the light in his eyes saying that he had arrived at a satisfactory conclusion.

"Miss Jess will know where Willow is. Tonight when she sits on the kitchen patio having a pipe before going to bed, we'll go talk to her. She'll let something slip."

Logan laughed to himself when the three rode off toward the barn. Only callow youths would think they could get something out of that old rawhide woman.

He was still sitting on top of the corral fence, studying the mustangs, deciding which of them would make good mounts, when Jules joined him. The rancher had bathed, shaved and donned clean clothes.

"You're looking pretty spiffy," he said with a grin, looking at Jules's snug-fitting black trousers and white shirt with the sleeves rolled up midway between his wrists and elbows.

"Why don't you come to town with me?" Jules asked as he led his saddled stallion out of the barn. "You need a few hours of relaxation too. You know—some drinks, a few dances with the saloon girls."

Logan studied the deeply tanned face a moment. It showed signs of recklessness and a readiness for violence of any kind. Jules would take his anger and hurt out on anyone who got in his way. A half-breed would be crazy to involve himself in a white man's brawl.

"Thanks, Jules, but all I want is a bath and a soft bed. I'm pretty beat."

"Suit yourself." Jules shrugged and climbed into the saddle. "You're going to miss a real good time."

"Maybe the next time."

Jules gathered up the reins, and with a lift of his hand he sent the stallion cantering toward town.

"I wonder what you'll look like when you get home, bucko." Logan grinned, and then, jumping to the ground, he walked toward the house to have a talk with Jess.

He found the old lady sitting in the kitchen, a bowl of potatoes in her lap, two of them peeled, a paring knife lying on top of them. "Hello, Logan." She looked up, giving him a weak smile, her tone gloomy. "Have a seat. I was going to make supper for myself and that idiot nephew of mine, but he has gone off to town to raise hell."

"Yes, I saw him. He thinks that drowning himself in whiskey will help him get over his hurt."

Jess nodded and muttered, "The damn fool," as she pulled her pipe and tobacco from her apron pocket. "I could have told him where Willow went, but he has to learn how important she is to him, how much he loves her and how badly he is going to miss her. When he gets rid of all his crazy notions, that arrogant pride of his, then I will tell him."

Logan waited until Jess had filled her pipe, struck a match to the tobacco and got it going. Then he asked softly, "Where did Willow go, Miss Jess?"

Jess took the pipe from her mouth, and without any hesitation answered, "I sent her to a small ranch of mine about fifteen miles from here." She sucked on the pipe stem a couple of times, then removed it from between her thin lips and said, "I want you to go look in on Willow in a couple days. See how she's getting along. Find out if she needs anything, if the Salazars have left, if the cowhands are doing as she tells them."

"I'll head out tomorrow." Logan stood up. He looked down at the basin of unpeeled potatoes. "Can I give you a hand making supper?"

"No." Jess placed the potatoes on the table. "I'll have a bite with our cook after the cowhands have eaten."

Logan paused at the door, a thoughtful look on his face. "Miss Jess," he began slowly, "three teenagers just rode in from the cattle drive. They're upset that Willow is gone."

"That would be those rascals, Jimmy, Sammy and Brian."

Logan nodded. "They would work their butts off for her. Don't you think it would be a good idea if I took them along with me when I ride out to your ranch?"

Jess puffed on her pipe a minute, the smoke curling up around her white head. Then, cupping the clay in her gnarled fingers, she said, "You may have something there, Logan. They have practically been raised on ranches and know every aspect of what it takes to run a spread. They can do a man's job, probably better than some older hands.

"When you go back to the bunkhouse, swear them to secrecy and then tell them where you're taking them." She gave a wry twist of her toothless mouth. "That will save me the aggravation of them coming up here later with the idea that they can trick me into telling them where Willow has gone." As Logan went through the door, she added, "And take that old hound with you. He goes around all the time looking for Willow."

The closer Jules came to town, the more he realized that getting drunk and brawling wasn't the answer to the emotions roiling inside him. He would only end up with a godawful headache tomorrow morning and maybe a battered face.

He turned the stallion around and headed home, a slight dejection in the droop of his shoulders. Women had come and gone in his life and he had never given any of them a thought later. Why couldn't it be that way with Willow?

Because he'd become besotted with her.

Jules's shoulders jerked erect. "Like hell I have," he grated. "There's not a woman on earth can do that to me." As he heeled the horse into a gallop, there grew inside him an anger and a determination to put Willow Ames with all the other women he had known.

By the time he reached the ranch, he had convinced himself that she was no better than the saloon women, that in fact she was worse. She had pretended affection for him when all along she had wanted to trick him into marriage.

Jess gave a startled jump when he stomped through the kitchen and on to his bedroom. When his bedroom door slammed, the old lady grinned. She was going to enjoy watching him try to get over Willow.

Chapter Fifteen

It was dark when Willow returned to the house, sweaty and dusty. She sighed with thanksgiving when she discovered that Rooster had made supper in the cookhouse where Sofia had cooked for the two cowhands.

During the last few days she had spent all her time acquainting herself with the surrounding land, locating Aunt Jess's cattle. Today, the Salazars had taken their leave of her. She was on her own now, running the ranch.

When Willow had cleaned up and joined everyone at the long table, she made a mental note that she had to hire a cook. She and Rooster wouldn't have time to make meals, and her mother wasn't up to it yet. She realized as she cut into a tender, juicy steak that she had to pay the cowhands' wages also. She sighed inwardly. She was going to have a number of unexpected expenses, no doubt. Things that she had little money for.

But looking across the table at the glowing face of her mother, the sparkle in the brown eyes, the smiling lips, she knew that somehow she would manage. To keep Ruth Ames happy would be her goal in life.

Maybe she could strike a deal with the men, and the cook she hired, she thought. She would ask them if they would be willing to wait for their pay until the fall roundup, when the cattle had been driven to market. They might do it if she offered them a bonus for waiting.

When the meal was eaten and the men were having a smoke, Willow discussed with them their duties for tomorrow.

"I want one of you to ride fence. You can decide between you which one will do it. The other one will help me and Rooster drive the cattle into one herd and bring them closer to the ranch. While I was riding around, I found the longhorns scattered all over the range. Many were alone, easy prey for a bear or coyote. It is too important that I don't lose a single head."

She smiled at Rooster and said, to his startled surprise, "Rooster will be my ramrod."

And while Rooster was gasping and liking the fact that he was going to be ramroding an outfit, Ruth asked, her expression eager, though a little worried, "Will I be the cook?"

"Not just now, Ma." Willow patted her hand. "Maybe when you're a little stronger. You have worked hard all your life."

"But I want to pull my weight too."

"Well, if you feel up to it, you can make up our beds and dust the furniture."

"Oh, I can do that." Ruth smiled at Rooster as though inviting his praise. He nodded at her and winked an eye as if to say, "Good girl."

When the two cowhands, Denny Prater and Hoot Welby, rose from the table and said good night, Willow followed them outside. "Men," she said, coming straight to the point, "do you think you could wait for your wages until after the roundup when I have sold some cattle?" She hurriedly added, "I'll pay you a bonus."

In the light shining from the cookhouse, she saw the two men look at each other a moment. Then Denny said, "I guess between us we've got enough pocket money to last until then." He didn't mention that he and Hoot would be unable to visit the bawdy house in town until they were paid.

"Thank you, men. That means a lot to me." She hesitated a second and then asked, "I don't suppose you know a cook I could hire under the same conditions?"

The men shook their heads, but then Hoot said, "Hold on a minute. I know someone you might be able to hire. It's a woman, but she's a good cook."

"You talkin' about good ole Corrie Mae?" Denny asked, wearing a wide grin.

"Yeah. Miz Jacobs fired her yesterday when she caught Corrie Mae and Mr. Jacobs in the barn foolin' round, if you get my meanin'."

"I think I do," Willow said dryly. "There's no husbands around here for her to fool around with, so everything should work out fine. Do you think she would wait for her wages?"

"Yeah, I think so. She's got a soft heart for anybody in trouble."

"Where can I find her?"

Denny's gaze lifted briefly to Willow, and then he said, "Me and Hoot are goin' into town tonight. We'll hunt her up and ask her to come out to the ranch and talk to you. If that's all right."

"That's fine with me." Willow smiled. Saying good night, she walked toward the house.

Hoot and Denny looked at each other, wide grins on their faces. "Can you believe our good luck?" Denny's eyes sparkled. "I can hardly believe that we may have Corrie Mae workin' here, takin' care of our needs every night."

"And it won't cost us," Hoot added to Denny's excitement. "I'm sure gonna make a hog of myself."

"Let's get goin'." Denny took off for the stables. "Maybe she'll come back with us tonight."

Ten minutes later they were galloping their horses toward town. Both men knew where they could find Corrie Mae. Between cooking jobs she worked at the bawdy house, satisfying two of her needs—money and a good supply of men to keep her content.

Willow was too tired and sleepy to drag in the wooden tub she had seen hanging on the patio wall outside, to fill it and take a bath. Instead, in her room she filled a washbasin with water from the pitcher sitting beside it and took a sponge bath. She slipped a gown over her head and crawled into bed. She fell asleep as she pulled the sheet up to her waist.

She smiled softly during the night, whispering love words to Jules, who entered her dreams and made love to her.

Fifteen miles away Jules was having the same kind of dream. Willow lay beneath him, her arms around his shoulders, her legs wrapped around his waist. Both grew angry at themselves when they awakened the next morning.

The first rays of the rising sun flashed across the prairie as Rooster shot his gun into the air and yelled, "Breakfast will be ready in ten minutes."

There came from inside the bunkhouse the noise of giggling and muted male laughter. Corrie Mae, naked, rested her back on the bed's headboard, watching Denny and Hoot scramble for their clothes, which lay in piles where they had hurriedly been discarded. She looked as fresh as the morning dew, while the men looked drained, with red-rimmed eyes from lack of sleep. They were a sorry-looking pair who gave the new cook a last, lingering look before leaving her.

"We'd better take a dip in the creek," Denny said. "Get the smell off us before we go into the cookhouse."

Willow was sitting at the table waiting for them when, with slicked-back hair, Denny and Hoot sat down at the table.

"Did you find the woman, Corrie Mae?" Willow asked after good mornings had been exchanged.

When Denny finished forking several flapjacks onto his plate, he answered, "Yes, we did. You'll be able to meet her when you ride in this afternoon. Most likely she'll have supper waiting for us."

"Did you explain how I'll have to pay her wages?"

"She's agreeable," Danny answered as he helped himself to the syrup.

"That's a relief," Willow said, and there was no more conversation as breakfast was eaten.

Fifteen minutes later, everyone was filing out of the cookhouse and walking toward the stables to saddle up. As Willow strode along, she was suddenly almost knocked over by a large dog throwing himself at her. As he danced around her, his whipping tail whacking her in the legs, she dropped to one knee. Putting her arms around the hound's thick neck, she exclaimed, "George, where did you come from?"

As she laughed and jerked her head away from the tongue that eagerly lapped at her face, a male voice spoke behind her. "He came with us."

Willow jumped to her feet and spun around. Had Jules found her already? Her face showed her relief when she saw Logan and the three teenagers smiling down at her.

When the three young men slid out of their saddles, she hugged each one of them and they all hung around her, talking at once.

"Miss Jess says we should work for you." Jimmy had a smile that threatened to split his mouth.

"We'll work real hard for you," Sammy was saying at the same time, and Brian was relating how upset they had been when they didn't find her at the Asher ranch on their return.

"I'll be real happy to have you fellows." Willow wiped at her wet eyes. "There's a lot of work to be done around here."

She looked at Logan and asked hopefully, "Are you going to stay, too?"

"I'm afraid not, Willow. Jules was cussing mad that Rooster left him. When he finds out he's lost these three yahoos, too, all hell is going to break loose." He grinned. "Not to mention his old hound deserting him."

Willow wanted to ask how Jules felt about her leaving, but was afraid what the answer might be. Jules would miss Rooster and the boys, and even his dog, but she could be replaced all too easily.

"Come to the cookhouse," she said instead, "and I'll make you some breakfast. After that, Rooster will set you fellows to some job. And Logan, Ma will want to visit with you."

Willow had forgotten how much teenagers could eat as she flipped flapjacks one after the other. At least it kept them from talking for a while, she thought wryly. They had been firing so many questions at her, she felt dizzy.

When finally their stomachs were full, she told them to go find Rooster.

"Why will Rooster tell us what to do?" Jimmy asked grumpily. "Miss Jess said that you're the boss here."

"I am, but Rooster is my foreman. I tell him what needs to be done and he decides who's to do it."

"That ole Rooster is tough," Sammy complained. "He won't let us work together like we're used to doin'."

"I imagine he won't." Willow grinned. "He probably knows that he'll get more work out of the three of you if you're not together horsing around. You can get together at the end of the day."

"I reckon," Jimmy grunted, and led the way outside to look for their new boss.

Ruth entered the cookhouse shortly after the boys had left, and as she and Logan greeted each other, Willow walked outside also.

An unbroken blue sky stretched overhead, and meadowlarks flitted about, their song an uplifting sound as Willow, Rooster and Jimmy rode along. The sun felt hot against their backs as they hunted cattle that had escaped from roundups and were now as wild as deer.

Two hours later, squinting against the sun, they spotted a small herd of longhorns. Willow counted fourteen. As soon as the cattle saw them, they were off running. The three touched spurs to their horses and took off after them.

"Chase them into the ground!" Rooster yelled. "They'll be easier to handle after that."

They chased the wild ones until the animals slowed to a walk. Then they had no trouble driving them the ten miles to the ranch, where a holding pen awaited them. Tomorrow morning they would be branded.

Denny and Sammy and Brian had arrived half an hour earlier, driving before them nineteen head.

When the three teenagers had gone off, arguing over who had ridden harder that day, and Denny disappeared into the bunkhouse, Willow and Rooster climbed to the top of the corral and viewed the bawling cattle.

Most were yearlings, Willow was pleased to see, weighing between six and seven hundred pounds, slick and vigorous. Buyers would pay good money for them in Wichita.

"I think we'll have a good-sized herd to drive to Kansas this fall if we continue to have the same good luck we had today," Willow said.

"Yeah. If we and the horses don't wear out from chasing the devils." Rooster laughed. "I don't know if I can sit down to eat my supper tonight."

Willow laughed too. "I think we all may eat standing up."

"You understand, don't you, Willow, that you must keep back your best cattle for breeding," Rooster said, turning serious.

Willow nodded. "I know that's very important. My father never thought that far ahead. He always sold our best animals and kept the scrubs for breeding. We had the worst-looking cattle in all of New Mexico."

Willow gave a sigh of weariness and climbed down from her perch. "I'm going to take a long bath and visit with Ma until it's time to eat supper. I'm going to ask the boys to put some kind of meal together for us. Jimmy learned a little about cooking from helping me on the cattle drive.

"I can eat anything put before me tonight, as long as it's hot and there's plenty of it," Rooster said. "I'm just not up to cooking it myself. I'm dead beat."

As Willow neared the cookhouse, a delicious aroma wafted through its door, accompanied by a rollicking, bawdy tune sung by a female voice. She turned toward the open door and got a face full of dirt and grit.

When she choked and coughed, the singing stopped and the dust settled down. "I'm sorry, miss," a husky voice exclaimed. "I've got supper all ready. The last thing I had to do was sweep the floor."

Willow gazed at the big woman. She wasn't fat, just big-boned. She stood at least five-feet-nine and had a mop of red hair she had tied back with the help of a neckerchief. She was barefooted.

"Come in." The woman's teeth shone white against her deep tan as she smiled, pushing aside the pile of dirt. "I take it you're Willow Ames."

"That's right, and you must be Corrie Mae." Willow returned the smile and offered her hand. "Something smells awfully good in here," Willow said when they had shaken hands.

"It's a beef roast. I just now added some potatoes and carrots to it. I figured everybody would be hungry after chasing wild cattle all day."

"You thought right, and I can't tell you how thankful I am that you're here making us supper."

"It's my policy to start a new job off right. That means make a hearty supper for the cowhands." Corrie Mae pulled a chair away from the table. "Sit down. I bet a cup of coffee would hit the spot right about now."

"It certainly would. I've been thinking about it all day."

While Corrie Mae filled two mugs with coffee, Willow looked around the kitchen. It had been clean enough before, but now it looked homey, too. The long table had been scoured until the grain of the pine wood showed through, and she imagined the black range hadn't looked so shiny in a long time.

But where had the woman found the bright, flowered curtains that hung at the two clean windows? When Corrie Mae brought the coffee to the table and sat down, Willow said, "You've certainly been busy, Corrie Mae. Where did you unearth those pretty curtains?"

"They belong to me. I bring them with me everytime I move to a new job. They, and rugs and bedcovers and pictures and other geegaws, make me feel at home right off."

Willow thought it was hard to believe that this big, rough-appearing woman would have such a sensitivity to what she had around her. Her gaze went to a basin of potato peelings sitting on a work bench. "Where did you get the vegetables for your roast? I didn't see a garden patch when I took a look around the house area."

"I bought them from a young man who sells vegetables and dairy products from his farm."

Could it possibly be? Willow wondered as she asked, "Is his name Thad?"

"Yes. Thad," Corrie Mae answered. She looked as though she was remembering something very pleasant. "Do you know him?"

"Yes. I used to buy his produce, too. Also his eggs and once a frying hen," Willow answered. She ignored the fact that Corrie Mae waited for her to go into more detail about her dealings with the handsome Thad. But this big woman could very well know Jules and might run into him some day. It was best if she knew of no connection between the rancher and her new boss.

Not that it would make all that much difference to him where she was. By now Jules had probably moved a new woman into his home. "I'll see you at supper time, Corrie Mae." She finished her coffee and left the cookhouse.

Chapter Sixteen

The sun had gone down, and the shadows were growing long. As Jules left the bunkhouse, a quail called plaintively off in the distance and he felt akin to it. He was tired, all the way to the bottom of his feet, and the horseplay of his men had aggravated the hell out of him.

It didn't occur to the whip-lean man as he strode toward the house that only a short while ago he would have enjoyed the cowhands' antics. Nor did he realize that he went around looking dark and brooding. He didn't even notice that his men stayed away from him whenever they could, that his presence in the bunkhouse made them uneasy. If anyone had dared ask him why he had a perpetual dark frown on his face, he would have answered that he was as mad as hell that four of his help had deserted him. He would not say one word about the cancer that was eating at his heart. He had convinced himself that he was a lucky man, discovering in time that Willow Ames had been out to trap him in marriage.

Jules was walking past the darkened veranda when his aunt called from the shadows. Taking a seat beside her, he asked, "Why are you having your pipe out here instead of in your usual place on the patio?"

"It's cooler out here." Jess knocked the remains of the tobacco out of her pipe. "I hope it rains soon to cool things off for a while."

"We need a real good gully-washer," Jules agreed, kicking off his scuffed boots and wiggling his toes. "The grass is beginning to dry up."

There was a companionable silence until Jules asked, "Have you seen Logan today? He didn't show up for supper, and I missed seeing him at breakfast."

"He's gone on a vision quest." Jess told her lie smoothly. "He said he'd be back sometime tonight."

A wry grin twisted Jules's lips. "Logan never struck me as the sort who would do those Indian things."

"You can never tell by appearance what lies in another man's heart."

"Nor a woman's," Jules said sourly.

"I expect by that remark you're referring to Willow." Jess peered at her nephew in the gathering darkness.

"Willow and her ilk. I've learned one thing—steer clear of the so-called decent woman. She's dangerous. She'll lead you to a preacher before you know what's hit you."

"Sometimes that's the best thing that can happen to a man."

"Bah! Putting a ring in his nose doesn't help him. It only takes away his independence, his freedom."

"That didn't happen to your pa when he married my sister. He remained the same strong-minded man he always was. As for his freedom, your mother allowed him to do anything he wanted to . . . except fraternize with loose women and whores. Of course he had no desire to do that. If he still wanted to whore around, he never would have asked your mother to marry him."

Silence settled between nephew and aunt as Jules thought back to when his parents were alive, remembering how much in love they had been.

He gave a start when Jess asked, "Do you still want to whore around, Jules? Is that why you're so dead set against marriage? Are you afraid you wouldn't be able to be true to your vows?"

"Aunt Jess, you can ask the damnedest questions," Jules snorted. Picking up his boots, he said a gruff good night and strode toward the door. As he was about to step through it, Jess called to him, "When you find time, will you ride over to my ranch and see how everything is coming along?"

"Logan and I are going up to the high country tomorrow to look for more wild ones. I'll check on your place after that."

The very tip of the sun was emerging in the east when Jules and Logan left the hacienda behind and rode toward the open range. They had a seven- or eight-mile trip ahead before they came to the area where they had found the last herd of wild ones. They had seen others that day, but had had their hands full with the ones they were chasing toward the ranch.

The air was close and humid, promising an uncomfortable day ahead. "Well, Logan, was your vision thing successful?" Jules asked, half joking.

"I think so."

"Well?" Jules waited for him to expound.

"In my dream I learned the foolishness of some men. Their fears that keep them from fulfilling the lives they were meant for. I saw them in their old age, alone and bitter with no one to care whether they lived or died."

"So you had a good look at your future, did you?" Amusement was in Jules's tone.

"Yes. And that of a friend of mine."

Jules's eyes narrowed suspiciously. "You mean me?"

"I did see a man who looked surprisingly like you."

"It couldn't have been me." Jules's amusement turned to irritation. "I won't be alone and bitter in my old age. I'll have some young thing to keep me company, and I sure won't be bitter about that."

"That young thing you speak of won't love you. She'll tolerate your old stove-up body for monetary gain. When you grow ill and are dying, she will leave you without a backward look. A loving wife wouldn't do that. She would hold your hand and help you to step over the Great Divide."

"Won't the same hold true for you? You don't yearn for hearth and home."

"After what my vision revealed, I may rethink my plans for the future."

"It was your vision, not mine. Do as you please," Jules grunted and kicked his horse into a brisk canter.

Logan grinned after him. "My friend," he said, "you don't like what I gave you to think about."

As Willow bridled the little mustang and cinched the belly strap, Rooster walked into the barn. "I think this close, humid air is gonna bring us the rain we've been wishing for," he said.

"I was thinking the same thing," Willow agreed. "I'm afraid an electrical storm will accompany it though, the air is so still. I hope we can find the cattle and drive them onto our range before it breaks."

"I think it will hold off until this afternoon," Rooster said, leading his horse out of its stall.

"Where's Jimmy?" Willow asked as she and Rooster mounted and rode off.

"He'll be along. He's horsin' around with them other two hellions."

"What do you think of our new cook?" Willow asked, switching to another subject.

"Well . . ." Rooster grinned. "She's a good cook, and she feels right at home with Denny and Hoot."

"I noticed that." Willow's eyes crinkled at the corners. "I got the impression this morning that she probably knows them in the biblical sense."

"I'm sure you're right. I could have got to know her that way last night had I a mind to. I had the invite."

"No fooling?" Willow laughed. She frowned then and chewed at her lower lip. "I don't want the boys hanging around her."

"I understand how you feel, them bein' almost like your own, but they couldn't find a better female to break them in."

"For heaven's sake, Rooster," Willow said, bristling. "They're only sixteen years old."

Rooster didn't comment on her outburst, but he was remembering that he'd been fifteen when he had had his first woman. But if the teenagers wanted to lose their virginity to big Corrie Mae, they'd better not let Willow learn about it. Brian was a couple of years older than Jimmy and Sammy, and he'd bet his spurs that the teenager was no virgin. If the boys ended up in Corrie Mae's living quarters, it would be Brian who would lead them there.

Willow and Rooster looked over their shoulders at the sound of a whooping yell. "That damn kid oughtn't to be racing his horse already," Rooster grumbled. "It's gonna get enough runnin' in this heat when we spot some cattle."

"You're right. I'll speak to him about that."

But when a grinning Jimmy rode up alongside them, and Willow began to gently point out that he shouldn't race his mount unnecessarily, Rooster glared at the teenager and had his say.

"If I ever catch you runnin' your horse in heat like this just for your own pleasure, I'll jerk you out of the saddle and knock you down. Is that clear, young man?"

With a sheepish look and a muted, "Yes, sir," Jimmy dropped behind them.

It was around noon and the three were scouting the edge of the foothills when a herd of ten head was spotted in a large thicket.

"Watch out for them devils," Rooster cautioned as they rode toward the longhorns. "They look red-eyed mean. Jimmy, you ride around behind them. Willow, ride upwind of them, and I'll stay here alongside them. When we're all in place, start yelling and popping your ropes. Spook them out of there."

Sweat rolled off Willow's brow, down across her eyelids, trickled between her breasts and soaked the back of her shirt as she and Jimmy and Rooster tried to chase the cattle from the thicket. Everytime it looked as if they would succeed, the longhorns would spin around and go back into the thorny brush.

One bull, big and mean-looking, insisted on following Willow's horse, blustering and bullying and pretending that he was going to charge it. She dropped her hand to the gun belt strapped around her waist, thankful that she wasn't afoot. Longhorn steers were very dangerous. They even challenged each other, making rumbling and moaning noises as they swung their horns about.

When finally the wild ones were driven out of their cover and onto the open range, Willow and the men were surprised at the overcast sky. They had been so busy with the cattle, they hadn't noticed the black clouds that had moved in.

"Damnit, Willow," Rooster yelled. "We're in for a storm that's gonna make all our hard work for nothin'. The first crack of thunder is gonna spook them ornery varmints and they're gonna make a beeline for them thickets again."

It was around two in the afternoon, the air hot and close, before Logan sighted a small herd of mustangs. He signaled to Jules to ride to the left of the stallion and mares while he drifted slowly to the right of them. When both men were in position, they drew their guns and began shooting into the air. With a plunging rush, the horses tore off across the range. With wild yells, Jules and Logan raced after them.

During the head-long dash, the air fanning across their faces grew hotter, and dark storm clouds gathered in the north. Neither man had time to notice the impending storm. Both were startled when suddenly the humid stickiness of the air was broken by a zigzag streak of lightning, then the loud crack of thunder.

"Damn!" Jules exploded as he was hit broadside by a blinding sheet of rain. "Forget about the horses," he shouted to Logan. "My Aunt Jess's ranch is in the area, if we can see how to find it."

"Give your mount his head," Logan shouted back. "If there's cover nearby, he will find it."

With the reins loose on their necks, the two quarter horses turned in unison. It wasn't long before they topped a butte and directly ahead, the riders could make out a group of buildings through the slashing rain. When Jules spotted three riders pounding toward them, he grinned. Someone else had been caught in the sudden downpour.

Willow and Jimmy had gladly left off chasing the longhorns and raced after Rooster as he led the way homeward.

Now, as they neared the barnyard, Willow saw through the rain the dim shapes of other riders racing toward the dry haven of the barn. The rest of the fellows were coming in, too, she thought, bringing her little quarter horse to a skidding halt only feet from the wide double door that someone had swung open.

She slid to the muddy ground and tugged the horse inside.

Willow heard footsteps pounding behind her and gave a grunt when she was hit by a heavy shoulder. She lost her balance and stumbled back against her mount.

"Watch where you're going, Jimmy," she said sharply, dashing the rain out of her eyes.

She heard a surprised grunt, then heard Jimmy, several stalls down, call out, "I'm all right, Willow." She looked over her shoulder to see who had bumped into her and stared right into Jules's hard, cold eyes.

"What are you doing here?" she gasped.

"I was about to ask you that." Water dripped off Jules's hat while his soaking wet clothes made pools around his feet.

"I'm running the ranch for Aunt Jess," Willow answered, her voice a little shaky.

"Hah! What happened to José Salazar?"

"He and his wife wanted to retire. They've gone back to Mexico."

Jules's eyes narrowed. It was all suddenly clear to him. Aunt Jess, the matchmaker, was trying her hand at playing cupid. Well, her plans weren't going to work the way she wanted them to, he thought angrily, even as he wanted to snatch the rain-soaked Willow into his arms and ravish her lips.

He ran his gaze over her slender body and sneered, "You'll never make a rancher even if you did steal four men from me to help you."

"Hardly four men," Willow snapped. "One man and three striplings. They all came because they wanted to."

"Yeah, because they knew they could get away without giving you a full day's work."

"You're wrong. The boys have been working very hard for me."

"And you had the nerve to take my hound."

"I didn't take him. He came with the boys."

Willow noticed Logan standing to one side and opened her mouth to say, "Ask Logan." But when the tall man gave a small shake of his head, she knew he was silently asking her not to let on that he had been here before. She looked back at Jules and said, "I'm not going to stand around here in these wet clothes and bandy insults with you."

She left her horse for Jimmy to unsaddle and wipe down, and without further words sprinted through the rain to the ranch house.

Ruth, who had seen them ride up, had dry clothes laid out for Willow, along with some towels. When Willow rushed in, dripping wet, she exclaimed, "Hurry up and change your clothes, child. Then come back in here and get some hot coffee inside you."

"Ma, Jules is here. He'll probably come to the house later."

"Oh dear. Is he angry with us?"

"He's not angry with you, but he's not very happy with me."

"Should I make extra for supper?"

Willow thought a moment about Ruth's question. It would be very uncomfortable, just her and her mother sharing a meal with the stony-faced Jules—feeling the cut of his frosty eyes on her, listening to his snide remarks. Shaking her head, she answered,

"I think we'll eat with the men at the cookhouse to-night."

Willow had pulled off her boots and was on her way to her room when the door was pushed open and Jules walked into the kitchen, a mist of rain blowing in behind him. He quickly closed the door and stood for a second, water dripping off his clothes. He took off his soaked hat and hung it on the wall, then smiled at wide-eyed Ruth.

"You're looking chipper, Ruth," he said in warm tones. "How are you feeling?"

"I'm ever so much better, Jules. How are you?"

Jules cut a look at Willow and drawled, "I couldn't be better."

As Willow, with chin in the air, disappeared down the hall, Ruth asked, "Do you have some dry clothes here that you can change into? You're soaked clear through."

Jules nodded as he sat down and pulled off his boots. "I've had a room here as long as I can remember. I'm sure I'll be able to find something to change into."

"Jules," Ruth said when he had placed his boots on the stone hearth to dry out, "I hope you're not angry with Willow for taking this job that Jess offered her."

Jules was somewhat surprised that Ruth didn't know the real reason her daughter had left him. What had Willow told the gentle woman? he wondered.

He decided that it would be too embarrassing to tell her the truth.

He smiled at Ruth and said, "I can't fault Willow for taking a better job." He couldn't resist adding, "It's only natural for a person to grab an opportunity that might better her future. Willow is the type of young woman who would take advantage of every opportunity."

Ruth smiled uncertainly. She was trying to decide if there had been a sour note to Jules's words, a hint of contempt.

She was still trying to decide when Jules stood up and said, "I'm going to get out of these wet clothes now. I'll see you at supper."

There was a strained silence in the cookhouse as everyone ate the evening meal. It was broken occasionally by Corrie Mae making some kind of jovial remark. The jolly woman wanted laughter and easy conversation in her kitchen.

She looked at Jules, who sat across from Willow, and took the coffee pot off the stove.

"Cat got your tongue, handsome?" She grinned down at Jules as she refilled his cup. "I can't remember ever seeing you so quiet. Don't you like your supper?" She gave him a flirtatious look. "Just tell me what you want and I'll take care of it right away."

Jules saw through his lowered lashes that Willow wasn't missing anything Corrie Mae had said.

He gave Corrie Mae a wicked look and, running his hand up her skirt, asked, "Right here and now? Shouldn't we wait until after everybody has gone?"

Corrie Mae gave a playful slap at his hand and retorted, "If you can wait, so can I."

The tension in the room eased as everyone laughed at the repartee between Jules and Corrie Mae. Everyone except for Willow and Ruth. Ruth looked bewildered, trying to figure it out, and Willow sat stony-faced, sure that every word out of Jules's and the cook's mouth was serious.

There was no doubt in her mind that after everyone had left, Jules would remain.

The ice broken, everyone started talking, Jules included. He let the resentment he felt toward Rooster and the teenagers go. Rooster was head-over-heels in love with Ruth, and it was only natural that he would go where she went. As for the boys, Willow was a mother figure for them, and as such, they would want to be around her. And his old hound—well, he, too, liked Willow's tender touch. He couldn't fault him for that. He had liked her tender touch too. Much to his displeasure, he had dreams of her hands on his body, soft and loving.

So, Jules laughed and joked with everyone except Willow. She didn't let on that she noticed this as she engaged her two cowboys in conversation. They responded to her attention by trying to out-talk each other and tell her tales of derring-do.

As she laughed and joked with them, seemingly enjoying herself tremendously, Jules gradually became quieter and quieter. Willow had received many hard looks from him by the time she and Ruth said good night and went home.

Once she left the cookhouse, however, her pretended joviality was wiped from her face. When they entered the ranch house, she sat in the dark kitchen waiting to see when Jules would leave the cookhouse. When the others all left without him, she went to her room, undressed in the dark and crawled into bed. She tried not to think of Jules and her cook in bed together, but she could think of nothing else. Her heart wouldn't have thundered so had she been able to hear the conversation going on in the cookhouse.

"What was that performance of yours all about, Jules?" Corrie Mae asked as she poured herself a cup of coffee and joined Jules. "Am I right in thinking it was for the benefit of my beautiful boss?"

"What makes you think that?" Jules raised an eyebrow at her.

"I'm not blind. While everyone else was eating, not paying any attention to the pair of you, I amused myself by watching you and Willow. The tension between you was so thick, I could have cut it with my butcher knife."

Jules's only response was, "You were imagining things."

"I don't think so. Someone mentioned that Willow used to keep house for you. I bet you coaxed her into your bed. Did you have a lover's spat?"

Jules narrowed his eyes at Corrie Mae. He must put that idea out of her head. He didn't want it rumored that he and Willow had been more than boss and housekeeper. He would not have Willow's reputation besmirched. "You only have it half right. I tried my damnedest to get her in bed, but she kept turning me down. I got mad and said some harsh words to her, so she left my employment."

"First time a woman ever turned you down, huh, big rooster?"

"Probably won't be the last either." Jules laughed and finished his coffee. "I'll see you in the morning," he said and left the cookhouse.

Chapter Seventeen

The rain had stopped during the night and there was a crisp coolness in the air as Jules and Logan rode away from his aunt's home.

Fifteen minutes before Jules's departure from the ranch house, Willow, Rooster and Jimmy had left for the day. Jules had purposely stayed in his room, waiting for Willow to leave first. He didn't trust himself to be around her. Last night, knowing that only a wall separated him from her silky, smooth body curled up in sleep, he had needed all his will power to keep from going to her room and begging her to marry him. If he stayed around her any longer, watching her laugh and joke with those two cowhands of hers, he would go crazy.

But would he be able to stay away from her, now that he knew where she was? He wished that he and

Logan could take off on another long hunt for wild horses, so he could occupy himself with something other than thoughts of Willow. But he had already neglected things around the ranch too long. He had to spend some time there. There was also the last herd of wild ones to be tamed. Before long they would be driving them to Wichita.

Willow and Rooster rode side by side in the early morning light with Jimmy, still half asleep, trailing behind them. Willow's thoughts were running in the same vein that Jules's were.

Jules had looked so good to her last night, even half drowned. When later he and Corrie Mae flirted with each other, she had wanted to attack her cook, fire her on the spot. This morning at breakfast she could hardly look at the woman, sure in her mind that she and Jules had made love in the cookhouse.

And last night, hearing him enter the room next to hers, she had been in danger of going to him, telling him that they would do it his way. That she would take the chance of him always wanting her. She had even told herself that she loved enough for both of them.

Luckily, reason had taken over and she had made herself stay in bed. She had told herself what a hellish life she would be letting herself in for if she did such a foolish thing. She would never feel there was any permanence in such a relationship. She would always have to worry that some day Jules would grow tired of her. And she would never be a mother.

She had given her pillow an impatient whack and had turned over and gone to sleep. Jules had invaded her dreams so often, she had made sure she left the house before he arose.

Weary of thinking about the man who had the power to hurt her so, Willow gave her attention to Rooster.

"Rooster," she began, "I've been thinking a lot about an idea that came to me. I want to tell you about it, see what you think."

"Fire away. I'm listenin'."

"The last time we hunted cattle, I saw herds of burros grazing. The first time I saw them, I remembered Jules saying how in Colorado, burros were much in demand to work in the silver mines. He said that their small size and surprising strength enabled them to work in the mines, whereas horses and mules were too large. He also said that the mine owners were paying ten dollars a head for them.

"Although Aunt Jess and I are sharing expenses and whatever monies we make on selling the cattle this fall, it isn't going to go far. I have to get the ranch built back up again. I suspect Mr. Salazar sold off most of the breeding stock. Consequently, as you have seen, we'll not be driving the best of cattle to Wichita. We certainly won't get top price for them."

Admiration for Willow shone in Rooster's eyes as he said, "You've got a good business head, young woman. You're gonna do just fine. When do you want to start hunting the little devils?"

"While we're driving the last of the cattle out of their hiding places, we'll watch for where the burros are grazing so that we'll know where to hunt them when we're ready."

* * *

It was near ten o'clock when Thad Wilson drove his produce wagon up alongside the cookhouse. Corrie Mae had seen him coming, and she wore a wide smile when she opened the side door to the kitchen and stepped outside. She and the farmer would spend some time together in her living quarters before they got down to the business of filling her list of vegetables.

Of all the men she had ever lain with, Thad was the best. He was a virile young man who never seemed to tire in seeking his gratification in lovemaking. They were a good pair in that respect. She was slow in tiring also. They would spend a good hour in her big, comfortable bed before she bought Thad's vegetables.

As Thad jumped down from the wagon, he said with a grin, "I hope you haven't made up your bed yet. I'm in a mood to tear it up if you have."

"I can see that you are." Corrie Mae smiled back at him, looking significantly at the bulge in his trousers. "It's ready and waiting. Come on, we'll tear it up together."

The bedsprings in the back room squeaked, and the headboard thumped against the wall for over an hour before Corrie Mae and Thad got back into their clothes and went outside to the wagon. It took Thad several trips to the kitchen to carry in all that Corrie Mae had bought.

When the last of her purchases had been set on the table and Thad handed her the bill, she said, "Wow, Willow is gonna have a heart attack when she sees this."

Thad's body went still. Corrie Mae must be speaking of Willow Ames. It was unlikely that there would be two women in the area with the same unusual name.

"Who is this Willow person?" he asked guardedly.

"Willow Ames. She's running the ranch for old Jess Miles now. The man that was here before retired to Mexico."

When Thad left Corrie Mae shortly after that, his mind was racing. He couldn't believe that he was lucky enough to be able to see Willow again. Also, he realized that if he was to court her again, he'd have to be very careful in dallying with her cook. He would have to learn when Willow would most likely be gone from the house and make his deliveries then. He didn't want to stop his liaisons with Corrie Mae, not even if he was lucky enough to marry Willow someday. For the past six years he and Corrie Mae had gotten together every week, no matter where she was working. He was afraid that the delicate-looking Willow could never handle his needs in bed.

Thad whipped up the team, planning when he could drop in for a visit with Willow.

Chapter Eighteen

Lines of worry creased Willow's forehead as she watched her bawling cattle being herded in among Jules's wild horses. Fall had arrived and it was time for the drive to Wichita. Would they all arrive safely at the stockyards there? It was so important that she not lose even one head.

Would Jules keep the drive at an easy pace? she wondered. His horses could travel longer and faster than her cattle could. If they were pushed too hard, they would lose a lot of the weight she had worked so hard at putting on them.

"Your cattle don't look half bad, considering the short time you had to fatten them up," Jules said suddenly beside her.

Startled, Willow twisted around and lost her seat on the narrow rail of the corral. As she started to fall,

Jules caught her arm and steadied her. Irritated at herself for responding to his touch, she answered sharply, "See that you don't run any of that fat off them on the drive."

Jules's eyes, narrowed in anger, watched Willow go into the cookhouse. He waited a minute, then followed her. Willow and Corrie Mae sat at the table, a cup of coffee in front of them. Corrie Mae gave him a wide smile of welcome, while Willow shot him a dark look.

"Are you going to miss me while I'm gone, Corrie Mae?" Jules asked, his eyes shining wickedly as he poured himself a cup of coffee.

A knowing smile, which Willow missed, lifted the corners of Corrie Mae's lips. "You know I will," she answered in sultry tones. "Will you miss me?"

"What do you think?" Jules fastened his eyes intimately on Corrie Mae's big breasts, where a good amount of cleavage was displayed in the low-cut neckline of her dress.

Corrie Mae leaned forward and, running her tongue around her lips, said huskily, "I'll be eagerly waiting for your return."

Willow kept her eyelids lowered to hide the pain in her eyes. Jules would be watching her, she knew, and not for the world would she let him see how deeply he was hurting her.

When Thad Wilson knocked on the door and walked inside, she was so thankful for his appearance, she greeted him more enthusiastically than she normally would have. The farmer's greeting to her was just as full of zeal.

Willow stood up. "Let's go outside and see what you have in your wagon."

"Yes, let's do," Thad said eagerly, and hurried to open the door for her.

The satisfied smirk on Jules's face rapidly changed to a dangerous frown when the farmer arrived. He knew that he was about to get a taste of his own medicine and knew he wouldn't like it at all.

"What's wrong, Jules? Don't you like to play tit for tat?" Corrie Mae teased. "You laid it on Willow pretty good."

"Yeah, but that sodbuster isn't fooling around. He was after Willow when she was working for me."

"He'll probably get her now. He's been hanging around here a lot. He's awfully good-looking, and the best lover I've ever had."

Jules jerked his head up to look at Corrie Mae in surprise. "Are you telling me that you have wrinkled the sheets with him?"

Corrie Mae nodded, a wide smile on her lips. "If Willow ever marries him, she's in for a treat, come bedtime."

"Why don't you shut your mouth, Corrie Mae." Jules jumped to his feet and stormed out of the cookhouse, slamming the door behind him.

Corrie Mae's eyes twinkled gleefully. *She's getting back at you, isn't she, bucko.*

Jules couldn't see Willow and Thad when he walked outside. Thad had pulled his wagon in at its usual place, alongside the building. But he could hear their laughter as he stamped off toward the barn.

A few minutes later he saw Willow emerge from behind the wagon. She looked toward the barn, hesitated a second, and walked to the house. It was plain she didn't want to see any more of him, he thought with a wry twist of his mouth.

When he saw Wilson carrying in a basket of vegetables, he leaned back against the corral, curious to see if the man would take his money and leave right away, or if he would stay a while with Corrie Mae.

When almost an hour had passed and Jules couldn't wait any longer, Thad was still in the cookhouse. *The bastard,* he thought as he walked away. *I guess he really does have the staying power Corrie Mae claimed.*

It was long before daylight when Willow lit the lamp in the kitchen and started a fire in the range. She wanted to start hunting the burros before sunup.

Her next act was to fill a basin with water from the pail on the worktable and to wash her face and hands. As she squinted into the small mirror hung beside the window and pulled a comb through her tangled hair, she thought how quiet it was outside. When she walked over to the cookhouse, the usual sounds of the men stirring about were missing. Only she and Brian and a stable hand had been left behind after she'd sent her cattle off to market.

As she started bacon frying, she sent up a heartfelt prayer that the drive would be successful. She remembered the amusement in Jules's eyes when he'd learned that she had taken over the running of his aunt's ranch. If for no other reason than to prove him wrong, she was determined to show him that she was just as capable as a man when it came to operating a spread. She had six willing workers to help her, and if Mother Nature and rustlers didn't intervene, she would wipe the smirk off his face.

Willow had just lifted the strips of crisp bacon out of the skillet and broken five eggs into the hot grease when Brian entered the kitchen. Knuckling the sleep out of his eyes, he reached for the washbasin.

"Morning, Brian." She smiled at the young man as he washed up. "How did you sleep last night, having the bunkhouse all to yourself?"

Sending a fast, uneasy look at the door leading to Corrie Mae's living quarters, he didn't answer for a second. Then he said, "I know it sounds crazy, but I had a hard time falling asleep. I missed all the snoring that usually goes on."

"You'll have to get used to it," Willow said and laughed. "The men will be gone for a while."

"I probably will, and then they'll be back and I'll have to get used to the ruckus they make all over again," Brian grumbled as Willow placed his breakfast in front of him.

Willow sliced half a loaf of sourdough bread, filled their coffee cups, picked up her plate of bacon and eggs and sat down at the table.

Neither spoke until they were halfway through the meal. Then after taking a swallow of coffee, Brian asked, "Where are we going to look for the burros?"

"I have in mind to start out in the high country and work our way down toward the ranch."

"They've been up there for years. The little devils will be as wild as deer. We're gonna have our hands full, herding them in."

"I expect so, but Rooster told me that a burro, alone on the range, is one of the most docile creatures in the world and will let anyone approach it."

Brian gave her a sceptical look. "Are you planning only to look for ones that are alone? Just walk up to them and put a rope around their necks?"

Willow had to laugh. It did sound ridiculous. "Not quite like that," she said. "You've seen that old burro that *Señor* Salazar left behind when he moved back to Mexico?" Brian nodded and she continued. "I plan to hang a bell around his neck and take him with us. I'm hoping that the ones we take charge of will follow him, and the sound of the bell will become like the voice of a mother. I know that it works for mules, and maybe it will be the same for their little cousins."

Brian chewed thoughtfully for a moment, then said, "I guess it's worth a try."

The sun was just coming up when Willow and Brian walked toward the barn. The air was chilly, and Willow pulled the collar of her jacket up around her ears as she watched some Canada geese honk their way across the sky, heading for a warmer climate.

When they rode away from the barn, heading for the high country, both were dressed for the job ahead. Besides the Stetsons pulled low on their foreheads, each wore a lightweight jacket, and heavy cowhide gloves were folded over their belts. Both wore scuffed leather chaps in case they had to ride through brush and thickets to get to the wiry little animals.

Brian was mounted on a buckskin gelding, and Willow rode a tough little quarter horse. Both animals belonged to the ranch's small remuda and didn't have names. A lariat was coiled on each saddle, and two hung around the horses' necks.

The old burro was tethered to Willow's saddle.

They had ridden for an hour, never seeing anything but a bear that went lumbering off with awkward speed when he spotted them. "He'll be lookin' for a place to hibernate before long." Brian grinned.

Another half hour passed and then they spotted their first herd of burros grazing in a shallow basin. Willow counted eleven. Unaware of the humans watching them, they were braying, kicking up their heels and playfully nipping at each other.

Willow felt a pang of regret that she was going to do her best to take away their freedom and send them to a lifetime of hard labor. If she didn't need the money they would bring her, she wouldn't do it.

"What do we do now?" Brian broke in on her gloomy thoughts.

Willow pushed away the guilt that had grabbed her, and after a sigh, she said, "Let's scatter them. Maybe we can come upon some that are alone then."

With a loud, "Let's go," from Willow, they dug in their heels, and yelling at the top of their voices, raced toward the little group.

The burros' shaggy heads came up, their pointed ears erect. The next instant they were racing out of the grassy depression, their sharp hooves tearing up the sod.

As Willow had hoped, the animals separated. In their alarmed state, some of them lost contact with the main herd as they ran blindly in all directions.

Willow pulled her horse to a walk. "We'll give them time to settle down, then see if my plan works. You go to the left and I'll ride right."

As Willow had hoped, she soon spotted a young

burro now grazing peacefully on the green, lush grass. She dismounted about five yards away from the youngster. With a rope in one hand, and leading the old burro with the other, she slowly approached the little animal.

It looked up at her, then shifted its gaze to the old burro. It twitched its ears at the sound of the tinkling bell. Willow couldn't believe her good luck when the little fellow trotted up to the old one and nudged his head against the old one's shoulder.

"Okay," she whispered, "let's see if you will follow your new friend."

She turned the old one around, and wanted to shout her elation when the little gray donkey followed after him.

After a couple of hours of riding the area, Willow had four burros following the tinkling bell. When she and Brian met at the spot where they had separated a few hours earlier, he had three more. In his case, however, the captured burros wore ropes around their necks.

"I could have caught more if I'd had more ropes," he bragged, very pleased with himself.

"Turn them loose and we'll see if they will follow the bell also," Willow suggested.

When the three were freed, they fell right in with Willow's four, and as if they had done it all their lives, followed along behind the tinkling bell.

"Well, Brian," Willow said, pleased at their catch, "we know how to do it now. You must bring more ropes with you tomorrow."

The days were getting shorter, and it was near sundown when Willow and Brian let down the bars of the corral next to the barn, and the old burro led the young ones inside.

Willow and Brian stood a moment, their arms resting on the top rail, watching the shaggy little animals milling around in their new home, sniffing out the corners. They noted, however, that the burros never stayed away too long from the one who had led them there.

"Seven in one day isn't too bad, is it?" Willow said.

"We can get three times that many a day when Jimmy and Sammy get back. They'll really enjoy rounding up the little devils."

Willow nodded in amusement. She could see the three teenagers whooping and yelling, making a game out of capturing the little animals. "I'm about starved," she said. "I imagine that by the time we wash up, Corrie Mae will have supper ready." She missed seeing the excited gleam that flashed in her young companion's eyes.

When half an hour later Willow and her mother walked toward the cookhouse, a displeased frown settled over Willow's features as Brian and Corrie Mae's laughter floated to her through the open door. She liked her genial cook a lot, but the woman's morals bothered her. It was none of her business how many men the woman took into her bed, but it was her concern if the cook started luring the teenagers there.

When she stepped inside the cookhouse, she found Corrie Mae's kitchen in its usual spotless condition. The floor was swept clean, and the lamp chimney sparkled, shedding its light on the red-and-white checkered tablecloth.

Corrie Mae looked up and smiled at Willow and

Ruth as she forked steaks from a skillet onto a platter. "Brian tells me that you had a very successful day with the little donkeys."

"Yes, we did," Willow answered as she and Ruth took a seat at the table. "And an exhausting one, too, I might add. I'm sure that Brian, like me, will want to go to bed as soon as he finishes his supper." She looked across the table at the young man. "Right, Brian?"

"Absolutely," Brian agreed solemnly. But when Willow looked away, he exchanged a conspiratorial wink with Corrie Mae. The fast glance they gave each other said that Brian would be going to bed early, but not in the bunkhouse.

"I hope that Rooster and the boys are eating as well as we are," Willow said, enjoying her tender piece of meat. "Jimmy is not the best cook in the world," she said, laughing. Then, looking at her mother, she asked softly, "Aren't you feeling well, Ma? You're not talking much."

"I feel fine, honey. I guess I miss Rooster sitting beside me." Willow patted the small hand lying on the table. "He'll be back before you know it," she reassured her mother. When she resumed eating, her thoughts were sad. She was thinking of all the wasted years her mother had endured married to a man she called husband, a bullier of women and those weaker than himself.

She wondered why some men were mean-spirited, why others were caring and giving of themselves. Did it have anything to do with the way they were raised, or were they just bad seeds from the day they were born?

She remembered her Grandfather Ames often saying that his son had always been a bad one, that he was glad Otto's Maw never lived to see how mean he had turned out.

Willow shook her head sadly. Her mother would never be able to find real happiness with Rooster. Although Otto Ames didn't love his wife, he would never allow her to divorce him.

I'm no better off, Willow reminded herself. What were her chances of a happy marriage? Jules would never marry her, and she didn't think she would ever love another man.

When Willow climbed into bed, she was still asking herself the same question. Was it possible for her to love again? Jules's strong face and laughing eyes swam before her and her feelings for him were as strong as they had been before. She would never love again, but maybe someday she might find a man she respected and liked, whom she could consider marrying. She did want to have children. What Jules had offered hadn't included them.

As she drifted off to sleep a fleeting picture of handsome Thad Wilson passed in front of her eyes.

Chapter Nineteen

The cattle had been driven into a circle, and most had been lulled to sleep by the songs Sammy and Rooster sang to them as they rode along, keeping watch over the herd.

A mare with a bell suspended from her neck kept Jules's horses together beneath a clump of birch growing beside the river where they were camped.

The two campfires had winked out about an hour ago; voices had faded and silence had closed in. Jules lay in his bedroll listening to the lap of the river hitting the riverbank, his thoughts, as usual, on Willow.

And, as usual, he was wondering if Thad Wilson was courting her. And if he was, was the randy farmer still visiting Corrie Mae? "I bet my string of wild horses he is," Jules said to himself.

As he dreamed on about Willow, longing to feel her

softness against his hard body, he realized suddenly that it wasn't only that he wanted to make love to Willow, he also missed seeing her around his home, the graceful way she moved as she cooked his meals. He missed the long talks they'd had out on the veranda in the evenings. He had told her things he had never told anyone else.

Would it be so hard to be married to her? he asked himself. Other women no longer appealed to him.

Before Jules could decide on an answer, the stillness was suddenly broken by the quick yelp of a coyote. He jerked erect, the bedroll falling to his waist. There was something about the sharp yowl that didn't quite ring true. He sat, listening for other sounds in the darkness. He jerked his head to the right when his horses began to snort and paw the ground. What had disturbed them? A bear? A coyote? A man? Perhaps an Indian.

He stood up, ready to go investigate, then quickly jumped behind a large boulder near the river.

The sharp, shrill war whoops of Indians rang out on the still night with yells fiendish enough to paralyze a man. As the men from both camps came running up, guns drawn, an unearthly din filled the air. There was the neighing of horses, drumbeats and a discharge of guns.

In the dim moonlight Jules saw the half-naked bodies of the Indians dashing about. He took aim at two of them, but was afraid he might hit his horses. When no shots were fired by his men, he knew that they had come to the same conclusion. Almost at the same time he realized that the Indians hadn't fired at them either.

It became clear to him then that the Indians' aim was to stampede the cattle so that they could steal some of them.

"No, you don't, you bastards," he yelled. "Willow needs every head of those cattle." This time, when a brave dashed past him, he took careful aim and squeezed the trigger. The Indian went down.

The men began following his lead and guns popped all around him. Suddenly then, as quickly as they had appeared, the Indians were racing their horses across the river, one having rescued the fallen brave.

Everyone's attention turned to the cattle then. The longhorns were on their feet, nervous and bawling as they milled around. It looked as if they might start running any minute. Jules ordered four of his men to mount and start riding around them, to push them into a tighter circle. It took about a half an hour before the animals settled down. Jules went to check on his horses and found that seven of them were gone.

But I didn't lose any of Willow's cattle, he thought as he rolled up in his blankets once again. Tomorrow they would arrive at the stockyards on the outskirts of Wichita. The cattle would be somebody else's responsibility then.

It was around noon the following day when the horses and cattle were delivered at the loading pens.

While Rooster saw to the selling of Willow's herd, Jules met with a man from Montana andfinalized a deal with him.

Jules and Rooster ran into each other at the ranchers' favorite saloon, and had a conversation for the first time since Rooster had left Jules's employment.

"I got a good price for Willow's cattle," Rooster led

off after a bottle and two glasses were put in front of them. "She's gonna be pleased. She worked like a little slave, fattening them up. She's determined to make a success out of Miss Jess's ranch."

Jules made no response. He was of two minds how he felt about Willow being able to bring the ranch around so that it was making money. On the one hand, he wanted her to succeed; on the other hand, if she failed, maybe she would come back to him.

But did he want her to return to him out of neccessity? he asked himself.

The answer was a firm no. He wanted her back only when she wanted to return to him. When she was ready to accept his terms.

He switched the subject to his success with his horses. "The buyer from Montana was pleased with my wild ones and wants more. I signed a contract with him to deliver another hundred head next spring."

While Rooster was congratulating Jules, their cowhands came in, rowdy and eager to spend their money on whiskey and saloon women. When Jimmy and Sammy squeezed in beside Rooster and said that they'd have a glass of whiskey to settle the dust in their throats, Rooster shook his head at the bartender.

"They'll each have a bottle of sarsaparilla."

"Sarsaparilla!" the teenagers exclaimed in unison. Then they pointed out that they had worked as hard as the older hands had and that they should get the same treatment.

"You'll be paid the same as them, but Willow would have my hide if I let you guzzle down raw whiskey."

Rooster saw the pair exchange a look that said they would buy a bottle after he had left for home. He waited until the boys drank their soft drink, then picking up his change, said, "Let's get goin', boys. We have a long ride ahead of us."

"But we plan on stayin' in town with the rest of the fellers," Jimmy protested in an agitated voice.

Rooster shook his head. "Not this time. Maybe in a couple years."

Amusement twitched Jules's lips as he watched the two sullen-faced teenagers follow Rooster out of the saloon.

It was dusk a week later, and Willow and Brian had just put eight more burros in the corral, when they saw Rooster and the teenagers riding their horses up the mountain. Their faces beaming, they ran to the front of the barn, waiting to greet the three.

Sammy and Jimmy were off their horses first, the wide smiles on their faces saying that they were happy to be home. They each took a turn giving Willow a bear hug that almost squeezed the breath out of her. And they thumped poor Brian so hard on the back, he went down on his knees.

With a grin and a shake of his head, Rooster dismounted. When he had exchanged greetings with Willow, he asked, "Everything go all right while I was gone?" Then his gaze went to the house. "Your Ma is all right?"

"She's fine. She's been missing you, though."

"I sure have missed her."

"Well, tell me, how did the drive go? Did you lose any of the cattle?" This last was asked anxiously.

"Nary a one. Let's get up to the house and I'll tell you all about it. Also"—Rooster patted his vest pocket—"give you this check."

After Rooster had handed over his horse to Brian, Willow followed him to the house. Ruth was sitting in front of a low-burning fire, a pair of knitting needles flashing in her nimble fingers as she knit a cuff for the wristband of a glove she was making for Rooster. Its mate lay finished in her yarn basket.

She looked up when Willow and Rooster entered the room, and the joy the flooded her face made Willow want to cry, for Rooster wore the same look. It was clear how desperately they wanted to run to each other, to embrace. But both were honorable people, so they only stood, smiling at each other.

When Willow and Rooster had shed their hats and jackets, the three sat down and Rooster told the women of the long drive and their encounter with the Indians. When he was finished, he took the check from his vest and handed it to Willow.

"I think you'll be pleased with its amount." He smiled at her.

Rooster and Ruth, watching Willow's face as she looked at the check, knew by her expression that she was more than pleased. She was ecstatic. "Oh, Rooster," she exclaimed, "I never dreamed the cattle would bring so much."

"We had a little luck there. The thing was, there hadn't been that many fall herds brought in, so the buyers were paying top dollar for those that were there."

"Ma," Willow exclaimed, "even after I split the profit with Aunt Jess, we will have enough money left over to see us through the winter." She looked at Rooster. "When Brian was in Bitter Creek last week, he brought home a newspaper. I read an ad in it that was placed by a miner in Colorado who is looking to buy burros. The ad said that if a person had a hundred or more for sale, he would send someone to collect them."

She gave her foreman a big smile. "I guess you know what our main priority is now."

Rooster grinned at her enthusiasm. "We'll get on it the first thing tomorrow."

"The first thing I have to do tomorrow morning is go to town and cash this check, then take Aunt Jess her share," Willow said, standing up. "Right now I'm going to get into some clean clothes. Corrie Mae will be announcing supper pretty soon."

"Will Thad come calling on you tonight?" Ruth looked at her daughter. When Willow gave her a blank look, she reminded her, "It's Friday night, the night he rides over to visit you."

"So it is. I'd forgotten. I'd better get a move on. Is there warm water in the reservoir?"

"Yes, dear. It's full to the top. I laid out clean clothes for you. With the air cooler these nights, I pressed your blue woolen. It will keep you warm if you go for a walk."

"Thank you, Ma," Willow said woodenly on her way out of the room.

"Is the farmer courting Willow?" There was a hint of a frown on Rooster's craggy face.

"Yes, he is, and I'm real pleased about it. He started coming over the Friday night after you left on the cattle drive. He's a very pleasant young man, and a hard worker. He's good husband material, I keep telling Willow."

"You can't always tell what a person is like by the face he shows the public. Sometimes a handsome, genial facade is not what it seems to be."

"You sound like you don't like him, Rooster. Is there a reason for that?"

"I only know him to nod at in passing. It's just that I've heard some rumors about him."

"What kind of rumors? Something bad?"

"Not bad. Nothing that would have the law looking for him. I guess he's pretty much a womanizer. And it's said that it doesn't matter to him whether the woman is single or married."

"The way I look at that, the women are just as guilty as he is." Ruth rushed to defend the man she secretly wished Willow would marry. "I'm sure Thad would never force himself on a woman."

"No, I don't think he would. He wouldn't have to. He'd sweet-talk her until she willingly fell into his arms."

"I'm sure he would stop romancing women once he was married."

After a short silence, Rooster asked, "Did you ever wonder why Wilson only comes to visit Willow on a Friday night? Why not on a Saturday or Sunday, which is normal for a courting man to do?"

"I admit it crossed my mind a couple of times. He seems so enamored of Willow. I decided that he works so hard all week, he needs to rest up on the weekends."

"I guess so," Rooster said and dropped the conversation about the young farmer. Let somebody else break Ruth's bubble about the man she so admired. Sooner or later someone would tell Willow about the woman who lived a few miles out of Coyote. That Thad Wilson spent his weekends with the woman and the five-year-old son he had sired on her. He hoped this person would tell her that this woman was crazy jealous of Wilson and that if she learned he had a romantic interest somewhere else, all hell would break loose.

When Rooster left Ruth to get cleaned up himself, he cussed Jules out for being a damned fool.

Corrie Mae had made supper a gala affair: a celebration of the sale of the longhorns. In the center of the cloth-covered table sat a sliced, ten-pound roast, and on either side of it were bowls heaped high with steaming vegetables: smooth mashed potatoes, the last string beans from Thad's garden, baked squash and sweet potatoes. A full gravy boat sat in front of the roast, ready to be ladled over the potatoes and hot biscuits. Waiting on the work bench were four pies, two apple and two pumpkin.

Willow looked around the table, smiling fondly at her boys, her mother and dear Rooster. All her loved ones were there. She had enough money to see her through the winter and a good start on rounding up a hundred burros. So why wasn't she enjoying the evening like everyone else?

She knew the answer. Jules wasn't sitting beside her. He never would be. It was time she began planning a life without him in it.

Half an hour later, coffee had just been poured when Thad stepped into the kitchen. Willow gave him a smile that was warmer than any she had ever given him before.

"Would you like a piece of pie and a cup of coffee?" she invited, making a place for him beside her.

"Just a cup of coffee, Corrie Mae." Thad smiled at the cook.

You little rat, Corrie Mae thought as she placed a cup in front of the farmer. *An hour or so from now you'll be in my bed, humping like a rutting buffalo. Willow is much too good for you. She belongs with that idiot Jules.*

It was but minutes later when the idiot arrived. The wide smile on Jules's face died when he saw Thad sitting beside Willow, his face clean-shaven and his hair slicked back. A pulse throbbed in his jaw when he saw that Thad had an arm drapped across the back of Willow's chair. Pride kept him from wheeling around and walking out.

Jimmy slid over on the bench, making room for Jules to sit between him and Sammy. That placed the seething rancher directly across from Willow. He shot her a fast glance, saw her talking and smiling at Thad, and didn't look her way again that night.

Instead, he gave his attention to Corrie Mae. When Jimmy left the table a short time later he slid to the end of the bench, and when the cook brought him a piece of pie, he swung his feet around and pulled her down on his lap. While everyone laughed at his action, he whispered in her ear, making her giggle.

"You naughty man," Corrie Mae scolded, pulling away from him, "having such thoughts. You know we can't do that now."

What none of the people at the table realized was

that all Jules had done was blow in Corrie Mae's ear. They didn't realize either that Corrie Mae was on Jules's side and that she knew how the stubborn mule was hurting inside.

The cook looked at Willow and knew that she was hurting also. What a pain in the rear this love thing was, she thought, and was happy she had never been bitten by that particular bug. It messed up a person's mind and made people do foolish things, not to mention the pain it caused.

When Corrie Mae put an arm around Jules's neck and blew in *his* ear, Willow could take no more. "Should we go, Thad?" She stood up and stepped over the bench before he could answer.

"Don't forget your jacket, Willow," Ruth called out. "It's real cool tonight."

"I agree. That's why I think we'll stay inside, sit in front of the fire."

When the door closed behind them, Corrie Mae slid off Jules's knees. There was no reason to pretend anymore.

Ruth and Rooster left almost on the heels of Willow and Thad, and the others left shortly after them. Willow's two cowhands gave Corrie Mae a knowing look as they left. They would be back later.

Jules gave Corrie Mae a roguish grin as she cleared the table. "Your bedsprings are going to squeak tonight, aren't they?"

"No more than usual," the big, attractive woman quipped saucily. "They squeak every night."

"Oh, yeah, what about all the time the men were gone on the cattle drive. There were no men here then."

Corrie Mae laughed as she filled a basin with hot water. "You forget that Brian was left behind."

"So I did." Jules chuckled. "Don't tell me that greenhorn kid could satisfy you."

"I hope to tell you he did. I'd always heard that a male reaches his peak when he's seventeen or eighteen. I firmly believe that now. Brian went after me every night, all night. If I had to choose one man on this ranch, it would be him.

"After Denny and Hoot have been here and gone, he will slip over here and spend the rest of the night with me."

"Why does he have to sneak to see you? Why can't he be open about it the same way the older men are?"

"Hah!" Corrie Mae gave a short laugh. "Willow would have a hissie if she learned that one of her boys knew how to hump. Brian even has to keep it secret from Jimmy and Sammy. If those two young devils found out that their buddy comes over here every night they'd be hotfooting it over here and not being discreet about it either. It wouldn't be long before Willow would know what was going on.

"I like this job, and I know that she would fire me if she learned I was taking her boys to bed."

When Jules picked up a dish towel and started drying the dishes Corrie Mae was washing, she looked at him from the corner of her eye and asked, "How far do you think Willow and Thad have come in their courtship?"

The cup Jules was drying dropped and shattered on the floor. He gave Corrie Mae a suspicious look and practically snarled as he grabbed a broom. "I don't know and I don't care."

Corrie Mae hid her grin as she continued to needle him. "Thad is a smooth talker. He's been seeing her for several weeks now. I'd say one more visit with her and he'll have her in bed."

It was plain from Jules's expression that he wanted to hit the cook as much as he wanted to bolt from the kitchen. He did neither. But he promised himself that he would geld the sodbuster the first chance he got.

Corrie Mae realized that she had almost pushed Jules over the edge and spoke no more about Willow and the man who was courting her.

"Do you want to play a few hands of cards?" she asked as she emptied the dishpan.

"I'm not in the mood for cards tonight," Jules said as he reached over to turn out the lamp on the kitchen table. "Let's just sit and talk for a while."

Corrie Mae started to ask, "In the dark?" but then realized what Jules had in mind. When Willow walked Thad to the door, she would see the cook-house in darkness and Jules's horse still tied up there. He wanted Willow to think that they were in bed together. Also, he could see when the young farmer left.

She folded her hands on the table and said, "Tell me about your cattle drive."

Willow kept shooting glances at the clock, wondering when Thad would leave. She was sorry now that they hadn't taken their usual ride tonight. They could have ridden for an hour or so, then returned home and she could have given Thad a quick kiss before sending him on his way home.

Her mother had spent only a few minutes with them before saying good night and going to her room.

The minutes had seemed like hours as they dragged along.

She was learning that she and Thad had nothing in common. He didn't know anything about ranching, and she knew little about farming, so the conversation between them was stilted with long stretches of silence between remarks.

She thought that Thad had read her mind when he said it was time he was getting home. It was almost rude, the way she ushered him into the kitchen and held his jacket for him. When she opened the door, she caught a sharp breath. The cookhouse was in darkness, but Jules's horse was still tied up in front of the building. She was so upset, she was hardly aware of Thad grabbing her to him and planting a passionate kiss on her lips. She didn't even feel his hardness pressed into her.

But she did become aware of his hand inching up toward her breast. She pushed herself away from him, saying "Good night, Thad."

He reluctantly released her and she went back into the kitchen and closed the door before he had mounted and ridden away. Blinded by the tears that had gathered in her eyes, she stumbled into her room.

Corrie Mae heard Jules's harsh intake of breath when Thad grabbed Willow and kissed her. It had been the kind of kiss that lovers exchanged and seeing it had torn Jules up inside, she knew.

You damn fool, she thought, *why don't you go over there and do something?*

On the heels of Corrie Mae's thought, Jules suddenly stood up and mumbled that he didn't feel like making the fifteen-mile ride home and that he would spend the night at his aunt's house. He left then, so upset, he forgot to say good night.

In the dark bunkhouse, the owners of two pairs of eyes sighed in relief when they saw the cookhouse door open and Jules step outside. They swore softly when, instead of mounting his horse and riding away, Jules led it toward the barn. Was he going to spend the night in the bunkhouse? they asked each other in a whisper.

Denny and Hoot had decided that they might as well go to bed when Jules walked past the window they had been peering through and went on toward the house. He was going to spend the night there.

The two cowhands had already tossed a coin to see who would visit Corrie Mae first, and Jules had barely closed the kitchen door behind him before Hoot, the winner, was hurrying toward the cookhouse.

Chapter Twenty

Tears of despair and self-contempt ran unchecked down Willow's cheeks and onto her pillow. How could she have been so completely wrong about Jules? What a fool she had been to think that she was special to him, that he loved her, would marry her. Right now he was in bed with her cook, doing all the things he had once done with her.

She had to face the fact that he wanted only one thing from a woman, whether it be a loose-moraled one, or a simpleton like herself.

Willow dabbed her eyes dry with the corner of the sheet, determined that she would get over the man who had made a fool of her. Exhausted, mentally and physically, from chasing burros all day, Willow was drifting off when she heard the soft click of the kitchen door being closed. She sat up in bed, terror filling her whole being. Her father and Buck had come to take her and her mother back to New Mexico! Would Jules hear her if she screamed, she wondered. The bunkhouse was too far away to hear a yell for help.

She threw back the covers and swung her feet to the floor. She would try to handle it herself, she thought nervously, as she stood up. She slipped noiselessly across the room to the dresser and picked up the Colt that lay there. From now on it would be kept under her pillow.

The gun in her hand, Willow eased out of her room and down the short hall. She heard a muttered curse as someone bumped into the table or a chair. She peered into the gray darkness of the kitchen and saw the shadowy figure of a tall man coming toward her.

"Stay right where you are," she ordered. The click of the Colt being cocked seemed to echo around the room. She heard the sharp ejaculation of a surprised curse, then hard arms were wrapped around her, holding her arms tight against her sides, rendering her helpless to shoot the intruder.

She opened her mouth to scream, but before she could, lips that she knew well were on hers.

Her first reaction was to relax in relief. But then the firm lips began to move urgently, and the arms that had held her prisoner were now across her back and around her waist. Jules was holding her so tightly, a feather wouldn't fit between them.

She unconsciously began to respond, opening her mouth to him, pressing closer yet. When she felt the throbbing of a male hardness against her stomach, anger replaced the passion that gripped her. This man who held her so tightly was a shameless, lustful animal. How could he come from one woman's bed and be ready to climb into another one so soon after?

Willow jerked her lips away and, raising her hand, slapped Jules hard across the face. The crack of her palm was loud in the room.

"Why in the hell did you do that?" Jules demanded, nursing his cheek.

"Think about it. It will come to you."

"No, it won't. I don't know what you're talking about."

"Do you think that I don't know where you've been and what you were doing the last hour?"

"Whatever you think you know is no excuse to haul off and hit me."

"Hah!" Willow gave an unladylike snort and, without another word, wheeled and ran down the hall to her room, where she bolted the door shut.

Jules stood in the hallway, fingering the welts rising on his cheek. A slow smile turned up the corners of his mouth. Willow had fallen for his ploy. She had believed, as he had wanted her to, that he had been in bed with Corrie Mae. She was jealous.

It had felt good, holding her in his arms again, Jules thought as he removed his boots and stripped down to his underwear before crawling into bed. Would it be so hard to be married to her? he asked himself again. He asked himself another question. Was he just being stubborn refusing to marry her? His father and Aunt Jess had always charged him with this unbecoming trait. They claimed that one day it would be his undoing.

Had that day arrived? He frowned into the darkness. Was the sodbuster replacing him in Willow's affections? The farmer would marry her in a minute.

And cheat on her all during their married life.

When Jules finally fell asleep, a war waged inside him. Should he marry Willow? Did he want to give up the freedom of bachelorhood? Was he being stubborn?

Willow had felt so right in his arms. Memories of all the nights of lovemaking came surging back. He didn't seem whole anymore without her.

Willow awakened to the morning sun striking her face through a two-inch gap in the drapes.

She had been a long time falling asleep last night, and this morning she had overslept because of it.

She slid out of bed, her toes curling away from the cold floorboards as she searched for her house slippers, which had been accidentally kicked away from their usual place beside the bed.

She was down on her knees feeling under the bed when a voice she would never forget drawled in amusement behind her. "Now that's a delightful sight, your little rear stuck up in the air."

Willow gave a startled jerk and hit her head on the high bedframe as she scrambled to her feet.

"What are you doing in my bedroom?" she demanded crossly, pushing the hair out of her eyes.

"Your door wasn't closed, so I thought I'd drop in and say good morning."

"Just because there's an open door doesn't mean you have to walk through it."

"But I've brought you some coffee," Jules explained, his hot gaze devouring the shape of her body, which was clearly outlined through the thin material of her gown. When his study of her reached her breasts, she remembered the buttons missing there. She started to cluth the edges together, but then said to herself that she'd be damned if she would. Let him gawk. She hoped that he would become so stiff and hard that he couldn't walk.

When Jules started toward her, Willow lost her bravado and grabbed up her robe. She barely eluded his hands as he reached for her.

"Aren't you going to drink your coffee?" Jules asked plaintively as she tied the belt of the robe around her small waist and headed toward the door.

"Yes, I am," she answered, "in the safety of the kitchen."

"Don't you think you would be safe drinking it in here?" His voice became soft and coaxing. "You know I would never hurt you."

Willow ignored his pleading tone. Her wish had come true. He was hurting.

But she was, too, she admitted as she walked down the hall. It had been all she could do to keep from throwing herself into his arms, to share the morning desire that had once started their day.

It didn't help her condition when just short of the kitchen door, Jules grabbed her by the waist and pulled her into the well of his hips. He ground his stiffness against her as he nuzzled her ear and throat.

"Think about this as you hunt your burros today," he said, emphasizing his meaning with a quick buck of his hips.

"And you think about this as you hunt your wild horses," Willow said softly, and reaching behind her, she caressed the edge of the hardness straining against his Levi's.

Jules gasped his pleasure, then his pain as Willow, with a taunting laugh, pulled away from him and entered the kitchen. "You teasing little witch," he hissed in her ear just before Ruth looked up from the stove and smiled at them.

"Good morning, children. Are you ready for breakfast? I was just about to start the bacon to frying."

"I'll do it, Ma. You go sit down."

"If you're sure, I'll go get dressed. It's quite cool this morning."

As Willow went about frying bacon, slicing bread and setting the table, Jules sat down, leaned back in the chair and stretched out his long legs as he watched her. He was still as hard as a rock and every time she glanced at him, he bucked his hips in invitation to her.

The fourth time it happened, Willow got her revenge. With her back to him she untied the robe belt, then undid the remaining buttons on her gown. Her firm breasts were fully revealed now as she turned to face him and pulled the robe apart. Then, with her hands beneath her breasts, she pushed them up and forward.

"Oh, lord," Jules rasped and sat forward, his gaze hot on the pink, pouting nipples. They seemed to be begging him to take them into the warmth of his mouth, to feel his tongue laving them.

Willow let him feast his eyes on her breasts, watching through lowered lids as the bulge in his Levi's grew and strained against his fly. When she thought the buttons would surely pop off, she gave a teasing laugh.

And that she shouldn't have done. Jules was on his feet in an instant, bending her over his arm and hungrily opening his mouth over one firm, white mound. His lips drew greedily on the hard, pink nipple, and Willow grew alarmed as thrill after thrill ran from her breasts to the core of her. Her mother could return to the kitchen at any moment.

"Jules, stop it." She tried to force his mouth off her.

But Jules wouldn't be persuaded. He had yearned too long for the taste of her flesh in his mouth again.

Willow was becoming panicky as she fought the fear of being discovered and the passion that was threatening to overwhelm her.

She was finally saved by a pounding on the kitchen door and Rooster demanding, "Willow, are you going burro hunting today or not?"

Jules reluctantly released her and hurried to sit down at the table to hide his condition. But the heat of desire was still visible in his eyes if anyone looked closely enough.

Willow was in the same state as she hurriedly tied her belt and stepped over to the stove. Taking a deep breath, she called out, "The door is unlocked, Rooster. Come on in."

"Good mornin' Boss," Rooster said when he stepped inside. Willow started to answer the same, but she realized her ranch foreman was addressing Jules. She gave a wry twist to her mouth. Rooster still looked on Jules as his boss.

"Have you eaten?" she asked.

"Yes. I just finished." When Ruth entered the

kitchen, Rooster's eyes lit up and he rushed to say, "I'll have a cup of coffee with you, though."

Willow and Jules hid amused smiles when he pulled a chair away from the table and took Ruth's arm to help her sit down. The little woman was no longer an invalid, but it pleased the rough cowboy to treat her as one.

Willow lost no time in eating breakfast. She had to get away from Jules's presence; she felt as if his hot eyes were stripping the clothes off her body. She finished her bacon and eggs while Jules and her mother were only halfway through theirs. "I'll be back as soon as I get dressed." She looked at Rooster.

Disappointment was in the eyes of the three left sitting at the table when she hurried out of the room.

Ten minutes later she was back in the kitchen wearing her usual work clothes. She dropped a kiss on her mother's cheek and, ignoring Jules, said, "Let's go, Rooster."

"I've been thinkin' on how you've been catchin' them little jackasses," Rooster said as they took off at a brisk canter. "Catchin' a half-dozen a day, we'll need months to gather a herd big enough to interest that company. You said they would want at least a hundred to make it profitable for them to come out here."

"I've thought about that." Willow slowed her mount down to a walk. "Have you thought of another way to take them?"

"Maybe. It's worth a try at least. I think that if we take all hands out to scour around, we could round up the little devils and herd them into a deep coulee that has only one openin'. We could have a fence we've knocked together waiting to close them in. We might be able to catch thirty or forty head a day. In a week's time you might have captured enough to interest that buyer in Colorado."

"I think that's a great idea, Rooster." Eagerness to get started danced in Willow's eyes. "Shall we go back and get the men?"

"Not today." Rooster laughed at her excitement. "First we've got to find a coulee deep enough so they can't climb out. Then we have to make the fence and get it out to the place we've chosen. It will take us all day to do that. We'll start the drive tomorrow."

Jules left his aunt's ranch shortly after Willow and Rooster rode off. As he saddled his black stallion, he swore he would never come here again. Although he knew he could stir passion in Willow, she had made it clear that she wasn't going to allow him to do it.

"Hell, I don't have to hunger after her," he muttered. "And I'll see to it that I don't. There are plenty of women eager to share their beds with me for an hour or so when nature demands it. And none of them will expect me to marry them."

Jules had ridden about a mile when up ahead he saw a rider coming toward him. He could tell from the small figure sitting astride the horse that it was a woman. When the sun sparked fire from red hair, he knew who she was. Thelma Grosman. The woman the sodbuster spent his weekends with.

"Good morning, Thelma." Jules nodded at the redhead when they stopped abreast of each other. "Did you want to see me about something?"

"I wasn't lookin' for you, Asher," Thelma answered coolly. "I was lookin' for that housekeeper of yours."

"Do you mean Nina?"

"No I don't mean that slut and you know it. I'm talkin' about the one that took her place."

Jules's eyes grew hard. "If you're referring to Willow Ames, she's no slut and I advise you not to call her that again."

"Why not? That's what she is. First she sleeps with you and now she's sleepin' with my man."

Jules leaned forward in the saddle and pinned Thelma with eyes that shimmered with rage as he ground out, "If you're talking about Thad Wilson, Willow would never sleep with a woman-chaser like him."

"What are you talkin' about? Thad is no woman-chaser."

"Hah! He's slept with half the women in a thirty-mile radius of Coyote. You're the only one who doesn't know it. But if you wait a half hour and then ride out to my aunt's ranch, you'll know it, too, when you walk into the cookhouse and catch your man plowing the female cook there."

Jules could see the uncertainty building in Thelma's eyes and hoped that she would take him up on his suggestion. He lowered his lids to hide the satisfaction that had came into his eyes. She was going to do it.

Thelma lifted the reins and said with her chin in the air, "You're lyin', and to prove it, I'll do as you say. And when I find out that you made it all up, I'll send my paw after you. He'll beat the hell out of you."

Jules watched the irate woman ride away, his brow furrowed. What if the farmer didn't keep his usual assignation with Corrie Mae? He didn't relish a fist-fight with Thelma's brutish father.

Chapter Twenty-one

When Willow and Rooster rode up to the barn, they gave each other a startled look at the loud ruckus coming from the cookhouse. The sound of angry female screeching and yelling rang out on the morning air. And above it all was a man's baritone trying to calm the combatants. They both thought of Ruth as they slid out of their saddles and rushed toward the angry din. Maybe Otto had come to take his wife away.

They arrived at the cookhouse just as a female body came flying through the door, landing hard on her rump. Corrie Mae followed, her face distorted in fury. She clutched her robe together at her throat; plainly it was the only garment she wore. Blood stained a large spot on her left upper arm. While Willow and

Rooster stared dumbfounded, Thad came rushing outside.

As he helped the woman to her feet, Rooster recognized Thelma Grosman and demanded, "What in the hell is going on here?"

When neither Thad nor the shaken Thelma answered, Corrie Mae, her eyes snapping, spoke up. "This bitch shot me and I knocked her through the door."

"Why did she shoot you? She must have had a reason."

"You're damn right I had a reason," Thelma screeched. "I walked in on them going at it in that slut's quarters. She lured Thad in there and coaxed him into bed with her. I wish I had killed the bitch, and I will if she ever tries her wiles on him again."

"You stupid bitch." Corrie Mae took a threatening step toward Thelma. "Thad and I have been wrinkling the sheets together for over five years. Not once did I ever have to coax him into my bed. Just look at him. You can see the truth of my words on his face."

As everyone looked at the farmer, including several hands who had rushed up, guilt was plain on his face. He knew that everyone there, except for Willow, was aware of his sleeping around. He also knew that if asked, they would all confirm the cook's charges.

Consequently, avoiding everyone's eyes, especially Willow's, he urged, "Come on, Thelma, let's go home. We'll have a long talk."

"You can bet we'll talk," Thelma snapped, jerking her arm free. "And my paw will be in on it too."

When the wagon rolled away, with Thelma sitting

stiffly beside Thad, her horse tied to the tailgate, Willow and Rooster walked into the cookhouse. Corrie Mae sat with her elbows on the table, her fingers pressed to her temples.

"Corrie Mae, let me look at your arm," Willow said gently. "Maybe you should see the doctor."

"I'm pretty sure it's only a flesh wound." Corrie Mae lifted her head and slowly slipped her arm out of the robe's sleeve. "The crazy bitch is a rotten shot."

"Didn't she turn any of her wrath on Thad?" Rooster asked as Willow carefully examined the wound.

"Hell, no. You heard her. It was all my fault. I took advantage of her poor Thad."

"I think she'll sing a different song from now on," Rooster said. "Today she learned that her Thad boy isn't as innocent as he lets on. I wouldn't want to be in his shoes when her father gets hold of him."

"I think you're right about this being a flesh wound, Corrie Mae," Willow said. "I'll clean it out, bathe it and put salve and a bandage on it. I think you'll be fine then."

"I'm glad it's my left arm," Corrie Mae said as Willow brought a basin of water to the table. "At least I can continue to cook for the men."

"If I were you, I wouldn't do anything else for the men for a few days," Rooster said wryly.

As he went through the door, Corrie Mae laughingly threw a biscuit at his head.

"I'm sorry you had to hear about me and Thad," Corrie Mae said as Willow finished bandaging her arm. "He's not worthy of you, Willow."

"Don't worry about it, Corrie Mae." Willow picked

up the basin and dashed the water outside. "I didn't have any romantic notions about him. To tell you the truth, I found him very boring, and I'm glad this happened. I don't have to think up an excuse to tell him to stop hanging around."

"I'm glad to hear that. I was beginning to feel guilty about going to bed with him."

Willow made no response to Corrie Mae's statement, but she wondered if her cook felt guilty about going to bed with Jules.

Why should she? she thought. She probably didn't know about her short-lived romance with him.

Willow said, "Well, I guess I'll see you at supper time. Rooster and I have some work to do at the barn."

She found Rooster on the veranda soothing Ruth's upset nerves. "Wasn't it awful, Willow, that young woman shooting Corrie Mae? I didn't know Thad had another girlfriend, but I was having second thoughts about him courting you."

"You were, Ma? How come?"

"He was spending too much time with Corrie Mae . . . in her quarters."

"How do you know that?"

"Sometimes when I'd go for a walk and pass by the cookhouse, I could hear them laughing and carrying on."

"And you didn't tell me, Ma?"

"Oh, I was going to." Ruth blushed. "Just as soon as I could find the right words. That woman Thelma didn't have any trouble saying them, did she?"

"No, she didn't." Rooster laughed. "She laid it right on the line."

"We're going to leave you now, Ma. Rooster and I have some work to do."

Willow and Rooster found the two cowhands and three teenagers discussing the fight between the two women. When Willow took Jimmy and Sammy into the barn to help her look for hammers and nails, Rooster discovered what was really troubling the two cowhands and Brian. Would Corrie Mae be able to frolic with them in bed that night?

"What do you think, Rooster?" Brian asked. "You saw her wound."

"Well," Rooster answered after a moment of sham serious thought, "does Corrie Mae use her left arm much when the two of you are going at it?"

"No," The three male voices answered at once.

"Then I think it will be business as usual," Rooster said, amusement in his eyes.

The three realized then that Rooster had been having fun at their expense and jumped on him, good naturedly pummeling his back and shoulders.

"Enough, enough." Rooster laughingly backed away. "Right now we've got to build a fence."

"A fence for what?" Brian asked.

"Come along and I'll tell you."

The rest of the day was spent in putting a sturdy fence together from discarded strips of lumber Rooster found stacked behind the barn.

It was nearing dusk as Willow sat her quarter horse and gazed down at the little burros milling around in the closed-off coulee. Rooster's idea had worked wonderfully well, she thought. Yesterday she and the men had corraled forty-eight burros, and today they had chased forty-three more into the deep gully. Added to the ones she and Brian had captured, she had over a hundred head ready for sale. All she had to do now was write a letter to that company in Colorado.

A pleased smile wreathed her face as she turned her mount homeward. When the buyer arrived, she would receive enough money from him to put aside a little nest egg for her and her mother.

The only thing she and the men had to do until then was to haul hay and water to the little animals. But right now she was hungry and weary from the day's hard work. She couldn't wait to eat supper and go to bed.

The dim lights of Coyote shone up ahead, and Jules lightly touched his spurs to the stallion. He was ready for the company of his rowdy friends. Logan had disappeared again, and he was tired of playing cards with the ranch hands. They didn't seem to like his company anyhow.

As the horse galloped toward the one-street town, Jules fell to wondering if Thelma had found Corrie Mae and the farmer in bed together. As usual, the sodbuster had showed up at the ranch yesterday, his wagon full of fall vegetables. His face had looked a little bruised, and there was a faint purplish shadow under his right eye. His usual smiling face had changed to one of sullenness. And for the first time, he had company. Thelma's father, Hiram, rode with him, a scowl on his rough-hewn face. In Aunt Jess's opinion, he was a watchdog, there to keep an eye on Wilson.

When Jules rode into town, he dismissed the

farmer from his mind as he dismounted and tied his horse to the hitching post in front of the saloon. But when he joined his friends lined up at the bar, he was forced to think of the farmer again. Everyone in the room was talking about a fight between Thelma and Corrie Mae. Jules felt bad that Corrie Mae had been wounded. He had thought there would be a catfight between the two women, but it hadn't entered his mind that jealous Thelma would actually pull a gun on the cook.

"And the best part," someone said with a chuckle, "was when Thelma sent her old man after old randy Thad. Hiram beat the livin' hell out of him, and he now rides along with the farmer when he makes his rounds. Like it or not, Thad has to keep his britches buttoned up."

Jules fell to wondering how Willow had been affected by the disclosure of what Thad Wilson was really like. Had she been disappointed that once again she had picked the wrong man to pin her hopes on?

The thought struck him that maybe she had really cared for the handsome young man. If that was the case, perhaps she would forgive him for sleeping with her cook practically under her nose.

Jules didn't like that idea, and when one of the saloon women pushed in beside him, he dropped an arm across her shoulder.

"I haven't seen you lately, Jules." The whore's painted face smiled up at him. "What have you been doing with yourself?"

"Working hard, chasing wild horses."

"Then you need some relaxation. Do you want to come to my room and have a little fun for a change?"

Rosy wasn't bad looking, Jules thought, and he had spent time in her bed on numerous occasions before Willow came into his life. He debated going to her room. Maybe Rosy would push Willow out of his mind for a while.

But when no excitement grabbed him at the thought, and there was no stirring in his loins, he knew he wouldn't be able to perform. Damn, he thought, he sure was besotted with the long-legged Willow.

Disgusted with himself, he said, "Some other time, Rosy. I'm dead beat tonight." He tossed some coins on the bar, said good night to his friends and left the saloon.

When Jules came to the fork that led to his aunt's house, he turned onto it. It was still early in the evening, and he felt like tormenting Willow for a while. Besides, Aunt Jess would be happy to hear some news of her little friend.

As he rode past the cookhouse on his way to the ranch house, it was dark inside. He was thinking that Corrie Mae had retired early because of her arm, but then he heard the rhythmic squeak of bedsprings.

I should have known that a gun shot wound in the arm wouldn't keep Corrie Mae from her favorite pastime, he thought with a grin.

He wondered which of the men was being entertained. Hoot or Denny, he decided. Brain, being the youngest, would have to wait until the others were finished.

The kid would have waited anyhow. He was smart. By now he had figured out that if he was the last, there wouldn't be anybody waiting for him to finish.

He could make the headboard pop against the wall all night if his strength held out.

Dismounting and letting the reins hang, Jules stepped up to the kitchen door, rapped once and then went inside. Rooster and Ruth looked up from their card game and smiled a greeting.

"What brings you here, Boss?" Rooster asked as he finished dealing the cards.

"I was in Coyote, and on my way home I decided to stop in and see how everyone was doing."

"We're all fine, Jules," Ruth answered in her soft voice. "Rooster and Willow have have been working hard to catch the little burros."

"How's that coming along?" Jules looked at Rooster, who was studying the cards he had dealt himself.

"We have over a hundred head waiting for the buyer from Colorado. Willow wrote the man a letter before she went to bed tonight. He'll probably send some men after the animals next week sometime."

Jules's spirits dropped. He wouldn't be seeing Willow tonight. And though he was glad that she had been successful in capturing the burros, at the same time he was disappointed. She would never return to him at this rate. Although it had been a small herd she had sent to market, she had managed to fatten them up and to receive top price for them. Now, on top of that she had over a hundred head of burros to sell.

She didn't need him . . . for anything. That knowledge left a sour taste in his mouth. He asked himself if he should go home and decided that he would. Willow would only give him the cold-shoulder tomorrow morning if he stayed, and that would get his back up.

Chapter Twenty-two

More than a week had passed since Willow had sent off her letter to the buyer in Colorado, and she was growing nervous because she'd had no response. To pass the time she made countless, needless trips to the barn.

"Stop worrying, Willow," Rooster said when he caught her staring down the rutted road toward town. "Those men will show up."

"But what if they don't? What if the owner of the silver mine has changed his mind about wanting the burros? What will we do with the little animals then—turn them loose after all our hard work capturing them? And that's not mentioning the chore of hauling feed and water to them."

"I repeat, Willow, the men will come. If not today, then tomorrow. Just be patient a little longer."

Patient, Willow thought sourly as Rooster walked away. She had been patient waiting for Jules to set a wedding date. Nothing had come of her patience. Was she to go through life waiting for something good to happen to her?

She even waited for something bad to happen. She waited in fear and dread that some day her father and Buck Axel would discover where she and her mother were hiding and that they would try again to take them back to New Mexico. That would be hell on earth.

"How much longer are you goin' to put off goin' for that daughter of yours?" Buck Axel demanded as he rode up to Otto. "You know where she's hidin'. Are you still afraid of that rancher?"

"I don't mind tellin' you that I am. Bein' hit by his fists is like bein' kicked by a mule. And you know yourself how fast he is with that Colt he always carries. When we go after Willow, we've got to be very careful or we'll both end up six feet under. We've got to make sure she's alone when we make our move."

"Well, when is that gonna be? The weather is gonna turn real bad any day now. I don't want to get caught in one of them sleet storms that part of Texas is known for."

"I've been thinkin' on it. I'm tryin' to think of a way that will make her come peaceably with us."

"Just don't take too long thinkin'," Buck said, a warning in his tone as he turned his horse toward his own ranch. "You might as well go home now," he said. "I've got a new squaw waitin' for me."

"But I thought—" Otto began. He'd been hoping

Buck would invite him to share the woman. Apparently there would be no more sharing until he came up with a time they would go after his daughter. Otto turned toward home, grumbling to himself.

It was shortly after noon, and Willow had only picked at her lunch, when she glanced out the kitchen window and saw four horsemen riding up to the house. It was all she could do not to rush outside and greet them with a welcoming smile.

She reminded herself that she was a businesswoman and should act like one. She took the time to tidy her hair and smooth some of the wrinkles out of her Levi's. When the riders drew rein in front of the house and dismounted, she controlled her excitement and walked out on the porch.

Appreciation of her beauty showed in the eyes of the men. All four men removed their hats, and one asked, "Are you Willow Ames, the owner of the burros we've come after?"

"I am," she answered, smiling at him. "Would you like something to eat before we go look at them?"

"We wouldn't say no." The leader returned her smile. "My name is Tom Garrett." Gesturing at his three companions, he introduced them as Yancy, Hartley and Gabe.

When the three nodded and smiled at her, Willow said, "Come on then, I'll take you to the cookhouse. My cook always has something on hand to feed a hungry man."

The men walked along behind her, their eyes glued to the gentle swing of her hips in the tight Levi's. As she opened the kitchen door, she hoped that Corrie

Mae wouldn't invite them all into her bedroom before they left. She didn't want these men thinking that she had a prostitute for a cook.

What Willow had feared, happened. As the four men filed into the kitchen behind her, Corrie Mae's face lit up like the first rays of the morning sun breaking over the mountain.

"Corrie Mae," she said, "these men are hungry. Could you rustle them up something to eat?"

"I surely can." Corrie Mae flashed each man a bright smile. "I have half a pot of stew left over from lunch. It's probably still hot. You men sit down and I'll dish it up."

As she flounced around, swinging her hips, her big, unfettered breasts bobbing up and down, the men watched her with interest. They understood the message she was sending them.

When Willow saw what her cook was up to, she frowned, and catching Corrie Mae's eye, she gave her a quick, warning shake of her head. Her cook's demeanor changed immediately. She repressed her excitement and moved sedately around the kitchen as she sliced a loaf of bread and filled four bowls with stew.

When Tom Garrett asked, "Aren't you going to sit with us while we eat?" she shook her head, answering that she had some work to do in her living quarters.

However, before she entered the room behind the kitchen, she couldn't help giving the big man a lingering look full of invitation. She saw Willow watching her then and quickly closed the door behind her.

Rooster entered the cookhouse just as the men finished eating. Willow introduced them all, and rising from the table, the men followed her and Rooster outside. Jimmy had Willow's mare saddled and waiting for her. Everyone mounted up and Rooster led the way to where the burros were penned up.

Half an hour later, Willow was clutching a check, her eyes shining with hope for the future. Tom Garrett had said that next spring he would be back to buy all the burros she could capture. Maybe things were going to turn in her favor for a change.

That evening after supper, Willow and Ruth sat before the fire, making a list of the items they needed from town, including warm winter clothing to replace items that were threadbare from many washings. Willow's scuffed boots would be replaced with new ones, and Ruth would get shoes and a warm coat.

The only luxury item they would allow themselves was a good supply of yarn for Ruth, who loved to knit, and for Willow, several bars of rose-scented soap.

It took Willow a while to fall asleep after she said good night to Ruth. She had to get to the bank and cash this check as well as the one from the sale of the cattle. Then she would take Aunt Jess her half of the money. She looked forward to seeing the old lady she had grown so fond of, but she dreaded the thought of maybe seeing Jules while she was there.

Jules was on his way to the barn when he saw in the distance a rider approaching the ranch. His pulse raced immediately. He recognized Willow. Even if he hadn't seen the sun turning her hair to gold, he would have known it was she. Something would tell him she was near even if he couldn't see her.

Was something wrong at the ranch? he wondered. He doubted that she was coming only for a visit. Although she cared for his aunt, he didn't think she would want to chance running into him. She didn't have much use for Jules Asher these days.

When Willow drew rein a few feet away from him and started to dismount, Jules stepped forward and, reaching up, grasped her by the waist to lift her out of the saddle. She reared back and frowned at him as he held her close against his hips a moment before sliding her to the ground. As soon as her feet hit the gravel in the barnyard, she jerked free of him.

Her face flushed from the close contact of their bodies, she started walking toward the house. He hurried after her, his eyes full of amusement. She had been aroused as much as he when their bodies met. She might tell herself that she hated him, but only her head thought that. Her body still remembered him and came alive every time he touched it.

For a split second he was tempted to turn her around, jerk her into the barn and cover her with kisses and caresses until she was panting for him to make love to her. But when their passion was spent, she might truly hate him, and herself as well, for that very passion he could always rouse in her.

"So," he asked, "what brings you here? I know you didn't come to see me. Is anything wrong at the ranch?"

"Everything is fine there. I've come to see Aunt Jess."

"She'll be happy to see you. She asked me this morning if I'd drop by and see how you are making out."

"So now you won't have to make that trip."

"Oh, I don't mind," Jules said lightly. "I haven't seen Corrie Mae lately."

Willow gave him a scalding look and retorted, "You'll find her in heat as usual."

Jules threw back his head and laughed loudly. Not only had Willow aptly described her cook, but a tinge of jealousy had crept into her voice. Even though she was determined never to make love with him again, she didn't like the idea of his doing it with another woman. He must remember that, work on that emotion of hers every chance he got.

They entered the small patio off the kitchen and Jules held the door open for Willow to step into the warm, sunny room. As he closed it behind them, there came the tapping of his aunt's cane coming from the great room.

The old lady's face lit up with a welcoming smile when she saw Jules helping Willow out of her jacket. "I've been wondering when you'd get over here to visit me," she said as Willow kissed her wrinkled cheek.

"I was meaning to get over here sooner, but I've been so busy at the ranch, I just couldn't find the time."

"Well, you're here now. Sit down." She pulled a chair away from the table, then looked at Jules and ordered, "Pour us some coffee, nephew, and set out that plate of cookies I baked yesterday."

Willow raised an amused eyebrow at how quickly Jules jumped to obey his aunt and thought to herself that the old woman was probably the only person in the world he loved.

Before she sat down, Willow walked over to where

Jules had hung her jacket and took from its pocket a long envelope.

"I've brought you something, Aunt Jess," she said as she sat down and laid the white square in front of Jess. "There's an inventory list of all the necessary items I had to buy for the ranch, plus the wages of the cowhands, the three teenagers, who earn less, and the cook who draws the same money as the cowhands. I added it all up and split it in half. I also did the same with the money the sale of the cattle brought us."

Jess didn't bother to look at the list of expenditures. She knew they would be right to the penny. But when she saw the thick sheaf of greenbacks, she looked at Willow, dumbfounded. "Are you sure I have this much coming to me?" she squeaked.

"Yes, I am. The cattle brought us top money."

"But I never got a third of this from old Salazar," Jess said, still in shock.

"I'm afraid Mr. Salazar was slack in keeping an eye on the men," Willow said.

"But you cracked the whip on them, didn't you?" Jules said with a humorless smile as he put the coffee and sweets on the table.

"I wouldn't say that I drove them too hard, but I saw to it that they gave me a good day's work," Willow said sharply. "The run-down condition of the ranch told me they had been doing very little for a long time."

"Good girl." Jess nodded her approval. "I knew you wouldn't let a man take advantage of you."

Jules knew his aunt's words were meant for him from the sly look that she slid him. He sat down and drew the sugar bowl toward him, then said smoothly, "Don't be too sure she's never let a man take advantage of her, Aunt Jess."

Willow gave him a stony stare and said coolly, "It might happen, but it hasn't yet."

"Is that right?" Jules's eyes mocked her.

"Yes, that's right if you're referring to Thad Wilson. He never had a chance of taking advantage of me. As for any other man who might have touched the edge of my life, I used him in the same fashion he used me. Our short encounter was of small importance."

Of small importance, was it? Jules gripped his cup, his face flushing an angry red. The little witch was lying through her teeth. When they had made love, their sweating bodies rising and falling together, climbing to the crest of mindless release, there had been nothing insignificant about their encounters, as she called them. The two of them had been as one, groaning and crying out their ecstasy as they floated back to reality.

Before she leaves here, I'm going to make her eat her damnable lie, he vowed.

Jules finished his coffee and pushed his chair away from the table. "I'd better get down to the corral and help the men break my latest bunch of mustangs," he said, then smiled crookedly at Willow. "I hope that soon you will meet a man who will be very important to you."

He was gone then, leaving Willow staring after him.

When Jules walked outside, he didn't go to the corral, but led Willow's mare into the barn. Sitting down on a milking stool, he waited for her to come looking for her mount.

Chapter Twenty-three

"I guess I'd better get started home," Willow said after finishing her second cup of coffee. "Ma always worries about me if I'm gone too long. We both live in fear that my father will come after us again."

Jess stood up when Willow did. "The law being what it is, I know that your father could force your mother to return home with him. But you're a grown woman, Willow. He has no jurisdiction over you. Our same law would forbid him to force you to go home with him."

"I know that, Aunt Jess, but I would never let my mother return to a life of hell alone. If you remember, the first time I left her alone with Pa, she almost died from his cruel treatment of her. And poor old Smitty lost his life."

As Jess followed Willow to the door, she said worriedly, "Make sure Rooster is always nearby. During the cold weather there is little to be done around a ranch. A man has a lot of time to just sit back and think. You know what your father will be thinking about."

"I know only too well." Willow sighed. "He'll be thinking of only one thing. How to sneak up to the ranch and grab Ma."

"You must always be alert and keep Ruth in the house as much as possible," Jess said before she closed the door behind Willow.

A cool breeze had kicked up, and as Willow walked toward where she had left the mare, she started to button up her jacket. Suddenly she dropped her hands, the buttons forgotten. The dainty little horse wasn't there, nor did she see her anywhere around. Had she strayed? That was unlikely. She always stayed where she had been left. Maybe someone had put her in the barn, she thought.

She pulled open one half of the wide double doors and stepped inside. She stood a moment, letting her eyes get used to the dimness. She smiled when she saw the mare's head sticking over the top of a stall.

"So," she said as she led the mount out into the barn's aisle, "some kind soul did bring you in out of the cold."

She gave a startled squeak when a tall man stepped out of the shadows. "I was that kind soul." Jules gave a husky laugh.

Willow tilted her chin in the air and said, "Thank you. That was very thoughtful of you."

"Is a thank-you all I'm going to get for taking care of your animal?" Jules's eyes shone wickedly at her.

"Yes, it is," Willow answered unsteadily. "Are you a stable hand looking for a tip? If I had a nickel on me, I'd give it to you."

"Am I worth so little?" Jules asked softly, taking her by the arm and turning her so that she came up against his body. "I'd settle for a kiss."

"Well, you can't have one." Willow tried to pull away from him. She knew too well that Jules's kisses always led her into trouble.

She opened her mouth to tell him to release her immediately, but before she could get one word out, Jules had dipped his head and the next instant his lips, hot and hungry, were devouring hers.

She stiffened her body, determined that this time it would not betray her.

Her body's desire was stronger than her common sense. It grew soft and pliable, leaning hungrily into the hard body it knew so well.

Still, Willow's mind tried to hold out against the warmth that was quickly building to a white heat. When Jules inserted a hand inside her open jacket and cupped his palm over her breast, she made a weak effort to pry his fingers away. But when he firmly but gently kept possession of the soft mound, rubbing his thumb back and forth across the nipple that had grown pebble-hard, she stopped resisting. Her arms came up around his shoulders and her fingers threaded themslves through his hair.

Jules pulled her tighter against his body, and she thrilled at his manhood throbbing on the spot that was eager to receive him.

Still, she whispered, "No," when he started to pull her down on a pile of hay.

"Yes," Jules panted, his desire to possess her at a fever pitch, almost uncontrollable. "I've suffered hell wanting you ever since you left me."

As if I haven't suffered, too, Willow thought, remembering the long nights spent alone. She was about to go down with him on the dry, fragrant grass when Jules whispered hoarsely, "I'll marry you if that's what you want."

As fast as Willow's body had softened, it now hardened. Before Jules knew what she was about, she had shoved herself out of his arms and stood glaring at him, her eyes shouting contempt.

"So, you randy tomcat," she said, "you'll marry me now if that's what it takes to get the use of my body."

"Come on, Willow." Jules took a step toward her, his hands outstretched to pull her back to him. "You know that's what you want."

Willow backed away, an emptiness building inside her. "You fool," she said, pity in her voice. "Going to bed together isn't the only thing that makes a marriage. If there is no love or respect between a man and woman, the marriage is doomed to fail. When I get married, it will be to a man whom I love and one who loves me back."

Blinking back tears, Willow was ready to place a foot in the stirrup when Jules grabbed her arm and swung her around to face him. Fury in his eyes, he grated out, "Are you foolish enough to think you can have happiness married to another man? You know damn well that when he's making love to you, you'll be thinking of me."

"Oh? When you make love to Corrie Mae and the saloon women, are you thinking of me?"

She jerked free of Jules's grip and was in the saddle and riding out of the barn before he could answer. He wanted to run after her, to explain that he had never done that. That he hadn't been with any other woman since making love to her. He even hurried outside to call to her, but pride stepped in. He had offered her what she wanted and she had thrown it back in his face. So to hell with the little witch. He was still of the opinion that when she made love to this husband she was going to have some day, she would be thinking of Jules Asher.

Willow let her tears fall when she was sure that Jules wasn't going to follow her. Not for anything would she let that devil know how deeply his words had hurt her. The words she had waited so long to hear had struck her in the heart like the sharp blade of a knife.

Her shoulders slumped in misery, Willow hunched against the chill as her mind continued to dwell on Jules. She must take her mother and move on. She must go to some place where she was sure she would never run into him. He had only to put his arms around her and she was responding to him.

Willow was so engrossed in planning where she would go after she and her mother left the ranch that she wasn't aware of the two riders who had been following her at a distance ever since she left the Asher ranch. It took the uneasy snort of the mare and the cocking of her ears to alert her that either man or animal was in the vicinity.

Straightening up and tightening her grip on the reins, Willow slowly looked around. When she saw nothing but the bare landscape, she turned her head and looked behind her. She saw two riders about a quarter of a mile away, loping along at an easy pace.

Cowboys from the Asher ranch, she thought, going to town for a few hours of relaxation. She went back to the problem of having to move again.

She gave no more thought to the two cowboys until she heard the rapid thuds of horses coming up behind her. She looked over her shoulder and a cold chill went through her. She recognized her father and Buck Axel thundering toward her. She dug her heels into the mare, sending her into a hard gallop. The ranch was not quite a mile away.

But the stamina and the speed of the two big stallions chasing her soon outran the spirited little mare. Her father and Buck rode up, one on either side of her, and Buck grabbed the reins, bringing her mount to a plunging halt.

"Let go of her," Willow ordered in a trembling voice. When Buck only gave her a leering smile, she raised her riding crop and struck him across the face with it.

The fat man glared at her a moment, his fingers on the welt that was beginning to seep blood. Then, leaning forward, he lashed out, catching her across the cheek. At her cry of pain, the mare reared excitedly, dancing around with nervous steps.

When Willow almost lost her seat, Otto ordered with a threatening look, "Settle down now. We'll leave your Maw where she is if you come peacefully with us."

"For how long?" Willow looked suspiciously at him. "Until you can sneak back here and grab her too?"

"I have no need for that weakling. As long as you behave yourself and do as you're told, she can stay at that ranch until she rots for all I care."

Willow knew with a sinking sensation in the pit of her stomach that her father spoke the truth. He really wouldn't care if he never saw his wife again. It was up to her to give her mother a chance at happiness.

But if she was to sacrifice her chance of someday being married to a good man and having a family, she wanted to secure that same thing for her mother. Ruth wouldn't be bearing any more children, but she could find happiness married to Rooster.

She looked at Otto and said frankly, "I will go with you, but neither of you will have any peace from me unless—"

"Unless what?" Otto growled, giving her a threatening look.

"Unless you see a lawyer and set Ma free through a divorce. Then there will be no trouble from me."

Otto looked at her thoughtfully for a few seconds, then nodded his head. "Agreed," he said. "I have to see a lawyer anyhow. It won't be any trouble to have him write up some divorce papers."

"I will want to see the papers," Willow warned. "I know how wily you can be."

"What business do you have with a lawyer?" Buck asked suspiciously.

"It's this way." Otto stared back at the man he didn't trust any more than his daughter trusted him. "I want it stated legally that you give me permission to water my cattle in that stream that runs through your property. And furthermore, you might as well know right now, you'll stay away from Willow until I get such a document in my hand."

Pure hatred stabbed at Otto from the fat man. Buck's right hand reached for a holster that wasn't there. His arm was useless, paralyzed from the bullet that Jules had put in his shoulder the first time he and Otto had tried to make away with Willow.

"Accept it, Buck," Otto sneered. "I've got you where the hair grows short. I'll call the shots from now on. You've had it your way long enough."

Buck said no more, but his slitted eyes promised revenge.

"Let's go," Otto said, and led off. Willow rode behind him, and Buck brought up the rear. Willow's shoulders drooped in defeat as the mare plodded along. She was getting a reprieve for now, but sooner or later she would be the wife of beastly Buck Axel.

It was an hour before sundown when Otto drew rein at the Rio Grande and announced they would make night camp there. He untied a grub bag from the back of his saddle and, dropping it to the ground, said, "As soon as I build a fire, cook us something to eat, Willow."

Nothing has changed, Willow thought wryly as she rummaged through the bag. *Paw barking orders as usual and me jumping to obey him.*

She paused a moment, gazing thoughtfully across the river. Ma wasn't here now. Before, she had always hurried to do as her father ordered to save her mother from being struck or kicked savagely. She no longer had to do everything he told her to do.

But right now she would rather make their supper

than sit idle where Buck could sit down beside her and give her those leering looks while he talked to her.

Unfortunately, she soon found that the way he ogled her every movement as she set a pot of coffee to brewing and fried salt pork and warmed a can of beans, was just as disturbing as if he were talking to her.

Night settled in as they ate the meal Willow had prepared, and the air turned bitterly cold. "You'd better scare up enough wood to last us through the night." Otto looked across the fire at Buck.

"Why me?" Buck asked, bristling.

"Because I gathered the wood that cooked our supper," Otto fired back. "We're gonna share the chores. You won't have any trouble finding some wood. There's a full moon coming up."

When Buck stamped off into the night, Willow said, "As you know, Paw, I don't have a bedroll."

"Don't worry about it. I brung one along for you."

Willow wondered if her father had a little soft feeling for her after all. She was disabused of that idea when Otto said, "I'm not taking a chance on you catching pneumony and dying on me before Buck signs that paper."

Shaking her head, Willow gathered up the dirty tin plates, pot and skillet, and took them to the river to scrub them out with sand. When she returned to camp, she found that in her absence Buck had gathered an armload of firewood and that her father was unrolling his blankets.

He looked up at her and said, "Roll out your bedroll here, next to mine. And, Buck, roll up in your blankets across the fire from us." He patted the gun he had tucked inside the covers. "I don't want you getting any foolish notions in your head tonight."

Buck gave him an evil look; then, unrolling his blankets, he crawled between them.

When Willow rolled out her bed of blankets, she gave a wry smile. Her father wasn't taking a chance on her catching pneumonia. He had wrapped a thick tarp around her rolled-up blankets. It was to go on the ground first to ward off the cold and dampness. Whatever his reason, she was thankful for the extra protection when she crawled beneath the covers. Her trapped body heat soon had her warm and cozy.

She lay on her back, gazing up at the full moon, listening to the steady slap-slap of the river against its banks. Her poor mother would be half out of her mind by now.

Chapter Twenty-four

The old Spanish clock on the marble mantle struck the half hour. "Four-thirty." Ruth dropped the half-finished sweater she was knitting for Rooster and stood up. "Willow should have been home an hour ago." She was near tears when she walked into the kitchen and stared through the window for the fourth time in an hour.

The sun had dropped behind the mountains and dusk was settling in. In order to see more clearly, Ruth stepped out onto the small veranda. She peered in the direction of the Asher ranch, but saw no rider coming toward the house. The frostiness in the air chased her back inside.

"Where is Rooster?" she whispered, holding her cold hands over the flames to warm them. He always calmed her, made her feel better. But he would be iome late today, she remembered. He and Jimmy vere riding fence, looking for breaks in the wires.

Ruth sat back down and gave in to her fear that her iusband and Buck Axel had grabbed Willow. They vere probably on their way to New Mexico right now.

Tears flowed down her cheeks. She would never see ier dear daughter again. Her only child would be orced to marry that beastly man. Any woman in-'olved with him didn't live long. Her mind went back o all the awful things she had ever heard about Buck Axel. She was almost hysterical when Rooster found ier sitting in the dark.

"Ruth, love, what's wrong?" He picked her up and at down in the chair, holding her on his lap.

"Oh, Rooster," Ruth sobbed, "it's Willow. She went o the Asher ranch this morning to give Jess her share of the money from the cattle, and she isn't home yet. know something dreadful has happened to her. She vould never let me worry this way if she could help t."

"Well now, honey," Rooster soothed, "maybe the nare threw a shoe and Willow is walking her in."

"And maybe Otto has her," Ruth cried fearfully.

That same thought had occurred to Rooster, and ie cursed himself for letting Willow go alone on her errand. He should have sent one of the men with her.

"I'll go ride a piece and look for her. I bet you one of your pies, I'll find her walking home."

"No, Rooster!" Ruth clutched his arm. "Don't leave ne. Send one of the men."

"All right." He patted her hand. "But first I'll light he lamp and build up the fire. It's icy cold in here."

Rooster could find none of the hands around; only

Jimmy sat in the bunkhouse. The teenager's face blanched when Rooster told him of his fears. "I want you to ride to the Asher ranch and find out what time Willow left there."

Before Rooster got back to the house, Jimmy had saddled a fresh mount and was riding out of the barnyard at a fast gallop.

He had only traveled about a quarter of a mile when he came upon a spot in the trail where sod and dirt had recently been trampled. He reined in, and sliding out of the saddle, he hunkered down to examine the hoofprints there.

He soon recognized a set of prints. There was a vee-shaped nick in the front left shoe. Willow had pointed it out to him last week, wondering if it hurt the mare to walk on it. Two other sets of prints were larger and bit deep into the sod. They had been made by large horses, the type that men were likely to ride.

He found the exact spot where the two horsemen had ridden up on Willow. He could tell that the mare had reared up, and the hoofprints milling around told him that one or both of the men had grabbed the little animal. He knew the whole story when all three sets of prints led off in single file, as they traveled south.

Rooster had been right in his suspicions.

Jimmy climbed back in the saddle and sat a moment, wondering what he should do. Should he ride on to the Asher ranch and tell Jules what had happened to Willow, or should he return home and tell Rooster what he had discovered? He knew that Miss Ruth would be beside herself, wondering what had happened to her daughter, so he turned the horse around and galloped back the way he had come.

Rooster was carrying wood into the house and ıeard him coming. Jimmy slid out of the saddle; his 'oice near to breaking, he said, "You were right, ⟨ooster. They've got her. She was almost home when hey grabbed her."

"Oh, Lord." Rooster doubled his hands into fists. This may kill Ruth." He looked at Jimmy. "You've ;ot to ride to the Asher ranch and tell Jules what ıas happened. He and Logan will go after the bas-ards. I pray that they will get to Willow before that 3uck—"

"I know what you mean, Rooster," Jimmy said as ıe swung back into the saddle. He touched spurs to he horse and it was off at a gallop.

Giving a sorrowful shake of his head, Rooster con-inued into the house to break the disturbing news to ⟨uth.

Jimmy's horse was winded and spent when he drew ein in front of Jules's sprawling home. A light burned n the great room, and dismounting, he stepped up ›nto the wide veranda and looked through one of the hree windows that flanked each side of the door.

Jess was sitting alone in front of the fire, her clay ›ipe clenched between her lips. Should he tell the old voman that Willow was missing? he asked himself.)r should he go straight to the bunkhouse in the hope ıe would find Jules with his men.

But the old lady was a strong-minded old bird, he old himself, and would take the upsetting news in tride. He took a deep breath and rapped on the door.

Jess's gray head jerked around and she peered hrough the glass. Her smile told the teenager that she recognized him. She rose stiffly and, picking up her cane, hobbled toward the door.

"What brings you here, Jimmy, at this time of night?" she asked, opening the door for him. "Is everything all right at the ranch? Willow was here this morning and she said everything was fine there."

"I'm here because of Willow, Miss Jess," Jimmy said. Then, as gently as he could, he told her what had happened. He ended by asking, "Where is Jules? I think Rooster wants your nephew to ride with him when he goes after Willow."

Jess dropped her cane and clutched at a chair back. "He's not here," she said in a breathless voice. "He and Logan decided to go on a last wild horse drive while the weather held. He said they would be gone for a week or two. I think they're going up into the high country."

"When did they leave?"

"Shortly after Willow left to go home. He seemed upset. Maybe he and Willow quarreled about something."

"They do that a lot," Jimmy said distractedly; then he asked, "Can I borrow a horse to ride back to the ranch? Mine is spent."

"Of course, son. Take any one of them you want. But don't you want a cup of coffee or something to eat before you go?"

"Thank you, Miss Jess, but I don't have time. Rooster is waiting for me."

"Godspeed then," the old lady said.

Rooster built a cigarette and stepped outside to breathe the night air as he smoked it. It was half gone when he heard the thunder of hoofs racing up to the house. He stepped off of the veranda as Jimmy slid off his mount. The animal stood, his legs braced, his head drooping, his muzzle and chest flecked with foam.

"I pressed him hard," the teenager said, compassion for the heaving animal in his voice.

"Did you speak to Jules?" Rooster asked, the red tip of his smoke arcing in the darkness as he flipped it away.

"He wasn't home, Rooster. He and Logan have gone up to the high country looking for the wild ones. Miss Jess said they might not be back for a couple weeks."

"Damn," Rooster swore grimly, staring unseeingly at the moonlit yard.

Jimmy waited a short while for him to say more. When the silence continued, he asked, "What are we going to do now? Will you go after them?"

"I'd like nothing better than to go after the bastards and shoot them down like the mad dogs they are. But I dare not leave Ruth now. She is overwhelmed with grief and is like a frightened little child. I need to be with her to keep her from going over the edge."

"What then?" There was a tone of impatience in Jimmy's voice.

Rooster sighed heavily and turned his attention to him. "I hate to ask this of you, Jimmy. I know you're exhausted, but would you take the hound and try to track Jules and Logan?"

"Of course I will. I'd do anything to get Willow out of those men's clutches."

Rooster slapped the teenager affectionately on the

shoulder. "I don't know what we'd do without you, son. Hustle over to the cookhouse and have Corrie Mae fix you a hearty meal before you start out. When you've finished, I'll have a fresh horse saddled and the hound will be ready. You'll have to start at the Asher ranch so the hound can get the scent of that black stallion Jules rides."

Jimmy trotted off for the meal his stomach was clamoring for, and Rooster called the hound and walked toward the barn.

A short time later a white blanket of fog hung over the land as Jimmy and the hound left the ranch, heading toward the high country.

Logan and Jules had camped beside a wide, shallow stream bordered with drooping willows. Logan had prepared a rabbit he had shot from the saddle and had roasted it over the low-burning flames. When they'd finished eating, the two men sat staring into the campfire.

"All right," Logan began when he finished building a cigarette, then lit it with a twig from the fire, "tell me what has put you in such a black mood. Every time I've tried to get a conversation going, you've only grunted."

"I guess I just don't feel like talking." Jules pulled his own bag of tobacco and papers from his vest pocket.

"That's a blazer, and you know it." Logan narrowed his eyes at the gloomy man tapping tobacco into the thin paper. "It's Willow, isn't it? You've argued with her again, haven't you?"

Jules passed his tongue across the paper, then

rolled the cigarette. When he had pulled a burning twig from the fire and lighted it, he said gruffly, "Yeah, it's that little witch again. She's driving me crazy."

"What has she done this time?"

"She refused to marry me."

Dry amusement danced in Logan's eyes, and with a hint of laughter, he said, "So you finally asked her to marry you. Did you ask her real nice-like?"

"Of course I did. I told her real nice that I would marry her if that was what she wanted."

"Those are the words you used to ask her to be your wife?" Logan looked at Jules incredulously. "No words of love, or anything like that?"

"I was trying to make love to her at the time," Jules answered testily.

"So that's what brought on your proposal. Willow wouldn't cooperate and you were so hot to have her, you thought to bribe her with an offer of holy matrimony?"

"That's what she's wanted all along." Jules tossed his spent smoke into the fire. "I thought she would be happy, getting her wish."

"I'm sure she was overjoyed," Logan said cynically. "I'm surprised she didn't take you up on your offer immediately."

"Go to hell," Jules snapped. "Why don't you mind your own business?"

The subject of Jules's wedded bliss was dropped as the two men rolled new cigarettes.

A wolf's chilling howl pierced the moonlit evening.

"He sounds like he's on the prowl," Jules remarked.

"Yeah. He's the majestic lord of wherever he roams. He answers to no one."

"He reminds me of you." Jules grinned at Logan. "I've never heard you answer to anyone." When Logan made no response, he asked, "Do you think we've been friends long enough for you to tell me a little about yourself? Your last name for instance?" He grinned, "Or were you whelped by a pair of wolves?"

Logan took the jibe in the same way it was given, good-naturedly. "My last name is Lapante. I am the only child of a French father and a Ute Indian mother. I was born and raised in northern Colorado."

"Where are your parents now?"

"Both dead. They were caught in a snow avalanche one day while running my father's trapline. I was ten years old."

"Who took care of you after that?

"My old Ute grandparents."

"Are they still alive?"

"No. They died from old age when I was eighteen. That's when I left the tribe and came down the mountain to see how white people lived."

"And?"

Logan snorted. "My father's people no more welcomed me than my mother's people had. A half-breed is scorned by both whites and Indians. He doesn't fit in anywhere."

"People are damn fools. I've never known a man more upright than you."

"Thank you, friend. That means—" Logan paused in mid-sentence when a big dog rushed into camp and made straight for Jules, his tail wagging a greeting.

"That's my hound," Jules exclaimed, coming to his feet. "He has tracked me all this way."

Both men slapped a hand to their holsters when a dark figure appeared out of the shadows.

"Jimmy." Jules recognized the teenager. "What are you doing up here? Is my aunt all right?"

"She's fine, Boss. It's Willow. Her Paw made off with her today."

"Oh, dear Lord." All the blood seemed to drain from Jules's face. "When did it happen? Where?" He fired the questions at Jimmy as he picked up his saddle and hurried to the stallion tied up beneath one of the willows.

"This afternoon after she left your place. She was about a quarter of a mile from home when they grabbed her," Jimmy said as he followed Jules. "I was able to read the signs," he added, pride in his voice.

"Has Rooster gone to look for her?"

"No. Miss Ruth is so upset, he's afraid to leave her. That's why he sent me to fetch you."

"I won't be going back with you, Jimmy. Logan and I will head out for New Mexico from here. Logan knows where the Ames ranch is. He used to work there."

"Can I go with you?" Jimmy asked eagerly.

"No, son. You've ridden enough for one day. There's some rabbit and hardtack and coffee left over from our supper. Take half the blankets from my bed-roll and spend the night here before the fire. There's enough wood to last you through the night."

In less than five minutes, Jules and Logan were galloping away from the fire, heading in the direction of New Mexico.

* * *

Willow had never felt so exhausted in her life as when she and her father and Buck approached the Axel ranch in mid-morning. They had ridden hard since leaving Texas, stopping only for a fast meal and a few hours' sleep. Her face and hands were dirty, and her long curling hair was a tangled mess. Her clothes were wrinkled from sleeping in them, and her feet felt swollen from being encased in her boots all this time.

As they rode up to the yard, overgrown with weeds that were now brown and bent, she ran a glance over the house. The roof of the porch was sagging; weatherbeaten boards were missing from the frame building, and three panes of glass were broken in the windows. Rags had been shoved in the jagged holes.

The place looked a far cry from what it had been when she had used to visit the former owners.

If it were possible, Willow felt even more dispirited at the thought of having to spend the rest of her life with Buck in this hovel.

"Get down, girl," Otto ordered as he swung to the ground. "Get inside and rustle us up something to eat. Me and Buck are hungry."

Willow noted that Buck was already in the house, having rushed there as soon as he dismounted. As if I don't know what his hurrying is all about, she thought as she climbed stiffly to the ground, every bone and muscle in her body aching. He's probably got some poor Indian or Mexican woman tied up to his bed.

As she followed her father into the kitchen, an angry-faced Buck came bolting in from one of the back rooms. "I think that dammed bitch is about to die on us, Otto."

"Did you leave food and water for her like I told you to? Did you put covers over her?"

"Hell, yes. I put water and some beef jerky on the floor, and I laid a blanket over her."

"*A* blanket?" Willow said disgustedly. "She probably has pneumonia. It's freezing cold in here. And beef jerky to chew on for close to a week? Our old hound is better taken care of."

"You'd better go take a look at her." Otto pushed Willow out of the kitchen.

The room was dark and cold, the shutters closed. Willow flung them open, then walked over to the bed and looked down at a sight that made her cry out in compassion. A delicate-boned girl lay tied on a dirty mattress, the single blanket bunched at her feet. Her light brown hair was matted and sundry bruises covered her small face. Willow judged that she barely weighed a hundred pounds.

The half-breed lay in a stupor, limp and motionless. Willow knew she was gravely ill, hanging on to life by a slender thread. She laid a hand on the flushed forehead, and it was very hot to the touch. The girl had a high fever.

Willow sensed that the men had entered the room, and without looking around she began to issue orders. "Get me a basin of cold water and a washcloth. And one of you prepare something for this poor girl to eat. And get some heat in this pigsty. And bring me more blankets."

When her father and Buck started making grumbling noises, she spun around to face them. "If this girl dies because of your treatment of her, I will report it to the authorities no matter how long it takes me. I will see you both hanged for this terrible thing you have done."

Fury stabbed out of Buck's pale eyes, and Otto could barely contain his anger. But without words, they stomped out of the room and seconds later there came the sound of cooking utensils being banged around and the smell of wood catching fire. A short time later, a basin of water was banged down on the rickety table beside the bed, then some blankets were dropped at her feet.

"Hurry up with the food," Willow snapped as Buck's heavy tread moved toward the door.

Her first act was to pile the extra blankets on top of the girl and to tuck them tightly around her narrow shoulders. She sat down on the edge of the bed then and began to bathe her face.

In just a few minutes the water grew warm from the heat of the raging fever. "I need more cold water in here," Willow's voice rang out in a no-nonsense tone.

"You're getting mighty bossy," Buck growled when he brought another basin of water into the room. "I hope you know that you will pay later on for every order you give."

"Hah," Willow snorted. "As if you'd need an excuse to beat me."

"I'll do more than beat you, missy." Buck licked his lips in anticipation.

"And I'll kill you the first chance I get," Willow shot back at him. "I'm strong, not like this poor creature. I will get my revenge."

"Bah," Buck growled. "I'd like to see the day when you can kill me."

For all of his brave words, Willow noted there was a hint of uncertainty in his tone.

Twice more Willow called for water. The last time Buck brought in a pail of water. "See if that will hold you for a while," he growled, setting it at her feet.

Willow noted as she continued to bathe the girl's face and throat that her skin felt less hot. Hope rose in her breast when she began to stir and moan.

"Please, Lord," she prayed as she smoothed the hair off the smooth brow, "Let her live."

The girl's eyelids flickered; then brown, pain-filled eyes looked up at Willow. At first she shrank against the pillow, but when Willow spoke soothingly to her, she relaxed some. "Don't be afraid," she said gently. "I won't let those brutal men touch you."

Thanksgiving and doubt battled in the soft eyes. Then terror took over when Otto entered the room, a bowl of steaming food in his hands. "It's all right." Willow laid a calming hand on the shrinking shoulders. "He has brought you something to eat."

The girl remained tense until Otto left the room. She relaxed then and allowed Willow to lift her head and prop the other pillow behind her and to sit her a little higher in the bed.

"Let's see what we've got here." Willow picked up the bowl Otto had set on the table. "Do you like beef stew?" she asked, stirring the spoon through the meat and potatoes. She sniffed at the bowl, then tasted the meat. "I guess this was cooked sometime last week, but it smells and tastes all right. I guess it has kept because it's so cold in here. Do you want to try it?"

The girl nodded eagerly, and Willow began to spoon the stew into her mouth, at first giving her only gravy and small bits of potato. She wanted her empty stomach to have time to accept the food. Slowly then, she fed her pieces of meat.

When the bowl was empty, the brown eyes asked for more. Willow shook her head in answer. She was afraid the girl's stomach would reject more.

She had just wiped the pale lips with the washcloth when Otto entered the room again. He held a length of coiled rope in his hand. "Me and Buck are riding into town to see the lawyer," he said. "I'm gonna tie you to the bed. I know you'll run the first chance you get. Hold out your hands or I'll beat that breed senseless."

Willow knew that he would, and with a sigh she sat quietly as he tied her wrists together and then fastened the end of the rope to a bed leg. "That ought to keep you until we get back," he muttered, and left the room.

"You are their prisoner too?" The question was filled with surprise and disappointment.

Willow nodded. "Although Otto is my father, I am, nevertheless, a prisoner, the same as you are. But"—she smiled—"maybe all is not lost."

When she heard the kitchen door slam shut, Willow stood up and found that the length of rope allowed her to walk to the window a few feet away. She stood to one side of it and peered out. In moments she saw her father and Buck ride away. She walked back to the bed, and propping her right foot up, she said, "Honey, there is a knife tucked in my boot. Do you think you can roll over on your side and fish it out for me?"

With wild hope blazing in her eyes, the girl slowly inched over on her side and reached into Willow's boot. She gave a weak, glad cry when her fingers closed over the long, heavy jackknife. She pulled it out and handed it to Willow, a proud look in her beautiful brown eyes.

Willow managed to free the long blade; then, dropping her foot to the floor, she sat down on the edge of the bed and held out her bound hands to the girl. "Do you think you have the strength to cut this rope?"

"I will do it." The answer came firm and determined.

With trembling hands she sawed away with the knife for a minute, then had to rest another minute before continuing. In all, it took about five minutes before the knotted rope fell apart. The girl lay back, exhausted. When Willow had cut the other end of the rope and sawed through the one that bound the girl, she wanted to take her and ride away at once. Logical thinking held her back, though. They would need food and water on their trip to freedom.

She hurried into the kitchen and rummaged through Buck's larder. She yanked from a shelf a slab of salt pork, a handful of pemmican and four cans of beans. Shoving them into a cloth bag that lay on the table, she added some hardtack that lay in the clutter of dirty dishes and scraps of dried food. She next grabbed a canteen off the wall and filled it with water from a pail sitting on the floor.

Willow hung the trail grub on the door handle, then at a half run she returned to the bedroom. "What's your name, honey?" she asked as she began wrapping the girl up in one of the blankets.

"Cailyn."

"No last name?"

"Just Cailyn."

"Cailyn, you must be brave now, and call on all your strength, for we are leaving this place."

Cailyn nodded eagerly and Willow helped her to a sitting position and then hefted her over her shoulder.

Steadying Cailyn with one hand and the food supplies with the other. Willow stepped out onto the decaying porch. She looked toward the tree where she had tied her mare. The little horse was not there. In a panic, she looked wildly around the immediate area. The mare was nowhere to be seen.

As Willow's brain raced, one thing was clear. They had to get away. If it meant walking all the way to Texas, then she would do it.

It was late afternoon when Logan led the way to the Ames ranch. He frowned when he saw no smoke coming from the chimney of the main house.

"It doesn't look like there's anybody here." Worried concern was in Jules's voice. "Where do you suppose the bastard has taken her?"

"There's smoke coming from the bunkhouse. Let's go see if the cowhands know anything about their boss's whereabouts."

When Jules and Logan walked into the mean quarters that housed Ames's help, three men looked up from their seats around a burning potbellied stove.

"Hiya, Logan," one of the men said. "Are you gonna work with us again?"

"Maybe. Where can I find Otto?"

"We ain't seen him for almost a week. He spends a lot of time over at the Axel ranch. You might find him there."

"Thanks. We'll go look for him there."

"We should have known that's where she would be." Jules swore savagely as they rode off, Logan leading the way. "How far is it to the Axel ranch?"

"Around four miles," Logan answered as he prodded his horse into a hard gallop.

They had covered about two miles when Jules drew in a sharp breath. Willow's mare was trotting slowly toward them, the stirrups swinging emptily against the animal's side.

Jules grabbed the mare's reins, imagining all kinds of terrible things that could have happened to Willow. He knew in that instant that the lovely young woman meant more to him than anyone or anything else in the world. He had stubbornly held on to his determination never to marry, never to give up his independence. What a damn fool he had been, he raged at himself as the stallion thundered on.

They arrived at the run-down ranch house and ran a glance over it. Everything was quiet inside. But smoke rose from the chimney and both men were wondering if inside, guns were trained on them.

They were dismounting when Jules saw the sudden flash of sun on metal. "Take cover," he yelled to Logan just as there came the whiplike crack of a rifle.

As the shot buried itself in a tree, Jules and Logan bolted for the doubtful protection of the dilapidated porch. They drew their Colts and crouched down, waiting. There was no doubt in their minds who was shooting at them, or that Willow was inside the house.

Jules was praying that she wouldn't come running out as the rifle spoke again, the bullet slamming into a rotting support post this time.

"When they get up the nerve to show themselves, I'll take Otto down and you take care of Axel."

"No. I'm going to kill Otto Ames," Jules declared. "His greed has caused all of this to happen to Willow."

"No, you're not." Logan sounded just as determined. "Although Willow may hate his guts, the bastard is, after all, her father. If you kill him, it will always be between you."

"All right," Jules agreed. "I'll take Axel."

There came a barrage of gunshots, and bullets sprayed the porch, splintering wood and breaking windows. When it grew quiet, Logan looked at Jules and said, "Either their aim isn't worth spit, or they can't see us."

"Can you make out where they are?"

"They're over there in that stand of cottonwoods east of the house. I saw movement there a couple of times."

Jules peered toward the trees. "I wonder why they've stopped shooting."

"It's my guess that they're either out of bullets, or close to it."

"What do you say we take the battle to them?" Jules suggested.

Logan nodded and said, "Remember, no matter what, I'm to get Otto."

Jules agreed with a nod of his head as he broke open his Colt and checked for spent shells. "When we hit the ground we'll separate, coming at them from two sides. That should spook them real good."

"I'll go right and you go left," Logan said, and then added, "Are you ready?"

"I'm ready," Jules answered and they hit the ground, running. Two shots rang out. One kicked up dust at Jules's feet and he felt sure that Buck Axel had shot at him. He had only the use of his left hand now, and most likely couldn't hit the broadside of a buffalo.

Jules's eyes widened when he saw Buck leave the protection of the trees and come at him in a lumbering run. He crouched, and the Colt in his hand grew steady as his wrist muscles stiffened. When the fat man was four yards away, his gun blazing, Jules slowly squeezed the trigger.

Buck staggered, dropped his smoking gun and clutched at his chest. He sank slowly to his knees and fell on his back, his open eyes staring sightlessly at the sky.

As Jules shoved the Colt back in its holster, two shots rang out from the trees. A minute later Logan appeared, reholstering his Colt.

"I got the bastard," he said grimly. "I put a bullet in his gut. He won't die easy."

Jules didn't hear Logan after his first announcement. He was running toward the house. Minutes later he was back outside, looking like a wild man as he rushed to his stallion. "The house is empty," he said when Logan came running up. "I can't understand it. If she's not here, where is she?"

"Maybe we should look in the barn," Logan suggested. "She might have escaped from the house and hidden there."

Jules began to realize that he wasn't thinking in a calm and logical manner. He should have thought of that. It should have occurred to him also that Buck might have bound and gagged her and left her in the barn while he went on some errand. He wouldn't want a neighbor coming along and finding her tied up in the house.

"Let's go look," he said, and started running toward the barn.

As Willow pushed on, every nerve tight with determination, Cailyn's weight grew heavier and heavier. She became breathless and stumbled occasionally. She feared she couldn't go on much longer without a rest.

But she dared not stop. She figured she had only covered about a half mile. Her father and Buck could ride her down within minutes. And by now her father probably had the signed document that gave him the rights to the river he needed so badly for his cattle. That would signal the beginning of her life of hell with the brutal rancher.

Willow staggered on, panting for breath. Finally she caught her toe against a rock and was sent sprawling into a deep coulee. Cailyn cried out as she was dislodged from Willow's shoulder, her head hitting a rock. Willow lay still, the breath knocked out of her.

When she could breathe again, she rose and bent over the girl. She sighed in relief when Cailyn gave her a weak smile. Getting down on her knees, she felt her forehead and frowned. The smooth skin was hot again.

"Honey," she said, "we'll rest here a little while. I'm going to carry you over to that pile of brush and rocks. It's a good hiding place for us."

Willow started to pick Cailyn up, but she paused when several shots rang out from the direction of the house. Hope beat fiercely in her breast. Rooster had come to rescue her. She held her finger to her lips when the frightened girl began to cry. "Don't be afraid," she soothed her. "A friend of mine has come to help us. Now be real quiet so I can hear what's going on."

There were several more shots with spaces in between, then a string of them, then a long silence. Willow was thinking about crawling out of the deep coulee and slipping up to the house to see what had happened there. She turned to tell Cailyn her intention, but then another flurry of shots rang out. The silence that followed this time lasted at least five minutes. When she heard no hoofbeats thundering along to track her down, she felt confident that Rooster had been the winner in the shoot-out.

She hunkered down beside Cailyn and struggled her onto her shoulder again. "I'm taking a chance that we won't have to fear my father or Buck Axel ever again," she said to the silent girl as she started climbing out of the gulch.

Willow hadn't gone far when she felt the light weight she carried grow limp. Cailyn had drifted into a fever-induced faint. She struggled on, her whole attention on putting one foot in front of the other. She wasn't aware when the ranch buildings loomed up ahead of her.

"What do we do now, Logan?" Jules asked, a tone of helplessness in his voice. They had searched every corner of the barn, even scattered a pile of hay, looking for Willow. She was not there.

"We start looking for tracks. Maybe she got away from the bastards and is hiding someplace. Come on, let's get going."

The two men stepped out of the barn, and stopped short. Coming toward them was the figure of a woman, bent almost double from the weight of a blanketed body lying across her shoulder.

"Willow!" Jules cried out when he caught sight of the golden hair. He loped off toward her, a prayer of thanksgiving on his lips.

When gentle hands took hold of her, Willow realized that at last she and Cailyn were safe. She gave in to her exhaustion and sagged against the hard body that welcomed her.

When Jules grabbed her to keep her from falling, Logan jumped forward to catch the body that was falling off her shoulder. He looked down at the bruised face and swore harshly.

"What is it, Logan?" Jules asked as, with Willow in his arms, he walked over to stand beside his friend. "You look ready to kill someone."

"Look at this poor girl. I wish Buck Axel would come back to life so that he could be killed again."

Jules looked down at the half-breed, and he also swore at the condition of her face. She had been used harshly and often. He wondered if there was a spark of life left in her.

"She's awfully sick." Willow tiredly lifted her head from Jules's shoulder. "She has been beaten and starved and is very weak. I'm afraid she has pneumonia."

"Let's get her inside and see what we can do for her," Jules said.

"No!" Willow objected firmly. "Don't take her back into that cold pigsty. Take her to my father's house. It's clean and we will find herbs and barks that my mother used to gather for medicinal teas."

When the men were mounted, holding the girls in front of them, Jules cleared his voice and said softly, "Your father is dead, Willow."

"Who shot him?" she asked, her body stiffening a bit.

Jules was thankful that he could say, "Logan's bullet got him."

Willow's body relaxed, and after a few seconds she said, "I am not going to pretend unfelt tears. My father was a mean, evil man and has a lot to answer for when he stands in front of his Maker."

"What about Buck Axel?" Jules asked.

"That one will go straight to hell." Willow shivered, just thinking of the rancher.

Cailyn stirred in Logan's arms, alerting him that she was still alive and giving him hope that she could be nursed back to health. There was something about the frail little thing that had appealed to him the moment he looked down at her.

But she was burning up with fever. He could feel

the heat of her body even through the blanket wrapped around her.

He heaved a grateful sigh when the Ames ranch came into view.

Willow had rested and regained her strength, and she, too, welcomed the sight of her old home. Her back ached from holding it stiffly away from Jules. It was bad enough to feel his hard thighs pressing on either side of her, but to feel the warmth of his maleness against her derriere was driving her crazy. Too many memories were flooding through her. Memories that she must flush from her mind.

When Jules reined in by the back porch, she slid off the saddle before he could dismount and help her down. She couldn't bear to have his hands on her.

As Willow mounted the steps and pushed open the kitchen door, Jules stepped down from the saddle and went to help Logan dismount with Cailyn in his arms.

"Bring her in here," Willow called from her old bedroom.

Logan found, on entering the room, that Willow had the covers of the bed laid back and was piling more quilts on it. When he laid his light burden down and started to unwrap the blanket, she grabbed his wrist.

"The poor little thing has no clothes on. While I take care of her, why don't you see to getting some fires started? There should be some wood stacked on the porch. Give me about five minutes and you can get some heat going in that little brasier over there in the corner.

"And, Logan," she said as he walked toward the

door, "heat me a pot of water as soon as possible. I've got to get some healing curatives inside her right away."

When Logan walked into the family room, Jules had just finished making a fire in the fireplace. "Willow wants some hot water for teas she's gonna make," Logan said. "I'll bring in the water if you'll get a fire going in the stove."

With three fires going, the house was comfortably warm in minutes. Willow had found her mother's bags of herbs, roots and bark and brewed two different teas.

"This tea is for her fever," she said to Logan, who stood at the foot of the bed watching as she dribbled a light brown liquid between Cailyn's pale lips. "And the tea I gave her before is to break up the congestion in her lungs.

"Is there enough daylight left for you to slaughter one of the cows? I want to get a lot of beef broth in her. The poor little thing is half starved. Common sense says that she should have been dead days ago."

"It's the Indian blood in her that keeps her hanging on," Logan said quietly. Then he left the room.

Twilight had settled in when Jules and Logan finished butchering a young bull. They cut a chunk of meat for broth and three steaks. Then they hung the rest of the meat in a tree. It would be safe there from any animal that might come prowling around.

While Jules started the beef to simmering in a pot of water, Logan went back into the sick room. "Let me spell you a bit," he said to Willow, who was sponging Cailyn's face. "Jules has brewed a pot of coffee. A cup of it would taste right good, wouldn't it?"

Willow shook her head. "I don't think it would be a good idea to leave you in here alone with her. She might wake up and become frightened. She's terrified of men."

And well she might be, Logan thought darkly, gazing down at the bruised and swollen face. "Has she told you anything about herself? Where she comes from, her name?"

"She told me her name is Cailyn. Just Cailyn, no last name."

As Logan prepared to leave the room, he said, "Jules is frying steak for supper. I'll bring you a plate when it's ready."

Fifteen minutes later, it was Jules who brought supper to Willow. Not knowing what kind of reception he would get from her, he wore a look of uncertainty.

When she didn't order him out of the room, only glanced up at him, he set the tray on the small table next to the two cups of tea. Willow looked at the thick steak, fried potatoes and canned string beans and her mouth began to water. She hadn't eaten since early that morning.

"It certainly looks good," she said as she moved the tray to rest on her knees. She picked up the knife and fork, cut off a bite-sized piece of meat, and popped it into her mouth. Her face lit up as she chewed and swallowed.

"It's delicious," she exclaimed, cutting into the steak again.

"It tastes that way because you're hungry." Jules laughed. "It's well known among the men that my cooking isn't worth a plugged nickel.

"How is she coming along?" he asked later when Willow had blunted her appetite. "Do you think she will make it?"

"I don't know. So far she has clung to life with the tenacity of a stubborn mule. What she has gone through would kill most men. At least her fever is going down and she's not so restless. I'll know toward morning if the bark tea is breaking up the congestion in her lungs."

"If she makes it, how long will she have to convalesce?"

"Quite some time, I'm afraid." Frustration was in Willow's tone. "I've got to get back to Ma, let her know that I'm all right. I'm sure she's beside herself with worry."

"When, and if, Cailyn recovers, maybe Logan can stay with her, and you and I can get back home."

Willow sighed. "That would be the answer if Cailyn wasn't so afraid of men."

"I think Logan can win her over. He has a way with children and abused animals. I don't know if you've noticed, but he's quite taken with Cailyn."

"Yes, I've seen that," Willow said. "A gentleness comes over his hard face when he looks at her."

Watching Willow covertly, Jules said, "I feel that way every time I look at you."

Willow sent him a cynical glance. "The only thing I ever see in your eyes when you're around me is pure lust."

"Then you don't look deep enough. Wasn't I always gentle with you when we made love? Did I ever hurt you . . . except for the first time?"

"Look," Willow said wearily, "that's in the past,

and I don't want to drag it up and discuss it at this late date."

Cailyn began to stir and moan and as Willow bent over her, she said in dismissive tones, "Thank you for supper."

Jules picked up the tray, a beaten look on his face. As he left the bedroom, he knew that the hardest feat he would ever have to accomplish in his life lay ahead of him. He must, somehow, make Willow believe that he felt more than lust for her. That he loved her with his whole being.

Chapter Twenty-five

The night was crisp and cold and Willow snuggled deeper into her bedroll. Behind her came the faint murmur of the Rio Grande moving slowly along. In front of her blue wood smoke rose lazily from the campfire.

How were Logan and Cailyn doing? she wondered. Her thoughts were never far away from the couple she and Jules had left two days before.

It had surprised them all how quickly Cailyn had accepted Logan. Willow thought that the sick girl had sensed the compassion and the gentleness in the hard man.

At any rate, Cailyn had allowed Logan to spoon tea into her mouth and bathe her face with cold water. In two days, when the teas began to work, it was clear that Cailyn would survive her sickness. From then on

Cailyn didn't like Logan to be out of her sight, even though she grew nervous when Jules happened to come into the room.

When, on the third day, Cailyn was receiving her first bath since she was sold to Buck, Willow said, "I should be going home soon, Cailyn. I know my mother is very worried about me."

"You should go, Willow. You don't know how lucky you are to have someone who loves you, who worries about you."

Willow heard the yearning in Cailyn's voice and she said gently, "Someday you will find someone who will love you and care for you."

"Do you honestly think so, Willow?"

"Yes, I do, honey, and I have a feeling it will happen soon."

"That would be nice," Cailyn said in a low voice, "but who would love me after—"

Willow knew she was thinking of Buck.

"Where will I go, Willow, when I'm able to travel? I don't want to go back to the Indian village. One of the braves would only sell me again."

"I would never let you go back to that life again," Willow promised. "You can come home with me if you want to. But let's not discuss it until we talk to Logan. He might have some idea where you could go."

"Do you think so?" Cailyn blushed shyly.

"You never know. He might."

Willow left off gazing into the fire and turned over on her back to look up at the stars. She and Jules had left for home early the next morning. She had felt a little nervous about spending nights alone with him on the trail. But when he made no mention of sharing her bedroll the first night, she relaxed.

However, she had known that he silently regarded her as she moved about the campfire making their evening meal. She also knew that it would only take one word or look from her and he would start using his charm on her. She wasn't about to let that happen. He had charmed her into thinking that she would have a loving future with him, and her hopes had turned to ashes in her mouth. He would not fool her again.

Willow watched Jules's tall figure as he piled more wood on the fire before disappearing into the trees. This was a ritual he followed every night before rolling up in his blankets.

When she found herself wishing that things could be different between them, she turned her back to the fire and coaxed herself to fall asleep. She mustn't let her thoughts go too far in that direction.

The next day, still following the river, Jules and Willow crossed into Texas. In the late afternoon, Aunt Jess's ranch appeared in the distance. They kicked their horses into a gallop. They were cold, thoroughly tired of being in the saddle, and hungry for a good hot meal.

As they drew rein in front of the house, the two cowhands and the teenagers came spilling out of the bunkhouse. Simultaneously, Corrie Mae rushed out of the cookhouse and Rooster hurried through the kitchen door. There was a babble of voices as Jules climbed to the ground and Jimmy rushed to help Willow dismount.

"What happened? How did you free Willow? Did you have a shoot-out with the bastards?"

All those questions were thrown at Jules at the same time. He held up his hand for silence. "Yes, there was gunfire. Otto Ames and Buck Axel will never terrorize women anymore. Let me get cleaned up, and I'll give you all the details while I get some food under my belt."

The men, though reluctant, nodded agreement.

As Willow and Rooster walked toward the kitchen patio, Willow saw Corrie Mae slap Jules on the back and say, "Come on, bucko. I'll take care of you."

Jules glanced at Willow in time to see the contempt that curled her lips. He swore under his breath. There would be no more of his pretending to share the cook's bed. He would never get into Willow's good graces that way.

"I've got to take a bath and get into some clean clothes first. I'll see you at supper time." As he walked away from the big woman, he thought to himself that he must tell Corrie Mae that there had been a change in his plans. There would be no more trying to make Willow jealous. It hadn't worked out the way he had thought it would.

Willow and Rooster walked quietly into Ruth's room and stood looking down at her sleeping face. It broke Willow's heart to see that her mother had relapsed into ill health again.

"Ruth, honey," Rooster said softly, laying his hand on her shoulder, "wake up and see who has come to visit you."

Ruth slowly opened her eyes and focused on Willow. "Willow," she whispered, holding up her arms. "You're home."

"Yes, Ma, I'm home." Willow knelt beside the bed and took Ruth into her arms.

"My dear child, are you all right?" Ruth pulled away from their embrace and looked into Willow's eyes. "Did that awful Buck—"

"No, Ma. He didn't have time. Jules and Logan arrived at his ranch shortly after we got there."

"Thank the dear Lord for looking after you." Ruth looked lovingly at her daughter.

"Ma," Willow began as she took Ruth's small hands into hers. "I've got to tell you something else."

"What, dear?" Ruth asked when Willow didn't continue right away.

Willow squeezed her hands and said, "Logan was forced to shoot and kill Pa."

Willow hadn't expected to see sadness come over Ruth's face, but she was unprepared to see the absolute joy that flashed in her brown eyes. "Free! At last I am free of that man," she cried. She reached for Rooster's hand. "Do you realize what this means, my dear?" She smiled up at him.

"I know what I hope it means." Rooster sat down on the edge of the bed. "Does it mean we can get married now and make a life together?"

"Oh, yes, dear Rooster, yes." Ruth looked up at Willow, her face glowing, and said, "I'm starving, daughter. Would you ask Jimmy to bring me something to eat? Rooster and I have a lot of planning to do."

"Right away, Ma." Willow stood up, thinking she had never seen her mother looking so radiant before. "Will you let me in on your plans later?" she teased Ruth, who couldn't seem to stop smiling.

"You know I will, honey. We'll talk before you go to bed tonight."

Willow felt almost normal again when she finished her bath and donned fresh clothing. All she needed now was a good hot meal and ten hours of sleep in a comfortable bed.

She went into the main room, and sitting down on the raised hearth, unwound the towel wrapped around her head and shook out her wet hair. As she pulled a comb through her curly locks, fanning them out so that the heat from the fire would dry them, she heard Jules enter the room and walk toward her. She would recognize his step among a hundred others. Hadn't she lain in bed enough times, listening for him to come to her?

Willow heard the chair creak as it took Jules's weight, but didn't let on that she was aware of his presence. She gave a pretended jerk when he said, "You have the prettiest hair I ever saw on a woman. I've missed seeing you brush it at night."

Willow knew what he was referring to. Most times she had groomed her hair before joining him in bed. There had been other times, however, when they couldn't get to bed fast enough, so great was their desire for each other.

I can't think about that, she told herself. So she ignored his compliment, the yearning in his voice, the charm he was trying to use on her. "I hope it dries quickly," she said. "I'm starving."

"Awfully good smells were coming out of the cookhouse when I passed by. I think Corrie Mae is preparing a feast in thanks for your safe return."

Willow was about to retort that the cook was celebrating *his* return, but thought better of saying anything when she realized it would give him an opening for some of his sly innuendoes.

"I wonder how Logan and Cailyn are getting along," Jules said in the silence that developed.

"I'm sure they're doing just fine."

"Logan is real taken with her, don't you think?"

"It appears that way," Willow said shortly.

"Wouldn't it be something if they got together?"

Willow pushed the almost dry hair off her face and gave Jules a stony look. "How do you mean, get together? Are you thinking that your friend will replace my father and Buck Axel with Cailyn?"

"No, dammit. I don't think that," Jules snapped angrily. "Logan is a gentleman and would never take advantage of Cailyn. When I said get together, I meant that they would get married. Find a contentment that neither one of them has ever had."

Willow was immediately sorry she had spoken so harshly about Logan. She had gotten to know the handsome man well enough to know that he wouldn't do what she had accused him of.

"You are right," she conceded. "Logan isn't the type to do that. But as for them getting married, I don't know. Cailyn has only known cruelty at the hands of men."

Jules shook his head regretfully. "That's true, but maybe Logan can show her that all men are not alike."

"Maybe," Willow said sadly. "I hope so."

Her hair dry now, Willow stood up and said, "I'm going to get Ma and go eat."

"I'll see you at the cookhouse then," Jules said, and left as Willow walked toward Ruth's room.

When Willow walked into Corrie Mae's domain, accompanied by her mother and Rooster, the aroma there said that her cook had indeed prepared a feast. The long table was so filled with platters and dishes of food, there was hardly room for the plates.

Jules and the help were already seated, waiting for their arrival. Jules and Jimmy jumped up simultaneously to seat Willow. She had a hard time hiding her amusement when Jimmy got to her first. She was hard-pressed not to laugh out loud at the dark look Jules sent the teenager.

"Everything looks delicious, Corrie Mae," Willow said as platters of roast beef and fried chicken and three different vegetables were passed around.

"I cooked everything I could think of in gratefulness that you were able to get home safe and sound."

"Thank you very much, Corrie Mae." Willow smiled at the woman she couldn't help liking.

When every platter and bowl had been handed around, the only sound in the room was the clinking of flatware as everyone started in on the banquet.

Later, when Corrie Mae had poured coffee for everyone, questions were asked and answers given. When Jules described the gun battle, how he had shot Buck Axel, and how Logan had been forced to shoot and kill Otto, Jimmy asked, "Where is Logan?"

There was a moment's silence, and then Willow said, "He stayed behind for a while to take care of a woman who came down with pneumonia."

"That's right," Jules agreed to Willow's half-truth.

"He'll probably come riding back in a week or so."

Willow sent him a grateful look. She didn't think it was necessary for anyone to know about Cailyn's misfortune. The woman would most likely be with Logan when he returned.

Willow had discreetly watched Jules and Corrie Mae during the meal. She had heard no plans to meet later. In fact, the cook paid Jules less attention than she did the other men.

While Willow was trying to figure that out, Ruth said, "Are you about ready to go to the house, Willow? Rooster and I want to talk to you."

"Sure, Ma," Willow answered, then laughingly added, "That is, if I can stand up after stuffing myself like a pig." Jimmy rushed to open the door for her, and a glance at Jules told her that he wasn't pleased with the young man's action.

It would never enter your mind to perform such a gentlemanly act, would it, Jules Asher? she thought as she stepped out into the cold night.

When Willow and Ruth and Rooster entered the house and walked into the kitchen, Willow sat down by the hearth and faced her mother and ranch foreman. She looked at their excited faces and said, "The pair of you are dying to tell me something. What is it?"

Ruth and Rooster started to speak at once, and then Rooster said with a grin, "Go ahead, Ruth, tell her."

"We're going to get married," Ruth burst out.

"That doesn't surprise me, Ma." Willow smiled at the beaming woman. "I couldn't be happier for you both. When is the big event going to take place?"

"As soon as possible," Rooster answered. "Before bad weather sets in."

"What has the weather got to do with when you get married?" Willow looked perplexed.

"Because, Willow," Ruth answered this time, "if it's all right with you, Rooster and I want to move back to our ranch and run it."

"That's a wonderful idea, Ma. Why should I mind?"

"You slaved so hard on that place for years—by rights the ranch should be half yours."

"You're wrong, Ma. There is no comparison between my hard work and your mental anguish all those long years. Tired muscles recover, but the damage done to the mind is a long time healing. Living in peace with Rooster will make a new woman out of you."

Rooster reached for Willow's hands, his eyes wet. "I'll take good care of your mother, Willow, never doubt that."

"I know you will, Rooster." Willow squeezed the work-roughened hands. "I guess you'll be talking to Reverend Moser tomorrow."

"No." Rooster shook his head with a grin. "I'm going to talk to him tonight. Me and Ruth would like to get married *tomorrow*."

Willow laughed and teased, "Everyone is going to think it's a shotgun wedding."

Rooster's face grew fiery red. "They'd have no reason to think that. I haven't even kissed your ma."

"Oh, Rooster, I was only funning you," Willow apologized.

"I see." Rooster gave an embarrassed laugh.

Willow rose from the hearth. "Congratulations to

both of you. If you don't mind, I'm going to bed now. I'm almost asleep on my feet."

Cailyn set the cup of deer broth she had been sipping on the table beside the bed. "Goodness," she said, laughing, "where did you get that armload of women's clothing, Logan?"

"I went through Willow's wardrobe and dresser. There's really not much you can use." He started removing the articles draped across his arm. "But there are a few pieces I think might fit you. They look like Willow must have worn them when she was a young girl."

Logan held up a faded calico dress. "I think this will fit you nicely. There are two more this size." He sorted through the garments he'd laid on the foot of the bed. "Here's some small-sized underclothes—petticoats, camisoles. And these," he said with a grin, holding up three pairs of thigh-length drawers.

Cailyn frowned. "They don't look like they'd be very warm. Not like my buckskins."

Logan had a hard time not to show his amusement as he said, "They're not to be worn outside, Cailyn. These three articles are to be worn underneath dresses, next to your skin."

"I have never worn so many clothes at once. I don't think I would like it."

"You'll get used to it."

"Why should I get used to it? I like wearing my doeskin shifts. My body has freedom in them."

"Look, Cailyn." Logan pushed aside the clothes and sat down on the edge of the bed. "The time has come when you must decide which race you will adopt. I don't think that you want to go back to the Apache village where you were treated as a virtual slave and would probably be sold again. So, what is your alternative?"

"The white race, I guess," Cailyn answered reluctantly, remembering her treatment at the hands of the white men.

"All white people aren't like Willow's father and Buck Axel," Logan said gently, reading her mind. "What about Willow and Jules? They were kind to you, weren't they?"

"Oh, yes." Cailyn's eyes lit up. "Willow has been very kind to me. I would be dead now if not for her."

"What about my friend Jules? Wasn't he nice to you?"

"I guess so. He didn't pay much attention to me. He only wanted to look at Willow. Does he want her to be his woman?"

"I think he finally does," Logan answered after a thoughtful moment. "I think he would marry her now."

"He didn't want to before? Willow is so beautiful and kind."

"He had some kind of notion in his head that if he got married he'd be giving up his freedom. I think, though, that he's finding his so-called freedom a cold bedfellow.

"Now, enough about my friend Jules. If I fix a tub of warm water and set it in front of the fireplace, do you feel strong enough to take a bath and put on some of these clothes? You've got to start moving around or you'll never regain your strength."

"You are right, of course. I have been in bed four days. It is time I was up and around."

"Good girl. I'll get your bath ready. When you're finished and dressed, I'll help you wash your hair. I have a feeling that beneath that bear grease you have some beautiful shiny hair."

A short time later, as Cailyn lowered herself into the warm water, she shivered with delight. She had never before bathed in warm water. In the warm weather she bathed in the river. But even on the hottest day the water was always cold.

It was with reluctance that she finally stepped out of the tub and toweled herself dry with a worn towel. It took her a while to figure out how to don the white woman's undergarments and to button up the bodice of the dress which was only a little large on her. She felt very awkward in it as she went to the kitchen to tell Logan she was ready to wash her hair.

When she stepped into the room, Logan stared at her so long, she burst out, "I look ridiculous don't I?"

Logan swallowed, and then said softly, "You look lovely, Cailyn." He took her arm and led her to the kitchen table, where a large basin and two pots of warm water waited. "I'll help you wash your hair now."

Two latherings and three rinses later, Cailyn knelt between Logan's knees as he towel-dried her hair in front of the fireplace. As it dried, the flames picked up highlights in the tresses that were now two shades lighter with the bear grease removed.

Her forearms resting on his thighs, Cailyn asked through the fall of hair hanging over her face, "What is to become of me, Logan?"

"I've been giving that some thought," Logan said as he picked up a comb and started drawing it through the silky strands. "How would you like to live in Colorado?"

"Where is this Colorado?"

"About two weeks' travel, northwest."

"Where would I live there? On another reservation?" Cailyn's throat closed nervously.

"No," Logan said slowly, combing the hair off Cailyn's face as he gathered his thoughts. "When I was just a baby, my French father staked a claim of a hundred acres. It's beautiful land of mountains and meadows, tall pines and quaking aspens. A river of fresh, clear water runs through a portion of it. I vaguely remember a boat docking at a certain spot once a week to buy the produce my mother raised in her garden."

"It sounds wonderful, Logan." Cailyn's sigh was a happy sound. "Who would I live with there?" she asked as she rose from her kneeling position and sat down on the hearth, facing Logan.

"With me, of course. Would you like that?"

"Oh, yes, Logan." Cailyn's eyes danced with excitement. "I feel so safe with you. When do we start for this Colorado?"

"As soon as you feel strong enough to travel. We get a lot of snow there, especially up in the mountains. It is probably snowing there now, and I'd like to get to my little cabin before the passes are blocked. Besides, now that Otto's dead, Willow and her mother will be arriving any day to resume ranching. I'd like to be gone by then."

"I feel almost as good as I did before—"

"That's fine, Cailyn," Logan broke in on her faltering words. "We'll start today getting our trail supplies together."

"Oh, Logan, I can't wait to start a new life." Cailyn looked at him, her eyes shimmering with happiness.

"I feel that way too, Cailyn." Logan patted her knee, but wondered inside if he was setting himself up for heartache.

Chapter Twenty-six

Willow yawned as she helped Ruth get ready for her wedding. Her mother had shaken her awake at dawn to help her decide what dress she should wear. She had first made herself a cup of coffee and had seen, through the kitchen window, lamplight in the bunkhouse. She smiled, wondering if Rooster was also trying to decide what to wear.

Ruth finally put on a dark blue suit; then it was time to fix her hair.

"Ma," Willow scolded, "If you don't sit still, I'll never get your hair fancied up."

"I can't help it. I'm so excited, I feel like I'm going to suffocate."

"You musn't do that. Rooster would be so disappointed, holding a dead woman in his arms on his wedding night," Willow teased.

Ruth's response was to reach behind her and pinch Willow on the bottom. She turned serious then. "Willow, I'm so afraid that old memories will interfere with my happiness in being married to Rooster."

"Ma, you musn't let them." Willow laid her hands on Ruth's shoulders and gazed earnestly at Ruth's reflection in the mirror. "You must put those nightmare years behind you. Happiness has been a long time coming to you. Don't let the memories of Pa ruin it for you."

"I keep telling myself that, but my hurt went so deep, I don't know if I can ever forget it."

"You will, Ma. Life with Rooster will be so different, in time you'll forget your old life ever existed."

"I hope you're right, and I hope that someday you'll be as happy as I am today. You deserve happiness too. I thought for a while that you might find it with Jules."

"Jules," Willow scoffed. "There's not a woman alive that one could make happy. He's too intent on what makes *him* happy."

Ruth shook her head sadly. "I would have sworn that he loved you."

"Be careful what you swear to, Ma," Willow said, a bitter note in her voice. "Especially if it has anything to do with Jules Asher.

"Now, *I've* got to get ready for your big day. I haven't even decided what to wear."

"You should wear that blue velvet dress you treated yourself to when you sold the cattle."

"Yes, I could wear that. I've regretted many times that I bought it. It was a needless extravagance, but it will come in handy now. I guess all I have to worry about is what to do with my hair."

"Your hair is lovely just as it is, curling around your shoulders and down your back."

"You're probably right. I'll just give it a good brushing," Willow said as she left Ruth still looking at herself in the mirror.

Willow hurried down the short hall toward her room. Rooster had insisted that everyone be at the church by nine o'clock, and it was already quarter after eight.

As she sped past Jules's door, it opened and she ran full-tilt into him.

"Hey, what's your hurry?" He laughed, taking her by the waist to steady her.

"I'm in a hurry to get ready for the wedding." She tried to pull away from him.

"I have to get ready too," Jules said thickly, his hands hot on her waist. "Rooster asked me to stand up with him."

"He did?" Willow's exclamation of surprise turned into a gasp. Jules had brought her so close to his body that she could feel the heat and the ridge of his full-blown maleness.

She pressed her hands against his chest, and her eyes shot angry sparks as she ground out, "If you don't let me go, I'll slap you silly."

"I think I'll chance that," Jules muttered, and transferring his hands to her bottom, he brought her up tightly between his legs. When she parted her lips to protest, his mouth swept down and seared hotly across them.

She was outraged one minute, her fists pounding

his shoulders and back, and then the next minute she was melting into him with a passion that matched his.

It took Ruth's call to bring them both back to earth. Jules dropped his hands and Willow sprang away from him. Wiping the back of her hand across her mouth, she hissed, "Don't ever try that again."

"Why not? You liked it."

"I did not!"

"Yes, you did, Willow. You wanted me as desperately as I want you."

"You're crazy," Willow retorted, and turning around, she hurried back down the hall.

"What do you want, Ma?" She looked at Ruth, who still sat in front of the mirror.

"I was wondering, dear, if it's too cold out for me to wear a hat. I hate to mess my hair, covering it with my woolen scarf."

"Wear the hat, Ma," Willow said, her voice a little shaken. "Take your scarf with you to wear back to the house."

Willow walked down the hall again, thinking how such a little insignificant thing as a hat had saved her from making a fool of herself.

The church was icy cold as Rooster and Ruth led the way into the large building. Following behind them were Willow and Jules and Corrie Mae and the ranch hands. There would be no one else attending the ceremony. There hadn't been time to notify their friends and neighbors about what was going to take place.

As everyone gathered around the potbellied stove,

whose heat didn't reach more than four feet away, Willow wondered why she and her mother had taken such pains about what to wear today. No one dared take off their coats.

Rooster looked toward the door. There was impatience in his voice when he said gruffly, "I wonder what's holding the preacher up."

Willow saw the mischievous look that popped into Jimmy's eyes and knew he was about to make some remark, like, "Are you in a hurry to start your honeymoon, Rooster?" She caught the teenager's attention and shook her head at him. He blushed and looked away and kept his mouth shut.

The door opened then, bringing in a blast of cold air behind Reverend Moser. "I'm sorry I'm late, folks," he said as he hurried toward the pulpit. "My milch cow decided to drop her calf this morning and she needed some help."

Removing a heavy shawl from around his balding head, Reverend Moser opened his worn bible and motioned Rooster and Ruth to stand in front of him. Willow and Jules joined them, and then the preacher began, "Dearly Beloved, we are gathered here . . ."

Willow felt a slight trembling in her mother's body. Was it nervousness or happiness? she wondered. She glanced at Rooster. There was no doubt that the big man was in the grip of pure happiness. His entire being shouted it. Behind her she heard Corrie Mae sobbing softly, and she wondered what was going through her mind.

It was time then for Rooster to place a ring on Ruth's finger, and Willow and Ruth and Rooster froze in place. In Rooster's rush to get married, there had been no time to purchase a ring, even if anyone had thought about it.

Willow's mouth parted a bit in surprise when Jules reached into his vest pocket and fished out a gold wedding band. He nudged Rooster and handed it to the grateful man. As he slid it onto Ruth's finger, Willow looked questioningly at Jules.

"It's Corrie Mae's," he whispered.

Willow turned her head and mouthed, "Thank you," to her cook. Corrie Mae nodded and smiled at her.

In just a moment the preacher was saying, "I pronounce you man and wife," and Rooster was finally allowed to kiss his love.

Ruth's cheek was kissed by everyone, and Rooster's hand was shaken and his back pounded. Everyone trooped back out into the cold again. Rooster helped Ruth into the buggy that Aunt Jess used to ride in when when she attended church.

When the entourage arrived back at the ranch and Rooster wanted to get started for New Mexico right away, Corrie Mae had something to say about that.

Her hands on her ample hips, she said, "Rooster, I'll put a hex on your marriage if you don't at least have a wedding breakfast."

Everyone loudly agreed. The cold air had whetted their appetites. Rooster grinned and nodded his head.

"Come on, Jimmy," Corrie Mae ordered, "you can give me a hand."

By the time Rooster had driven the buggy back into its place in the rear of the barn and unhitched the horses, Jimmy opened the kitchen door and yelled, "Come to breakfast."

Willow and Ruth had spent the time in the warmth of the big kitchen, and they were already sitting at the table when the men came inside and took their seats.

Fried potatoes, ham and bacon, scrambled eggs, red-eye gravy, and hot biscuits were passed around. When only a strip of bacon and a spoonful of potatoes were left, and the men sat back with filled bellies, Corrie Mae poured coffee.

When the men lit up their cigarettes, Ruth whispered to Willow, "I'm getting nervous about tonight."

"Don't be, Ma," Willow whispered back. "Rooster is the gentlest man in the world. I think you're going to be in for a pleasant surprise."

"Do you really think so?"

"I wouldn't lie to you, Ma. Just relax and enjoy your honeymoon."

"I believe I will." Ruth's eyes sparkled.

"Well," Rooster said, drinking the last of his coffee and pushing away from the table, "me and Ruth will be on our way just as soon as Ruth changes into something warm."

When he helped Ruth out of her chair and escorted her to the door, Willow wanted to go with her mother, to have a last few words alone with her. But it was obvious that Rooster was going to accompany Ruth into the house. So later, she stood with the others, waving good-bye to the newlyweds.

"Rooster will take good care of her, Willow," Jules said as he stood beside her.

"I know." Willow blinked away a tear. "It's just that I'm going to miss her."

"Do you want to go to the house and talk about it?"

"No, I don't!" Willow glared at him. "Shouldn't you be getting home?"

As she walked away and disappeared into the house, Jules muttered with clenched fists, "Yes, it's time I got home, and I'm not coming back."

But later, as he took the trail home, he knew that he would be back. Again and again until he wore her down. He had learned earlier that she still had feelings for him and he was going to work on that.

When Willow entered the house, she went to her mother's room to tidy it up. As she made up the bed and picked up discarded clothes, she wiped often at her tearing eyes. The tears weren't for her mother, however. They were for herself. Was she never to get over Jules Asher? It had felt so good to be held in his arms again.

She consoled herself with the thought that he had gone home, and not back into the kitchen to spend time with Corrie Mae after the others had left.

I've got to stop grasping at straws, she admonished herself. *For all I know he took the branching trail to Coyote. Corrie Mae isn't the only woman who can comfort him.*

At that thought Willow gave way to a flood of tears as she ran to her room and slammed the door behind her.

Chapter Twenty-seven

When Willow had cried herself empty of tears, she sat up and swung her legs over the edge of the bed. As she wiped her wet cheeks with the heels of her hands, she yawned. She was so sleepy. The day was only half gone, but she felt as if it had gone on forever. Ruth had awakened her before the sun was up, and the run-in with Jules, then her tears, had worn her out. All she wanted to do was find oblivion in sleep.

She noted then the wrinkled condition of her blue velvet. She must get out of it before she took a nap. She stood up and pulled the dress over her head. Then she got out of the rest of her clothing. She picked up the robe lying at the foot of the bed and slipped it on. She would get dressed again when it was time to go to the cookhouse for supper. Tying the robe's belt loosely around her waist, she crawled back onto the bed and fell almost immediately into a deep sleep.

The stallion took advantage of the loose reins lying on his neck and plodded on at a leisurely pace.

Jules sat in the saddle, his body swaying with the slow motion, his shoulders drooping as he stared unseeingly ahead. He was having second thoughts now. Just because he had stirred Willow to passion didn't necessarily mean that she wanted anything more to do with him. Any skilled lover could probably rouse her as quickly as he had. Hadn't he taught her body to respond to hot kisses and caressing hands?

Jules groaned at the thought of another man bringing Willow to that fever pitch. He closed his eyes against the vision of her in bed, her arms and legs wrapped around a male body, not his own, calling another man's name in ecstasy as she had once done with him.

As he rode along, he remembered how it was making love to Willow. It could still be that way if he hadn't been such a stubborn fool, clinging to an old determination that marriage wasn't for him, that his freedom was more important than being tied down to one woman. He knew better now.

"But I was a young fool when I thought those things," he cried out to the emptiness around him. "There's nothing I want more in the world than to be married to Willow. To love and cherish her, like the preacher said to Rooster today."

Suddenly Jules picked up the reins and turned the stallion around. His mouth firm with stubborn determination, he headed back toward Aunt Jess's ranch.

Today Willow was going to listen to him. He couldn't go on without her.

The late afternoon sun was shining through the bedroom window when Willow came slowly awake. Her lips parted sensuously in a lazy smile. She had been dreaming that Jules was stroking his hand down her hip and thigh.

She lay quietly, her eyes still closed, trying to recall the dream, to continue the pleasure of it. Suddenly her eyes flew open and she rolled over onto her back, coming up on her elbows. She had recaptured her dream, but it was no dream. It was real. Jules was sitting on the edge of the bed, his hand slowly caressing her from her hip to her inner thigh.

"What do you think you're doing?" she squeaked, slapping his hand away. "I thought you went home."

"I started to," Jules said, but he got no further. His gaze, simmering with passion, was fastened on her chest.

Willow looked down and grabbed at the edges of her robe. It had fallen open to her waist and half her body was bare to where the belt held the material together.

When she reached with her other hand to pull the robe together, Jules caught her hand, whispering, "No, Willow."

"Turn me loose," she panted, struggling to free her wrist.

"In a minute," Jules said softly. He bent his head until his mouth came down on the velvet softness of her inner thigh.

"Stop," Willow cried in near panic. His lips were

only inches away from the curly thatch that was still covered by the robe.

Jules only shook his head. A delicious warmth began to build inside her as his tongue laved and his teeth tenderly nipped at her trembling flesh. She pushed at his head, even pulled his hair. When his arm snaked out and grasped her other hip, holding her firmly to him, she gave up and lay back down.

Willow felt the robe's belt being undone, felt the cool air on her body and knew that he had parted the material. She stiffened when she felt his fingers in her crisp curls and knew what they meant. He was feeling for the little nub hidden there.

She sighed when he parted her feminine lips and transferred his mouth to them. All other thoughts left her. She could only concentrate on the ecstasy his darting tongue and nibbling teeth were creating inside her. It had been so long since he had done this to her. Since she had done the same thing to him.

Willow felt her passion building and tried to prolong the eruption that was sure to come. She didn't want the titillation of his tongue ever to stop.

Then, as she had known would happen, her body's need would no longer be denied. Her soft cry of exultation followed the shuddering of her body when Jules brought her to a climax that shattered the world around her.

Jules held her close, his hands stroking her, soothing her. When her breathing was more normal, she felt him stand up, heard his belt buckle being undone, then the rustle of his clothes being removed. When she heard his boots hit the floor, she scooted down in the bed. When he knelt on the edge of the bed sh reached for him.

Jules gave a groan, almost of pain, when her lip closed over him. It took but a minute until he wa pulling himself free of her. Willow opened for him and he knelt between her legs. She took his harc throbbing erection in her hands and guided it insid her.

"Ah, Willow," he whispered as her hot, moist wall closed round him, "how I've longed to be inside yo again."

He grasped her small bottom and pulled her snugl into the well of his hips. Holding her there, he whis pered huskily, "Work with me, honey," and began long, slow pumping of his hips inside her.

Her feet braced on the mattress, Willow reache eagerly for each long drive of his manhood. Perspi ration sheened their bodies as the minutes passe and they rocked together. When Willow's body bega to stiffen, alerting Jules that she was fast climbin toward the little death, he increased his pace an drove deeper inside her. In just seconds her soft crie mingled with his deep groaning as they found a relie that left them mindless.

Willow had barely regained her breath when Jule started adoring her body. He rained kisses all ove her, from her shoulders to her feet. At last he settle down to stroking and kneading her breasts, and fi nally taking one in his mouth. When his lips bega to suckle a nipple, she bucked her hips at him, silentl saying that she wanted him again.

Two hours later, it was totally dark outside. Wor

ut, they wrapped their arms around each other and ell asleep.

They were jerked awake by a pounding on the bed-oom door and Jimmy calling to Willow that supper vould be ready in ten minutes.

Willow gathered her wits together, and praying hat the teenager wouldn't open the unlatched door, he cleared her voice and called out, "I'll be right here."

"I'll wait for you in the kitchen," Jimmy called back s his boot heels clicked down the hall.

Willow felt around on the bedside table, searching or matches. When she got the lamp lit, Jules was lready dressed and was pulling on his boots. He rinned wryly. "I'll have to leave through the win-low."

"Have you had to do that before?" Willow asked, alf joking, half serious.

"No," Jules answered as he pulled on his jacket. I've never fooled around with married women, so onsequently I've never had a husband gunning for ne either."

He grinned crookedly. "I've had a few irritated boy-riends come looking for a fight, though."

It flashed through Willow's mind just how many vomen Jules had slept with. And just as quickly came he thought that not once had the word love crossed ules's lips as he moved over her, working the passion out of his body.

She felt an empty sickness in the pit of her stom-ach. Her damn lustful body had betrayed her again. t was her bad luck that it had found in Jules's body a perfect match for its lust. The body cared nothi about what the heart might feel.

Willow rose from the bed and took her time dra ing on her robe. Let him leave there with an erectio she thought grimly as Jules's hot gaze raked over h bare body.

As she tied the belt around her waist, she sa coolly, "You'd better leave before Jimmy comes here and wants to fight you."

"The young devil probably would, too." Jul laughed, but there was a tone of uncertainty in h voice. It worried him that suddenly Willow had go back to her cool, aloof way with him.

"I'll come by in a couple days," he said as he pull up the window sash.

"Maybe you shouldn't," Willow said as he threw leg over the sill. "I'm going to be pretty busy for while."

"Doing what? There's not much to do around ranch in the winter."

"There's always something to be done," Willow sa and walked over to the wardrobe to choose som thing to put on.

"But, Willow—" Jules started to protest, the stopped when Jimmy banged on the door agai "Damnit," he muttered and climbed on out of th window.

Willow and Jimmy had no sooner sat down at th table than the ranch hands hurried into the coo house, closing the door against the biting wind th had come up. For a second Willow thought of Jules long ride in the changing weather and how chilled h ould get. She chastized herself then for caring. A ›oling off would do him good.

The meal was, as usual, delicious, and those gath-ˈed around to eat it were, as usual, in high spirits. /illow had noted that each night the group picked n one of the men to be ragged and teased. Tonight was Brian. Sly remarks were made and innuendos ‹changed. She didn't understand their meaning, but ıe wondered why the young man looked at Corrie Iae and blushed.

The meal was eaten and the coffee finished, but the ıen still lingered. Willow thought that perhaps they idn't want to go out into the cold weather. But it ˈasn't that chilly, for heaven's sake.

Finally, Corrie Mae said briskly, "The coffee pot is mpty, so you fellows might as well leave."

When all the men but Jimmy gave the cook a woe-ıl look, she grinned and relented. "After Willow and visit a while, maybe I'll make a fresh pot, and you ˈho care to can have another cup."

Male faces brightened and there came the sound of hairs being pushed away from the table. When the ıst one had passed out the door, Corrie Mae picked p the supposedly empty coffee pot. "I had to tell ıem all the java was gone"—she grinned as she re-lled their cups—"otherwise they'd sit here until mid-ight.

"Now," she said, sitting down, "tell me why you ›ok less rested than you did when you went to the ouse for a nap."

"I just couldn't fall asleep." Willow shrugged.

There was a short silence; then, as Corrie Mae pooned sugar into her coffee, she shocked Willow by saying, "Jules wouldn't let you sleep, would he?"

"What are you talking about?" Willow gaped at h cook.

"I saw him go into the house this afternoon, and never saw him come out. I imagine that Jimmy's a rival sent him out the window. I tried to keep the k from going over there, but he insisted that you h to eat."

Corrie Mae glanced at Willow's fiery red face a said softly, "Don't be embarrassed, Willow. He's cra about you. He might not tell you that, but in tho nights when we sat here in the dark, all he talk about was you."

"You mean he didn't . . . you didn't . . . go to b and . . ."

"Not one time. Jules and I are only good frienc Like I said, all we did was sit in the dark drinki coffee while he talked about you. He hoped that yo would think we were in bed together and be jealou

"His plan did work to a degree. I was jealous. I al learned to hate him."

"But that hate for him is gone now, isn't it?" Corr Mae looked hopefully at Willow.

Willow toyed with her spoon, making circles on th oilcloth-covered table. She needed so badly to confi her heartbreak to someone. It had been out of th question to tell her mother all that had happened b tween her and Jules, how she had foolishly thoug he was going to marry her. So she had kept her hu and disillusionment bottled up inside her.

Sitting across from her, however, was the o woman who would understand her pain and tormer She had thought for some time that Corrie Mae's g ughter and careless attitude were a cover-up for me painful happening in her life.

She looked up at Corrie Mae, started to speak, and en broke into tears. The big woman scooted her air up beside her and put tender arms around her oulders and held her.

When Willow had wept away most of her bitter-ess, she was handed a dishtowel and told to wipe er eyes. When she had done as ordered, Corrie Mae id softly, "Now tell me all about it."

For half an hour, with her head on the cook's com-rtable shoulder, Willow unburdened herself. When e finally grew silent, Corrie Mae gave a harsh snort. think most men are the sons of Satan. They work different ways. Some will beat you, break your ones, batter your face. Then there are the others ho will inflict pain to your heart and mind. I don't now which is worse. I do know that it takes longer heal mental pain."

Neither woman spoke for a while, each dwelling on ast pains they were unable to put behind them.

Corrie Mae broke the silence. "What you need, Wil-w, is to get away from the ranch for a few days. Go omeplace where you can be alone and think things rough. You must come to some kind of decision bout Jules. You must either give in to his terms, or ave Texas. Go so far away he'll never find you."

"I admit I've longed for some solitude, but I don't now where I'd go to find that around here."

"I know of a place," Corrie Mae said. "It's a spot here I go when sometimes life seems unbearable."

"Where is that?" Willow questioned, interested.

"I have a small cabin almost on top of the mountain. Only wolves and eagles and a few Indians kno that it's there. I keep it well stocked with supplies ar there's plenty of chopped wood. It's the perfect pla for healing the mind, Willow. The men can hand things here at the ranch."

Willow debated for a minute, then smiled at Corr Mae. "Thank you, friend. It sounds like just what need."

"Good," Corrie Mae said, beaming. "You go on bed now and get a good night's sleep. I think yo ought to get an early start in the morning. Leave b fore the men are up. I'll have a hot breakfast waitin for you, and directions how to get to the cabin writte out."

Chapter Twenty-eight

'illow referred often to the map Corrie Mae had ·awn for her as the mare climbed higher and higher ɔ the mountain.

Thank goodness the directions are clear, Willow ıought, *or I'd have been hopelessly lost after leaving ·e foothills.*

The first instructions said she was to turn left at the ghtning-blasted pine. Then a mile later she would ›me to a spring whose water trickled from within a ıve. She was to turn right then and ride in a straight ne until she came to a jumble of loose boulders. here she was to turn left again and ride to where ıe'd see a stand of pines growing off by themselves. nd in the center of these trees she would find the ttle cabin.

Willow sighed as they continued to climb. She had

passed the lightning-struck pine, the spring and th boulders. She was almost at the top of the mountai Surely the cabin wasn't far away.

The mare continued upward for another half hou before Willow gave a sigh of relief. The stand of pin she had been looking for stood a few yards ahea Her back was tired and the mare was becomir winded.

She steered the little animal into the thick growtl its hoofs making no noise on the thick carpet of pir needles. She uttered a little cry of delight when sh saw the sturdy cabin half hidden by the tall pine Corrie Mae was right, she thought. She would fin her solitude here. The only thing that would distur it would be the birds flitting among the trees, c maybe the hoot of an owl at night. That wouldn bother her, though. She loved both those sounds.

Willow was dismounting when she wondere where to put the mare. Corrie Mae had said ther were wolves about. Then she spotted a corral and horse shed adjacent to the cabin. When she led th mare into the pen and carried the saddle into th shed, she discovered a pile of hay and a keg of oat Her mare would do just fine.

She walked stiffly to the cabin then, excited to e: plore it inside. Pushing the unlocked door open, sh stepped inside and could only make out the dir shapes of furniture. Of course, she thought, the shu ters are closed. When she swung them open, she spu around to survey her new quarters.

The cabin consisted of one large room. Her eye sparkled at the coziness of it. One wall was taken u by a huge fieldstone fireplace. It had a wide mant ith a couple of pictures on it, and a rifle hanging at m's reach over it. The hearth was raised, an inviting ace to sit and stare into the flames. The makings of fire lay on the grate. Taking a match from the man-l, she struck it and held it to the shredded bark that y beneath the logs.

When they burst into flames and burned brightly, e turned her attention to the rest of the room. In ont of the fireplace was a brown, leather-covered uch with a table and lamp beside it. On the other de of the table was a rocker.

Against the opposite wall a bed sat in a corner with small chest of drawers beside it. In a corner of the me wall was a cookstove. On one of the shorter alls was a table and two benches. The door and a indow took up the wall across from the table.

Colorful Indian and Mexican rugs were scattered out: one in front of the hearth, one beside the bed id a large one in the center of the room.

Willow went to the kitchen window and looked out-de. The red flash of cardinals and the blue of jay-rds flying about brought a smile of contentment to r lips. She was going to love the wild solitude here ı this mountain. Here she could get her muddled oughts together and make up her mind about Jules. nd whatever she decided, she would stick to it. here would be no more switching back and forth e a March wind that blew first one way and then e other.

Willow walked back to the fireplace and added ore wood to the fire she had lit. When she straight-ned up, she noticed a framed picture on the mantel. ne took it down to look more closely at it, and gave a start. Three smiling faces looked out at her. A b man and a pretty woman posed behind a young gi who looked ten or twelve years old. The girl look like Corrie Mae.

What had happened to those parents, she wo dered, and what had put their daughter on the pa she now traveled?

Willow put the picture back, understanding a litt the sadness she sometimes glimpsed in Corrie Mae eyes. She sighed and picked her saddlebag off t floor. Life wasn't easy for women, especially those li ing on the western frontier. Too many times th were at the mercy of some uncaring man.

When she had put away four changes of unde wear, two pairs of woolen socks and three clean fla nel shirts, and laid her gown and robe on the foot the bed, her attention turned to the clock on the ma tel. She gave it a tight winding, then checked the tin on the small watch broach pinned to her shirt. Sh moved the hands to read quarter to three and set th pendulum to swinging.

Willow walked to the door then and took down h jacket. She had close to an hour before the su started going down. She would take a short walk ou side and discover where the woodpile was, as well the water source for the cabin's use.

She picked up the wooden pail sitting on the tab and stepped out into the biting cold. Walking behir the cabin, she came upon the wood and a spring clear water trickling from beneath a large boulde Someone had walled up a wide, deep basin wi rocks. It held a good supply of water before spillir over and disappearing into the ground. She dippe

: pail into its depth and carried the full container the porch, where she set it down.

She stood a minute, and then struck out walking. r footsteps took her out of the pines and onto the ountain proper. Earlier she had been intent on oking for landmarks that would lead her to the bin, but now she was free to gaze at the magnificent auty that surrounded her.

Willow sighed softly as a great peace came flowing er her. The solitude of the mountains would help r to think through problems, come to the right de- ions, and heal her broken heart.

It was near sundown when a sudden, sharp wind me up. Willow shivered and retraced her steps to : cabin. She picked up the pail of water and carried nside. The big room was in shadow, but the danc- g flames in the fireplace lent it a warm coziness. She nevertheless lit the lamp on the table after she ok off her jacket. Her empty stomach growled, and e started a fire in the kitchen stove.

Willow's next act was to go through the supplies owed in a tall cupboard. She took from it a smoked, gar-cured ham, two potatoes, a can of beans and a ece of hardtack. When she had placed the items on e table, she filled the clean coffee pot with water om the pail she had brought inside.

While it heated, she took a coffee grinder and a bag coffee beans from a shelf next to the stove. As she ound the hard little beans, a delicious aroma afted through the room. When she poured the ounds into the boiling water, she could hardly wait r it to brew.

The coffee taken care of, Willow sliced a thick slab

off the ham, then peeled and sliced the potato When she had started them frying, she opened can of beans, and dumping them into a pan, set th on the stove to heat.

Twenty minutes later, when Willow sat down eat, she felt sure she had never before eaten anythi so good or drunk better-tasting coffee.

As she washed and dried and put away everythi used in preparing her supper, she could hear wind growing in volume. When she went to the ot side of the room and sat down in front of the fi place, the rising wind swirled down the chimn causing the fire to smoke and ashes to fly onto hearth. She wasn't frightened, though. The lit cabin was sturdy and could stand against rou weather. Even the chilling yowl of a wolf did bother her.

It was still early in the evening when Will banked the fire and got into her gown and crawl into bed. She curled up in the feather bed, and once her dreams of Jules were sweet and loving night long.

Jess secretly watched her nephew as he sat stari moodily into the fire. There were signs of dissipati beneath his eyes and at the corners of his mouth, a a heavy stubble of whiskers covered his jaw.

For the past two nights one of his men had had help him into the house and into bed. He was so f of raw whiskey, he couldn't walk alone. The woman remembered the times she had railed at hi claiming that some day a woman would come alo who would bring him to his knees, and that s ɔped that female wouldn't have anything to do with ım.

She took the pipe from her mouth and sighed. Her rediction had come true, and her nephew was hurtıg more than she wished him to. If he didn't stop his rinking and carousing, something bad was going to appen to him. Her greatest fear was that some night hen he was riding home full of drink, he would pass ıt, fall from his horse and freeze to death. She ıanked God that they hadn't had a blizzard yet.

Jess was wishing that she could help this nephew ho was like a son to her when Jules stirred and ood up. "I'm going to take a ride into town," he said, is tone warning her not to give him an argument.

Helpless tears glittered in Jess's eyes when she eard the kitchen door close behind him. Would he rive safely back home tonight? She wished that she ɔuld talk to Willow, tell her that Jules was slowly lling himself.

Corrie Mae sat at the long table in her kitchen, a ıp of coffee in front of her, an envelope in her hand. mmy had brought it from town yesterday. It was ddressed to Willow, a letter from her mother.

The big woman lifted her head and stared out the indow. The letter gave her an excuse to ride up to er cabin. She wanted to see how Willow was doing, lone on top of the mountain, but mostly she wanted tell her what was going on with Jules, that the ıncher was on the path to ruin. If the heartsick girl ɔuld see him now, she would have no doubt in her ıind that the man lying in Corrie Mae's quarters ɔved her desperately.

Corrie Mae shook her head, remembering bein awakened by a heavy thud on the cookhouse doo around three o'clock that morning. As she left he warm bed and slid her feet into a pair of slippers, sh wondered which of the cowhands had a little lovir on his mind.

She opened the door and exclaimed, "Oh, dear, when Jules fell inside. He was passed out and hal frozen. As she managed to drag his big body fa enough into the room so that she could close th door, he kept mumbling, "Is Willow home yet? I gott talk to her. I have to tell her that she has to marr me."

As Corrie Mae grabbed him by the ankles an started dragging him toward her room, she sai wryly, "If she could see you now, she would neve marry you."

It took her about five minutes to lug Jules onto th bed, remove his jacket, boots, and gun belt, then pil blankets on his shivering body.

The last time she'd looked in on him, the shakin of his body had stopped and he was snoring. Sh hated to think how sick he was going to be when h woke up.

Corrie Mae brought her attention back to the er velope, her mind made up. She was going to mak the climb up to her cabin. At some point in her co versation with Willow, she would mention how muc Jules was drinking.

As Willow had done, Corrie Mae saddled her b gray and rode away from the ranch before anyor was awake.

* * *

Willow pulled the mare in when she came to a gap ı the trees. Away in the distance she could see the ange land stretching out of sight. She couldn't make ut the ranch buildings, but she knew that some-here down there were Jules's and Aunt Jess's hold-ıgs.

Since arriving at the cabin, she had ridden all over ıe mountain, and the beauty and solitude were now ld and familiar friends. In her exploring of nature's onders, and the long evenings spent in front of the replace, she had retraced in her mind every day om the time she'd met Jules. She recalled how it ad been with them at first: the time spent together n the cattle drive once they stopped fighting and be-an to love. She realized now that Jules had used his ody to show her how much he cared for her. If her tubborn pride hadn't stood in the way, she would ave accepted his proposal, and maybe by now she ould have heard those three words that had once eemed so important to her. Now, just knowing that e loved her was enough.

She wasn't going to make it too easy for him ıough. After all, he had caused her much mental ain with his pretense of sleeping with Corrie Mae. he would let him stew a few more days and then ide out to his ranch. She would pretend that she'd ome to visit Aunt Jess. All she would have to do then as give Jules one tiny smile, and he would be all over er.

"Let's get back to the cabin." Willow patted the ıare's neck as she looked up at the clear blue sky. here had only been that one spell of wind to mar her therwise perfect days.

She was just entering the clump of pines when s heard her name called. She frowned as she turn her head to look over her shoulder. Who was invadi her solitude?

Her furrowed brow smoothed out and Willo smiled. Corrie Mae. Her cook had come to check her, no doubt. She reined the mare in and waited f the big woman to join her.

"Well, you're looking mighty good," Corrie M said by way of greeting. "This old mountain can cu a person of whatever ails them, can't it?"

"It sure can," Willow smilingly agreed. "I can't r member ever feeling so relaxed and at peace with m self. What brings you up here? Were you afraid th by now I'd burned your cabin down?" she asked on teasing note.

"Well, you never know what a loco woman mig do," Corrie Mae said with a grin. "But I've climb this mountain to bring you this." She pulled the e velope from her jacket pocket. "A letter from your M I think. I figured you'd want to read it as soon as po sible."

"Thank you, Corrie Mae." Willow's eyes lit u "Let's ride on to the cabin and warm up with a cu of coffee."

Willow took the time to unsaddle and stable th mare before following Corrie Mae into the cabin. H cook had poured coffee already, and as soon as s shrugged out of her jacket, she sat down at the tab and began to read Ruth's letter.

Dear daughter,

My prayer is that someday you will find the

happiness that I have with Rooster. I still can't believe that marriage to the right man can bring so much happiness and contentment to a woman.

We only arrived yesterday, and you can imagine the work Rooster and I have ahead of us. But we will enjoy every minute of it as we work together to bring the ranch up to its full potential.

Rooster is waiting to take this letter to town, so I must get it to him. Don't work too hard, dear heart. My thoughts and prayers are always with you.

Love,
Mama and Rooster

As Willow put the single sheet back into the envelope, Corrie Mae said, "I can see by the smile on your face that everything is well with your ma."

Willow nodded. "Finally Ma has found happiness. She adores Rooster." She picked up her cup of coffee, took a sip, and then asked, "Is everything going all right at the ranch? Are the boys behaving themselves?"

"Things are running smoothly. Jimmy misses you. He rags me every day about where you went. I can't convince him that I don't know where you are. I told him and the others that you left me a note saying that you'd be gone for a few days and not to worry about you. I knew that if I didn't tell them something, they'd be out scouring the range for you."

"That was good thinking, Corrie Mae. I never considered that they might worry about me."

"They are all very fond of you, Willow. Especially that Jimmy. He looks on you as a big sister."

Willow's lips stirred in a soft smile. "I couldn't wish for a better brother."

"So, has the mountain helped you, Willow? Has it straightened things out in your mind? You have lost that harassed look. There's a serenity about you now."

"You were right about me coming up here. The solitude I needed so badly has worked wonders for me. I've been able to think things through where Jules and I are concerned. I have plotted a new life for myself: one that I'm going to start working on as soon as I return home."

For a moment Corrie Mae idly stirred a spoon in her coffee. Then, looking up at Willow, she said, "I hope you're coming home to let Jules know where he stands. Good or bad. He's killing himself with drink. Although he probably doesn't deserve it, I think you ought to let him know once and for all what you really feel for him."

Jules's disregard for his health was added proof to Willow that he did truly love her. Guilt gripped her for a minute that she was causing him so much grief. She couldn't help remembering then that he had done the same thing to her many times. But it was time they both stopped hurting each other.

Willow spoke none of her thoughts to Corrie Mae. She only remarked, "I'll be home tomorrow. I want to spend one more night here. I may never again feel the peace I've been experiencing up here."

"I know what you mean," Corrie Mae agreed. "I always hate having to leave here. I look forward to the day when I can get myself a rugged old mountain man and settled down in the cabin for keeps." She sighed and stood up. "I've got to get back down the mountain and start supper for the men. They'll be as hungry as wolves."

Willow walked with Corrie Mae out onto the porch and waved good-bye to her until she disappeared into the pines.

Chapter Twenty-nine

"Where have you been all day?" Jules complained when Corrie Mae walked into the cookhouse, her cheeks and nose red from her cold ride down the mountain.

"I had to go see someone," Corrie Mae answered as she took off her jacket and then held her hands over the hot cookstove.

"He must be a very important fellow to bring you out on such a cold day. It's freezing out there."

"It is that," Corrie Mae answered and said no more on the subject.

Jules ran a palm over his whisker-stubbled jaws. "I guess I ought to get home, take a bath and shave."

"The sun will be down in another fifteen minutes." Corrie Mae looked out the window. "Why don't you stay another night and go home tomorrow?"

"I don't know." Jules looked out the window too. "Aunt Jess will be worried about me."

"If she could see you now she would be more worried if you started to ride home at this hour. You look like hell."

"Thank you," Jules growled as he gave the cook a baleful look.

"You can take a bath in the bunkhouse and borrow a razor from one of the men."

"What about Aunt Jess?"

"Send one of the men to tell her that you'll be home tomorrow," Corrie Mae said as she began peeling a large basin of potatoes.

"I guess I could do that," Jules agreed, but he continued to sit at the table. After a minute or so of silence, he said, "I haven't seen Willow around the place. I went to the house and found it stone cold. I got the feeling that there hasn't been any heat in the place for a few days."

"There hasn't been. Willow went away for a while. She had a lot of thinking to do. A person can't think straight around here."

"Where did she go?"

Corrie Mae only shrugged her shoulders. She didn't want anyone else to know about her hideaway.

"Do you know when she'll be back?" Jules asked impatiently.

"Tomorrow sometime." Corrie Mae put the peeled potatoes in a pot, added water, and then placed them on the stove to boil.

"What did she have to think about that was so heavy she had to leave the ranch?"

"I have no idea." Corrie Mae placed a frying pan on

the stove and then started dredging a dozen porkchops in a plate of flour.

"Did she ever mention me to you?"

"A couple times."

"Well, what did she say?" Jules demanded when Corrie Mae didn't elaborate.

"You don't want to know."

"Yes, I do."

"Well, one time she said that you're a lean, long-legged wolf, always chasing after a bitch."

"What else?" Jules growled, a dark frown on his brow.

"Well"—Corrie Mae had to pause to think up another lie. "She said that golden rod you're so proud of isn't all that much. Then she said—"

"That's enough. I don't want to hear any more of her lies," Jules barked angrily. He jerked to his feet and slammed out of the cookhouse.

Corrie Mae's eyes glittered with amusement. Although she loved men and the pleasure they could give her, she never missed a chance to put them in their place.

She went about preparing supper, directing worried glances out the window. Darkness was coming on early because of the dark clouds gathering in the west. By the time the sun dropped behind the mountain, total darkness would descend.

A half hour later when the men came bursting in to eat, their hands clamped over their ears, the air had turned cold and sharp. "We're in for a blizzard sometime tomorrow," one of the men said.

Corrie Mae, her hand holding a fork poised over the frying pan, ready to stab a porkchop, grew still.

Would Willow know enough about Texas sleet storms to leave the cabin early tomorrow morning?

She went ahead and forked the meat onto a platter. When the men were ready to leave later, she would detain Jules and tell him of Willow's whereabouts and that she was worried her young friend might get caught in the impending storm.

"What do you want to talk to me about?" Jules asked when the last man straggled out of the kitchen. "You look worried about something."

"I am. I'm worried about Willow."

"What about her?" Jules sat forward, an anxious look on his face.

"I lied to you about not knowing where Willow went. She didn't want anyone to know. But now that a blizzard is bound to break tomorrow, I've got to tell you. I know that she's going to need help getting down the mountain if she doesn't start out early."

His face tight and his fists clenched, Jules grated out, "Where is she, Corrie Mae?"

"I'll write down the way to get to her."

"You don't need to write anything down. I've been all over the mountain hunting the wild ones. Just tell me the direction to go."

When Corrie Mae had told him about the lightning-struck tree, the spring and then the stand of pines, Jules pushed away from the table. "I'll leave at first light."

When Willow came awake, she knew the temperature had dropped. Her nose was cold.

She scooted deeper into the warmth of the feather mattress. She dreaded making the dash to the fireplace where red coals gleamed through the ashes she had covered them with before retiring last night.

Two thoughts ran through her mind as she lay staring at the dim outline of the curtainless window. She hated the idea of leaving the peaceful mountain to return to the ranch where some crisis or other was always happening.

The other emotion that gripped her was excitement. She couldn't wait to get down the mountain to make make peace with Jules, to marry him. It wouldn't always be a smooth marriage, this she was aware of. They would be at loggerheads many times about something or other. They were both strong-willed people. She grinned. Their life together would never be dull, that was for sure. For one thing, the many children she hoped to have would keeps things lively.

The clock began to strike and Willow counted its soft bongs. "Six o'clock," she exclaimed. "That can't be so." It was still night outside, for heaven's sake.

She leaned on one elbow, fumbled for the matches on the table and lit the lamp. She peered at the clock on the mantle and couldn't believe what she saw. It was indeed six o'clock. She scrambled out of bed and, shivering, hurried into her robe and house slippers.

When she had built up the fire, she went to the window that looked eastward. There were patches of gray trying to break through dark, rolling clouds. She shivered. A storm was brewing, and she couldn't start down the mountain until it was light enough for her to find the landmarks that would lead her home.

"Now I mustn't panic." She spoke aloud her thoughts as she made a fire in the cookstove. "While

I'm waiting for it to clear up, I'll cook myself a hearty meal and tidy up the cabin."

As the stove heated up, Willow got dressed, then packed her clothing into the saddlebag. By the time she had made up the bed, heat was flowing from the stove.

Willow kept an anxious eye on the window as she sat at the table eating a slice of ham and hardtack and washing it down with coffee.

"Will daylight never come?" she cried when the clock struck seven. Then, to increase her anxiety, a wind came up, whipping the pine branches outside the window into a frenzy.

"I've got to get off the mountain," Willow half cried. "I'll give the mare her head. Maybe instinct will lead her to the ranch."

It took less than a minute to wash and put away the plate, knife and fork, and the frying pan and coffee pot. Another minute saw her in her jacket, a heavy scarf tied over her head. She blew out the lamp, picked up the saddlebag and stepped outside.

The icy wind almost took her breath away. She ducked her chin and mouth into the folds of the scarf and looked in the direction of the horse shed. She could barely distinguish its shape as she struck out toward it.

The little building was warm and when Willow fumbled the saddle and halter on the little mare, the animal balked at going out into the cold. She gave in to her mistress's soft coaxing, though, and out in the whipping wind she stood still so Willow could mount her.

Willow pointed the little animal's head west, and

letting the reins lie loose on her neck, said as she kneed her into motion, "It's up to you, girl. Get us home."

Willow hadn't realized how the pines around the cabin had blunted the force of the wind until she rode out of their protection. As soon as the mare broke free of the trees, she and Willow faced a howling, hissing wind. Minutes later snow was whirling before Willow, dancing crazily in the icy wind. The flakes were small, stinging her face like hailstones.

The snow was affecting the mare the same way. She grew nervous and upset as she was half-blinded by the snow that clung to her thick lashes. She dropped her head and continued to pick her way down the mountain's frozen path.

Finally, a dark gray daylight dawned. Willow heaved a sigh of relief. They were on course. The spring, one of Corrie Mae's markers, was only a few feet away.

Suddenly her relief was shattered. At the same time that she caught the blurred sight of an animal dashing through the trees, the mare saw it too. She gave a terrified squeal, reared straight up and Willow was flying through the air. The mare went tearing down the mountain.

Willow landed on her back, the wind knocked out of her. As she scrambled to her feet, she saw the rear end of a deer bounding off through crags and boulders. A timid deer had spooked her mare.

What to do now? she asked herself. The answer was there was nothing she could do but strike out walking. With any luck, she would come upon her mount.

She took one step and then crumpled to the ground

vith a sharp cry of pain. Her right ankle was either roken or badly sprained. Either way she couldn't valk. She must find some kind of shelter and pray hat Corrie Mae would send somebody up the mounain to check on her.

Willow peered through the snow, looking for a lace that might shelter her from the storm. She ound that the best place was the large boulder from vhich the stream flowed. She painfully crawled up to t and sat hunched against its roughness, the scarf ulled down over her face.

Chapter Thirty

The sound of sleet striking against the window pane awakened Jules. He felt that it was daylight becaus he felt refreshed. But when he rose and pushed asid the heavy curtain at the window, it was still as blac as night outside. He looked down toward the cook house and saw its illumined window. He made ou the dim shape of Corrie Mae moving about. Sh would be making his breakfast.

He felt his way to the kitchen and lit the lamp o the table. At the dry sink he pumped water into basin and splashed it onto his face. When he had tow eled it dry, he went back to his room. As he pulled o a fresh set of long-legged underwear, he wondere what the weather was like up on the mountain an imagined that it was snowing up there. He praye that Willow hadn't started out in a blizzard.

Dressed in his warmest clothing, Jules, his head ducked against the icy pellets of sleet, walked across the yard to the cookhouse. He pushed open the door and caught the aroma of the freshly brewed coffee Corrie Mae was pouring into two cups. A steaming plate of bacon and eggs and hot biscuits also waited for him. He wrestled the door shut against the howling wind and took off his jacket and hat.

"We're in for a bad one," he said, sitting down at the table and picking up his fork. "I guess it's too much to hope that Willow will stay put until the storm passes."

"I doubt that she will. She will know that the trails and passes could be closed and she'd be stuck up there all winter. The cabin doesn't have more than a week's supply of grub." Corrie Mae sat down and picked up her cup of coffee. "She'll head down the mountain as soon as it's light."

Jules started eating faster then and refused a second cup of coffee. Something told him that Willow was going to need him before the day was over.

When he was pulling on his jacket again, Corrie Mae handed him a pint bottle of whiskey. "This may come in handy," she said. Jules nodded his thanks and put the bottle in his pocket. "Good luck," Corrie Mae added as he walked out into the storm.

Entering the barn, Jules quietly saddled his stallion and led him out into the sleet-filled air. Swinging into the saddle, he heeled the big animal into motion, heading him toward the tall, black shadow of the mountain.

The whipping wind was blowing the sleet sideways, and in no time Jules's brows and lashes were ice encrusted. Every few minutes he had to wipe his eye with his gloved hand. White steam snorted from th stallion's nostrils, and Jules's breath hung in the ai He had long since pulled his neckerchief up acros his mouth.

Both he and his horse grew weary, but Jules kne that they must keep on. To stop meant death on th icy, windswept range.

Full daylight finally came, a white sun trying t shine through the clouds. Jules wanted to shou aloud his thanks when he saw the beginning of th foothills only a short distance away.

When Jules reached the edge of the timber, as h had expected, the sleet turned to snow. With the co lar of his heavy mackinaw still pulled up around hi neck, he put a hand in front of his eyes to ward o the stinging snow. As the stallion began to climb, h stared through his fingers, looking for Corrie Mae' first landmark.

As the stallion climbed higher and higher throug twisting trails and rocky passes, anxious sweat gli tened on Jules's forehead despite the freezing col He had passed the lightning-struck pine some wa back and been expecting to meet Willow comin down the mountain ever since. Corrie Mae's secon marker couldn't be far away.

The big mount suddenly pricked his ears. Jule stiffened and sucked in his breath. Willow's littl mare was advancing slowly down the trail, her hea hanging low. But where was Willow? Jules felt th gut-wrenching sensation of fear in his stomach. Wha had spooked the mare? Had Willow been set upon b a pack of hungry wolves? He told himself that wolve vouldn't attack humans unless threatened.

He let the mare move on down the mountain, nowing that she would head straight to the barn. He need the stallion, and it began to climb again. Jules ooked carefully on both sides of the trail, searching or Willow. When they came to the spring and he still aw no sign of her, he began to fear that when she vas thrown from the saddle she had tumbled down he mountain. He envisioned her lying at its bottom, er body broken and bleeding.

He drew a long, shuddering breath. There was a lim chance that he might find Willow at the cabin.

Jules had almost ridden past the huge boulder vhen he saw what he thought was a snow-covered iece of windfall. On a closer look, hope swelled in is breast. A wisp of blue material lay up against the tone. He pulled on the reins and left the saddle, run-ing. Willow owned a blue scarf. Two swipes of his and through the snow revealed Willow's face.

It was as pale as her hair; the only color on her still eatures was the darkness of her long lashes. Calling er name anxiously, he brushed all the snow off her nd pulled her into his arms. When she made no re-ponse, he remembered the whiskey Corrie Mae had iven him. He took the bottle from his pocket, un-orked it and held it to Willow's pale lips. The liquid an out the corner of her mouth. He tore off his glove nd laid his finger on the inside of her wrist. He gave smothered cry of relief and joy when he felt a slow ulse. She was alive.

Cradling her in his arms as he would a baby, Jules rabbed the saddle horn with one hand and managed o pull himself and Willow onto the saddle. With both arms wrapped around her and her face turned in t his chest, he spoke to the stallion and it moved ou heading back down the mountain.

After what seemed like hours to Jules, he sa through the sleet the outline of the ranch building Nothing had ever seemed more beautiful to him tha the smoke rising from the chimney of the hous Blessed heat was waiting for them there. Corrie Ma must have lit the fire. The stallion stepped along mo quickly, as though the smell of smoke alerted him t the fact that nearby was a warm stall and a pail c oats.

When Jules drew opposite the bunkhouse, tl shout he gave brought the men hurrying through tl door. They stared up at him, and at Willow claspe tightly in his arms. None had been aware that he ha left the ranch to go look for their boss.

Jimmy, his face full of concern for Willow, reache for her. When Jules passed her down to him, he fel more than dismounted, from the saddle.

"Take her to the house," he ordered, and then sai to Sammy and Brian, "Gather up several large rocl and bring them to the house."

Jules hurried ahead of Jimmy to open and hold tl door for the teenager to pass through. When he ha closed the door behind Jimmy, he led the way dow the hall and entered the bedroom next to his.

"Go into the family room and build up the fire a you wait for the rocks," Jules said to Jimmy when l had laid Willow on the bed. "Bury them in the h ashes to heat up."

"What are you going to do with them, Jules?"

"Down at the end of the hall is my aunt's line

closet. You'll find a stack of towels there. When the rocks are hot, wrap them up in towels and bring them to me."

Jules shed his jacket, then got Willow out of her wet one. He turned to taking her boots off. The left one came off easily, but every time he tugged at the right one, a soft moan of pain fluttered through Willow's lips. He realized that her foot and ankle were swollen. She had either a bad sprain or broken bones. He took the bowie knife he always carried from his boot. The broad blade quickly cut through the leather, and her slender foot was freed. He gently probed the swollen ankle. It was badly sprained, but not broken.

He was bending over Willow, unbuttoning her shirt, when Corrie Mae came hurrying into the room. She stood at the foot of the bed, frowning.

"Shouldn't I be doing that?" she asked.

Jules looked up at her, his lips twisted in a half smile of amusement. "We have been lovers, Corrie Mae. Don't you think that I already know every inch of her?"

"I guess I never thought of that." Corrie Mae grinned, a little embarrassed that she hadn't remembered that. She walked over to the dresser and took from a drawer a long, high-necked, flannel nightgown. With the garment over her arm, she went back to the bed to watch Jules continue to undress Willow.

"She certainly has a beautiful body, doesn't she?"

Jules made no response to her remark. He had known for a long time the beauty of Willow's body. The only thing that interested him about it now was getting it thawed out.

He held out his hand for the gown. He had jus pulled it over Willow's head and eased it down to he toes when Jimmy entered the room, his arms full c towel-wrapped rocks. "Line them up on either side c her and put two at her feet," Jules said. "Corrie Ma get some more blankets out of the linen closet."

When the hot rocks had been placed around Wi low and the blankets were tucked tightly around he shoulders, the three stood around the bed, waiting.

When low moans began to come from Willow' lips, all three heaved happy sighs. She was in pai because her body was heating up. They also nov knew that no part of her body had frostbite.

"Come help me start supper, Jimmy." Corrie Ma smiled at the teenager hanging over the bed's foc rail.

Jimmy sighed and reluctantly followed the bi woman out of the room.

When Jules was finally left alone with Willow, h pulled his chair up close to the bed and inserted hand under the covers. Finding her hand, he held i while his other hand stroked her brow and hair.

As the room heated up, the rigorous day he ha spent caught up with Jules. Suddenly he was dea tired and overwhelmingly sleepy. He took off hi boots and stretched out beside Willow. He lifted he head to rest on his shoulder, and then fell into a dee sleep.

It was dark and someone had entered the room an lit the lamp, when Jules came awake. He looked dow at Willow and found her smiling at him.

"How do you feel?" he asked softly.

"Washed out, and my ankle hurts."

"It's swollen. I'll bathe it with cold water later."

"Much later, please. I've had enough cold to last me . lifetime." Willow raised her head to look up at Jules. I was so frightened when my mare threw me and ran .way. I thought that I was going to lie in the snow nd freeze to death."

"Don't say that." Jules hugged her fiercely. "When found you, all I could think of was that you were lead and that I had never said I loved you."

"And do you love me, Jules Asher?" Willow asked oftly.

"Sometimes I actually hurt, I love you so much."

Willow stroked his whisker-rough cheek. "I know 'ou do, love. And I love you. I suffered greatly when 'ou never said those three little words to me. I hought that you had used me the same way you were n the habit of treating all the other women in your ife. Then, at Corrie Mae's urging, I went up to her abin to think things through. I wanted to decide vhether I would stay on here, or go away.

"As I walked and rode over the mountain, I retraced very day of our relationship from its beginning. Two lays ago I realized that maybe you didn't know it, but 'ou did love me. When I started home this morning, intended to go to you and accept your proposal of narriage."

Jules leaned over and gazed down at her, love shinng in his eyes. He gave her a crooked grin then and eased, "Do you mean to tell me I said those words vhen I didn't have to?"

Willow lifted her arms around his shoulders and aid huskily, "That's right, bucko. Now give me a iss."

The heated kiss was broken when Corrie Mae en tered the room and said in mock anger, "That will b enough of that, Jules Asher."

Jules lifted his head. "I'll never get enough of that, he said, and before he bent his head to capture Wil low's lips again, he added, "Get out of here and clos the door behind you. Willow and I have some seriou talking and working to do."

"Hah," Corrie Mae snorted as she walked towar the door. "There will be working but precious littl talking done."

When the door closed behind the cook, Jules sai thickly, "That's right." Standing up, he got out of hi clothes. Willow sat up and whipped the gown ove her head.

"Be careful of my ankle," she said, laughing, whe Jules slid in beside her and folded her in his arms.

"I have no interest in your ankle, lady," he said, hi voice thick with desire.

Epilogue

As soon as Willow was able to hobble around on her strained ankle, she and Jules were married by the same preacher who had married her mother and Rooster. Corrie Mae was Willow's attendant and Jimmy was Jules's best man.

As Mrs. Jules Asher, Willow moved back to the large hacienda. Jimmy, of course, went with her.

A man was hired to run Aunt Jess's ranch, and Corrie Mae stayed on as cook.

Although Jimmy was a little old to be adopted, Willow insisted that he should carry Jules's name. The papers were drawn up, and the homeless teenager who adored Willow finally had a family and a home.

Sage
NORAH HESS